The Unforgotten Promise

To a fellow Julie—
Please enjoy and be blessed - and
continue to rock the crazy socks!

J. Anne Lezsley

The Unforgotten Promise

J. Anne Lezsley

Text and cover design by Karen Webb

ISBN: 978-1507785072

For Worldwide Distribution, Printed in the U.S.A.

My Deepest Thanks

If I were to take the space to thank by name everyone who has influenced me in the three years it has taken me to get to this point, these acknowledgements would consume more pages than the story itself. I'll make a valiant attempt to keep it brief.

Dave Hess, Senior Pastor of Christ Community Church – Your papa-heart for the House is evident. Your wisdom, insight and childlike playful humor (yes, even the puns!) are a true delight. My thanks for indulging all the requests to check the several instances herein that I've quoted and borrowed from your sermons, your many prayers, and your enthusiastic support of this pursuit.

The leadership and family at CCC – I came to you broken and unknown, and so many of you took it upon yourselves to love, walk alongside, and instruct me as a person, to speak God's words of promise over my life, and to share in my passion for this writing. I have learned and gained so much from so many of you. Special thanks to my small group, who have supported me and this in prayer from the beginning.

A.R. Mitchell – You were willing to spend months submerged in an unfamiliar genre, learning and keeping mindful of that ever-important cadence. Every writer should have an editor who will both rake them over the coals and pull them back from the brink. I'm ever grateful for your friendship… even if I *am* the basis upon which you normalize your crazy.

Joy Henley of Inkstained Editing – *You reminded me of the importance of retaining my voice.* Nearly as importantly, you allowed me to compensate you for your assistance by buying you dinner. Next time, I promise I'll pay cash. I'm thankful to call you a dear friend.

Karen Webb of Webbdezyne – I had no idea this story wasn't yet half complete when I met with you to pitch it a year ago, but you've been both patient and persistent with me. Thank you for believing this needed to happen.

And to so many other friends I've known from here, there, and everywhere – My life is enriched by the "dear people" I collect wherever life takes me. I would name names if there weren't so many of you. Some of you have walked with me through dark days, and some have prayed with me in pursuit of the hope that has been promised. Some of you have read early stages of portions of this story and assisted me in exploring my characters. I'm grateful for all of you, for all of it.

Saving the best for last: My Lord, God, My Lover – You have made me what I am, and are teaching me to love who and what that woman is. Three years ago on a December night I prayed, "I want to write, but I don't have a story – I need You to give me a story," and You have answered in a very profound way. This has been an incredible journey of learning to hear from You in ways that pious prayers could never achieve, of falling in love with You, of believing for the impossible, and of learning to be dependent upon You in all things. I am eager and grateful to receive all that You have promised for my life.

The LORD has done this,
and it is amazing to [me].

Psalm 118:23 ESV,
Author's Paraphrase

By the mid-22nd century, the physical landscape and shape of America have been so drastically changed that it no longer resembles its 21st-century self. An apocalyptic-seeming series of earthquakes and other geological events in the mid-21st century have torn the Midwest asunder. They have left in their wake a wide basin of land, once flat and expansive, but now ridged by mountains, valleys, and canyons. Into this wasteland, a people were exiled for their faith, with the intent of their demise. Three generations hence, however, they have brought forth life from their new homeland, isolated from the world that rejected them. Having decided to be selective in their use of technology, and taking an alternate view of the function of economy, they've reverted to simpler days with the benefits of their modern era.

Chapter 1

June 2145

"This is *not* the life I desire!" The confession exploded from the deepest place in Caeleigh's heartsick soul as, arms flung askance, she spun a single rotation to take in her surroundings to emphasize her point.

The haste of the turn pulled her feet from beneath her, dropping her to the ground as the soft rush of the voice of God answered her complaint. *Nor is this how I desire your life to be.*

"You promised that I would know love here, and receive healing of the phantom ailment which has plagued me for nearly half of my life, both of which I have yet to find," she wept. "I'm well aware that You don't operate on quid pro quo terms ... yet all that is before my eyes is the fear that I had incorrectly heard Your promise regarding the deepest unmet desire in the core of my being."

Examine your heart, My child. Recall that My instruction to you was to leave your home to come dwell in this place, to seek Me here and I would make Myself found by you and known to you. How long have you resided here and still you do not yet ***dwell****? I would have* ***all*** *of your obedience, to release all of the blessings I have prepared for you.*

Palms and knees pressed into the mossy earth, Caeleigh flushed with the heat of conviction. She could conceal the truth from herself no longer, now that it had been stated so plainly: she'd not been *dwelling* in her new home these past eighteen months; she was merely inhabiting the place and pantomiming through the behaviors of having a life, rather than truly living. She had taken residence, and found herself an occupation as well, but still in a year and a half Caeleigh had yet to fully set her heart in the place where she abided. The only party she could blame for the complaint she'd shouted at Heaven was herself. "My Lord…" she whimpered into the sylvan glen to which she'd fled.

Gentle laughter rolled over her. *It has been a great many years since anyone has called Me by that name, especially in this country.* Sunlight reached down through the branches overhead, dappling the ground beyond her fingertips. Its warmth spread up her arms and over the back of her bowed head, illuminating her strawberry-blonde hair to appear as spun copper as it hung loose before her eyes.

Contrition muted and made way for gratitude.

"Then it is good I've come all the way out here to meet with You in secret," she replied to the presence that had embraced her, referring to the distance she had walked – in excess of a mile beyond the outlying border of the Settlement that had taken her in. This copse of trees, with a clearing at its heart, was the secret place Caeleigh had made for herself for those times when she felt a need to escape and speak freely with God, whom she'd learned to call by a new – in reality an *old* – name: Kadosh.

For a year and a half she had lived in the Settlements, with no trouble adopting the manner of speech characteristic to the people thereof. Yet she continued to fear that she might revert to her ways of speaking from life prior, and utter a phrase or expression unfamiliar to those around her, the need of which to explain she did not welcome. Thus, she had wandered and explored the wild land beyond the outlying boundaries of the fields and orchards, until she'd found the hidden grove. Here, so far removed, there stood no risk of being overheard, or witnessed in any way.

Taking and releasing a deep breath, she collected herself and stood, brushing the debris from her skirt and straightening the lightly corseted bodice that had become twisted when she doubled over. As her hands passed over both garments, taking in the textures of the fabrics, the smart hems and the fine details, Caeleigh knew where – and with whom – she would begin to set things right.

The afternoon was not yet near its end when she returned to the home of the tailor who had taken her on as an apprentice, a widow by the name of Adeline. This woman, petite in frame and diminutive in stature, had lived half a century in the Blue Creek Settlement and had offered on multiple previous occasions to aid Caeleigh in adjusting to life there.

"Did you not request the entire day off?" the elder woman asked unaccusingly.

Caeleigh stood in the doorway between the front parlor and the dining room of Adeline's home, her eyes on the worn hardwood floor. "I did, but Kadosh sent me back under reprimand."

"Reprimand? Whatever for? ... If you don't mind my asking."

Where previously she would have bristled at such inquiry, Caeleigh refused her heart to close against the woman who had shown her nothing but kindness. "For as long as I've lived among this community, I have not dwelt in it as though to take it for my home. In so doing, I've only half-obeyed Kadosh's instruction when He directed me here."

"Far be it from me to speak in contradiction to Kadosh," the elder tailor twittered maternally, "but one could scarcely fault you for suffering homesickness after moving to a new place entirely on your own."

"That's the issue at hand – " Caeleigh nearly felt a need to kneel for the confession, opting instead to perch upon the edge of the nearest chair. "I haven't been homesick. I was glad to come here; I *desire* to be here."

Adeline set aside the work in her hands to give her apprentice her undivided attention. "Then what has held you back?"

"I'm not altogether certain."

"My dear girl, when the children of Israel arrived in the land promised to them through their father Abraham, they were obligated to *possess* it. They could not simply arrive at the place and receive all the blessings Kadosh had stored up for them; they had to enter in, conquer fears, and actively take possession of what was theirs. So, too, must you. I've watched you linger at the periphery of life since you arrived. It's time for you to enter in and take possession of the place Kadosh has prepared for you here."

"Where would you advise me to begin?" If there remained yet something undone for Caeleigh to accomplish that stood between her and the attainment of what had been promised her, she was avid and determined to apply herself to the expeditious completion of that task.

The dining chair creaked softly under the shifting of Adeline's slight weight as she leaned toward the younger woman. "Make friends closer to your own age. Much as I delight in your company, I'm old enough to be your mother nearly twice. You're far too young to engage in the life of an old maid. Beyond that, practice your talents and share them – Do you truly wish to grow in skill as a storyteller? You have an acuity for it. I've observed you with young children in the Settlement – your tales enchant them."

"I would like that, yes." Caeleigh watched her mistress rise and cross to the breakfront set against the side wall.

Lifting a small basket filled with scissors and shears of assorted types and sizes, Adeline handed it to Caeleigh with an impish grin that belied her years. "Then take these to Abram the coppersmith for sharpening, and ask him to instruct you. He was once the shyest man I'd met in the full span of my life, until he learned the art. Now there isn't a soul in the entire Settlement who doesn't know him as a storyteller."

Half an hour later, Caeleigh had followed Adeline's directions and found herself in the doorway of the coppersmith's workshop. Timidly she rapped on the frame of the open door, clutching her basket of scissors and shears. Caught mid-task, the proprietor bid her enter without rising from his seat. Looking at the man, Caeleigh recognized Abram as a dear friend of Adeline's, one with whom the elder woman frequently sat during the Settlement's communal meals, and shared leisurely walks on summer evenings.

"Will you tell me the history of how the Settlements came to be as they presently are?"

"What brings about such a peculiar request from a young lady such as yourself?" Abram looked up from the tools in his hands to search Caeleigh's eyes for an explanation.

"I am fascinated by the stories of history, and it's one I've not heard before." After a moment's hesitation, she added, "I'm also hoping to learn more of the art of storytelling from you, in the process."

The coppersmith attempted to conceal his astonishment, not wishing to give offense to a family he did not know. "Your parents never told you any of the history as a child?"

"I came to the Blue Creek Settlement alone, nor do I have family in any of the nearest-by Settlements."

"Well, then." Abram smiled. "You've brought me enough work to last through the telling, so have a seat. I will be required to break one of the rules of storytelling to sharpen these, however," – he lifted a pair of pinking shears from her basket – "as there are some things that cannot be done while maintaining eye contact."

Caeleigh found an out-of-the-way place to sit, on a stool at an adjacent side of the worktable where the coppersmith had begun to line up his tools. She smiled as he set the shears aside. "I understand. I would not have you lose a thumb for the sake of the story."

The older man chuckled appreciatively. "Now, where to begin? Are you familiar with the history of the cataclysms of the earth that afflicted what was known at one time as the United States of the North American Continent more than a century ago, and the sociopolitical retaliations of the balance of the nation's population against the followers of Kadosh in those days?"

Unwatched by the coppersmith, the tailor's apprentice permitted her eyes to explore his workshop. Across the large room was less a door than the majority of an entire wall panel set in a sliding track to open wide in the summer months, lest the heat turn the workshop into an oven. At present she estimated it to be at approximately the halfway point, affording them a scenic view of pear and apple orchards on a not-so-distant rise.

Drawing her gaze in from the vista, Caeleigh watched the coppersmith as he drew a ceramic honing rod along one, then the second, of the blades of a large pair of shears with sweeping, fluid movements which she described to herself as being *lyrical*. "I've heard and read some stories, yes. That far back, the followers were yet identifying themselves as 'Christians,' and one book I found likened what happened to them to the European Holocaust of the Jews during the Second World War in the twentieth century."

Abram nodded in cadence with the movements of his hands. "That's a fair metaphor, though I'm grateful to say there were no death camps or gas chambers at the end of these rail lines. The land now occupied by the Settlements long ago once comprised parts of the midwestern states, torn asunder by earthquakes originating east, west, and south of here. Rendered seemingly uninhabitable and by all appearances a hostile environment, it was considered a fitting punishment for the Christians to be exiled to this land."

"Punishment for what?" She hoped he didn't mind her interrupting to ask.

"The answer to that depended upon whom you asked," the coppersmith reported plainly. "Some claimed it to be retribution against those who had called down the wrath of their God upon the nation. My grandfather, who was brought to this land as a young man, felt it was more likely a rebellion against the moral compass that had been legislatively forced upon them by a well-intentioned but misapprehending government."

"Such a harsh rejoinder for a nation in whose origin the precepts of Kadosh were the foundation."

The remark gave her tutor pause. Abram smiled upon the items on the worktable before him, unexpectedly pleased. "You *do* know history – as it was, not as it was subsequently rewritten."

"I have a fondness for old books." Caeleigh blushed under his commendation.

"You are correct, though." Abram continued his task. "Yet over the centuries, the young nation turned away from Kadosh, praising evil as good and despising good as evil. Those who called upon the name of the Christ did not fight in defense of

His statutes with ardency, and so their cries were outshouted by their lusty adversaries." His disappointment in his ancestry, though mildly intoned, was not unmissed.

"Thus began the ephemeral death of that society," Caeleigh murmured thoughtfully, lost in the tale.

"Of an entire culture, it could be said," Abram returned with a smile, pleased with his pupil. He set aside the honing rod and picked up another tool for the jagged-edged blades of the pinking shears. This smaller tool required smaller rhythmic movements, which flowed more from the wrist than the elbow and shoulder, as had the prior. "Before the cataclysms of the earth, Kadosh sent other signs, and a prophet to interpret them. Every seven years to the day by the Hebrew calendar, a sign of judgment and warning was visited upon the nation. The prophet raised his voice to the winds. Sadly, not all who heard believed. Of those who believed, not all heeded. Of those who heeded, too many remained silent. So after many years passing in this way – "

"The stones and the earth cried out, as the Christ said they would," Caeleigh interjected, scarcely aware she'd spoken aloud. After having watched Abram continue his task for a few moments, she'd understood why a greater portion of his attention was required.

Abram spoke without looking away from the work before him. "Indeed they did, in a manner. Though the cataclysms of the earth themselves were no less a sign than any other that had preceded them – the epicenters of the geological events were not along any known profound geological fault, but rather at the birthplaces of the decline of life as Kadosh had ordered and established it. In the weeks and months that followed, riots and fires grew pandemic in what remained of many of the affected cities. Humanity bared the darker side of its soul."

"How terrible… !" Caeleigh gave silent thanks that Abram's attention remained on the task before him, preventing him from observing the shudder that rippled through her frame.

"Indeed." Abram nodded mildly, his eyes yet on the pinking shears. "My grandfather once told me that someone called it a mercy when the Christians were sent here, to be removed from all such circumstances. Facing hardship is altogether different from being surrounded on all sides by abomination."

His last comment, Caeleigh understood only too well – it had been a significant motivator in her decision to abandon everything she'd known and found familiar to relocate to the Blue Creek Settlement. This, however, was not information she could share. Fortunately, Abram had not provided her an opportunity to respond, as he continued to speak.

"Many were in agreement with that point of view, from what I have heard told," the coppersmith continued. "The First Elders, however, were concerned with other matters. They believed that how one's life is lived bears more weight than from where one had come and how or why. They are the ones who established the rules of the Settlements, many of which are connected to covenants they made with Kadosh for us as a people."

"How could they find agreement and unity when they, as well as the people they led, had come from a number of different creeds?" Her desire not to betray what knowledge she *did* possess on the matter of this history was insufficient to countermand her curiosity.

"That's my favorite part of the history." Abram beamed, his delight evident. "Kadosh *met* with them. The eight men had gathered to pray in a crumbling mansion in a community where there were structures yet standing, in which these figurative exiles had sought refuge. They convened to pray together despite their pragmatic and doctrinal differences, seeking wisdom for how to lead the people in their newfound circumstances. The matters upon which they might have disagreed in the past were trivial to them now – they'd become united by their shared grief over what had happened to them all, and by unanimous faith that what had been done with the intention of their demise, Kadosh would use ultimately not only for their good, but to bless beyond them. They fasted, prayed, and searched the scriptures for guidance.

"They came to understand that the beginning of everything – the fullness of the decline in societal circumstances and the then-recent events – which had led all of them to where they had fallen was the compromise of their hearts. It is from this revelation that the First Elders determined to make with the people the same covenant that Moses made with the sons of Israel before they entered the land promised them, as recorded in the thirtieth chapter of Deuteronomy regarding the keeping of the Lord's commandments, as it is phrased in that part of the scriptures."

The coppersmith's favorable acknowledgement emboldened Caeleigh to be more forthcoming in her return. "I believe I've heard it recited on remembrance occasions – Is it true that the First Elders omitted from *their* covenant the line about inflicting curses on their enemies that was in Moses' covenant?"

Abram turned toward his guest and leaned forward, hands braced upon his knees, no longer merely telling the *story* of their history, but engaging the *truth* of it with the young woman seated in his workshop. "That's correct. They were adamant in their refusal to sow seeds of bitterness and vengeance in this new people from their very outset. We may not have officially established sovereignty, but we are, in effect, as a people, a nation – not unlike Israel in her own early days in the land promised to Abraham, after having been released from Egypt."

"Perhaps one day it may be so for us, as well," she mused.

"It may well become so. The nation surrounding abandoned us to a dead and desolate land with the intent that its hardships should consume us. They could not have known that Kadosh would flourish this wasted desert under our hand and prosper what by all reports was naught but come to ruin." The elder man waited eagerly to see what reply was forthcoming. His instincts told him to expect a rebuttal to the suggestion he had offered, to open his eyes in new ways to the deeds of Kadosh.

Caeleigh did not disappoint him, suggesting that history would again repeat itself in the lives of the chosen followers of Kadosh. "He has done here exactly as He did also in Israel, then, as you said – He's planted His people in a place deemed undesirable by all who oppose them, and made a rose to bloom in the desert."

Chapter 2

June 2145

The following afternoon, Abram welcomed Caeleigh into his shop with a warm smile.

"I apologize if I left too quickly yesterday and forgot to collect everything I had brought to you before I departed," she stammered.

"You neglected nothing, my dear." Abram held up a pair of scissors so small they were dwarfed by the size of his hand. "I retained these to straighten them – one of the blades was bent."

Caeleigh thanked the coppersmith, then flushed with mortification as she realized the question she had never asked the day before. "Forgive me – I suppose in the excitement of your instruction, and the story itself, I completely forgot myself. What do we owe you for this work?" At his direction, she resumed the seat she'd taken on her previous visit.

"Your learning our history and passing it on as a storyteller for your generation will be compensation enough," Abram assured.

"Are you certain? Is there not even some small mending I could do for you in exchange for having given me so much in your work and your time?"

Abram looked on the young woman before him with what she could only call paternal regard. "Adeline's late husband was as a brother to me. Before he passed into eternal reward, I promised him that I would take care of her in whatever way she would allow. As someone she considers to be the daughter she never had of her own begetting, this promise is yours as well by extension."

Caeleigh was set back by this. Truly, Adeline showed her affection of the nature Abram had described, but she hadn't known that the widow had spoken of it to anyone outside the two of them.

Abram compensated for her awkward silence by asking an uncomfortable question of his own: "There is a greater reason I asked Adeline, when I spoke with her last evening, to send you back here today. Something from our conversation yesterday has been troubling me." He held up a hand to still the apology that began to spill from her lips. "I was so impressed with your knowledge of the history of the outside world that I betrayed my own. I made a comment that anyone else, had they heard it, would have caught and called me to answer for it. You didn't. Why was that?"

He moved to the workbench to which the bench shears were bolted and began cutting strips of metal, rather than continue to stand holding eye contact with the young woman, lest his inquiry appear confrontational.

"I'm not certain I understand." Had Caeleigh not been so worried by the question, she would have celebrated not stuttering in anxiety. "I recall that I was flustered when you praised me openly. Beyond that, I don't know that I know to what you are referring, exactly." Notwithstanding the lack of the coppersmith's scrutiny upon her, Caeleigh had no fewer than six times untied and reknotted a length of silk cord idly tied about her wrist.

"The Settlements have been our home, our isolation, for nigh one hundred years or more," Abram explained patiently as he continued to work. "Exceptionally few people, including among those who carry our history from one generation to the next as storytellers, have much knowledge of what the outside world has recorded in its history of the events that brought us here – never mind that it might differ from the truth of what happened. For one so young as you to have such knowledge is veritably impossible."

Caeleigh stumbled within her mind, searching for an acceptable honest answer to supply. "Old books, as I said before. Physical books cannot be withdrawn or rewritten." She fervently hoped that she had not stammered as much as she felt she had.

"Too true. Yet such items are in short supply among us here."

"Then how do *you* know?" The question escaped Caeleigh's lips before she had sufficient notice of her own curiosity to bind her tongue.

This query Abram chose to ignore.

Caeleigh persisted no further, for his impasse of confession was her own as well.

"I beg your forgiveness if I have been disrespectful in my questioning." She started nearly out of her seat at a loud noise from behind; Abram's apprentice had dropped an anvil in the center of the open floor.

The warmth of Abram's smile upon her could be felt despite his back being turned to her. When he returned to face Caeleigh, it was confirmed. "No, dear girl, you have not been impertinent. I'm simply seeking to remember where in the tale I left off yesterday." His hand was likewise warm on her shoulder as he passed by, moving around the shop in the rhythm of his work while she sat out of the way.

"You had briefly mentioned the covenants." Caeleigh watched the coppersmith return to the workbench with a pair of pliers and small acetylene torch and begin shaping the strips of metal.

"The covenants, yes. You are a faithful student of the scriptures?" This question Abram benignly posed.

"I do my utmost to be." Caeleigh found herself twisting the index finger of one hand in the pinch-grip of the other, praying that Abram wouldn't quiz her for a recitation. As often as she read the scriptures, she suffered a deplorable inability to commit them to memory. Her spirit held the truths, but her mind could not hold on to the exact wordings or their locations, is how she articulated the problem to Adeline.

Her mistress and friend had laughed – but compassionately so – and assured her that this did not give a poor reflection upon her efforts.

Abram broke into Caeleigh's rumination. "And we already covered one, I believe – the one borrowed from Moses' covenants in Deuteronomy, correct?"

"Yes, the one from the thirtieth chapter, regarding blessing for remaining faithful."

The coppersmith nodded. "That was the covenant the First Elders made with the people, as I had said yesterday. They – "

"The First Elders?" Caeleigh interrupted to clarify. Moments later she restrained a giggle when she realized that the shapes Abram had been forming were cookie cutters. What other purpose could there be for the rudimentary outline of a daisy?

Abram nodded in the affirmative, unperturbed by the disruption. "They also covenanted with Kadosh on behalf of the people. Or rather, *He* made a covenant with *them*. The First Elders had come to Kadosh seeking guidance for how to unify a group of people from disparate heritages and creeds, and He was honored by the covenant they had made with the people.

"With the words of the prophet Jeremiah, He pledged: *I will bring them back to this place, and I will make them dwell in safety. And they shall be my people, and I will be their God. I will give them one heart and one way, that they may fear me forever, for their own good and the good of their children after them. I will make with them an everlasting covenant, that I will not turn away from doing good to them. And I will put the fear of me in their hearts, that they may not turn from me. I will rejoice in doing them good, and I will plant them in this land in faithfulness, with all my heart and all my soul. 'For thus says the Lord: Just as I have brought all this great disaster upon this people, so I will bring upon them all the good that I promise them. Fields shall be bought in this land of which you are saying, "It is a desolation, without man or beast"…' "*

"He answered all of their unspoken fears!" Caeleigh exclaimed quietly. With a glance of permission from Abram, she continued aloud her thought. "They must have been timorous of so many unknowns, of what would become of them in what was a new and essentially foreign country. How were they to establish society and order life? What were they to do to provide for themselves and those dependent upon them? How would they keep their hearts right with Him?..."

Abram picked up where she trailed off. "Yes, with this covenant and the Bonding, all of their principal concerns were addressed."

At last, the subject had been raised upon which Caeleigh had most wanted to inquire, but had been too embarrassed to ask. She fervidly seized upon her opportunity. "Tell me of the Bonding, please."

This request, implored in earnest, took Abram by surprise; he set down his pliers and the newly-formed silhouette of a snowflake. "You mean you haven't yet... ?" Hastily he abridged the query when he noted the pain it raised in her eyes. The question had plainly stung to such a degree that it could only mean that she had not.

The coppersmith began anew in a gentler tone. "Forgive me. It usually occurs for most young people by the time they have reached their early- to mid-twenties. I oughtn't have made the assumption, however. My apprentice, Thomas, has yet to experience the Bonding either, so I have reason to have known better. I apologize."

Abram cleared his throat and resumed: "The Bonding is something the First Elders requested of Kadosh. You recall from yesterday that they had determined that it was a departure from family, as Kadosh had intended and ordered it, that allowed the beginning of compromise in the hearts of man and in society. In order to preserve themselves against recurrence of such a departure, the First Elders asked Kadosh for a means to ensure that His will for marriage and family would be carried out, without breach." Abram reached for his pliers to resume working, then rethought the impulse. The project was one without deadline, and some matters were of greater consequence. "His answer to their request was the Bonding. A man will Bond only with the woman Kadosh has purposed for him, and him for her, and only in the proper time according to His will. The Bonding is an activity of the Spirit of Truth within the human heart and cannot be coerced by human effort, nor can it be counterfeited."

"What is it like?" Caeleigh felt a fool to need to ask, and to ask a middle-aged bachelor at that, but something in Abram's fatherly demeanor gave her the courage to pose the humiliating question.

The coppersmith's answering smile quickly dissipated Caeleigh's unease. "Different men express it different ways, depending on how well they handle words. The best I've heard it articulated is that it's a stirring, a whispered confirmation in the depths of one's being: 'I have found the one created for my soul to love.' "

Caeleigh sat awestruck. "So beautiful..." she whispered, her voice tinged with longing.

"Beauty and love are at the core of the heart of Kadosh. They are His greatest gifts to us." Abram, having completed the last of his tasks for the afternoon, began to put away his tools and tidy his corner of the workshop. "After a man has Bonded with his Beloved – how soon after is of his choosing and discretion – he approaches her and makes a declaration of intention to court her. This isn't publicly done, but it *is* forthright. 'Another error of the past learned-from,' it was called when this part of our history was passed down to me."

The tailor's apprentice nodded with a greater understanding than she desired to speak.

"At some point in the course of their courtship, the woman Bonds in reciprocation. Not being a woman, I can't tell you firsthand how that experience occurs." He grinned. "You may prefer to ask Adeline for a female perspective." Abram toured the room, confirming that Thomas had set the rest of the workshop in order before sitting down to complete the last of his own tasks for the day.

"Kadosh did not, however, strip away our free will," Abram continued, "nor did the First Elders. It is yet permitted that a man may choose his own wife without waiting on the Bonding. Such is referred to as a Pledged marriage. In Pledged marriage, however, there is less certainty and more risk that the match might be less than ideal… For that reason, the First Elders decreed that only those with marriages from Bonding may hold positions of leadership in the Settlements, for those marriage partnerships have been set by Kadosh Himself."

Haltingly, Caeleigh dared pose one final question to the man who had grown to earn a measure of her trust in the past day and a half. "What of the way we speak? I understand that the land itself – and this isolation in it – has caused us to seemingly move backward in time in regard to the practice of trades. The physical means for much industrial technology became lost to us. But that doesn't explain why we speak as we do. I've noted that in the Border Settlements, at least the one I was in before I came here, there isn't this level of formality of language..."

She added this last statement in haste, lest the entire question appear too conspicuous.

If Abram caught any part of the blunder, he made no indication of it. "It was a conscious choice on the part of the First Elders. They were quite aware of the degradation of contemporary spoken language and they abhorred it... so they took advantage of their separation from the outside world and determined that we as a people would take pains to speak intelligently and choose those words which best convey the meaning we desire to express. I believe it is – at least in part – an outward symbol of the overall higher principles by which Kadosh has called us to live our lives."

Caeleigh nodded her understanding, as well as a request that Abram continue.

"You are correct, however, in your assessment that some of the Border Settlements have not upheld this standard as highly as we have here; I fear their proximity to the outside world leaves them vulnerable to its influences in more ways than simply this relatively harmless one." The coppersmith dropped himself upon his work stool, nearly dejected with the weight of woe. He studied the tailor's apprentice watching him, estimating her character, and when next Abram spoke, Caeleigh was uncertain whether his trail of thought had much changed with the subject of his conversation:

"A woman so young and full of life as you cannot enjoy the association of an old man like myself. Please tell me you've done as Adeline asked of you and taken up company with your peers. There are a number of young ladies who could benefit from a friendship with you... as would young Thomas, over there." This last suggestion was muttered conspiratorially so as not to be heard beyond the two of them, between the intermittent clangs of Thomas' rhythmic hammering as he crafted a bowl upon the anvil with which he'd frightened their guest the half-hour before.

Chapter 3

September 2146

"I thank you for your willingness to help me with this." Elizabeth spoke from inside one of the meetinghouse kitchen's large refrigerators, emerging with a juggled armload of the items she'd been seeking therein.

Caeleigh cleared space on the countertop and aided the lovely young blonde in setting everything in place without a spill as she replied, "I've wanted for a long time to learn how to bake, so this benefits me, as well, you know. Besides, I couldn't see one person preparing a sufficient number of pies to feed hundreds in the course of a single afternoon. There simply aren't enough hours in the day."

"It's merely dessert, not an entire meal." Elizabeth eyed the floursack leaning against the cabinetry beneath the counter. "I have no desire to suffer the backache that will come with repeatedly bending over for that. Let's set it up on the back of the counter. You're taller than I am – you'll be able to reach into it."

Together the two women attempted to lift the forty-pound sack of flour from the floor to the countertop, only to drop it from a height of two feet as the load proved too heavy and awkward for them, given how they grasped it. The top seam of the cotton sack pulled loose in their precarious grip and erupted in a cloud of white powder when it thudded between their feet.

As the dust settled and their coughing subsided, Elizabeth began to giggle.

"What?"

The baker pointed at the stainless steel refrigerator door's reflective surface. "I've become an old woman! I knew that feeding so many, and having to work so quickly around the schedule of the kitchen staff, would give me white hair one day – I only didn't think it would happen so quickly!"

"You're too young for white hair," Caeleigh returned, as they dusted themselves off.

"You say that as if *you* aren't. Mind, you're not *that* much older than I am." Elizabeth slid the floursack aside, resigned to intermittent bending, and scooped a substantive quantity of its contents into a bowl.

"Spend five years somewhere you don't want to be – it will quickly feel like an interminably long time," Caeleigh muttered acerbically, more to herself than to her best friend, while squinting and rubbing the offense of flour from her eyes.

Elizabeth tucked an errant curl behind her ear. "Truly, Caeleigh, there are moments when you say the most confounding things and I never know whether to take you seriously."

Not for the first time, Caeleigh was thankful to have befriended the very embodiment of grace, as Elizabeth had altogether disregarded her tone and chosen to address only her words. Redirecting the latter alone was more easily done with the former forgiven. "I simply meant to say that, once I knew Kadosh desired that I should live here, nowhere else would satisfy me. No other place could possibly be home, not for so much as an interim."

"Hm. I *do* love living here, I'll grant that," Elizabeth agreed as she guided Caeleigh in the measurement of dry ingredients to be combined.

Chapter Three

"How many more pie crusts do we need? I'm afraid I've lost count again." Striving with little more than dubitable success not to confuse the quantities of what she was to portion, Caeleigh had within two hours lost track of the other number she'd been responsible to remember.

Elizabeth quickly counted those they had already prepared. "Another four after these three we're working on at present. It shouldn't take long – we've been moving much more quickly since we began our little assembly line." As if to emphasize her point, Elizabeth set aside another pan, crust pressed into place and impeccably fluted with her fingertips. Though ostensibly simple, the process of manipulating the edges of the dough from both sides into the perfect symmetry that only Elizabeth could achieve had so intimidated Caeleigh that the latter woman had suggested a division of the tasks in order to avoid it. That so doing had improved their productivity had been an unintended blessing.

Immediately upon the completion of another panned crust, Elizabeth took the prepared dough from the bowl between them and began rolling it out, as Caeleigh mixed ingredients for the next.

Within an hour and a half, they were opening jars of canned strawberries, dicing rhubarb, and assembling large batches of pie filling to be ladled into the waiting pie crusts.

"It'll be a treat to have something prepared with strawberries after the season has ended," Elizabeth enthused. "When I saw how many jars were in the storehouse, I knew straight away this is what I wanted to do."

"How did they come to be there?" Caeleigh asked, altogether innocent of how such things were orchestrated.

"They likely were given in the first-fruits offering – no pun intended – when all of the farmers gave a portion of their first yield in faith for a full good season at the beginning of the harvest," Elizabeth explained. "The chief coordinator in charge of the kitchen would have had them canned as quickly as possible. After that, once the jars are crated and stacked, they sometimes are overlooked and forgotten. Hence the opportunity for out-of-season surprises!"

The two women continued chatting on light subjects until they set the first pies in the oven to bake. With less to demand their attention for a short while, they could afford themselves deeper conversation.

"Is there yet no one occupying the other half of your room in the lodginghouse?" Elizabeth enquired.

Caeleigh had not expected the question. "Not presently. Why do you ask?"

"I've sought my parents' permission to move into the lodginghouse and they have granted it. It's my hope that we might be roommates." The younger woman submitted her appeal with slight diffidence.

This announcement disconcerted Caeleigh; any woman who had the opportunity to live with her parents remained under their roof until marriage. For an unwed woman to leave her parents' house approached scandal. "What prompted you to make such a request?"

Elizabeth answered frankly. "A kindred spirit. I perceive in you the same soul-deep need for friendship that I myself have been experiencing."

"Are you certain, though, that you ought to do something as extreme as leave your parents' home without marrying?" Caeleigh's question, by contrast, was directed more to the countertop she was wiping clean of the flour that had coated much of the room.

"To be entirely forthright, I believe it will serve to bring peace between my mother and me. We're equally strong-willed, and for as much as we love one another and I desire to honor her, nearly every day holds some form of conflict," Elizabeth confessed. "We're simply too alike to remain in close quarters without tension. My father agreed when I spoke privately with him on the matter. He has given me his blessing to do this."

Within a fortnight, Elizabeth had moved into the women's lodginghouse to share the double-occupancy room Caeleigh had been placed in upon her arrival in the Blue Creek Settlement.

Elizabeth picked up one of the many hardcover novels Caeleigh had stacked about the room. "Charles Dickens. I'm beginning to understand why at times you speak a bit oddly. You're influenced by the writings of those whose speech was vastly different from ours."

"I'm sorry if they're underfoot," Caeleigh apologized. "I suppose I took advantage of the extra space so for long that I allowed it to become a habit." She began collecting the volumes that encroached upon the space that was rightfully now her friend's.

"You could have shelves built, or a bookcase, perhaps," her new roommate suggested. "My friend Peter has a man he calls brother who is a carpenter. You could ask him to build one for you. Young men often enjoy doing such things to earn the favor of women."

"I – I don't know…" Caeleigh stammered. "I'm not terribly confident with men."

"Why ever not?" Elizabeth straightened from the stack of books on the floor she was picking up and turned to her friend.

Caeleigh pointed to the mirror on the wall. "Look at yourself, and then look at me. You're a beautiful woman. Curly flaxen hair, lovely features, nicely proportioned all through your figure. My hair can't decide what color it is, red or blonde, and my build is just as indecisively mismatched. I won't bother to comment on the state of my face – there's nothing to remark upon there." She dropped her armload of books on the bed and dropped herself beside them.

"Don't judge yourself so unkindly. 'Man looks on the outward appearance, but the LORD looks on the heart,' as the scriptures say." Elizabeth sat beside her friend and put an arm around her shoulders. "Kadosh made you to look as you do, and *He* says you are lovely. Do you wish to contest His decision? I think the *true* problem with your appearance is that it hasn't been affirmed. So stand up and I will tell you what *I* see." Gently she nudged Caeleigh off the bed.

Caeleigh looked at Elizabeth as though the younger woman were mad.

"Go on, stand up," Elizabeth insisted, pushing a bit harder until her friend obeyed. "It's only me; it's not as though you have an audience."

"*Please* don't ask me to turn in a circle."

"Fair enough." Elizabeth studied Caeleigh for a moment, then offered her evaluation: "My father's sister has hair similar in color to yours. She calls it auburn, and she is in fact rather proud of it. When her husband was courting her, he would take her out into the sunshine and proclaim that he saw tones of rose gold and yellow gold in her hair – he's a jeweler, and uses the colors of gemstones and precious metals as metaphors quite often.

"To answer your complaints regarding your face ... smile. You're moping at the moment and that helps you none at all. ...Much better. Your face is what my father likes to call 'a blank canvas' or a plain-faced beauty. I know both of those terms may sound a bit harsh, but those are the type of face he most enjoys sketching, because the beauty issues from within – it isn't contained within the features; it bears out in the emotions that convey more easily than on 'other' types of faces. 'An artist puts forth his best work when he begins painting on a blank canvas, rather than one that has strict lines drawn upon it from the beginning,' he says.

"As for the last complaint, I blame you." This Elizabeth said not unkindly. "You begin from a place of self-doubt and dress to hide it. The result is that you exacerbate your appearance rather than flatter it. You're a tailor, aren't you? *Tailor* your clothes. Thin out the lines of your skirts to make them less full at the waist. Try a more fitted blouse; all that loose material is adding bulk. Bring in the lines of your bodice a little more. All that extra 'you' that you despise is made of fabric!"

A week later, Elizabeth took Caeleigh to meet Peter. The man she encountered surprised the tailor's apprentice – not for his winsome, jocular demeanor; such was the personality type Elizabeth naturally gravitated toward as a carefree individual herself. She was mildly surprised to learn that, despite his Anglicized name, the stonemason was Hispanic in heritage. She was well aware and well at ease with the wide and variant range of ethnicities that made up the body of their community. She was less at ease with how conscious and comfortable Peter seemed to be regarding how attractive he was.

Tall and broad-shouldered, with dark laughing eyes and naturally tightly-curled black hair, he was a man who Caeleigh could see considered himself suave, and who was confident that women agreed with his self-assessment. She was hard-pressed to impugn him, however, seeing how readily charmed Elizabeth had become, a woman who was otherwise quite sensible. He greeted Caeleigh cheerfully as their mutual association introduced them, complimenting her generously on both her appearance and the kindness she'd extended in providing a place for Elizabeth to live outside of her father's home, as well as issuing florid praise for the strawberry pies the two women had prepared together.

Despite Peter's equal meting out of attention to both women, Caeleigh, self-conscious in her recently altered clothes, refused to speak beyond saying hello, leaving Elizabeth to make the request.

"My friend and roommate has more books than can be contained in any way we've been able to manage. Do you think your friend the carpenter would be willing to build a bookcase for her?"

"Andrew? I don't see why he wouldn't. He likely won't ask for compensation, either, knowing him. I'll ask him about it at the evening meal."

Fewer days than anticipated later, an older woman whom Caeleigh considered an unofficial housematron of the women's lodginghouse made her way down the hall, instructing everyone to keep to their rooms with the doors closed. Arriving at Caeleigh and Elizabeth's door, she informed the pair that a male would be granted temporary permission to enter, to carry in a piece of furniture, and that she would escort him and they were to wait outside the room. Having already made space for the bookcase, the young women stepped into the hall as they'd been bidden.

Minutes later the housematron returned, leading the young man as promised. He bore the frame of the bookcase on his back in the likeness of a turtle shell, and she carried a number of boards meant to serve as shelves. He strode into the room, seeming to take care not to cast his eyes about, and set the case beneath the window in the space prepared for it. Kneeling, he relieved the housematron of her burden and inserted the shelves in their places. Quickly and efficiently he finished the task and rose to leave.

Elizabeth thanked the carpenter on behalf of her once-more-stoic friend as he passed them.

"You're Elizabeth, correct?" he asked in reply, tucking loose strands of long, dark hair behind his ears. "Peter speaks well of you."

Elizabeth nodded both to him and to the housematron's cautioning glance. "We'll see you out." She tugged Caeleigh along by the hand.

The housematron followed, supervising, until the trio exited to the porch. At her friend's continual prodding, Caeleigh spoke at last. "What do you ask in compensation for the bookcase?"

The carpenter turned to her, an indeterminate ardent light flashing in his eyes. "To know your name is all I would require of you."

His expression, which might potentially have been considered innocent had she been better disposed toward him, combined with the merest hint of husk in his tone, raised her guard. Promptly she determined to distrust the man and wanted nothing to do with him.

To Caeleigh's misfortune, Elizabeth had not read him similarly. "Her name is Caeleigh."

"Caeleigh," he repeated, trying the name as though tasting a delicacy. "That's quite an unusual name. And quite lovely. I'm Andrew."

Caeleigh despised the smile he offered. It far too closely resembled those she had received from men in the Border Settlements on her way west, men whose intentions had been less than favorable. Brushing past his hand extended in obeisance, she retreated once more into the lodginghouse where, his task completed, his presence was no longer permitted.

Chapter 4

Late February 2147

"Elizabeth, I haven't the words to convey how *pleased* I am for you. This is a remarkable opportunity for you to practice your talents," Caeleigh enthused as she transferred trays from the oven to the stainless steel counter. Not yet oriented to this new environment, she turned two or three circles in search of the peg upon which she was to hang the towel she'd folded to protect her hand from the hot metal.

In so doing, she took in again the sight of the nearly-completed bakery that had been built for Elizabeth. Recent visitors from the Cypress Ridge and Cedar Rapids Settlements had sampled her desserts and asked if she would be willing to bake to order. Without her meaning it to, Elizabeth's baking had become a vocation – one that could not efficiently share space with the preparation of meals for the Blue Creek Settlement. Peter had been the one to recommend building a separate bakery adjoining the meetinghouse kitchen, providing Elizabeth her own workspace as immediately as possible, yet affording her the accessible use of the existing appliances while waiting for her own to be ordered and installed.

Pointing to a hook beneath the wall-mounted shelf overhead, her petite friend snickered. "You 'haven't the words to convey'? You've been reading Jane Austen again, haven't you?" she teased. "Only you would find enjoyment in reading what the rest of us consider taxing to the mind."

"It's a superb story, else it wouldn't have remained a classic across the span of centuries, unlike other, less-well-written piteous attempts to pass themselves off as great literature," Caeleigh defended. She took up a broad-bladed dull knife and joined Elizabeth in the task of applying thick, sweet frosting to the warm cookies between them on the counter.

"Is she speaking English?" The question was grunted from behind the industrial refrigerator inching its way through the door.

"Peter! That was *worse* than unkind!" Elizabeth rebuked him. "Simply because Caeleigh is as a sister to me and you are as a brother to me does *not* make the two of you brother and sister and give you license to ridicule my dearest friend!"

Peter bore the reproval in silence while maneuvering the refrigerator into its place and setting it up. "My apologies to you both. *Hermanita,* you're fortunate I chose to pay no mind to your pique and leave this for you to plug in and finish moving on your own," he upbraided with a sternness that may or may not have been genuine.

Elizabeth bowed her head in apology. "You'd have been right to do so, Elder Brother; forgive me," she responded to his Spanish affectation with its English counterpart. As Peter stepped nearer, she continued, "I will be striving for quite some time, I think, to fully express my gratitude for all that you've done to assist me in setting up the bakery."

Peter grinned puckishly as he replied, "Thanks are not necessary – but I *will* accept a cookie." Standing as notably taller than she as he was, he reached over the petite woman's head and plucked up two of the freshly frosted cookies from the counter.

Elizabeth grabbed the nearest benign object within reach – the quarter-folded towel she'd used to hold the trays while removing the cookies – and with it swatted Peter's arm.

Peter laughed and winked before making his escape with the pilfered cookies.

As the two women watched his departure, Caeleigh remarked to Elizabeth, "I believe he's beginning to be inclined toward you."

Elizabeth blushed at the suggestion. "That's absurd! Peter regards me as a younger sister, nothing more. That's what his epithet for me means."

Caeleigh raised her hands in surrender, despite the fact that Elizabeth remained armed with nothing more than the towel. "Rest easy; I wasn't suggesting he's infatuated with you, nor you with him. I was merely observing his affection for you."

"Peter has been an invaluable help to me with this bakery. He has given so much of his own time and labor, and convinced those of other trades to refuse compensation for their work as well. Truly, I can't say what state I'd be in if not for all the aid he has rendered." Elizabeth paused momentarily to take in the sight of the bakery – *her* bakery. "I cannot believe this has truly come to be. I feel as though I am walking through a dream."

"It isn't a dream, my friend. This is real, and no one deserves the blessing more."

The baker shook her blonde curls vigorously. "Truly it was a practical matter – sharing the meetinghouse kitchen interfered with the preparation of meals. And their schedule was equally disruptive of mine. It simply made the most sense for me to work in a separate space."

"Don't speak so, Elizabeth," Caeleigh reprimanded gently. "If you persist to entertain such thoughts, you may dissuade yourself of your talent."

Peter arrived at the work site, yet in high spirits, and offered one of the two cookies to Andrew with a flourish. "My Brother, I present to you the latest sweet achievement of the exceptionally sweeter Elizabeth."

"Is the bakery now complete?"

Andrew compensated for his ineludible lack of shared enthusiasm by accepting the confection and pouring himself a cup of coffee to complement it.

Peter likewise partook of the coffee Andrew had brought to the work site. "It is. I completed the last of the appliance installations this morning. I can't deny I'll miss having a reason to spend a measure of time in her company daily."

Not long after, the two men resumed the task of setting the frames for the foundation of a new home to be built.

"You sound as though you're beginning to grow infatuated with her. Is she aware of your affection?" The carpenter retrieved another beam from the pile of lumber and set it in place.

Peter downed the last of his coffee, wishing he'd had a second cookie to offset the bitter dregs that had settled at the bottom of the mug. He contemplated returning to the bakery for another cookie... and another glimpse of its creator. "I address her only as 'younger sister.' I don't believe my heart toward her has grown strong enough to be given more voice than that."

Andrew momentarily paused his hands and gave the young stonemason a chastising frown. "The Spanish word has both that meaning *and* the greater endearment. By addressing her thus without informing her of both meanings of the word, you're misleading Elizabeth regarding the nature of your intentions, Peter."

"You've taken quite nearly the same tone Elizabeth directed toward me earlier," the younger man quipped, attempting to dispel the tension.

"What did you do to earn it from *her?*" From his limited acquaintance with her, Andrew knew Elizabeth to be a woman of mild temperament. He anticipated that Peter's answer would amuse him.

"Nothing more than a bit of harmless jesting, directed toward her friend Caeleigh."

"How did *she* respond?" Andrew's grip flexed involuntarily tighter on the handle of his mallet, the impulse to safeguard rising like bile in his throat.

Peter was altogether ignorant of the carpenter's response. "She didn't say a word the entire time I was there."

"It sounds to me as though your jesting may have wounded her. You might want to consider treating Caeleigh more kindly... if you wish to remain in Elizabeth's good graces."

Several wordless minutes later, Andrew set aside his tools, his frame of mind perceptibly altered. "You'll have to continue without me," he spoke gruffly. "I am required to intercede in prayer – it may take a significant amount of time."

"The same individual again?" Peter's response to Andrew's sudden change in disposition was neither alarmed nor discompassionate. This had become a routine occurrence.

The carpenter nodded. "As always." With these words he departed, seeking a place where he might find solitude for the travail that he knew would soon be upon him.

Hidden in a place of which only she had knowledge, Caeleigh screamed out all of her agony and frustration.

"Tell me truly, do You *delight* in my misery?!" she shouted into the trees around her hidden clearing. "Does it *amuse* You to taunt and mock me?! Do You *enjoy* it when every time that You give that which I desire to another, *right in front of my face,* it drives me ever deeper into despair?!

"*Why* do You do this to me?! *Why* do You allow such things to happen?! Do I matter *so little* to You?!" she demanded of the sky. "This is a tribulation of the heart which *I haven't* the strength to bear!

"*You said* that You came that I might have *life,* and life to the *full* – yet my life is *empty!* You instructed that I should delight myself in You and You would give me the desires of my heart! ... I have *done* that! I have *followed* You where You led me, and *obeyed* You to my utmost, and yet my heart's deepest desire remains *unmet!* Whether the words mean that You will give me what I long for, or that You would make my heart long for the proper thing, is *irrelevant* – The desire is *still* there, and it is *still ignored!*

"This is *not* the life I *desire!*" Caeleigh raged between sobs. "You spoke to me and *told* me that You crafted my heart *specifically* and *deliberately* for the love partnership of marriage! And yet the *very thing* for which You *purposed* me, You *withhold!*

"I have *begged* and *pleaded* and *sought* after You for *some purpose* for my life to which I could apply myself ... so that the emptiness of my heart will not always be before my eyes, so that I can *know* how to serve and seek You instead of always bemoaning my loneliness – but even *this* You do not grant me!

"*Why* should I persist after You, when *all* I can conclude from what I see is that You *despise* my heart?! You *promise* blessing, and peace, and contentment, and I have found *none* of these!"

Caeleigh sank her knees, utterly spent.

"There is nothing – absolutely *nothing* for me!" Caeleigh sighed. "…'Though he slay me, I will hope in him.' …Though my flesh waste away and my heart wither within me, still I will praise His name…

"I *beg* of You… if You *truly* have *meant* the things You've told me – if You *truly intend* to keep the word You gave to me – Won't You *please* bring into my life the man You have *said* You have prepared for me?"

Locked in his workshop, Andrew groaned as one suffering the pains of death. Gathering the last reserves of his strength of will, he pushed back against the tidal wave of despair, slamming white-knuckled clenched fists against the hardwood floor as he prayed.

His final entreaty was for himself: "Kadosh, I *cannot* endure in this manner any longer! I *beseech* You – there *must* be *some* other way that I can help her!"

Chapter 5

Early March 2147

"Friends!" Governor Caleb called from the head of the room. "Before we offer thanks for this evening's meal, it is my joyous privilege to announce to you that our brother Peter has informed me today that he has Bonded with a young woman and declared to her his intentions of courtship." A middle-aged African American of trim physique and average height, the Governor of the Blue Creek Settlement always seemed taller and fuller in his build when he made these announcements, as though his joy at another marriage soon to come would not physically be contained within him. Exceptionally romantic himself, Caleb routinely took a moment during the ensuing cheers and shouted congratulations to steal a kiss with his own wife of thirty-plus years, further provoking his friends and adult children and their families.

Anything said after Caleb's initial pronouncement, Caeleigh missed entirely. Unlike many others in the room, she had no need to speculate as to the woman's identity. At her right hand, Elizabeth did her best not to appear flustered under the significant glances Peter was casting their way from where he stood, not far from Caleb. Caeleigh had suspected for some time that Peter might Bond with Elizabeth; her friend was sweet, kind-hearted, and nurturing – there was nothing not to love about her.

Now, as Peter took a seat across the table from them, Caeleigh surreptitiously observed her best friend. Elizabeth's countenance lit in response to Peter's smile. Theirs would not be a long courtship, Caeleigh decided, before Elizabeth would Bond in kind with Peter. Regardless of her own emotions, she could not begrudge them their happiness. The Bonding was, she believed, one of the great blessings Kadosh had bestowed upon the people of the Settlements. Uncertainty was absent in the confidence that those who Bonded with one another had been chosen for each other by Him and ordained by Him to be together. Of added benefit was the fact that the Bonding was impossible to counterfeit; no cause for insecurity or fear could stand before it.

Thus, it seemed to Caeleigh, that a man's Bonding with a woman was as good as an announcement of betrothal, for the latter was a foregone conclusion and a question of nothing other than time. She did celebrate with genuine gladness for Elizabeth – and for Peter, as well. Yet she could not altogether ignore the hollow feeling of having been left behind. Elizabeth was five years her junior. If younger women were being chosen now, then her own chance must be becoming significantly less.

Sensing that she was being watched, Caeleigh looked up and caught sight of a tall young man of Native American complexion, who sat further up the table from Peter, staring at her with an unreadable expression. She quickly suppressed her despondency, smiled brightly and forced herself to join the conversation around her with more enthusiasm than she felt.

As soon as it was possible to do so both discreetly and politely, Caeleigh excused herself. She made her way to the shadows at the end of the meetinghouse porch and leaned the side of her face against the corner post, wrapping her arm around the post and gripping it and the rail with both of her hands.

"Oh, Kadosh, *why* must this pain me so deeply?" she spoke into the stillness of the evening. "I *am* sincerely happy for them. But I feel as though I have been passed over. Is there no man who would love *me?* Am I destined to forever be alone?" She sighed. "But if that is what You have chosen for me, then I will obey and forbear it. I am sorry for my self-centered thinking, and I thank You for gifting me with a trade by which I am able to provide for myself." Eyes closed, she stood motionless and quiet for several minutes, reordering the attitude of her heart.

"Are you alright?"

The unexpected voice nearby startled Caeleigh back into the present moment. She turned to see who had approached. The man beside her looked vaguely familiar, but she could not place from where she knew him.

"I'm sorry if I frightened you. I'm Andrew. Peter's friend," he offered in explanation, tucking loose strands of his long hair behind his ears.

"Oh. Yes. Hello." Caeleigh spoke haltingly as recognition dawned. It was the young man who had spent most of the evening meal watching her.

"Are you alright?" he asked a second time.

"Yes … no ... I …" Caeleigh sighed as Andrew leaned backward against the banister. "It's …" She gestured toward Peter and Elizabeth as they walked up the street. "I suppose I'm feeling a bit envious."

"You care for Peter?"

"No, not him specifically. Every time there is a Bonding, especially for someone younger than I, it leaves me feeling … wistful. Lonely."

Andrew smiled enigmatically. "Your turn will come, in the proper timing."

"Please don't ply me with platitudes and promises of baseless hope." Caeleigh clenched her eyes shut and tightened her grip on the rail.

Andrew smiled again, more genially this time, intending to reassure. "I'm not. I'm saying that Kadosh has told me that He has chosen a man for you."

"I don't mean to be rude, but I have increasing trouble believing people who say that, the longer it continues *not* to happen."

Andrew recoiled slightly at Caeleigh's biting words and tone, causing her to wish that she could retract both.

"I'm sorry … You didn't deserve that. Please accept my apology."

He stepped a bit closer. "All's forgiven. You're hurting, and such pain is bound to express itself sooner or later."

"Rather *later* than sooner; now I'm certain I've given a terrible first impression to you."

"Not at all." When Caeleigh remained unconvinced, Andrew furthered, "This is the first impression I have of you: that you have both an immeasurable capacity and a great desire for love. That your heart toward Kadosh is both honest and obedient. And that, if I may be so forward to say it, you could use a friend."

"So you heard my prayer a moment ago." Caeleigh turned in Andrew's direction but cast her eyes to the floorboards of the porch.

"A lot can be learned about a person from what she says when she prays in earnest," he offered gently, his tone imploring that Caeleigh might meet his eyes and there find him to be sincere. "But that wasn't why I followed you. The way you left the table, I thought something might be wrong. I wanted to help, if I could."

"I was trying to slip away unnoticed – I suppose I didn't succeed as well as I thought I had." As the conversation turned less intimately personal, Caeleigh was able to look into the man's face. He seemed open, honest, and ... afraid of frightening her. The last of these surprised her, for he was otherwise a confident man, so she called out the point. "Am I correct in surmising that you're worried about alarming me by having approached me as you have?"

The observation gave him pause. "Yes, a bit," he admitted. "I might not have approached you at all, but that I caught a look in your eyes that gave me concern for you. I read people well – it's one of my gifts." He made the statement plainly, without pride or boasting.

Caeleigh nodded. "I will be fine, but I thank you for your concern."

"If it helps at all, I understand what you are likely feeling. Like Elizabeth and you, Peter is younger than I, yet he will be married much sooner. Kadosh has told me, quite specifically, that I must yet wait for what He has promised me." Though Andrew had not intended to disclose so much immediately, he dared do so in hope that it would provide a foundation upon which he could build.

Softening with empathy, Caeleigh dropped her guardedness. "How do you endure the wait? Is it, perhaps, something I could try to make this ache less?"

Rewarded, Andrew replied with earnest candor. "I pursue the heart of Kadosh. His love is ever-available and never-failing. Seek His love, and let it be sufficient. It *is* more than sufficient, truly."

"Thank you," she said with a sincerity that told him she had accepted his words.

"Do you mind if I change the subject?" Andrew asked, mindful that he needed to take care to direct the conversation toward more neutral themes before matters ran beyond his control; he needed to *earn* Caeleigh's trust, not presume it.

Andrew's very apparent desire to be a friend to her made Caeleigh smile. "I'd be grateful if you would." Her smile grew as her response was received by him as if it were a reward.

"You are one of the tailors of the Settlement, correct?" This was something Andrew had heard, but considering his source was Peter, who was understandably distracted of late, he wished to confirm the fact.

Caeleigh nodded. "Yes, I am. Is there something you need made? Or mended?"

"Mended, I suppose. I can stop by where you work, tomorrow, and show you. I don't know how to describe in the terms of your trade what the problem is."

"I'm certain that would be the simplest approach, yes. I work from the home of the widow Adeline – it's easier than attempting to work from the lodginghouse."

"I see," Andrew nodded. "Especially since men are not permitted to enter the women's lodginghouse."

"Exactly. It benefits Adeline, too, though, because I'm present and available to help her when she needs assistance. I *did* apprentice under her, as well. She's the one who recognized that I'd been gifted with the skills of the trade, and she taught me nearly everything I know." All of this tumbled forth at increasing speed, accompanied by a rising brightness in the young tailor's eyes.

"Very well, then." Andrew admired openly Caeleigh's passion for her work, so vibrantly different from the loneliness that had overshadowed her minutes before. "I shall see you tomorrow morning before I start my own work for the day."

Caeleigh agreed to the appointment, then asked, "May I request a favor of you?"

"Of course." Andrew smiled. "That's what friends are for."

"Would you escort me back to the women's lodginghouse? Usually I walk with Elizabeth, or some of the other women, but I think everyone has already left without me." She had stunned herself with the boldness of the petition, considering how little she knew the man. Yet for reasons unknown, Caeleigh felt safe with him.

"Afraid of the dark?" Andrew could not resist to quip.

Caeleigh tipped up her head in defiance of his teasing. "It isn't a matter of fear; it's a matter of preference and sensibility."

Andrew laughed. "Indeed."

The following morning Caeleigh looked up from her sewing machine when Adeline answered the door and ushered Andrew into the dining room, which had been converted into first her, then also Caeleigh's, workspace.

"This young man says he has an appointment," Adeline announced.

"He does," was Caeleigh's apologetic reply. "I forgot to add it to the written schedule. Good morning," she greeted Andrew. "What is this 'indescribable' repair you need?"

He unfolded a pair of denim trousers on an open space on the dining-table-turned-work-table, and stepped back to allow the women to see for themselves. Both knees of the trousers were worn threadbare and shredded open; the outside leg seams strained against the stitching holding them together. Evidence of other tears and previous patching covered nearly half of the fabric.

"What do you do?" Adeline asked, astounded at the extent of damage. "Wrestle wild tigers?"

"I'm a carpenter. I lay wood floors and install cabinetry, mostly. Can these be mended? Three others are in equally bad condition."

"I don't see how." Adeline raised her hands in surrender and informed Caeleigh, "This is *your* appointment; it's *your* project."

Andrew turned to Caeleigh, who paid him no attention. "Dungaree is obviously insufficient," she mused aloud. "Sailcloth would be tougher, but unsuitable for garment-making. ...Leather," she finally concluded.

"What?"

"There's no point in repairing these – the material is so distressed that, even if repairs *would* take hold, they wouldn't withstand the strain. Simply replacing them with the same thing again would bring you directly back around to the same point when the new ones wear out. I'll have to try buckskin leather – it's the only thing durable enough that won't be uncomfortable."

"Have you ever worked with leather before?" Adeline interjected. "I know I never have."

"There's a first time for everything," Caeleigh replied. To Andrew she said, "Has the mercantile shopkeeper expressed any desire for work you could do?"

"Possibly." His tone requested explication.

Caeleigh retrieved her electronic tablet from the sideboard, opened a new file, and began making notations for the job as she spoke. "Leather is purchased on a large roll that would be more than I'll need for this one job. It will also require tools that I don't have. If you purchase the leather and the tools I'll need, I'll make four pairs to replace all those that you've indicated are in this bad a condition. I'll retain the tools and excess leather as payment, and calculate an amount of credit for your future use, based upon the difficulty of the work once I'm able to assess it. Is that agreeable to you?"

Thoroughly impressed by this point, Andrew would have agreed to a higher price, had Caeleigh quoted him one. "Abundantly fair. Let me know what you'll need, and I'll barter my work for it."

"I'll go to the mercantile this afternoon or tomorrow, and make a list of the items to order." Saving her notes, Caeleigh thanked Andrew with a shy smile.

After Andrew had departed, Adeline questioned Caeleigh. "Don't you think you underpriced the job? Even with a margin for error if you can't guarantee the quality of work you've never done before ... a *credit* on top of four garments?" Adeline had spent years coaching her apprentice on the value and quality of the work she produced; the quote she had moments before witnessed was a distant departure from that teaching.

"Not for the size of the roll of leather I'll be ordering, not to mention the quantity of needles and the cutting tools." Caeleigh rummaged in a sideboard drawer for the manual to her sewing machine. "This project isn't going to end with one carpenter – the stonemasons, the metalsmiths, and who knows how many other manual labormen will all be wanting the same. Truly, I don't know *why* I never thought of using leather before."

"Because I never taught you to be so creative." Adeline smiled, patting the younger woman's hand. "I know you haven't been my apprentice anymore for a few years, but you truly are coming into your own as a tradeswoman."

Caeleigh smiled thankfully at the older woman. "Save your compliments for after I've completed the job and earned them."

Early / Mid May 2147

"I owe you sincere thanks," Caeleigh told Andrew two months later as they walked to Adeline's home.

Adjusting the load he carried, he grunted as it bounced on his shoulder. "This roll of leather is taller and larger than you are," he replied. "I couldn't see you attempting to carry it yourself. I'm simply glad to have been in the right place at the right time, to be able to help you."

"That isn't what I meant." Caeleigh shook her head with a smile. "Ever since that sewing job I did for you, it seems half the men in the Blue Creek Settlement would rather have trousers of buckskin than plain cloth. I have had no shortage of work, due to the trend you began. I suspected that the manual labormen would find it preferable given their work, but it hasn't stopped there. It's gratifying to know I'm making a contribution to the community of the Settlement, and I've been able to provide amply for Adeline as well as myself. So, thank you."

"You're welcome. I've always believed that you were the one who did *me* the favor, finding a means of making clothes that could survive what I put them through. To see you blessed beyond a single job … well, all I can say is that you deserve it." Andrew allowed Caeleigh to precede him up the porch steps of Adeline's home.

Caeleigh held open the door for Andrew and guided him to where he could set down the leather. She then immediately ushered the carpenter to the door, picking up a package from the table beside it on her way.

"Adeline isn't home?" he asked as she closed the door behind them.

"She's visiting her sister on the far other side of the Settlement for a few days," Caeleigh replied. "She – the sister – hasn't been well, and needs help until she's fully recovered."

"I see. And where are *you* off to, now? You aren't following me, are you?" Andrew teased, since Caeleigh had stayed close at his side as he proceeded toward his own shop.

"Of course not. I have a delivery to make to the blacksmith." She held up the brown-paper-wrapped bundle in her hands. "I don't mind to go unescorted in the daytime, but I wasn't going to pass on the opportunity to not have to walk across town alone. Besides, I'm not entirely certain I remember the correct way to get there."

Andrew smiled at his companion. "Fair enough. What did you think of this morning's teaching?" He had observed her taking notes during the teaching that daily followed each communal morning meal.

The day's teaching had been on the subject of persistence. David, an engineer by trade, had read from Luke's gospel and spoken on the need to persist when presenting requests to Kadosh and not receiving an immediate reply. The seeming resistance was not a *refusal,* David had said, but rather for the purpose of building character in the requestor, to make them more in nature like the Christ.

Caeleigh returned the carpenter's smile as she shifted her burden from one arm to the other. "I enjoyed it. David's teaching always challenges me to think."

"He challenges *me,* as well. I wouldn't be surprised if he were to become Governor of the next Settlement to be Planted, or at least one of the candidates, as wise as he is."

Andrew's comment, casually made, stirred Caeleigh's curiosity. "Do you suppose another Settlement will be Planted in the near future? I've never witnessed a Planting before."

Andrew shrugged, his hands opened upward in a display of nescience. "I don't know. What I *do* know is that the Blue Creek Settlement is growing larger than most other Settlements of which I have knowledge. Whether or when a Planting is sent out is a matter of the Governor's discretion – and Kadosh's command, of course."

Caeleigh nodded her agreement.

For a time, they walked in silence, until Andrew spoke once more. "Are you alright?"

Caeleigh focused her gaze on the cobblestones before her, choosing where to place her next steps on the well-worn street. "What makes you ask?"

"You have that haunted look in your eyes again, the same one you had the night Peter's Bonding was announced." He stopped and took hold of Caeleigh's elbow, halting her as well. "You know you can confide in me," he told her softly.

The tailor struggled to meet her friend's eyes. "I know. I oughtn't say anything, since nothing has been publicly announced, but … Elizabeth has Bonded with Peter."

"Last evening – I know. Peter told me." Andrew took care with the information he knew would injure Caeleigh more deeply than it had him. "He's planning to propose marriage within the next few days. That's why I was at the mercantile this morning – he wanted assistance in choosing the betrothal ring." Seeing that the news had borne the effect he'd warranted it might, Andrew changed the subject somewhat. "While I was there, I saw the roll of leather and knew it must be yours, so I waited there for you, to be truthful."

The unexpected admission plucked Caeleigh momentarily from the despair into which she'd been rapidly descending. "You delayed the start of your workday so that you could *happen* to be there when I arrived to pick up the leather, so that you could carry it for me?"

By the tone of her response, Andrew realized he had redirected their conversation too far, causing Caeleigh to misunderstand his intentions. Speaking gently so as not to belittle, he clarified, "I knew Elizabeth would have informed you of her Bonding, the same as Peter told me. I wanted to be certain that you were alright, having heard the news. I know how deeply it affected you when *he* Bonded with *her*."

A solitary tear slipped unbidden down Caeleigh's cheek. Her voice broke as she told him, "I will be fine."

Heartache dried Andrew's throat as he was forced to accept Caeleigh's lie by his inability to speak words that would bring the comfort he longed for her to have. "I'm here if you need a friend to lean on. Remember, I understand exactly what you're going through."

"I know." She wiped the tear away with her sleeve, cleared her throat, and stood a little straighter. "Would you please instruct me how to find the blacksmith from here? I have a great deal of work to be done today."

Andrew gave her the directions, then before she turned to leave, he put a hand on her shoulder and bowed his head near to hers in low-spoken prayer. "Kadosh, Your scriptures tell us that not so much as a sparrow falls to the ground without Your notice and care. I ask that You would let my friend know that You notice her, and that You would draw her close to lean upon

You in the present and coming days. Allow her to feel Your care for her in this season."

Caeleigh thanked him, then with some hesitation asked, "It isn't a sin of selfishness, is it? To hurt so deeply as this?"

"Of course not. Wounded though it may be, your heart is in the proper place. Don't allow your pain to turn you bitter, and you will be fine." There was infinitely more Andrew could have said, but daren't, instead pulling back with every available ounce of strength on the reins of self-restraint until the bit cut into the flesh of his own conflicted spirit.

Turning to leave, Caeleigh looked back. "Thank you, Andrew. For your friendship, and for everything else."

"It's my pleasure," he replied with a solemn smile.

To say that Marcus the blacksmith was pleased would be an understatement. Lifting his leather apron from the wrapping and shaking it out, he laughed aloud. He set down the apron just long enough to remove and cast aside the old one – pocked with singed holes from wayward cinders despite the heaviness of the canvas – then gleefully picked up his new gift and pulled it over his head. Slapping himself across the belly as he continued to laugh, he caused Caeleigh to smile more broadly than she would have thought possible that day.

"This is wonderful!" the large man boomed while tying the leather strings behind his back. "What do I owe you for it? I know I didn't order it, and I can't expect you to be simply giving away your work."

Caeleigh withdrew from her handbag a metal disc one-and-a-half inches in diameter and a quarter of an inch thick. "Four dozen of these weights, made exactly like this one." She handed it over for his inspection.

"Only four dozen?" The bid seemed far too low. Marcus worried that he was expected to make a counter-offer. He'd heard of the tailor willing to work with leather, who, despite a reputation for being generous, was neither so inexperienced nor foolhardy as a businesswoman to make such an insignificant barter.

Caeleigh stood her ground, equally as confident of what she was asking as what she was offering. "Per *each* of the aprons, *plus* the referral of anyone who asks you who made them."

Marcus reached again for the opened package. *"Each? Them?"*

Caeleigh further unfolded the wrapping and produced a second apron. "I took the liberty of making one for your apprentice, as well, while I was already started."

"You've got yourself a deal," the blacksmith grinned as he heartily shook her hand. "And if I may say so, you've also got a very good mind for business. I'll be happy to refer anyone who shows interest. As far as I know, you're the only tailor in all of the Blue Creek Settlement willing to work with leather."

Marcus' praise ducked Caeleigh's head nearly halfway to her shoulders. She hand-pressed open a fold in the brown paper in which she'd packaged the aprons. "I only work with suede, though. I can't work with any of the tougher types."

"What you do is already more than anyone else does, Miss. As long as you do that much, you don't need to do everything. Besides, if you *did* start making other items, you'd put my wife's brother, the leathersmith, out of work!" Marcus laughed again, then called for his apprentice.

Having concluded business, Caeleigh found her way back to a familiar street and returned to Adeline's home and the work that awaited her there.

The day promised to be long, and was only beginning.

Chapter 7

Mid May 2147

That evening, as Caeleigh had expected, Elizabeth's Bonding was announced to all gathered for the evening meal. Having been pulled aside by their male and female friends, respectively, Peter and Elizabeth spent the duration of the meal apart. Swept up among the women surrounding her best friend, Caeleigh found herself promising to make the dresses for both the bride-to-be and the as-yet-unnamed woman who would stand up as witness for her during the marriage ceremony.

After the dishes from the meal were cleared, Elizabeth took Caeleigh aside as the two of them went to the kitchen to help serve the dessert the baker had prepared. In the brief moment the two were alone, Elizabeth professed her sisterly affection for Caeleigh and asked if she would stand as her witness. "I know I am asking more of you than is asked of most brides' witnesses, by asking you to make the dresses as well..." she began.

Caeleigh interrupted her friend. "You have no need to apologize. I *offered* to make the dresses. They will be my gift to you," she added as they joined the servingwomen from the kitchen in picking up large trays of portioned-out desserts.

Navigating between the tables to serve, Caeleigh was stopped by Peter as she passed him. At his inquiry, she confirmed that she had agreed to Elizabeth's request to stand up for her as witness.

"I'm glad to hear it," Peter responded. "Elizabeth has told me many times that she considers you to be the sister she never had." He turned to the man beside him. "Allow me to introduce you to the man I've asked to stand up as *my* witness – Andrew has been as much my brother as you are my Beloved's sister."

"We've already met," Andrew informed Peter. "She is the tailor I've told you of – the one who works with leather." The statement was delivered with the sort of elder-brotherly warning look that meant *'Do not repeat what I have told you.'*

Peter's expression carried mischief.

Andrew spoke before Peter took the opportunity. "Please tell me you're not conniving to play at matchmaking. I've told you before that I am waiting on the Bonding – I have no interest in being paired with anyone other than the woman Kadosh has chosen for me."

"I intend no such thing," Peter rebutted with less-than-complete innocence. "I am only thinking of the *way* you've spoken of – "

Andrew cut him off abruptly. "As your man and woman of honor, it falls to the two of us to plan your betrothal party," he clipped as he rose and took the serving tray from Caeleigh's hands and passed it to a woman from the table behind them. "From what you've told me of your intentions, we haven't a moment to lose – so if you will excuse us, we'll take our leave to begin making plans." With these curt words, he followed Caeleigh out the nearest side door.

Caeleigh felt as though she had barely escaped in time. She was pacing along the far end of the meetinghouse's large rear deck when Andrew approached her. The deck was spacious enough to span the full width of the meetinghouse and wrap around both sides as far forward as half the length of the dining room, extending equally as far behind the building, besides.

Caeleigh had retreated to a far corner from the door through which they both had exited.

"Thank you for providing the excuse to leave," she spoke without looking up. "I don't think I could have lasted any longer."

"I could tell. Don't worry; no one else noticed," Andrew added in response to her alarm. "I knew what to look for – they didn't."

"Thank you, then, for your quick thinking." Caeleigh turned away and rested her arms on the deck's railing. The world before her blurred, as tears filled her eyes. A small part of her mind fretted over *how* Andrew could've known she'd been so near to her breaking point, but that soft voice was vastly over-shouted by the ache in her heart.

Andrew pressed a handkerchief into her hands. "I'm sorry if anything I said to Peter was hurtful to you. That wasn't my intent." He leaned against the rail beside her, his eyes fixed upon the distant tree line to afford her a small measure of privacy.

"It wasn't that."

"No?" Though meaning to keep his voice even and soothing, the carpenter found his pitch rising in surprise.

"If anything, I'm angry with myself, for having such an emotional response to something I clearly knew was coming." Caeleigh raised her fist and tapped it repeatedly against the rail as though she meant to slam it and had slowed the motion for fear of injuring her hand. "I've taken the advice you gave me the night Peter's Bonding was announced, and put it into practice. ...I've been doing much better – or so I had thought. It's *completely frustrating* – *why* must I have these emotions?! Why must *any* of us have emotions, when all they do is cause us to live according to the desires of the mortal will rather than according to the aegis of the Spirit of Truth?!" Her tears resumed, causing her to mop haphazardly at her eyes, embarrassed at the scene she had made of herself.

Andrew let out a brief, sympathetic chuckle. "I can see how you would think that way. Emotion *does*, however, have a greater purpose to serve. Love isn't *love*, without emotion… it would be no more than a strange muddle of duty and congeniality … Nor would we be able to fully engage with or enjoy Kadosh and His creation. Think of how your heart soars with joy when you worship – would you *truly* be willing to forfeit that, in order not to feel a bit lonely this evening?"

"You're right – I wouldn't," Caeleigh conceded, her emotional outburst finally coming once more under control. "Truly, Andrew, I *am* sincerely happy for our friends. But I am unsure of how well I can weather being so intimately involved in a marriage ceremony, when I'm so painfully alone."

"You won't *be* alone." Andrew encased one of Caeleigh's hands in both of his own. "I will be by your side throughout the entire process."

Caeleigh wondered at the sensation of his hands over hers. She was uncertain whether such a gesture carried any significance for him, but absolutely certain of the comfort she received from it.

"Phileo," Andrew murmured, withdrawing his hands.

The word and its insight left Caeleigh altogether stunned and perplexed. "How did you know that's what I was speculating?"

"Kadosh," Andrew explained. "He told me that you had need for reassurance that you – and especially your heart – are safe with me." The moment had grown far more emotionally charged than Andrew had intended. He cleared his throat and quickly changed the subject: "We had best begin to make some of the plans we told Peter we came out here to make – he intends to propose to Elizabeth within days."

"Then it would be best not to plan anything elaborate," Caeleigh replied, eliciting a tension-relieving laugh from him.

"Indeed. Do you have anything in mind?" Much about Caeleigh, Andrew had been discovering, was atypical in comparison to his admittedly limited understanding of women. He hoped that these charming differences did not extend to the otherwise general feminine affinity for sentimental celebrations.

"Yes, I think I do. Elizabeth loves the outdoors. She would appreciate a garden party, held out here. Strings of lights, potted flowers, simple table linens… there wouldn't be much required, and it could all be prepared earlier in the day, hidden from most opportunities of sight by putting blinds in the meetinghouse windows to block the view outside." Caeleigh left the rail and began pacing the open space as she thought aloud, planning the placement of the to-be-borrowed furnishings.

Andrew remained where he'd stood and observed the woman as she moved in a semicircular pattern, talking with her hands in small, confined gestures. The variable shift in her disposition had been both subtle and abrupt, though not unwelcome. Not only in evidence was genuine enthusiasm for this assignment entailed to their roles in their friends' nuptial celebration – a notable degree of artistic talent was likewise apparent in the ideas Caeleigh presented.

"Don't forget, this celebration is as much for Peter as it is for Elizabeth," the carpenter cautioned, as the male participant in the planning.

Caeleigh accepted the correction unruffled, adjusting her plans nearly seamlessly and without disruption to her stream of thought. "Very well, then, I'll add some rustic elements to the decorations, so that the overall effect will be less feminine. Will you oversee having the tables and chairs moved out here?"

With a sweeping gesture of her hands, she followed the inquiry with gesticulated instruction regarding their placement as she moved with nimble steps amid the broad open space.

"Of course," Andrew blinked several times in rapid succession, reclaiming his own attention. Despite the brevity of Caeleigh's described intentions, he had been able to visualize everything perfectly. "It can be done earlier in the afternoon so that you'll have time to set up the decorations without having to fear being trampled by men moving the tables. It's simply a matter of choosing the day."

"How will we justify moving the evening meal outside without ruining the surprise?" Caeleigh worried as the thought occurred to her. Though the betrothal party itself wouldn't be a surprise, the couple couldn't anticipate *when* it would take place – that was the sole element of surprise available, and stripping the meetinghouse dining room of all its furnishings would quite decidedly impede that.

Andrew gave the matter some consideration, then broke into a grin. Canting his head toward the very large stone fire pit Peter himself had built, he said, "I'll speak with one of the blacksmiths about constructing some grills. The ladies who serve in the kitchen ought to have some evenings off this summer." He winked conspiratorially at her.

"Ask Marcus, if you don't mind," Caeleigh requested. "I've established what I hope is a good business relationship with him, and I'd like to continue to build upon it."

"So I've heard. You and I have a mutual friend in his apprentice, Thomas." Andrew turned and leaned his back against the railing, taking in the full sight of Caeleigh as if evaluating her.

She fidgeted under his steady gaze and enigmatic smile. "What? Is something wrong?"

Andrew's grin only widened and deepened in its equivocality. "Nothing at all. You've made quite an impact, is what I was thinking."

"Upon whom?" Caeleigh's question was voiced in so innocent a tone that Andrew doubted she could have been coy if she had meant to be. She tilted one foot on side until her ankle met the ground, then brought her foot upright once more and repeated the movement with the second, while stroking the pad of one thumb along the length of the nail of the other, her brow furrowed in soft disquietude. "Marcus?"

At such extensive attestation of her discomfiture, Andrew directed his gaze to a point beyond her elbow. "...Among others. I was referring to myself at the moment. The more I observe you, directly or indirectly, the more you ... impress me. I must confess, I'm looking forward to becoming better acquainted – in a closer friendship – with you."

Chapter 8

August 2147

"Good morning," Andrew called through the open front door of Adeline's home as he knocked on the frame of the screen door. "I hope you don't mind my stopping by. I was placing an order for supplies at the mercantile and I noted you had some things waiting for you, so I thought I would bring them to you, since I know how busy you are."

Caeleigh stood and waved him entry, continuing about her work. "Adeline stayed at the meetinghouse to take a turn to help wash dishes after the morning meal today."

Her tone and choice of conversation confirmed for Andrew everything he'd intuited on his walk from the mercantile. He wasted no words. "Tell me what's wrong."

"I cannot *do* this! I am so ... *wrecked* ... that I am on the threshold of blaspheming to – to – so much as *begin* to find the words to express what's in my heart! It's too much for me! I simply cannot!" Trembling, Caeleigh thrust her hands, empty of the things she was unable to articulate, toward the floor.

Dropping the package on a small table beside the door, Andrew stepped into and across the room, hoping that Caeleigh's tears would blind her to how quickly and deliberately he moved toward her as he took her shoulders in his hands. "You *can*. You can, you must, and you *will*, Caeleigh."

The tailor faltered, swaying forward into his solid frame. Without a word, he welcomed her into his arms and allowed her to weep. Standing immovable as she clawed and pounded against his chest and arms, Andrew waited for Caeleigh to exhaust herself to quiet sobs before he began to speak. "I understand," he told her gently. "I know how difficult this is."

"*Everything* I've longed for, Kadosh gives to someone else – and I am forced to watch it happen *immediately* in front of me!" she bewailed, pushing away. Andrew kept his hands at Caeleigh's back, lest she stumble and fall. "*All* of it! To know what it is to be loved *exclusively* above all others by someone, to have the companionship of a love relationship, of *marriage,* the hope of children, to find relief from the *loneliness* that *consumes* me. To be *pursued* by someone who has *chosen* me, who *desires* me above all other women and causes me to feel as though *I alone* have a unique value *worth* treasuring. *All* of these yearnings Kadosh has stitched into the most central essence of my *soul,* and then fulfills *none* of them! I assume based upon the fact that those Bonding now are so many years younger than I that I have been passed over for the Bonding – and I am *certain* that no man would condescend to *choose* to Pledge with me. Andrew, I feel as though Kadosh *Himself* has rejected me, by how He has made these seemingly *empty* promises!"

"I could issue the same remonstration," Andrew intoned calmly. "In fact, I have, and others beside it. Life does not always follow the path we map out for ourselves. But the ways and plans of Kadosh are higher than our own, Caeleigh. He wouldn't withhold that which He has promised in order to punish us." His next words, he chose tactfully. "I cannot speak for your circumstance, but He tells me that there are other things He wishes to align in *my* life before bringing this promise through."

As he had spoken all of his confession and gently reprimanded them both, the carpenter had released Caeleigh to retrieve a thin towel from the tea service on the sideboard, with which to dry her eyes. Having so done, she returned to him, tea towel in hand, and attempted to blot his shirt where she'd assaulted him with her tears. "I've soaked it completely through!" she apologized.

Andrew took the towel from her still-trembling hand, turned her back toward the table, and ushered her to sit once more before the work he had interrupted with his arrival, unable not to chuckle in slight bemusement that in her deep grief, this woman could yet manage to find consternation at her behavior. "I'll be several hours out in the sun today. It'll dry quickly," he assured her. "Show me what's upset you, and I'll pray while I'm working." Subtly he swept his damp shirt front with the tea towel while Caeleigh moved aside a few sheets of paper containing measurements, sketches and notations. From hidden beneath them emerged the pattern for a bridal gown.

"Are you concerned at the complexity of the detail involved?" Andrew rested the heel of his free hand atop the back of Caeleigh's chair as he leaned forward for a better view of the printed image. "I confess my ignorance both of women's garments and the full extent of your skill in your trade, but I see nothing of which I would presume you incapable."

Caeleigh's hands shook violently enough to cause her to need to elevate them, lest her fingertips hammer audibly against the tabletop. Andrew's behavior in the aftermath of her latest outburst, and, truth be told, the three prior over the previous weeks, had given her a slow-growing confidence not to hide from him. "May I confess to you?" she requested, her voice quaking to match her hands.

"Of course," Andrew returned, easing into the empty chair beside her. "Allow me to be a brother to you. Your secrets are safe with me. The trust is already between us, since I've given you one of mine."

"I've owned this pattern for nearly ten years." Confessing though she was, Caeleigh yet found it difficult to meet his eyes. Both studied the images of the dress design, to spare her the unease. "It's what I'd chosen for myself after Kadosh had spoken to me and told me that He intended for me to be married. I love so many things about the design, the details, the layering and textures..." Trailing off, she closed her eyes momentarily, inhaling and exhaling deeply before she continued. "I'm giving up. I'm surrendering all hope that I'll ever have need for this, in offering it to Elizabeth."

Andrew smiled in his nescience of the subject. "Forgive the impertinence of the question, but two women cannot wear the same gown?"

The innocence of his delivery coaxed something of a smile to emerge. "No. Especially not friends as close as she and I are. And with her being so much slimmer and more petite than I am, the pattern will be cut too small for me to reuse for myself, were I to wish to do so despite it being poor form. Once I begin cutting, that's altogether the end of it for me."

"Why, then, did you offer it?" Andrew could not imagine that Elizabeth would have initiated the request.

Caeleigh traced her fingertips around the perimeter of the envelope. "I've waited a painfully long time on a promise with no sign of its fulfillment on the horizon. I've prayed diligently and persistently for rain. I've prepared the figurative fields. No rain has come. I've given up daring to hope, anymore – all it ever yields me is disappointment."

Unable to find appropriate words with which to reply to this flat pronouncement, Andrew made hasty excuses and took his leave.

His prayers, proffered while setting the frame for Peter and Elizabeth's marital home, were fervent and strewn with burning tears. So virulent was the carpenter's misery that nails were sunken flush under a single blow of his hammer. Determined not to shout aloud, he bit his tongue until he tasted the bitter copper of blood, and spat its stain in the dust.

"Bad day?" the blacksmith assisting with the labor ventured to enquire.

"Bad travail," Andrew returned dully, not desiring to punish Thomas for an innocent question. "I oughtn't be attempting to work through it, but if I take any time away from this project, I'll fall too far behind schedule."

Thomas nodded his understanding. "Give yourself half an hour. I can complete for you what you've started while you afford yourself that small respite. You'll never forgive yourself if you present less than your best work in your brother's home."

Andrew raised a wary brow. "*You* will complete my trade's work?"

His friend grinned. "I test your tools after I cast them, you do realize. How else do you think they're always so optimally balanced?" Thomas handed the weary carpenter a copper tumbler of cold water from the crockery pitcher he'd kept in the shade of a nearby tree.

Begrudgingly, Andrew accepted the refreshment, the rebuke, and the kindness. Seating himself against a pile of lumber, he continued to pray in utterances varying between anger and agony.

Thomas left the carpenter to himself undisrupted for most of an hour. When Andrew raised his head and noted the time, he chided the man for neglecting to rouse him after thirty minutes as promised.

"I made no such promise," Thomas qualified, surrendering Andrew's hammer and finding another. "And it was considerably apparent that whomever you've been appointed to uphold in prayer has substantial need of it."

"True enough," Andrew conceded, his tone and mood returning to equilibrium.

"A burden shared is halved, my friend," Thomas offered with compassion. "Will you allow me to assist you in interceding? You've undertaken more than enough for one man to uphold for the next several months."

"The truth is I have been engaged in this intercession for more than a year. Six months ago I told Kadosh I could no longer endure to interpose anonymously as I had been. It had become a regular tribulation that left me believing that my prayers had no effect."

"How did He answer that for you?" Thomas asked, after the pause induced by his own need for a drink of water.

Andrew considered by what means to best approach the matter. "You're acquainted with Caeleigh, the tailor who works with leather," he began.

"I am," Thomas confirmed. "She apprenticed under Adeline, whose husband was as a brother to Abram the coppersmith."

"I know her through Peter and Elizabeth – she is to stand up for Elizabeth in their marriage ceremony." Andrew volunteered no further information than this.

"Is she ailing or ill?"

"She's become increasingly forlorn over the past weeks, over the matter of a promise Kadosh has not yet fulfilled in her life. I've taken to checking on her daily out of concern, the turns have grown so downward. She told me this morning that she has renounced all hope for the promise."

Andrew's groanings, half from the duress of his spirit on Caeleigh's behalf and half from the physical exertions he had not discontinued as he spoke, perplexed Thomas. "I wasn't aware you knew her well enough to care so deeply," the blacksmith replied in a measured tone.

"She has become as dear to me as a sister in the course of several months. I agree, I wasn't anticipating it, either. But now that she's come to have such import to me, to see her in so hopeless a state breaks my heart on her behalf." Andrew paused briefly to rest, wiping sweat from his brow with the back of his hand. "She confessed three months ago to fearing that she would not have the endurance to forbear this, and I promised that I would walk beside her through the challenges as she faced them. I am only now coming to understand the ramifications of what I asked of Kadosh."

Chapter 9

Early October 2147

"You've done well today," Andrew praised Caeleigh as he handed her a glass of young wine.

She accepted it gratefully and drank before responding. "No, I haven't. My thoughts have been selfish for most of the day."

"I know exactly what you mean," he admitted as he seated himself beside her; Elizabeth and Peter, surrounded by a small multitude of Peter's relatives, would not be returning to the bridal table anytime soon. This left the bride and groom's man and woman of honor to themselves, their duties for the day at long last complete. "Celebrations like this make me wish that Kadosh had told me how long *I* must wait."

His unexpected candor so surprised Caeleigh that she looked up from her concentrated study of the weave of the tablecloth. He smiled almost appreciatively at her expression, as if she'd done it deliberately with the intention of cheering him. "Yes, once in a while men have such longings just as women do."

Feeling a tug in her spirit, Caeleigh turned to him and spoke the words she felt compelled to say: "Kadosh has plans for your life, Andrew, and He will keep the promises He has made to you, for those promises are part of His plan. Is He a man, that He would lie to you? No. You shall receive as has been promised. Be encouraged and trust that the day will come when you see His word fulfilled."

"And so shall it be for you, as well," he returned with firm surety. With a raised hand and gently stern look, Andrew stopped her before she could protest. "No bitterness or argument today. Today we celebrate the happiness of those we love. 'Rejoice with those who rejoice,' as the great apostle has instructed."

Caeleigh fidgeted with the stem of her wineglass. "I still have difficulty rejoicing when everything I have most deeply longed for is given to someone else. I *am* glad for their blessing and I don't begrudge their happiness, but to *rejoice* is asking more than I can manage." She visibly winced at the cheer that arose from the other side of the room as husband and wife kissed yet again.

"But you *must*, Caeleigh," Andrew insisted. "Do you remember what David stated in his teaching last week? We forestall our own blessings when we fail to rejoice in the blessings of others. You *must* rejoice in Elizabeth's blessing if you wish to position yourself to receive your own! As David said, your destiny is directly relative to your posture – you will receive *nothing* if your heart is not positioned in receptiveness and gratitude!"

"What is behind your urgency? You speak as though *your* happiness is tied up in *my* blessing."

Andrew plucked the glass from her hand and set it beyond her reach. "No more wine for you; it makes you morose and paranoid." Standing, he extended his hand to her, saying, "Come with me."

"Where?" Despite the question, Caeleigh slipped her hand into his and rose to follow him. This man had done nothing if not earned her trust in the past several months.

"To celebrate."

Leading her to the open floor, Andrew spun Caeleigh into his arms and led her in a slow, four-step waltzlike dance. "The reminder was as much for my benefit as for yours," he told her softly when she remained cold and distant. "It's out of character for me to openly speak of my longings in such a manner as I have with you."

She studied him from the corner of her eye. "Am I to take that to mean that you trust me with something personally precious?" Though intrigued and rather touched by his expression of confidence, she remained wary.

"That's *exactly* how I mean for you to understand me. Caeleigh, you've entrusted me with much these last few months. In so doing, you've earned my trust in kind. You've become as a sister to me, and – " As Caeleigh's heel caught in the hem of her skirt, Andrew paused, then reversed his steps to provide that he would be the one moving backward and she, forward. "... *your* desires have become *my* desires *for* you. That's why I felt such urgency to remind you of the great apostle's instruction and the consequences of failing it. I truly *do* long for the fulfillment of your promise as though it were the fulfillment of my own." The altered light in her eyes told Andrew he had broken through her defenses.

"Thank you for caring so deeply as to set straight my wayward course." She managed a small smile, the first that hadn't looked forced or pained in hours.

"I *do* understand, I hope you realize. Would obedience be so chiefly and so often commanded throughout the scriptures if it were *easy* to do the right thing?" Andrew shifted his hold on Caeleigh, affording her the emotional comfort of a bit more space between them and allowing them to maintain eye contact while they spoke.

"Fair point," she conceded. "...Have you truly suffered loneliness and ached for your promised companion?"

Andrew raised their joined hands, guiding his partner to turn. He kept the rotation slow, aware that she felt insecure of the dance steps. This also afforded him an opportunity to take in her beauty without her notice, while her back was turned and her attention on being in motion. He'd never before seen her with her hair down, and he had to confess that he was delighted by what he saw. "Are you referring only to today, or the past five months?"

"Either. Both." Watching Andrew contemplate his reply, she hastily added, "You needn't answer if you'd rather not. I know the question was terribly intimate."

Caeleigh's choice of words prompted another of the inscrutable smiles that had become increasingly common to him. "Yes."

Andrew paused only long enough for the insufficient answer to be fitted to each of her questions, observing Caeleigh's eyes as she strove to determine what he'd meant in saying so little, before elaborating. "Yes, the question was intimate, but I'll allow it, because you've become so dear to me. Yes, over the past five months as I've helped Peter build the house that will be his home together with Elizabeth, *and* today standing up with him as they were knit together in marriage, my soul has been pierced in the vacant place yet to be filled." He allowed some truth of his pain to enter in at the corners of his smile.

Caeleigh made no immediate reply as they continued to dance, other than to match and return his mien, empathizing, understanding. Moments later, a lone tear escaped her eye and rolled down her cheek. When he noted it, she quickly turned her head aside and dabbed it away with her shoulder before he could comment or act.

A fleeting pained expression in Andrew's eyes piqued her curiosity, prompting her to ask, "Are you alright? You look as though there's more you wish to say."

"May I confess something to you in the utmost of strictest confidences?" he asked as the music slowed.

"If you so desire. I won't obligate you to speak anything you'd rather not share."

Following the cue of the music, Andrew relaxed his frame and drew Caeleigh closer, pulling in her outstretched hand to rest against his shoulder, as if to confine his admission from advancing any further than necessary. Lowering his voice and leaning in close for his confession, he told her, "It has not been being alone that has pained me, but rather the knowledge that *she* is alone. As long as *I* must wait, so must she. Every one of these events that I have walked through alone without her, she has had to walk through alone without me. After standing by your side, I understand better how painful and difficult this is for women … and the thought of the one Kadosh created for my soul to love having to suffer that pain – *that* is what pains me most deeply."

Caeleigh stumbled, staring at him as if uncomprehending. Quickly she thrust herself out of his arms, mumbling an excuse about having grown overwarm, and fled the meetinghouse.

Ten minutes of tearful prayer later, footsteps approached from the opposite end of the porch.

"I owe you an apology, Andrew," Caeleigh spoke without turning as the footsteps' source neared. "You've been more than a friend to me, asking nothing in return, and I failed to serve you in kind. Please forgive me."

"I'm not Andrew, but I've no doubt he'd agree that you have no cause to apologize."

Startled by the unanticipated voice, she turned and looked into the face of Marcus the blacksmith's apprentice. "Thomas –"

The man who'd known her for two years approached with care, speaking with the concern of a friend who wished to see peace restored. "Andrew asked me to see if you were alright.

He fears he may have misread the understanding he felt he had with you and caused offense."

Caeleigh flushed and raised her hands to her cheeks. "No. Oh, no," she sighed. "Not at all. Please – I must apologize to him."

"Wait here." Thomas produced a handkerchief from his suit coat pocket. "Dry your eyes and I will direct him to meet you here."

"Thank you, Thomas."

Caeleigh attempted to repair the state of her face as Thomas' broad shoulders disappeared around the corner. Pressing her fingertips against her cheekbones, she found that her eyes had swollen from the deluge of her tears. Knowing that such evidence could not be erased, Caeleigh stepped beyond the reach of the porch light, where, she hoped, it could less easily be seen.

Andrew's arrival was silent enough to be unnoticed beneath the sounds of the autumn evening. "Caeleigh," he spoke softly. "Forgive me. It was not my intention to distress you."

"*I* am the one who must apologize, for failing to be as steadfast a friend to you as you have been to me." She rubbed her bare arms, more out of discomfited anxiety than cold.

Giving no forethought to his actions, Andrew removed his suit coat and held it out until she'd slipped her arms into the sleeves. Gently he asked, "Why did you run? If I've said or done anything inappropriate, tell me and allow me to make amends. I want no injury between myself and my sister."

"That isn't it at all, Andrew," she assured him, repeatedly stretching and bending her arms until her hands emerged from within the too-long-for-her coat sleeves. "I simply needed to get away – to pray – because of what you said. It was too much to bear. I needed to set my heart aright before it was overcome with longing that would make it impossible to rejoice as I ought."

"So you came here?" With his eyes Andrew traced the lines of the rail and post, irony tugging his mouth into a grin.

After a few moments, she caught his allusion. They stood again in the very place they'd first spoken when she'd slipped away to pray over the attitude of her heart on the evening of Peter's Bonding announcement. She answered his smile with one of her own. "I have a way of turning full circle in these manner of things."

Rogue tears dropped from Caeleigh's lashes as she blinked. Andrew raised a hand to brush his thumb across her cheek, while simultaneously she dabbed at her eyes with the handkerchief. They laughed softly as their hands collided and she stuttered an attempt at explaining how she had come into possession of the handkerchief.

"It's mine, actually," Andrew admitted somewhat abashedly. "I had a feeling you would have need of it, and gave it to Thomas to pass on to you." His hand hovered alongside her jaw.

"Thank you for your foresight, then," Caeleigh murmured, her eyes darting back and forth between his face and the handkerchief she held in both hands.

Briefly Andrew closed his eyes, took a deep breath and expelled it slowly. Stepping back half a pace, he lowered his hand to Caeleigh's elbow, loath to break the connection but desirous to be obedient. "I must ask of you, so that I don't cause something of this nature to happen again, what was it I said that had such an effect on you?"

"When you spoke of your deepest pain being the thought of the pain your Beloved endures alone without you in her life – " Caeleigh's words were cut off abruptly as she choked back a sob. She regained control of her emotions and began anew: "Your words, your sentiment, your compassion were so *beautiful,* Andrew. I was overwhelmed with yearning for a man who would feel that way for *me*." Tears welled up and spilled over once again, as she looked into the face of the man who had become the brother whose love she relied upon in the course of facing life with that yearning unmet.

He opened his arms to her, offering solace, but also in part so that she would not see his own eyes flood. "Then I have not only *not* provided comfort, I have done you a tragic disservice. Truly, I am deeply sorry for having placed this obstacle in your path and caused your stumbling. If you would rather keep company with someone else for the remainder of the evening, I'll understand." Releasing her from the embrace, Andrew leaned away to wipe the moisture from beneath her eyes. "Tell me what you need, and it shall be yours."

Chapter 10

Early October 2147

"Dare I *ask* how this happened?" Thomas enquired late the following morning as he examined the chipped axe blade Andrew had brought to him for repair. "Or perhaps the more appropriate question is, dare I ask whether what happened to *this* is connected to what happened last evening at the marriage celebration?"

Andrew shrugged noncommittally.

Patiently Thomas laid the axe aside. "You *know* I know you better than to allow you to get away without answering that. For you to work so hard in a single morning that you've done this much damage to your tools" – he lifted the axe for emphasis – "you're punishing yourself for something."

"I have a great deal more work to be done yet today," was Andrew's pointed reply.

Thomas tested the axeblade's edge once more with his thumb. "You'll destroy this if you continue to use it as it is. I'll need to melt it down and recast it for you. Meanwhile…" He set down the damaged axe and removed his leather apron. Setting them both on his workbench, he chose two axes from a selection of those he had made.

Andrew left the smithy with his friend at his side. Neither spoke until they reached the wooded area where Andrew had spent the morning cutting down trees. Immediately upon their arrival, Andrew lifted the new axe Thomas had handed to him and began attacking the tree he'd earlier been in the process of chopping down.

"You know the woodcutter usually does this. Why are you out here, truly?" The blacksmith hated the tactless tone he employed, but Andrew's obstinacy would be challenged by no less.

"That's an interesting question, coming from a man who's yet an apprentice at the age *we* are." Andrew continued to swing vengefully at the tree trunk.

Thomas joined the effort, alternating the timing of his swings with Andrew's. "You confirm my suspicions of self-retribution." Under doubled effort, the tree soon was felled.

Thomas stood leaning upon the handle of his axe, watching as Andrew continued moving, clearing the trunk of branches. "Not that it bears any relevance to whatever sense of futility you're wrestling right now, but the apprenticeship under Marcus has been my second. When I first came of age I apprenticed under Abram the coppersmith, and later decided I wanted to know more of the smithing trade in general, about a year or so after I completed that first apprenticeship. As for my apprenticeship under Marcus, it was completed nearly a month ago – he and I now work in concert, much like Caeleigh and Adeline, under whom she apprenticed."

The steady rhythm with which Andrew had been working abruptly halted at the mention of the young tailor; Thomas knew he had struck a raw nerve, though he'd not done so deliberately.

"What happened last evening, Andrew?" Thomas pressed. His involvement in the situation, whatever it had been, had been limited, and he hadn't felt it his proper place at the time to ask questions. As he watched the aftereffect being had on his friend, however, Thomas felt compelled to intervene. He wrested the shaking axe from Andrew's hands and waited for an answer.

"I lost my wits and wounded the poor woman." The words ground out through clenched teeth.

Thomas set aside both axes against a previously felled tree and positioned himself between Andrew and them, lest the bitter man attempt once more to hide in activity rather than confront his demons. "That isn't how she seemed to have interpreted whatever passed between you, from the few words she and I exchanged. In the moment she mistook me for you, she apologized, quite sincerely, for having failed to be as unselfish a friend to you as you have been to her. I perceived in her no sense that she felt in any way injured or wronged."

Andrew scoffed self-reproachfully. "On the *rare* occasion Caeleigh might acknowledge she felt such a way, she'd *never* behave accordingly. The woman has an inordinate measure of grace to endure."

"So you claim upon yourself the fault for the failure which last night she told me was hers?" Thomas raised his eyebrows to alleviate any suspicion of acerbity that may have unintentionally conveyed in his words.

"Of any perceived 'failure' on her part, *I* was the sole cause and architect." Andrew stripped off his leather work gloves and threw them to the ground at his feet before stalking a few yards into the nearby trees, leaving Thomas to call after him.

"I respect that you and I don't have the brotherhood-friendship you enjoy with Peter," Thomas allowed, before pressing his entreaty. "But Andrew, I *urge* you, for your own sake, not to withhold from me simply because I'm not him. Allow me to be a brother to you while Peter is not available for counsel. In truth, I believe I may understand your situation better than Peter could, were he here to speak with you."

These latter words lured Andrew back into the clearing he had created, cautiously intrigued. "Upon what grounds do you claim this deeper understanding?"

"Upon the grounds that Peter is too young and now also too *married* to fathom what it is to be yet unwed – and yet waiting for the Bonding – in one's thirties, and to find oneself loving a woman while in that position."

Though delivered as a retort with utter calm, the statement was also in some measure a confession; as such, it deflated Thomas' confrontational posture until he sat upon the trunk he'd aided Andrew in bringing down.

Andrew sat beside him. "You loved – truly *loved* – a woman with whom you hadn't Bonded?"

"I didn't believe such a thing was possible, either, until it happened. Perhaps that's how and why I recognized the signs in you."

Andrew ran quaking hands through his hair. "She is as a sister to me. It must be no more than that."

"One would hope a man would love his sister," the blacksmith rebutted, the trace of a smile lifting the corner of his mouth.

The carpenter would not be dissuaded of his malfeasance. "*Phileo* does not behave as I apparently have."

"Nor does it *recriminate* itself as you've done here, Andrew." Thomas, with a broad sweeping gesture, indicated all of the trees he'd brought down over the course of an obviously long morning.

"My actions of last evening *justify* recrimination, Thomas!" Andrew shouted, propelling himself to his feet and pacing in the agitated manner of a caged beast. "I *sinned* against the First Elders' covenant with Kadosh for the Bonding, by willfully attempting to create an opportunity for the Bonding to occur, when I know *full well* that is *not at all* how Kadosh instituted the Bonding to work in our lives."

Thomas sat in contemplative silence, absorbing the half-blurted confession. When at last he responded, it was with a plainly posed question. "Would she agree?"

"Whom?" Lost in his self-directed vitriol, Andrew had forgotten whom else he and Thomas had been discussing.

"Would Caeleigh agree with your assessment of the circumstances, were she to hear it?"

Andrew began collecting the small branches he'd cleared and casting them aside, seeking to dispel some of his churlish energy. "I'm certain she'd object vigorously to the accusation I have leveled against myself. She refuses to believe me capable of such atrocity."

"Then find the means to extend yourself as much as half the measure of grace she has given you."

"You'd *agree* with her?"

"If you've truly done as you say, repent of it and go forth forgiven. Though I must say I agree with *you*, as well, that she's a woman worthy of love. Take care to find the balance."

Andrew recognized both the words and the voice of the Christ when he heard them in his friend's rejoinder. Penitent, he resumed his seat. "Did *you* find it easily?"

Thomas expelled a long, deep sigh, the last of his fair humor departing him along with his breath. "Benia was lost to me before things had progressed that far."

"Lost in what way?" The near-immediate deflation of his friend's demeanor extracted Andrew from his own mire of troubles.

"She passed into eternal reward a few years ago." Thomas seemed to contemplate for a moment whether and how much to disclose. "Benia and I had known one another since our youth and shared a mutual infatuation since before we'd come of age.

I was beginning to entertain thoughts of asking her whether she would be willing to Pledge with me if I did not Bond with her, when she fell ill. Her family left the Settlement with her and moved south to a Settlement in northern Texas, where she could receive constant care in a hospital there. For a time it looked as though she was much improved, and then she was suddenly" – he swallowed back the emotion that had mounted as he spoke – "gone..."

"I'm sorry," Andrew murmured. "I had no idea."

Thomas, altogether lost in memories, continued unhearing. "The last opportunity I had to speak with Benia, I must have wondered aloud about having not Bonded with her. She told me it was better, if the number of her days was to be few, that I had not – she would rather I suffer the lesser pain of regret than that great loss. Though she did say, at our final parting, that she had loved me, as much as she had comprehended love in her brief life. The news of her passing is what prompted me to forego my former plans and undertake a second apprenticeship, to be truthful – I could not continue my life, unaltered, without her. To this day, she is the one my soul holds as beloved, despite her absence."

By the time Thomas had finished, Andrew was nearly bereft of speech. "I owe you more than a few apologies," he choked out at length. "Forgive my heedless tongue, especially."

"You had no way of knowing this is what I've carried," Thomas forgave with a doleful smile. "None have known; it has been my choice to keep these things to myself. Benia's family chose not to return to the Blue Creek Settlement, and she has since been forgotten here. She has no grave, no memorial, no mark here that she ever lived but the one she left on my heart. It is better – easier – the less is said on the matter."

"Yet you've told me..." Andrew replied, growing to realize the full extent of the kinship Thomas had expressed by confiding in him.

"That you might know me as a brother. *Trust me* as I have trusted you." Andrew caught from Thomas' inflection that it was known he had not yet been fully truthful.

Both men stood as Andrew extended his hand, and the two men pressed hands as though sealing an oath. "Truly this day you are my Brother," Andrew declared, "for you see me more clearly than I see myself. Those things I have not divulged, or have spoken only in part, I withhold upon the behest of Kadosh. What He has asked of me regarding love is unlike anything He has asked of our fathers or their fathers before them, and He has commanded me not to speak of it."

This, Thomas accepted. "Then tell me of your heart for your sister. Perhaps I may offer some counsel."

"She aches to be loved. In the months leading up to Peter and Elizabeth's marriage ceremony, I've spent much time in prayer for her, and many of those prayers have become regular travails on her behalf." Andrew gesticulated abjectly with one hand and massaged the back of his neck with the other, tension rising with the memories that flooded his mind. "My soul weeps with the loneliness that pains her, as if it were my own. I have borne her to the foot of heaven's throne so often that my heart has been turned toward her more than I wish it to have been." He sighed heavily. "The events of last evening prove that these sentiments *cannot* be expressed – in truth, not a word of what I spoke to her betrayed my affections, and *still* I wounded her deeply."

Thomas offered a sympathetic wry grin. "I understand, now, why we're out here."

Chapter 11

Mid October 2147

Nearly a week had passed before Andrew again spoke to Caeleigh. He approached her as she exited the meetinghouse after the midday meal. "Thomas has counseled me that I ought to explain my behavior the other evening."

"Andrew, I've told you before, you needn't apologize for a simple misunderstanding. Though if it sets your conscience at ease, I forgive you – again." Caeleigh's tone on the last word was not one of exasperation, but rather one of affectionate teasing, and coaxed a smile to his countenance.

He searched her eyes, seeking more true forgiveness than the levity he'd been granted. "There's more to the situation than you know. Can you spare some time before returning to work?"

The unexpected weight in his voice gave her pause. "Is this truly urgent?" Taking one look at his face, she shook her head and corrected herself. "Forgive me. You wouldn't've asked if it wasn't important. I will make the time."

Caeleigh followed Andrew to the stables and waited outside the western paddock as he climbed over the fence and whistled. A still-half-gangly yearling barreled toward him at the call.

"This is Noya," Andrew turned over his shoulder to say.

"Business must be continuing to improve if you've needed to purchase a second horse."

Andrew returned to the fence, Noya following in search of more of the treats she'd received. "I purchased her in preparation for the future. I'm not at liberty to speak of it, though I will dare to say that the community meeting that's been called for a few weeks from now will clarify what I mean."

This comment worried Caeleigh – never had Andrew been anything but entirely forthright with her. "Then speak of what has troubled you, my friend. *I* will dare to say that your eyes carried a rather nearly haunted expression a short while ago – the same one I've seen these last days while you've been avoiding me."

Noya's persistence wore Andrew down at last; he pulled an apple from his coat pocket, cautioned her that it was the last one in his possession as he offered it, then retreated over the fence. "Participating in Peter's marriage ceremony was more difficult for me than I cared to admit at the time, I'm afraid. Supporting you through the troubles you were enduring provided me a convenient excuse not to face the truth. It wasn't until you'd run off in tears and caused me to realize exactly *how* out of turn I'd spoken that I began to examine my heart at all. " He leaned heavily against the paddock fence. "A very deep old wound in my heart was reopened. I was speaking out of a pain I thought I would never again experience as more than a distant memory."

Caeleigh reached between the fence rails and tentatively stroked the yearling's muzzle. "Was it due to the involved role you had to play? There've been plenty of other marriage ceremonies in the past half-year that haven't affected you this deeply."

"Perhaps. Or perhaps it's because Peter is as a younger brother to me." Andrew scoffed a wry chuckle. "Particularly a younger brother who cannot resist reminding me of my age."

"Is that what you're speaking of when the two of you jest in Spanish?" Quickly Caeleigh withdrew her hands as Noya's head whipped toward Andrew when he withdrew the additional apple he'd been concealing in an inside pocket of his coat.

This query surprised Andrew. "I wasn't aware you knew Spanish."

"I don't – not fluently – but I understand enough to grasp the inferences."

Andrew cut the apple into quarters with a pocket knife and offered them to the yearling one at a time. "So then you've understood all along the dual meaning of his endearment for Elizabeth…? There's no wonder you've been so aggrieved since before their Bonding."

"What do you mean?" Caeleigh began to toy with the hem of her wrap, picking at the thread where a few stitches had begun to come loose.

"I saw you, before we met, in Elizabeth's company when Peter pointed her out to me. You seemed to carry a deep pain that you didn't wish her to see. If you've witnessed their interactions, as I have, it only serves to reason that you've heard him call her by that endearment."

"What has troubled you so deeply, Brother?" she redirected their conversation to its original vein. "Out of what pain were you speaking that evening?"

"Abandoned hope." The low-uttered words sounded alien emerging from Andrew's throat as he stared after Noya, who was gamboling back across the paddock, finally satisfied that no more apples were forthcoming.

Caeleigh thought she saw tears in his eyes. "I don't understand. That same evening you spoke of what Kadosh has promised you as though you're certain of its fulfillment."

Folding and pocketing the knife, Andrew blinked several times, clearing his countenance of whatever the tailor suspected she may have witnessed. "I *am* – now. I haven't *always* been."

Caeleigh waited patiently.

Andrew continued to speak to the horizon, one foot propped on the lowest rail of the fence, his hands hanging from wrists draped over the top rail. "Two years ago I was in the same despair I've been aiding you through these past months. All of my peers had married and were beginning to grow their families. I was desolate. My answer to the circumstances was to apply myself to the admonition of the great apostle in his first letter to the church at Corinth. I insisted to myself that I was better to be undistracted from seeking whatever Kadosh had purposed for my life."

"But that didn't diminish the desire, did it?" Only too well did Caeleigh understand.

"No." His voice grown rough, Andrew coughed to clear his throat, with no improvement. "The longer my desire for marriage and a family continued unmet, the more disheartened I became, until I reached the point where I simply gave up all hope. So far beyond the customary age of marriage at that point, I began to say that Kadosh must have other plans for me – something greater than what I had requested." Andrew shocked himself by how easily he said so much.

Caeleigh forced her hands to stillness. Andrew *never* spoke so freely from his heart. That he was doing so now was no insignificant matter. "That sounds very much like the lines of reasoning I've used to appease my own soul's wounds," she replied. "It's a shameful thing when we mismanage the truth so that we end up resenting it."

"Indeed." His confession seemed to have exhausted Andrew for words, reducing him to the utmost minimum of emotional and verbal responses.

Each, in turn, shifted as though intending to close the physical distance between them as an entirely other form of distance crept in amidst the silence. Yet both remained where they stood.

"It would seem we have found the purpose for which Kadosh has given us to one another as friends," Caeleigh submitted.

Andrew's response to the suggestion was a sharp, cryptic chortle. "That's *one* possible explanation, I suppose."

Caeleigh hesitated only briefly before stepping closer to the carpenter and laying a trembling hand on the back of his shoulder. "I am truly sorry if my struggles of late awakened the memory of yours. I never once thought that you might... And that was selfish of me. Please, forgive me."

As on previous occasions, the tremor in her voice apprised Andrew that the care he'd taken to guard his words had done more harm than good. "No, don't think yourself at fault for this. I ought to have minded my heart better. Kadosh has since shown me a bit more of His plan for me – enough that I firmly hold to peace and hope. I meant what I said about the waiting, but truly I *do* bear it better than I behaved about it that night."

"Don't feel ashamed before *me,* Andrew. Certainly not after as many tears as I've cried on your shoulder for the same reason."

At last he met her eyes. "When did *you* become the strong one between us?"

Caeleigh withdrew her hand and rested her forearms against the fence rail beneath her chin. "What strength I have, I've learned from you. You have instructed, counseled, and admonished it into me." She offered a smile that traversed from joy to sorrow, and every emotion between.

If his coloring hadn't been naturally ruddy, she might have accused him of blushing. "I hope you've learned well. You'll need to stand on that strength on your own, in the coming months."

"Do you mean to say that you intend to *leave* the Blue Creek Settlement?" Caeleigh managed to keep her composure in light of such news by staring straight ahead, across the paddock and beyond.

"Again, I am not at liberty to speak freely – not quite yet, anyway." Studying her from the corner of his eye, Andrew silently congratulated her exhibition of strength. As little as a fortnight prior, she might have been in tears. "Were I able, I would tell you everything right this moment, you know. For now I'll say this much: it isn't an intention in the sense that you're thinking. You needn't fear that."

Despite her dear brother's assurances, fear of abandonment nullified Caeleigh's inhibitions. "Will you extend me the courtesy of an explanation once you *are* free to speak on the matter?"

"Do you *deliberately* endeavor to break my resolve when you know I am obliged to keep silent?" Andrew replied, nigh too quickly, grinning nigh too widely, hoping that the jest would prevent her from noting how she'd pierced his heart with the question.

"Not *deliberately,* no…" Caeleigh's smile faded as she confessed, "I suppose, if I must admit, I fear I'm about to be left behind by yet another of those dearest to me."

Andrew sobered, the ache in his soul both deepening and taking on a new dimension. "I would *never* deign to abandon you, Caeleigh, no matter where Kadosh would have me go." Upon turning to face her, he knew he could refuse her no longer. "I must choose my words with care, and you must promise to keep them in confidence. Will you do that?"

She nodded.

"I *will* be gone for a time. Though it may seem long, all I can tell you now is that it *is* necessary. I am being sent – Kadosh has set a path before my feet, and I must walk that path. There are things He has promised me, as well as things I have asked of Him, and this is something that must be done before any of them can be released into my life. I will be toiling both in the land and in my spirit while I am away, without many of the comforts I often turn to."

The hands he'd been clenching at his sides in order to keep them to himself reached out and took hold of her shoulders. "It would bring me peace to know, during this season, that I am held in the prayers of one who knows me as well as you do. Will you do that for me? Will you pray for your brother in his absence, not knowing my need from one day to the next and trusting Kadosh not only with my wellbeing but also to guide your prayers therefor? Has your courage grown that strong?"

Caeleigh swallowed, cleared her throat, inhaled and exhaled deeply, and blinked slowly. "I suppose we shall find out."

Chapter 12

Late October 2147

"My friends! It is time – " Governor Caleb surveyed the assembly gathered before him in the meetinghouse, drew a hand over his short-cropped salt-and-pepper beard, and repeated in a lower pitch and volume, "It is, indeed, time." Raising his voice once more, he proceeded with the announcement for which he'd gathered them. "It is time for our Settlement to send out a Planting. We have so grown in number that we are near to outgrowing all we have built here. The blessing of it is, we've at the least two or three tradesmen practicing every trade, so we will be able to send a full complement, that they may start well.

"As is the custom, three sons of the Blue Creek Settlement were sent out to search for a large plot of land where this new Settlement might be set. I have visited all three of the sites they found, and prayed to seek which of them Kadosh would choose. The new Settlement will be slightly beyond two hours' ride east and south of here. The land there is wild, however, and will require some breaking labor before it will be ready for the usual preparations. As a result, I will be sending more than the three for the Planting's initial shared leadership and toil. These are the men to be sent: Simeon, Andrew, Ezra, Philip, and David."

Those named stood, stoic and solemn yet subtly excited.

Caeleigh wondered at the susurrations that began to fill the room around her. Few words were perceptible, though she thought she heard "Governor" repeated by a man behind her. The disruption immediately hushed as Thomas rose from his seat and stated boldly yet humbly, "I volunteer to join them in their toiling in the land." Already confounded by the announcement that their Governor was breaking with the tradition of sending no more than three men, the community waited to see how the submission of a volunteer would be received.

After notably little conferrence with his fellows around him, Andrew stepped forward and responded. "We accept our brother Thomas' offer. It is good that we should have another, that we may grant turns of leave to return home to those among us who must not neglect their responsibilities to their wives and families, yet have enough hands to keep the work apace."

Caleb considered Andrew's words briefly, nodded his approval, and indicated that Thomas should step forward beside the others. "Agreed." He offered a prayer of commissioning over them all, Thomas among them: "Kadosh, our Father, these men are Your *sons*. You have given me charge over their lives and the lives of all our community here in our Settlement – and now You say it is time for these few to go forth and prepare a *new* Settlement, the community and lives in which You will give them charge over." Caleb moved along the line as he prayed open-eyed, spending a few moments before each of the now-six, placing a firm right hand on each man's shoulder. "They have responded to Your summons in obedience and courage, willing to face the days ahead, certain to be filled with challenges and hard labor, for the sake of their people – Your children, all. Father, my heart swells with pride for these sons – I would call them my own. Guard their comings and goings, as I know You will, and let not a single one of their feet strike a stone in the path You lay before them. Strengthen their hearts, their minds, and their bodies as they toil with their hands and their spirits to prepare this new land in which You will plant them and those who follow. I commit these, *Your* sons and mine, into Your care as they follow where You lead them, to do the work You have set for them to accomplish. As You will, may it be so."

Caleb allowed the men to be seated as he announced, "The usual preparations for the Planting will commence in the spring, with the first volunteers being sent after the summer solstice. This affords you more than sufficient time to prayerfully consider whether you desire to volunteer to join the Planting."

Two hours after the meeting concluded, at the evening meal, Caeleigh chose a seat beside Adeline and waited for the opportunity to ask her questions.

"Normally when a Planting is announced, no more than three men are initially sent," the elder woman explained. "For Caleb to be sending twice that number is a break with custom."

"He *did* say that the land requires extra laborers to prepare it for the work of the Planting," Caeleigh suggested. "Is that perhaps a circumstance that has not previously been encountered?"

"It *is* possible," Adeline allowed. "I was quite young when my parents brought our family here as part of the Planting of the Blue Creek Settlement, and I have lived here all my life since, so I have never participated in a Planting at an age that I can remember well. However, it is my understanding that the rule of three has never before been broken." No one else was yet seated near enough to the pair for them to ask.

Caeleigh related to her mentor and friend the suppositions she had overheard when the men had been presented, that at least three of the five were to be the new Settlement's candidates for Governor.

"I cannot say for certain what the truth of the matter is," Adeline replied. "Quite likely all of them will be set in leadership positions in the new Settlement once it is established. The three who were sent ahead when the Cypress Ridge Settlement was Planted became the candidates for Governor there; *perhaps* three of the five will be the new Settlement's candidates."

"Is there any way of knowing?" Caeleigh's eyes strayed across the room and alighted on Andrew, seated between Simeon and Thomas.

"It is never spoken of this early in the process." Adeline followed her former apprentice's gaze. "Do you intend to volunteer?"

"I already have." Caeleigh had yet to remove her contemplation from the man who so held her implicit trust that she'd been willing to follow him at the least prompting by Kadosh.

"Take care to be mindful of your reasons for following him," the older woman cautioned. "If he is indeed to be in a leadership role, *any* leadership role, he cannot Pledge with you. The rules of the Settlements require all men who hold positions of leadership to be Bonded and married."

"I have no such expectation," Caeleigh immediately responded, without petulance. "He is among my dearest of friends, and is as a brother to me, but nothing more. I entertain no illusions or fantasies for more than what stands between us at present. My purpose in volunteering to join the Planting is to follow Kadosh wherever *He* leads and calls me. If I allow myself any personal reason for going, it would be to join Elizabeth – Peter has volunteered as well, which means she will be accompanying her husband, whether or not she is at ease with the idea of leaving here, herself."

Something in the manner of her young friend's report of this news gave Adeline concern. "Did he not speak with her before volunteering?"

"He did, but it seemed more to inform than to consult."

Adeline shook her head, disappointed and disapproving. She said not a word further, however, lest the conversation turn to gossip.

Knowing that to change the subject would be appropriate, Caeleigh asked the question she'd been harboring since she put forth her name as a volunteer: "Do you believe I am ready to serve a Settlement as tailor, on my own?"

Adeline patted Caeleigh's hand reassuringly, smiling with pride. "Without a doubt. You have proven yourself inventive and capable, dear girl. There will be enough to keep you busy at all times, but by the time the Settlement's numbers will have grown enough to produce more work than you can handle by yourself, I expect you'll be ready to take on an apprentice of your own."

The remark gave Caeleigh pause. To be on her own, working without Adeline beside her daily, was one matter and a step she could feel ready to take. Training and overseeing an apprentice, however, far surpassed what she imagined herself capable of achieving so quickly. She spoke her thanks for the compliment and hoped that her discomfort was not apparent.

After the conclusion of the meal, Caeleigh attempted to linger in the meetinghouse dining room, waiting to be taken aside. She assisted the servingwomen in clearing dishes away to the kitchen and wiping down the tables, working slowly at the latter task as she watched from the corner of her eye the group of men still deep in discussion at the center of the head table.

They had fallen silent when the plates before them had been taken away, she'd observed, and she was reluctant to disturb them again, for the risk of her own embarrassment as much as for the likelihood of prolonging the conversation further.

"You're liable to scrub a hole through that tabletop if you keep at it," a familiar voice broke into her rambling thoughts.

Startled by having been spoken to, she turned so quickly that she tripped on the hem of her skirt. Andrew caught her elbow and steadied her before she could fall.

"I've kept you waiting," he observed apologetically.

"I wanted to apologize for our last conversation," Caeleigh stammered. She swallowed her anxious emotions before continuing, "I now understand, as you promised I would, why you couldn't speak before now. I'm sorry for having forced your hand as much as I did at the time. I know I said some things that, retrospectively, had to have been rather cutting."

Andrew nodded agreement, but his expression forgave. "They were. I might have said them myself, though, were I in your position. Don't harbor bitterness toward yourself for it. I have no desire to leave you here with any ill between us. I'm counting on your prayers – there is much hard labor before me."

"Yet you're eager to go." Caeleigh's voice faltered with dismay.

For her sake, Andrew did his utmost to temper his elation. "How could I *not* be? I'm following in the will of Kadosh and His plan for my life. As I told you the other week, these are the first steps on the path He has set that leads into promises that I have been waiting on for longer than I can say. Wouldn't *you* be the least bit eager, in such circumstances?"

She blinked back her tears. "I would that I *was* in such circumstances..."

"I know," Andrew empathized. "Believe me when I say I know that desire intimately well."

"When will you depart?" Caeleigh asked, praying that the question and its tone had not conveyed interdependency.

Andrew kept his words few and neutral. "By the end of the week."

"That's only a matter of *days* from now!" The hushed protest burst from Caeleigh's lips before she had the opportunity to restrain it.

Again, Andrew remained calm and patient, with his mind incontrovertibly on some further goal. "The sooner the work is begun, the sooner it will be complete. There is much that must be done before the winter sets in."

Caeleigh acquiesced. "Then go, with my prayers as promised." Caeleigh collected and folded her scrub cloth from the tabletop. "Have you any parting words of wisdom, since you're certain to be busy from now until the time when Governor Caleb sends you and the others off?"

Andrew smiled indistinguishably. "I'll offer you one better, dear Sister. A word of wisdom *and* a word of prophecy. I've been informed that you have already volunteered to join the new Settlement. I feel quite assured that as you enter this new season, Kadosh means to deliver on some long-awaited promises, including some that you've forgotten about."

"How can you be certain?"

Andrew clasped his hands behind his back in order to occupy them against other things they might attempt. "I trust the heart of Kadosh, and I know His voice. Now heed me in this: do not seek after the promises and set them higher in your heart than Him." He spoke as one who had journeyed the more difficult course to obtain the wisdom he now imparted. "Kadosh ought always to be your first pursuit, your first desire. Seek Him first always, and allow all other things to be added into your life."

Caeleigh nodded, no longer trusting herself to speak.

"Remember one other thing?" Andrew waited for Caeleigh to make eye contact before continuing. "I *will* be returning at some point. Don't say goodbye as though you're sending me into eternal reward."

Three weeks later, Caeleigh garnered the courage to join the wives of the married men who had been sent when they gathered in the chapel to pray for their husbands. The four women looked up curiously upon her entrance, tempting Caeleigh to regret the decision. Remembering the promise she had made, she forced herself not to turn and run.

A woman she remembered to be Simeon's wife invited Caeleigh to sit beside her.

"What brings you among us?" the sweet-faced woman asked.

Caeleigh smoothed her skirts and tucked her trembling fingers beneath the backs of her knees. "Your husbands all have you to lift them up before heaven's throne as they labor in the land for the new Settlement," she began. She feared how she might be judged for her next words, but could not fail the promise she had made. "Andrew has plenty of women pining after him, but none who are praying for him in the manner of his need. Simply because he is unwed does not make his need of prayer any less. Nor is Thomas' need, for the same reason. Before they departed, I gave my word that I would fill that duty for them, as a sister."

While one or two of the others seemed to be evaluating her answer, Simeon's wife accepted her much less warily. "Then you are welcome to join us. My name is Beth."

Chapter 13

Early November 2147

"Caeleigh, this letter for you was included with Philip's letter to me, this week." Carinne, Philip's wife, handed the tailor a folded letter as the two women approached the chapel for what had become their daily early-morning prayer meetings. "Ezra brought them back with him when he arrived last evening. Philip assures me that he has not read its contents, and I know that neither have I – it was concealed within the folds of my husband's letter, so no one other than we knows that it was there."

"Thank you, Carinne." Caeleigh received the letter as something precious; quite rare were the occasions upon which Andrew wrote to her. She'd known immediately the letter was from him; there could be no mistaking the origin of the meticulously spaced block lettering that spelled out her name. The two women took their seats, opining that Sophia would likely not be joining them whilst her husband was home.

Aware that they had arrived early enough to have given themselves a few private minutes, Caeleigh unfolded the letter and began to read its contents.

"What news does he send?" Carinne enquired. "Philip sent no significant news, only mostly a love letter speaking of how dearly he misses me and the children."

Caeleigh chose fragments of Andrew's letter to report. "He states that Thomas has proven himself lacking as a farrier –

which explains why Ezra brought back two additional horses to be tended to along with his own," she commented before reading verbatim, "... 'so we must seek to recruit one for the new Settlement.' I do hope they'll be alright with only three horses between the five of them for the next few days."

"I'm certain they'll be fine," Carinne assured. "One thing Philip *did* mention was that Ezra would've brought an additional horse, anyway, to carry them back replenished supplies when he returns." Though Carinne was respectful enough not to seek to read the letter not addressed to her, she had come to care enough about its recipient to wonder what transpired in the correspondence between her and the unattached man who had sent it. "What else does he say?"

Despite not desiring to stonewall a recently-made friend, Caeleigh chose the most benign of the personal remarks in the letter. "He and Thomas both send their wishes that I would have a pleasant birthday. They've both known me for quite some time, and are aware that I find my birthday a generally unpalatable event."

Carinne's maternal instincts had already begun assembling the pieces of the larger puzzle. She chose, however, to defer the potentially distressing conversation as Beth, and David's wife Lydia, arrived.

"Do we expect Sophia to join us?" Beth asked as they approached. Caeleigh tucked Andrew's letter beneath herself.

Carinne shook her head. "I anticipate not," she replied. "Micah and two of the girls have had fevers for a few days now. She likely wouldn't rather leave Ezra to contend alone with three ailing children during his respite. Will you be requesting that Simeon be the next to return?"

"Goodness, no. He's already been, and we've found it easier not to torment ourselves with interim visits during this time.

David may take the next turn if he prefers," Beth offered to Lydia.

Lydia blushed and grimaced. "I feel terrible for saying this, but I've slept better since David has been away. I love him dearly, but he *snores*."

The confession elicited giggles from the other two married women.

"Honestly!" the dark-haired Lydia continued. "I feel simply dreadful for complaining or daring to so much as *potentially* speak ill of my Beloved, but there is something to be said in defense of a quiet night's sleep!"

"Perhaps, then, one of the other men would like to have an opportunity?" Carinne directed the suggestion toward Caeleigh delicately.

The tailor shook her head. "Their minds are too much in the work. When Thomas wrote last, he confided that he has been feeling useful in ways he never has before. He intimated that he has no cause to surrender that, not even for a few nights in a comfortable bed. He has, however, asked that we pray for his recovery from a persistent pain he's developed in his shoulder."

With this as the last comment spoken, the group's attention was directed upon their purpose. Beth held before them a letter Ezra had brought her from Simeon, in which had been detailed the men's progress to date, their successes, setbacks, and challenges yet ahead. This the women used as a list to guide their prayers, adding Thomas' request for his injured shoulder when seeking for continued good health for all of the men.

As their time of prayer concluded and the group disbanded, Caeleigh lingered in the chapel, withdrawing Andrew's letter from its concealment and rereading the last lines on the page: *I am aware you might read this, at first, with others present. Knowing you as I do, dear Sister, I caution you that you may wish to reserve the second page for a moment of privacy, as I cannot guarantee that what I say next will not cause you tears, for which I understand you do not care to have witnesses.*

Glancing back from the door, Carinne ushered Beth ahead of herself through the exit, whispering to her friend, "I believe we may have upset her with so much discussion of our marriages."

Alone at last, Caeleigh turned over the thick, fibrous paper. There, Andrew's words continued.

Those of us who are out here count ourselves fortunate that David is among our number. Despite our removal from the Settlement, we are yet able to have the benefit of daily teachings. I have been learning much these past weeks of the Hebrew concept of the go'el, the kinsman redeemer. The best example of it in human relationship in the scriptures is the account of Ruth. We have been discussing also how the Christ has ultimately performed that role for all of us as His followers. I was reading on this subject in Matthew's gospel this morning, and as I came upon his quotation of the prophet Isaiah, my eyes fell upon a single line that seemed to speak resoundingly of you: "a bruised reed he will not break." Caeleigh, I understand the wounds that are borne upon your heart, the aches and longings of unfulfilled promises. I know well what you consider the torment of being surrounded by those who are enjoying that which has been promised but has yet to be realized. You are a bruised reed in this season of your life, dear Sister. You have this promise before you now: Kadosh will not break you. He will not allow despair to so overcome you that you feel wholly swallowed by it. Take heart. Be brave, Caeleigh. This season must and shall end, as all seasons do. Winter, no matter how bitter its cold or heavy its snows, always capitulates to spring, sooner or later. I know your preference is for the sooner, but rest in the assurance that it is coming at all, and allow that to be sufficient, knowing that Kadosh will provide you the grace needed to forbear for as long as He asks that you do. I can tell you firsthand that this is a request He will gladly and generously oblige.

Hold fast to these truths, Caeleigh. I know all too well there will be days when these words I've written will be the last you will want to hear. You will have no desire to welcome them – do so anyway, despite what you may feel. The strength to persevere grown in you by your endurance of the darker days is what James the brother of the Christ says leads to perfection. Dwell in the first few verses of his letter to the church scattered abroad. Meditate on them. I have done the same and the Spirit of Truth has ministered unspeakable peace to me through those words.

As had been predicted by Andrew himself, his neatly block-lettered words began to blur and swim. Caeleigh cared little to miss the requests to pass on his greetings to Peter and Elizabeth, as well as to enjoy on his behalf the frosted apple cookies that Elizabeth had begun making annually as part of the Blue Creek Settlement's Thanksgiving celebration feast. Andrew had spoken directly to Caeleigh's deepest and foremost present sorrow.

By the time Caeleigh composed herself once more and felt able to face the day, she arrived late to the morning meal. As she attempted to slip unobtrusively into the meetinghouse dining room, Beth waved to her from the nearest table, indicating a vacant seat between herself and Lydia. Cautiously, Caeleigh accepted the invitation.

It was Lydia who was first to speak as Caeleigh took the reserved seat. "We owe you an apology, Caeleigh," she offered in sincere contrition. "We spoke without consideration of your feelings, this morning, when discussing our husbands."

Caeleigh wondered why she was at all startled that this reparation had been extended by David's wife. The man she'd come to affectionately address as *Rabbi* for his insight as a teacher of the scriptures frequently characterized his Beloved as a peacemaker. Caeleigh supposed that it had simply been a matter of the fact that she'd not quite felt accepted by Lydia, not as openly as Beth and Carinne had welcomed her among them.

"Please don't be distressed," Caeleigh forgave. "I'd received a letter with some troubling information, as well," she further excused the morning's situation.

"Oh, dear," Beth worried. "I hope nothing too terrible."

"Is there anything we may do to help?" Lydia likewise expressed her inclined concern.

Caeleigh sighed. "I was reminded that my birthday is approaching. I *loathe* observing my birthday."

The admission confounded the two women beside her. "Why?" Beth asked.

"I will be thirty-two this year... and still unmarried."

"Oh," Lydia murmured, her voice intoned low with sympathy. The common age for marriage in the Settlements was nearly ten years younger.

It was this tone that broke through to Caeleigh, in a manner not unlike that by which Andrew's letter had reached her half an hour prior.

Caeleigh lowered her fork to her plate. "I have no example of a lifelong unmarried woman leading a full and happy life, to pattern myself after. And regardless of whether or not I have such an example, I yet have the desire for marriage and family..." She glanced further up the table to where Carinne sat with her daughter and son, the young boy seated between his mother and older sister.

"Then we shall pray for you," Beth promised, Lydia readily agreeing. "We shall seek that Kadosh provide according to your need in whatever way He sees fit, and mend this quite apparent ache in your heart."

"And we shall take care not to speak so carelessly in your presence, lest we provide opportunities for envy," Lydia added. "We have no desire to set a stumbling block in your path." After a moment's pause, the engineer's wife smiled with a light of mischief in her eyes. "We will, however, insist upon celebrating your birthday with you. The two of us, Carinne and Sophia. Name how you would like to spend the afternoon, and we will make arrangements to see that it's done. *No one* should be permitted to have their birthday be a loathsome experience."

Chapter 14

Early – Mid December 2147

With the exception of a two-day furlough for Thanksgiving, the men sent ahead remained in the place that was to become the new Settlement until after the first light snow of the winter. Only those of the men with wives and families returned intermittently in turns to the Blue Creek Settlement to visit them; having no such ties to draw them back, Andrew and Thomas remained in the land of their labor for seven continuous weeks.

It was plain they would have continued to labor in the wilds through Christmastide had the snows not driven them back to shelter. In truth, it could be called into question whether they had indeed returned: Those five who had been sent and named to leadership of the new Settlement disappeared for significant portions of each day – save the Sabbath – behind the closed doors of Andrew's workshop.

Simeon, an architect, worked closely with Andrew, the carpenter, in structural design. As an engineer, David had much to contribute in regard to construction planning. Philip and Ezra, a vintner and keeper of fruit orchards, respectively, provided agricultural insight. Though Philip and David's input was considered essential and highly valued, the lead of the work within this closed circle was shared between Andrew, Ezra, and Simeon. Only they knew the full extent of the leadership these three men shared in the development of the new Settlement, as the candidates for Governor thereof, though that selection had not yet been made public. Until one man was chosen and appointed, they would share the responsibilities of leadership as anonymously as possible, relying on the nature of their trades in relation to the Planting of the Settlement to explain the way they took charge in tandem.

After a week, the group's number was reduced by two. Simeon and Ezra, however, continued meeting with Andrew as Christmastide approached and winter deepened. The former two, however, did so without neglecting their families and the whole of the community, in contrast to the latter.

Midway through the second week of this, Caeleigh took her concerns to the one man she thought might be able to help her.

"What happened to Andrew while you were out there, Thomas? This ...*distant*... behavior is entirely contrary to his nature." Though the word *antisocial* rang in her mind, she could not bring herself to speak it in connection to Andrew. She could not connotate the man she'd known with such aberration.

"I can't say for certain what's causing him to act as he has been. Although..." Thomas paused in reflection. "There was an afternoon, early last month, when he and I were clearing an overgrowth of brush from what's to be farmland. He confided in me that Kadosh had spoken to him regarding his future. He seemed quite certain of things that are to come to pass with the establishment of the new Settlement – undeterrably so, in fact. As I look back now, from that day forward he has been indomitable regarding the work of the Planting, to the point of working himself to exhaustion."

Caeleigh considered her friend's words. "...I believe I understand the situation," she concluded at length.

This news brought Thomas both relief and newfound desperation. "By all means enlighten me, that I might be of some aid to my Brother."

All he received in response to his plea was an apologetic smile. "I'm truly sorry, but to do so, I would reveal things that were confided to me with the understanding that they would be kept to myself. But I *will* speak to him," Caeleigh grasped Thomas' workworn hand in both of her own as she promised, "and I'll be certain to express that the concern for him is yours as well as my own."

So it was that later that same day Caeleigh knocked on the door of Andrew's workshop, knowing that Philip and Ezra had within the hour prior left for the afternoon.

Though no call bade her enter, she stepped out of the snow and into the warmth of the workshop. She was unprepared for the state of the place. Contrary to what she anticipated she might find, every wall, worktable, counter – and a few additional surfaces invented with sawhorses and sheets of plywood – were covered with large sheets of paper: plans, maps, and diagrams. Andrew sat on a stool at his primary worktable, bent over one such hand-rendered map, sketching.

Caeleigh spoke his name and was ignored. She tried again, adding, "I've come to speak with you."

This at the least garnered a grunt of acknowledgement. "I'm busy."

She studied the man before her, appalled at what she found. He was neither clean-shaven nor unshaven, but rather inattentively shaven, it seemed, and had grown alarmingly gaunt and pale despite his naturally darker tone. If his own care escaped his attention, she would be required to behave uncharacteristically in order to obtain it. "I see that. Busy *and* distracted. You picked up the wrong parcel off the counter at the mercantile yesterday. You have my tailor's chalk pencils."

Andrew spoke dispassionately to the tabletop before him. "If I have your parcel and you have mine, switch them and go.

Please leave me to my work; I don't wish to be impolite, but I have much that must be done and no time to talk."

"I would speak with my *Brother,* not this aloof and indifferent man who's come back from the wilds in his disheveled likeness." Caeleigh spoke in a warning tone, hoping to shock Andrew to attention.

Andrew dropped his pencil and watched it roll toward the center of the table. She'd *reprimanded* him. The woman he'd been certain would have been distressed by his behavior of late was angry. Now he genuinely was at a loss for how to conduct himself in her presence. He continued to stare at the pencil, which had come to rest several inches beyond his reach. "Pardon me?"

"You heard me." Her tone remained as it had been.

Andrew stood and retrieved his pencil, then turned to face the angry tailor. "On what grounds do you level such strong words at me?" He kept his tone even, though he admitted to himself there was a great deal more tension in his shoulders than simply the accumulation of having been hunched over maps all day.

She narrowed her eyes at the carpenter's effrontery, her head tilted to a forward-leaning angle upon not merely one axis, but all three. "I don't do so lightly *or* eagerly. You ought to know me well enough to trust that."

"Cae – " he began, but she cut him off before he finished so much as her name.

"*No.* I won't allow you the opportunity to argue or make excuses. When I'm through, *then* you may make your apologies." Caeleigh took a step nearer, her right hand raised at eye level, index finger sharply extended. "*First,* you listen. For two months I have prayed for you, faithfully, as you asked. Not simply *because* you asked – also because I wanted to. I watched the other men's wives gather daily in the chapel to intercede for their husbands while the six of you were gone, and it didn't seem *right* to me that you and Thomas had no one standing before heaven's throne for you when you were toiling just as hard, if not harder. So I joined them, despite the mistrust and suspicion it earned me. I don't say it that way to paint it as a hardship, but to make you face the reality of what I endured." Her hand slowly fell to her side as her admonition fell upon a slowly-growing-receptive spirit.

Caeleigh's left-hand fingers unconsciously found their way to the chain hanging from her neck and began sliding the sandstone pendant from side to side along its free length as she continued, "I know Kadosh has spoken to you in your time in the wilderness. He told me that He had – not *what* He had told you, only that He had spoken to you. And I'm glad for that. I've *rejoiced* with you, Andrew, to know that Kadosh has spoken straightforwardly to you to direct the course of your life and make that journey a partnership. I can understand, as well, how such an experience would make one rather introspective for a time."

Andrew continued to stare, his expression unreadable. Unable to bear more than a few seconds' silence when he remained unresponsive, Caeleigh spoke further.

"However, I spoke with Thomas earlier today. He betrayed no confidences, but he did say enough to tell me what it is you've been doing." Through her speech so far, Caeleigh had softened ever so slightly, gradually. Now came through the heartbreak Andrew had been anticipating from the beginning – yet not in the manner he had expected. She closed her eyes and breathed deeply before continuing, "Do you recall your confession the day that you introduced me to Noya?"

"I recall, yes." Andrew's compliant tone caused Caeleigh to open her eyes and study him.

"You implied that day that I know you well, better than most, perhaps any. Am I correct?"

He nodded, waiting for what she might say next.

"What word of wisdom did you give me before you departed?" Whether by miracle or by the sheer depth of her anger, Caeleigh succeeded in keeping the tremor out of her voice that had threatened to slip in and give her away.

Andrew did not answer the question aloud; he understood.

Caeleigh approached the table and studied the map – a plan for dividing allocations of farmlands. "You have been doing the work that is yours to do. But what are the motives of your *heart,* Brother? You have been working *not* 'as unto the Lord,' as the scriptures instruct, but with the aim of causing your promised future."

The carpenter forced himself to step away from Caeleigh, to put the stool between them.

She interpreted this as a retreat and pursued not physically, but verbally. "You have been living so much for the future that you have become disconnected from the present moment. Forgive the redundancy of the phrasing, but you aren't *present in* the present. Life goes on all about you, good and bad alike, and you're *missing* it.

"Peter needs the influence of his elder brother to correct him, lest he make any more unilateral decisions that wound his marriage. Philip's wife Carinne told him only this morning that she is again with child. And your own body has been crying for days that it needs more rest – you have been wearing the pallor of deep illness almost since you returned. If you expect to be a figure of strength and authority in this new Settlement, you *cannot* conduct yourself like this … and you certainly must keep up your physical strength."

Andrew's hands shook; he clenched them in an attempt to still them, only to snap the pencil he'd long forgotten he still held. The splinters of wood and graphite piercing his palm cleared the last wisps of fog from his mind.

The minor utterance when his flesh tore, too quick for him to stop, also caught Caeleigh's attention. Without seeking permission, she took his hand to examine the wound. She commanded him to sit on the stool once again and demanded her parcel from the mercantile.

"I must admit I thought you had concocted that tale to create an explanation for your intrusion here." Andrew half-smiled at her back as she retrieved first the parcel from the shelf he'd indicated, then a box of matches from the drawer where they were stored. Reluctantly he admitted to himself that he had missed her.

"I'm a *storyteller,* not a liar," she retorted sharply, though without shouting, her anger not yet fully dissipated. "You're fortunate that I purchased needles along with the pencils." Untying the string and pulling back enough of the brown paper to slip out the packet of needles, she chose one, struck a match and held its tip in the flame to sterilize the metal.

After she blew out the match and could find nowhere safe to set it, Andrew took it with his free hand. "I know; I've made a mess of this place. I've made a mess of a great many things, it would seem."

"None of them irreparable," Caeleigh replied while bowed over his other hand with the heated needle, gently prodding, coaxing the splinters out of the wound. He flinched, prompting her to add, "I didn't say it wouldn't hurt." She tipped up her head and looked up at him, half-smiling apologetically.

"That, you didn't," he conceded.

Caeleigh finished clearing the wound, then cleaned and bandaged it, having retrieved a first aid kit from the same drawer the matches had been in. She gave Andrew's palm a sound thump, directly on the worst of the wound, before returning the first aid kit and matches to their drawer.

Andrew wrenched his hand away from the assault it had received. "Ow! What was that?"

Caeleigh smirked over her shoulder. "An anchor to hold you in the present moment. The future will wait until you arrive there."

Andrew thanked her while fighting regret. She was both invaluable and impossible to him. He had been right, he decided, to keep his distance these past two weeks. He would have to continue to do so, knowing it carried great potential to wound her. Though, perhaps with what he'd seen in her in this exchange, their friendship might well weather this difficult season yet.

Chapter 15

Mid June 2148
through Very Early September 2148

Winter departed quickly, as it did every year. By the end of January, the world had thawed and the six men who had been sent ahead in the Planting returned to the new Settlement to execute the plans they had been preparing.

Throughout the spring, tradesmen of all applicable trades had begun processing the raw materials that streamed into the Blue Creek Settlement in addition to what had been accumulatively stored in the months since Governor Caleb's announcement. Lights glowed in workshops up and down the streets in the evenings when the sun set before the day's work was completed. Those who had no other contribution to make preserved food to be sent with the volunteers. Few hands were idle.

As summer drew nearer, Caeleigh turned again to Abram for instruction. Those she might have asked months earlier had been too busy at the time, and were markedly busier now. Her storytelling mentor, however, was more than pleased to spend an afternoon imparting more of the traditions of the Settlements to the young tailor.

The coppersmith was glad to once more instruct his favorite pupil. "Construction begins with the principal streets, the chapel and meetinghouse, as well as the digging of wells both for water and geothermal heat for all structures."

"That's why, then, everything has been mapped out in advance?" Caeleigh thought of the many maps that had littered Andrew's workshop.

Abram nodded. "Ordinarily the planning of placement of these things would be happening now. However, the fact that an engineer was one of those sent initially has set this new Settlement ahead in that regard."

Caeleigh scowled thoughtfully, attempting to process and organize the information. "Pardon my impertinence, but how do you know all of this? I was under the impression you'd lived the majority of your life in the Blue Creek Settlement."

Her instructor chuckled affectionately at the young woman who still believed herself capable of showing him disrespect, which to him was an outrageous impossibility. "You understand correctly. I did, however, give the skills of my hands to the labor of the last Settlement that was Planted, the Cypress Ridge Settlement, north and not quite so far east of us as this new Planting will be. My nephew is an engineer, as well; he was one of the volunteers who went out in that Planting. He has volunteered, along with his apprentice, to assist David with the placement and drilling of the geothermal wells, since they possess the necessary equipment for the job."

"What is there that *I* may do at this stage?" Caeleigh shifted in her now-customary seat. "Certainly there must be *some* way that I may offer the skills of my hands, though my trade is not directly involved and the present labor is not suitable for a woman. ...I don't have any skill in the kitchen – or, at the least, not enough that I could be more help than hindrance were I to try. My only opportunity to be of useful service is through the work of my trade."

Abram gave this plea consideration. "My *knees* have not aged well. Many of my friends who have assisted with Plantings suffer the same complaint. We've attributed the pain to the many long days spent kneeling on bare ground setting the cobblestone pavers of the streets."

"Isn't that the work of the stonemason?"

"You would have a single man build an entire city unassisted?" Abram posed the question with raised brows and a jesting tone. "Any man who is capable contributes to the work, regardless of his own trade."

"How, then, might *I* be able to help? I doubt I would be permitted to participate in such a task." Abram had implied that Caeleigh might have a contribution to make, yet offered nothing of which she was capable – not in the society in which she now resided.

"Most certainly you would not. However, you could *equip* those who are." Abram indicated the shawl Caeleigh held in her lap. "You have been expanding upon what you can do with leather, I see."

She turned over the edge of the wrap to examine the lining she'd sewn inside the outer layer of buckskin leather: the material she'd used was warm, soft, and *thick*. "If you'd had something to kneel upon, a sturdy cushion perhaps, to protect your knees..." she thought aloud.

Abram grinned. "Better than that," he suggested, "would be one that wouldn't have to be moved by hand every time it's necessary to shift position, as that happens frequently while moving and setting the cobblestones. Could you design such a thing?"

"Give me two days," she replied. Springing from her seat, Caeleigh hugged the coppersmith impulsively on her way to depart. She paused in the doorway. "Thank you, Abram."

"Go on, get to work," the coppersmith shooed her with a smile.

Toward the end of that week, Caeleigh found a team of men loading cobblestones into a wagon behind Peter's workshop. With a look and a nod, Andrew delegated Thomas to speak with her while he kept himself busy.

"What have you brought us?" Thomas eyed the ungainly floursack that Caeleigh had dropped the moment she approached.

"It's for you to take with you." Caeleigh cast a significant look at the bundle at her feet.

Peter stood taller on his knees inside the bed of the wagon to better see over the side. "My wife *does* know I prefer my food a bit less raw than that, I would hope…" he remarked, he himself not altogether certain whether he was jesting.

Caeleigh shook her head at her best friend's husband, rather than extend the disrespect of rolling her eyes. "Elizabeth gave me an empty floursack from the bakery to make carrying these easier." She opened the floursack and withdrew two of the items therein. "To protect your knees during all the time you'll spend kneeling on hard-packed earth," she told them, handing the items as a pair to Thomas for his inspection.

Thomas turned and tossed one of the two to Peter, keeping the other to inspect himself. "What is it filled with?" he asked, pressing the thickness between his thumb and forefinger and finding greater resistance than he expected.

"I've packed them with uncombed wool," Caeleigh answered, "as well as added a second layer of leather on the outer side to improve resilience."

Peter, who had tied on the guard and found that it covered not only the knee but the upper shin as well, gave his approval. "This will make the work far less uncomfortable."

"There are enough here for the three of you and two more. I've already taken another five pairs to Simeon at John's workshop," she named the other stonemason in the Blue Creek Settlement who, though not volunteering to go in the Planting as Peter was, had turned all his efforts of late to creating cobblestones for the new Settlement.

"What happened to your hands?" Peter asked as she handed the floursack to him to be packed into the wagon.

Caeleigh looked at her fingertips, nearly all of which were covered with bandages. "Some of the sewing had to be done by hand. I was hurrying to get these finished before you left. I'm not worried; they'll have healed long before it's time for me to join the Planting and I'll need to be able to work. *This* was the contribution I could make *now*, and I didn't want to miss the opportunity."

"Thank you," Thomas replied for the others as well as himself, leaning over the side of the wagon to return the guard he'd still held to the floursack. His back momentarily toward Caeleigh, he issued Andrew a warning look, to which the carpenter subtly shook his head and refused to speak. "This is thoughtful and generous of you. I can't imagine how much of your own expense you put into these – beyond the damage to your hands, which I will pray heal quickly."

Four months passed as though they were four weeks.

Given that Elizabeth's bakery abutted the meetinghouse kitchen, the carpenter Matthias cut and installed a doorway between the two, making the bakery an extension of the kitchen until such time as someone would wish to run the bakery again.

Caeleigh stood with Elizabeth as she locked the outer door for the final time, having left the key on the ledge above the sink. "This isn't cause for sadness, you know," Caeleigh reminded her as they departed through the meetinghouse. "You'll have a new bakery built, and I've heard Peter say he intends to ask Simeon about doing a few things differently to improve upon what you've had here."

The thirty volunteers from the Blue Creek Settlement arrived at the new and as yet unnamed Settlement with few possessions – they would be sleeping in auxiliary rooms of the meetinghouse until construction of the men's and women's lodginghouses and initial homes was complete. The lodginghouses were intended to have – at the least – been begun; however, a debate over building methods had arisen amongst the engineer, architect, and carpenter. Until a consensus could be reached within all members of the Settlement's leadership, construction was at a standstill and other work scheduled for the interim.

That first late morning, Caeleigh watched those married among the men who had gone ahead of them greet their wives who now joined them – the storyteller in her began drawing out metaphors of parched men in a desert arriving upon the site of an oasis, as she watched their expressions. The vintner Philip's wife, well into her fifth month of maternity, had elected to stay behind until after the birth of the child; in her place had come their twelve-year-old daughter Sarah. The vintner took up his firstborn in his arms, spinning her as though she were much younger – her resultant laughter was clearly his great delight.

A young farmer by the name of Nathaniel distributed several written messages to their recipients.

Ezra stood in the bed of one of the wagons and called order from the minor chaos. "On behalf of those of us who have been here for the past months, I welcome you to the Willow Springs Settlement. The work ahead of us means long days and, at times, hard labor – but the reward promises to be great."

Toward the end of the day, as they gathered for the evening meal, Thomas approached those in leadership. "I must leave immediately and return to the Blue Creek Settlement," he informed them.

Andrew looked to the others for confirmation before taking the smith aside as friend. "You haven't been yourself all day," he observed. "What can be done to help you?"

Thomas handed him the letter Nathaniel had delivered earlier in the day. "My father has fallen ill. They believe he's not long from passing into eternal reward." Briefly he offered a cheerless smile. "I appreciate that you place emphasis on the value of my contribution here, but I cannot stay – I'm needed by my family. My father has asked for me, for whatever time he has left. And after that… I will need time to ensure that my mother will be cared for, before I can return."

Andrew saw in Thomas' eyes that there was much more this had brought to light upon which he wasn't speaking. "Then go with our blessing and our prayers, Brother. I wouldn't have you do anything that may leave you with regrets."

Chapter 16

Mid September 2148

It seemed to Caeleigh that the Willow Springs Settlement was to be a pioneering Settlement in more than a few ways. As of yet, nearly a year after the first men had been sent to break and prepare the land for the work that was now taking place, there had been no establishment of which three of the five Caleb had named would be the candidates for Governor. All five continued to share the responsibilities of leadership, each contributing according to his gifts and the skills of his trade. They were willing to hear requests and proposals to alter the ordering of the new Settlement from that of the Blue Creek Settlement. Decisions were made by the five together as a committee, and they had chosen to open some decisions – particularly those which directly or potentially affected several individuals or families – to the community for vote.

Since several farming homesteads were the first additional buildings to have been constructed over the past several weeks, the community of those living on-site now numbered eighty, many of them working to establish the farms and orchards that would provide food for the Settlement at large. The leadership had determined this course from a desire for the Willow Springs Settlement to be self-sustaining as quickly as possible. It had meant an industrious summer for all who could apply themselves to the work, and delays in other regards – most notably the prolonged lack of men's and women's lodginghouses – but few were the complaints. One of the youths, a boy soon to come of age, had suggested that the circumstances lent them all a sense of adventure not found in everyday life, and the disposition seemed to have been adopted at large.

Another innovation of the new Settlement's leadership was that the whole of the community all met weekly on the eve of the Sabbath to discuss, plan, and pray over their progress; it was a practice to which many attributed the growing unification of those who had given of themselves to the work of the Planting, and a sound foundation for the community of people who would live there.

At this evening's meeting, in fact, Caeleigh had proposed that rather than one general mercantile for all needs, with space constraints limiting how much of any one thing may be available, that specialty shops be allowed for some trades. The events that had spurred the construction of Elizabeth's bakery in the Blue Creek Settlement as an independent vocation had begun to open eyes, Caeleigh suspected, and she had sought both Adeline and Abram's counsel on the matter of requesting a millinery for herself several weeks prior. Standing before the five members of the council, as the community had come to view them, Caeleigh held the multifolded page of their letter in her hands, gleaning courage from their words of support as she spoke.

"Relying on the mercantile to supply and acquire the necessary tools and materials of my particular trade not only inconveniences the mercantile shopkeeper, but also both limits my readily available options – due to the mercantile's limited available space for those items – and delays me for specialized work." Fearing that such a contention might be considered a complaint, Caeleigh quickly added, "I also find myself in need of a workspace. In the Blue Creek Settlement, I was able to work from the home of another while residing in the women's lodginghouse. It was acceptable there and then, because I had been her apprentice. Here, I have no right to expect the same of anyone. A millinery would provide ample space for both the wares and the work."

A bemused and cheshire smile had perked the corner of Andrew's mouth at Caeleigh's mention of the disadvantage presented by living in the women's lodginghouse. Discomfited, she quickly turned her eyes to Simeon. "I acknowledge and respect the choice the First Elders made, which we have since upheld, to choose a simpler life than that offered and pursued by the outside world. However, simplicity does not necessitate primitiveness," Caeleigh argued, "and opening this possibility would allow more people, especially unmarried tradeswomen, the opportunity to support themselves and serve the community with greater opportunity to practice and barter their trades."

Clutching Abram and Adeline's letter until the paper began to crumple, Caeleigh turned to the crowd behind her while the council conferred. Elizabeth winked. Lydia, David's wife, nodded and smiled. Caeleigh returned to her seat beside Beth, who squeezed her hand encouragingly, as the council opened the subject for discussion amongst the community.

The proposition was received well – in part, Caeleigh suspected, because Andrew supported it. Between his oft-demonstrated wisdom and his irresistible charm, people were always inclined to accept whatever earned Andrew's endorsement. A vote was taken and the motion passed. Caeleigh was gratified that her proposition was accepted and glad that she would have a means of providing for herself in the new Settlement.

Distracted by her thoughts as everyone gathered around the tables for the evening meal, she was surprised when Andrew stepped ahead of her and pulled out a chair to seat her. He truly shocked her, though, when he took the seat beside her. Though Andrew frequently seated himself beside different people each time the community came together for a meal, he had never before chosen Caeleigh. A year prior she would have called them close friends, but Andrew had returned from the initial labor of the Planting with an altered demeanor that had left them little more than cordial familiar strangers. Their last conversation, sometime in the weeks before Christmastide, had been terse at best, and he had made concerted efforts, it seemed, to avoid her since.

Smiling warmly, he congratulated her success and praised her wisdom; she thanked him shyly and searched around her for other familiar faces. Though they had been good friends for a few years – and she deeply regretted what had been lost of that friendship – suddenly Caeleigh found his attentions disconcertingly attractive. Suddenly she was noticing everything about him anew, such as how shirtsleeves rolled back to his elbows revealed arms taut with muscle – every inch of him exuded strength, physically and spiritually.

Peter and his wife Elizabeth, Andrew's and Caeleigh's best friends, respectively, were seated across from her. Peter picked up on Andrew's remark complimenting Caeleigh for her insightfulness and, determined not to be outdone, further extolled her virtues. "Caeleigh is not only wise, but talented in both trades and arts, and gifted in other ways besides! With all of her many abilities, she could be Governor herself were she a man; being a woman, though, she may have to settle for marrying one, and aim to leave something for him to do in the role. Don't you think she would make an excellent Governor's wife, Andrew?"

Flushed with embarrassment, Caeleigh rebuked the man: "Peter, it's cruel of you to tease me in such a manner. Andrew, please tell him not to spoil my evening with his aggrandizements." As she addressed him, Caeleigh turned to Andrew and placed a hand on his forearm, purely out of long-dormant impulse. In that split-second of contact, three things happened all but simultaneously.

An involuntary joyous cry that could best be expressed as 'Yes, you are the one my soul was created to love' resounded in Caeleigh's spirit, followed immediately by a breathless cry from her mind of a terrified *'No!'* Andrew jolted at her touch as though receiving an electric shock.

Mortified, Caeleigh jerked back her hand. Hastily whispering, "I'm sorry!" she pushed back her chair and fled the room and the building.

"Did I do something to offend her?" Andrew asked Elizabeth as Caeleigh flew out the door.

Equally perplexed, Elizabeth replied, "I don't know."

"If I've upset her, I must apologize. Excuse me." After grabbing his coat from a hook by the door, Andrew likewise left the meetinghouse in haste. He stepped off the end of the porch in time to see someone duck behind the next corner at the far end of the building. "Caeleigh!" he called after her.

Knowing that he would follow her, Caeleigh took up fistfuls of her skirts and ran across the meadow toward the copse of weeping willows for which the new Settlement had been named. She neither slowed nor dared to look back until she reached their cover. So winded that her lungs burned, Caeleigh released her skirts but continued to trudge further into the shelter of the willows' drooping branches in search of a hiding place, her hands dangling listlessly at her sides.

The moment her breathing began to be less labored, however, she began to weep. She had Bonded with Andrew! Something *had* to be wrong – it was impossible for a woman to Bond with a man who had not first Bonded with her, and Andrew had never shown her any more interest than he had shown any other unmarried woman. Perhaps less – particularly of late. And it was widely known throughout the Settlements that he had not declared to have Bonded with anyone. The only possible conclusion was that something was wrong with Caeleigh, that she had misperceived what had happened just now. Overwhelmed with grief and confusion, she pressed her hands against her abdomen, striving to quiet her sobs.

"Caeleigh?" Andrew spoke gently as he approached from behind. "If I've offended or upset you, I'm sorry."

Wrapping her arms around her midsection, she fell to her knees. Unable yet to speak, she shook her head.

Immediately Andrew knelt at her side. "What's wrong? Why did you run?"

"I was frightened," she whispered.

"Of me?" he worried.

She rocked back and forth in an attempt to camouflage her trembling. "Of the way you responded when I reached for you. You shuddered as though I repulsed you."

"No, Caeleigh, that wasn't it at all. When you laid your hand on my arm, it was so cold that you gave me a chill," Andrew gently explained. "I was shivering; that's all."

"Truly?" Caeleigh finally looked into his face.

Andrew hesitated for a brief moment, then instructed, "Give me your hands." Caeleigh did as she was told, and he took her hands in his. "See?" he said. "Your fingers are cold as ice." Releasing her hands, he rubbed his together briskly to warm them, then grasped her fingers a second time, moving his hands up hers to her wrists. "You're *freezing*, poor thing." He shrugged off his coat and placed it around Caeleigh's shoulders while she wrung her hands.

The whimper that escaped her lips called to mind for Andrew the last occasion upon which he had put his coat on this woman. This time, however, he knew the circumstances *were* different – he *had* been given the right to claim her and behave toward her in the manner of a *go'el,* a kinsman redeemer, a concept he had been studying under David's tutelage for several months. Still, rights aside, he needed not to approach her brashly.

"Please tell me what's upsetting you?" he requested.

"I'm not sure I can. I don't understand it; the very *idea* makes no sense at all ..." Frightened by what had transpired between herself and the man she had once upon a time called Brother, and his suddenly-resumed unconstrained behavior, Caeleigh shifted uneasily within the confines of Andrew's coat. Had she not been in need of its warmth, she would likely have refused the garment. Despite his attempts in this moment, he had not for most of a year been the man she had known and trusted with her heart. The man he had become in the interim had left her uncertain whether she might ever find in him that former man once more. Yet as she stared at the ground ahead of her, she found herself wishing for nothing else more greatly than exactly that.

"Caeleigh, look at me." Andrew waited for her to meet his gaze before continuing. "Something happened to you; I saw it in your eyes. Did you experience the Bonding?"

"I can't have," she argued. "It's impossible. You never – "

"I did," he interrupted. "I never said anything because I didn't know you well enough at the time and I didn't want to frighten you. I Bonded with you the first day I saw you. Then Kadosh spoke of you to me, and told me that I needed to wait. I thought I would have more *time,* that we would get to know each other better first ... and then the Planting was announced and I was sent. My intention has been that after the labor of this Planting was completed I would tell you and could seek to court you, the way it's usually done. I wasn't expecting this."

Caeleigh stared, uncomprehending. "This can't be happening. I can't be ..." She stopped without completing a thought that would only lead to a confession she wasn't ready to make.

"But it is." Andrew gripped her shoulders gently. "It *has* happened, and it's beautiful."

"I need time to think," Caeleigh begged. "*Please,* I need time."

"Of course." Andrew stood, pulling Caeleigh to her feet. "For now, let's get you indoors and warmed."

As the two of them walked back to the meetinghouse, Caeleigh found herself saying, "I don't want to have to give up my trade. Especially after gaining permission to have my own shop, tonight." It shocked her to hear herself speak as though she'd already accepted that which her mind still struggled to conceive.

Having been disciplining himself to provide the physical space that she clearly needed, Andrew dared to close that space and lightly place a hand behind the shoulder of the woman he could now call his Beloved. "I would never ask that of you, Caeleigh. You are too gifted to simply throw your talents away. I might ask that you take an apprentice to share some of the work, but I would never allow you to give it up entirely." He found it an overwhelming relief to speak with her as he once had, before his affections had become insuppressibly strong and necessitated absolute separation.

"Do you truly mean that?" She looked at him with wide eyes. Her fears began to melt in the warmth of the assurance in his features.

The carpenter smiled, gladdened by the freedom newly afforded him to openly profess his full intentions. "Of course I do. I'll help to build and prepare the millinery, for you, to prove it. Anything you desire, simply name it and I will do whatever

I can. I was already planning to make that offer – I thought we could use the time to become reacquainted from the distance I'd had to deliberately allow to grow between us in the last year – then by the time it's complete, perhaps you'll feel ready for me to openly court you." In the course of this rehearsed speech, Andrew had removed his touch from Caeleigh's back, desiring to take her hand. The opportunity to do so, however, had not presented itself as she kept her arms wrapped tightly around her waist. He settled, alternatively, for extending his hands, palms upward-facing and open, in a gesture of peace offering.

"You would wait through the whole autumn and winter?" Caeleigh was stunned by the selflessness of what he'd suggested. Few men, if any, entered courtship intending that it should last more than a few months. No man had been heard of who was willing to delay courtship after Bonding with a woman; yet hadn't Andrew said that he'd done exactly that already?

"I'll be getting to spend much of that time with you, and the work of my trade will be my gift to you – I'll ask nothing in compensation for it." By this time they had stepped onto the porch of the meetinghouse. Andrew opened the door for Caeleigh, and as she passed him through it, he winked at her and murmured, "Besides, it will help to ease all the young ladies of the Settlements into the idea that I have Bonded with someone."

At this, Caeleigh laughed. It was no secret to anyone that Andrew was the object of more than a few wistful – and some *ambitious* – daydreams.

They returned to their seats, Andrew again holding Caeleigh's chair for her. Peter, now suspicious, looked from Caeleigh, still wearing Andrew's coat, to Andrew himself, and back again. "What was the problem?" he queried.

"A simple misunderstanding. Amends have been made and all is well," Andrew replied. "However, I am going to be making some proposals regarding construction at the next meeting. We cannot continue to allow our Settlement's women to freeze indoors." He gave Caeleigh a grin that carried significance only she understood.

"Thank you!" Elizabeth interjected. "I haven't wanted to complain, but lately I have felt as though there's *no difference* between *indoors* and out!"

Andrew grinned at the blonde seated opposite him. "We have eschewed a great deal of the modern technology available in order to live as simply as we do, but as Caeleigh so well put it earlier tonight, living simply does not mean we have to live primitively." Wanting to rest his arm across the back of her chair as he spoke his Beloved's name, but sensing that so much physical attention would both overwhelm her and betray the secret he'd promised to keep a season longer, he opted rather to stretch behind her and then retract his arm. "There are technologies and materials that it will not hinder us to take advantage of, including the building methods I intend to propose. I'm certain I can easily win Simeon and David's agreement; given that the three of us had been entertaining the idea in earlier stages of planning, half of the research is already done."

Chapter 17

Late September 2148

A few weeks after that portentous evening to which she refused to refer aloud, Caeleigh sat together with Elizabeth on the swing on the side porch of the newly completed women's lodginghouse, sharing an evening of one another's exclusive company such as they hadn't had since before Elizabeth and Peter were married. In the quiet serenity of what Caeleigh called an 'Indian Summer' nightfall, a term foreign to Elizabeth, but which the latter presumed to have been appropriated from one of her dear friend's many favorite books, the pair enjoyed the comfortable silence of kindred friends who needed little more than the presence of one another to find contentment.

"I know you and Peter miss each other, being separated in the men's and women's lodginghouses," Caeleigh confessed to her friend, "but I've been glad of the opportunity to spend time with you again."

Elizabeth kicked with the foot that she hadn't tucked beneath herself, propelling the swing into gentle motion. "I know. *I've* been glad for it, too, truthfully. And I know that spending so much time in the company of Andrew and the other men is good for Peter, as well."

"I can't help but wish they wouldn't keep progressing so quickly on your home, though, because then you'll be taken away again." Mournfully Caeleigh joined her friend in perpetuating the swing's steady rhythm.

"Not *that* far away," Elizabeth reminded her. "Besides, Peter told me this morning that the next structure to be built is your millinery – *That* will be exciting, and no doubt keep you busier than I will be in setting up house."

A boom of thunder caused both women to jump in their seats. The falling light of day's end had misled them regarding the truth of the darkening sky. Caeleigh sighed as they relaxed once more. "Storms like this make me wish I had a man in my life to share them with," she confided. "I find them terribly beautiful."

"This one may be merely terrible," Elizabeth spoke over the intensifying wind, as lightning splintered the rapidly blackening sky.

Within minutes Elizabeth was proved right. The storm continued to thrash the landscape, though without a single drop of rain. Both women were about to retreat indoors after a lightning bolt stretched toward the earth not far away, until a cry rose above the wind: "Fire! The meetinghouse is afire!"

The call beckoned everyone within its hearing, men and women alike, Caeleigh and Elizabeth among them. As the two approached the meetinghouse, they caught up with the men who had outpaced them. The sight before them all brought everyone to a halt. The tree which stood overshadowing one wing of the meetinghouse had been split in two by the lightning strike and sent crashing through the roof, where it ignited.

"I need five men! *Now!*" Peter shouted from the front of the gathering crowd. Drawing water from the nearest well, he doused himself before charging into the building. The recruited men followed suit; Elizabeth caught the daughter of one of them as she ran in pursuit of her father.

"You *must* stay here," Elizabeth commanded the girl.

"But my father – " came the protest.

"Sarah, your father knows what he is doing and will be safe. It isn't safe for you."

A loud clap of thunder thrust the girl into Elizabeth's arms.

Beside them, another woman, Michelle, who had been inside the meetinghouse when the tree was struck, quaked under the power of the storm. "This is *judgment!*" she wailed. "We have wrought the displeasure of Kadosh by beginning the Settlement without a Governor. Now His wrath will be brought to bear upon us!"

"Not so!" Michelle was rebutted. "Kadosh instructed the Planting of this Settlement at this time. He would *never* punish us for obeying Him!"

Unwilling to be proved to have no cause for her terror, Michelle immediately retorted in near-hysteria: "Well, *someone* is displeased, or this would not have happened!"

"Nonsense!" Caeleigh shouted at her over the whistling of the wind and crackling of the flames. "Will you show preference to the trauma over the deliverance that has brought you safely out? Have you spoken here only to induce your spirit of fear among the people? I *rebuke* your cowardice!"

As Michelle skulked away still bemoaning the situation, Peter emerged from the building, darkened with soot which caused the dismay in his eyes to stand in stark relief. "We have no means of stopping the fire. At the present it otherwise would not stand to consume the whole building and everything inside, but in this wind it likely will spread, and fast."

A call from one the men still within the building summoned Peter back.

"Pray for deliverance – pray for rain!" Peter shouted over his shoulder to his wife and the others near her as he re-doused himself from the well and ran back into the meetinghouse.

The group accosted heaven as they had been instructed to do. Heaven's initial response was to issue no more than the cannonfire of additional thunderclaps. Those assembled huddled closer to better hear one another as they shouted their prayers. Andrew, having not entered the meetinghouse alongside Peter, had been about to take charge within the chaos when Caeleigh stepped forth.

"Kadosh!"

Andrew was amazed when Caeleigh raised her voice to a level of which he had originally deemed her incapable. He was soon to find that her volume would be not only matched but bested by her boldness.

Caeleigh threw her head back and thrust her pointed finger skyward. "I *ask* You for *nothing!* Instead I *call* You to *remember* Your own promises to this Settlement! Your word was given that You mean to build us up and cause us to *thrive* – *not* to cut us off before we've scarcely begun!" She pointed toward the flames rising from the roof of the meetinghouse. "We are utterly dependent upon *You*, Kadosh! It falls to *You* to deliver us!"

Caeleigh's fearlessness in address animated those around her to pray in kind. Several of the men who had arrived from the men's lodginghouse continued to draw water from the well, filling buckets and heaving their contents as high as they were able.

Before long, their pleas and efforts were answered with a hot and heavy rain that began to pour down into the valley. This came in addition to the storm that raged on still, the ponderous torrent thrown about in every conceivable direction by the thrashing winds that had been tearing asunder the surrounding vegetation, as the sky lit brighter than midday with every flash of lightning. The majority of the assembly fled for shelter; Elizabeth, Caeleigh, and a few others remained, though they sought the tenuous shelter of nearby trees.

Thick black smoke billowed from every outlet of the meetinghouse, driving out all of those within. By the time the men had regrouped with those standing watch for them, the fire had been extinguished.

The rain continued to pummel the compromised meetinghouse, heedless of the end of its necessity. In due time the weight of such force proved overpowering, and those yet present watched as the roof and one of the walls caved in with a crash that outthundered the storm.

"There is no more we can do now," David shouted to be heard over the wind and rain. "We had best let it be until the morning." With these words of dismissal from the engineer, the small band dispersed, the men and the women each to their separate lodginghouses and Sarah and her father to their home in-between, all of them running.

"It seems now that the millinery will have to wait," Caeleigh thought aloud as she wrapped her wet hair in a towel. "The meetinghouse is much more necessary to the Settlement." The thought she kept to herself was that she was grateful for such a delay. The more time she had until completion of the millinery was more time before needing to face Andrew, a prospect that had given her anxiety severe enough to effect increasing loss of sleep and appetite since the evening she had fled from him, and he'd pursued. Despite Andrew's inexhaustible patience and her own deep-seated desire for marriage with a man who inarguably would possess many of his finest traits, Caeleigh could not reconcile that Kadosh had intended him for her. Caeleigh was insufficient for Andrew's deserving; the thought of explaining to him *why* filled her with a terror that the truth would cost her not only Andrew's affection, but his friendship and loyalty as well.

"Do you suppose it will take the men long to repair it?" Elizabeth replied from where she sat on one of the beds in their shared room in the women's lodginghouse.

"I truly don't know. With the entire roof caved in, it may be beyond repair. I feel terrible."

That Caeleigh would take upon herself any measure of fault for occurrences clearly to be blamed upon natural events left Elizabeth more perplexed than the evening's excitement had rattled her. "It's only a building and no one was injured. What cause could you have to feel guilt?"

Caeleigh eyed the closed door before speaking further, massaging the moisture from her hair into the towel swathed over it. "Shortly before the tree was struck, we were discussing your home. I was thinking about the fact that it, like the lodginghouses, public buildings and other homes, is built by that new method Andrew proposed, whereas the meetinghouse was not. The new-method buildings are much better insulated against heat and cold alike, and my last thought before the lightning strike was a regret of the fact that the meetinghouse lacked that benefit."

"So you blame yourself for the destruction of the meetinghouse based upon one fleeting thought? It isn't possible. Don't be silly," Elizabeth admonished her friend, smiling.

Shortly thereafter, both women retired for the night, knowing they would be needed in the morning to assist in the recovery efforts after the damage had been assessed.

The next morning dawned sunny and clear, though the ground was strewn with evidence of the previous night's tempest. Caeleigh caught up to her friend and looped their arms together, after having given Elizabeth a chance to greet her husband, who had jogged off moments before.

"Where is Peter going?" Caeleigh asked as they made their way to the home of Philip the vintner, who had opened his kitchen for the preparation and serving of the morning meal.

"He said something about needing to tell Andrew what you said last night. Please don't be cross with me for telling him," Elizabeth pleaded as Caeleigh's dismay grew.

"I could never be cross with you," Caeleigh squeezed Elizabeth's hand. "But if your husband embarrasses me…"

They were interrupted by the sound of Andrew's laughter. He and Peter approached them with long, quick strides.

"*Peter* – " Elizabeth began to scold.

"No, Beloved. It isn't what you think." Peter turned to Caeleigh's icy stare and explained, "I don't repeat everything my wife tells me, but this time I *had* to. You see…"

"We had the same conversation that you did, last night," Andrew supplied with a poorly suppressed grin that was remnant of his laughter. "As we were finishing work on their home last evening, I mentioned to Peter that I wished for an opportunity to go back and rebuild the meetinghouse in the new method. Then in the next moment, lightning struck – literally."

"You see this disaster as an *answer* to *prayer*?" Caeleigh couldn't believe him.

"Absolutely. How can you two, the women who found the meetinghouse too cold *before* winter has set in, disagree with that? Kadosh has given us the opportunity to start over with the meetinghouse." He continued to grin as though spilling over with eagerness to disclose a secret.

"So it's irreparable, then?" Elizabeth asked Peter, who had been one of the men charged with inspecting the building.

"And everything inside is lost?" She sidestepped a puddle, the hem of her skirts lifted above her ankles to keep them dry and free of mud.

"Yes and no," was Peter's response. "Yes, the building will need to be torn down. The foundation is sound, so we can rebuild in the same spot, and most of the furnishings can be salvaged. The kitchen was miraculously spared, and the dining room suffered only smoke and water damage."

"Nathaniel is giving use of his barn," Andrew added. "Everything will be moved there for storage and cleaning, until the new meetinghouse is built. The fact that so much survived, except for the structure itself, tells me that this was no coincidence."

Seeing that Caeleigh was beginning to lag behind the rest of them, Andrew stopped until she caught up while Peter and Elizabeth continued without them. "Truly, I *wasn't* laughing at you, *or* at what you said to Elizabeth last night," he assured her. "I was responding to the revelation that Kadosh provided what apparently a number of us were wishing for."

"You say that solely to attempt to comfort my bruised feelings." Caeleigh stared only straight ahead as she spoke.

Andrew remained patient and gentle. "No, I say it because it's the truth."

Her only reply was to quicken her steps.

"*She* is the one!" was the bitter cry that greeted Caeleigh when she stepped into Philip's home. She followed its sound to the resentful glare and pointing finger of Michelle, whose quailing the night prior Caeleigh had reprehended.

Simeon, one of the presumed candidates for Governor, stepped between the two women. "You stand accused of taking liberty over a weaker brother with harsh words," he informed Caeleigh, speaking in the firm authority of a position to whom one must give answer. "What say you to the claim?"

"I say that I did no such thing." Speaking with a calm greater than she felt and standing with her arms dropped straight at her sides, Caeleigh collected fistfuls of her skirts, the tight clenching of her hands concealed by the folds of fabric. "Michelle bewailed the fire as retribution from Kadosh, and I reprimanded her for it, because I knew that wasn't the truth. I spoke strongly because she would not hear gentler words when they were used."

"I will vouch for Caeleigh's account," asserted Elizabeth.

"As will I." Sarah, Philip's daughter whom Elizabeth had stopped from rushing after him into the meetinghouse, came forth. "I was there and heard the exchange. It was as Miss Caeleigh says."

Simeon nodded thoughtfully. "I agree with you. What cause would Kadosh have to punish us so? None."

Caeleigh's accuser, however, would not so quickly be dismissed. "*Someone* acted against the Settlement last night! If not Kadosh, then some other, perhaps. I was *in* the meetinghouse last night, and I am *telling* you, there is something to be feared at work!"

"Not so." Andrew stepped forward as if to physically shield Caeleigh from the woman's words. He spoke authoritatively: "Witnesses saw you safely out of the building before any genuine danger presented itself."

"The meetinghouse was *afire*!" Michelle continued to protest with vigor.

"Peace, now," Simeon told her. "The matter is settled. Your complaint is dismissed by the testimony of witnesses." He nodded to Andrew, confirming that the two men were in agreement.

Andrew turned toward Caeleigh, only to find that she had shrunk back – though not from that against which he had stood, *for* her, as he supposed… but rather from how near he had stood *to* her.

Chapter 18

Late September 2148

"I find this dreadfully boring," complained one of the dozen or so children who were helping the following day to scrub clean all of the chairs salvaged from the meetinghouse.

Caeleigh could not argue that the task was anything but monotonous. It was, however, the only thing the children present in the Willow Springs Settlement could do to contribute. Simeon and Peter had forbidden them entry into the vicinity of the devastated building. Several men were bringing the furnishings outside, to be carried to Nathaniel's barn by the older boys and youths. There, the few girls, and younger children old enough to work, were washing away the soot and ash. Caeleigh had volunteered to be the adult supervising them, primarily because she knew that Andrew would be needed elsewhere and could not be spared for so menial a task – thus she could both be useful to the recovery efforts and avoid him without rousing his suspicion, at the same time.

"Would it help the time pass more quickly if I told you a story while we work?" Caeleigh offered.

Simeon's daughter Laurel bounced on her knees with excitement. "Yes, please!"

"Please do!" cried another of the girls.

"Very well, then, what ought the story be?" Caeleigh asked as she plunged her scrub rag into a bucket of soapy water and wrung it out.

"Would you tell more of the story of the maid who went to the wedding feast at the king's castle?" Sarah requested. "It's my favorite."

"Only if we *all* keep working as I talk," Caeleigh stipulated. "We *must* get all of these chairs cleaned before they bring us too many more." The storyteller gestured to the two and a half dozen chairs that surrounded them.

"But it sounds as though to be a *girls'* story!" protested Micah, a boy of seven.

Caeleigh smiled at Ezra's youngest child and only son. "Not *all* of it," she told him. "And certainly *not* the part I'm going to tell now." She chuckled softly as the boy's eyes lit with excitement. With three elder sisters fairly close to him in age, Micah had little opportunity to hear anything other than girls' stories.

"The king was giving a wedding feast for his son the prince, and everyone in the kingdom was invited. The maiden, who was from a village far away from the castle, had been brought there in a carriage sent by the *king* himself, simply so that she could be in attendance. She was quite poor, and unaccustomed to all of the fine things to be found in and around the castle. She also was exceptionally shy around strangers, and the disapproving looks the courtiers gave her made her feel unworthy and unwanted."

During this opening of Caeleigh's story, Andrew appeared in the doorway, carrying the tools he would need to repair those several chairs and a table that had been damaged. Caeleigh knelt with her back to him, and her audience was focused on the task before them as instructed. As a result, all present neither saw nor heard the carpenter enter the barn. Quietly he set down his tools and settled in to listen to the storyteller's tale.

"...So the maiden found a quiet spot along a nearby creek, and enjoyed the peace of her solitude all alone. She had no shoes, so she stuck her bare feet in the water, allowing the current to tickle her toes. Suddenly she heard a rumbling noise approaching from over the next hill. She turned to look, and saw an enemy *army* approaching! The soldiers were small, no taller than a child of perhaps eight years of age, and their weapons were blown darts the length of my hand." Caeleigh held out the palm of her hand to the children, allowing them to imagine all that she was describing.

"In the next moment, the prince appeared! *The prince!* But rather than wearing his royal robes, he was dressed as a warrior, and carried a double-edged sword."

Micah beamed. This was decidedly *not* a girls' story. There were no swords in girls' stories.

"The maiden stood and watched as he defended against the army and turned them back. When they had been driven all away, he turned back to her where she sat on the bank of the creek, plucking out of her arms and legs the darts that had hit her. 'I am pleased,' declared the prince. 'My father the king and I are *honored* whenever one of our subjects trusts us to protect them.' The maiden said nothing, and the prince spoke again, hoping to draw her to speak to him. 'You are *quite* brave,' he complimented her. The maiden did finally reply as she continued plucking darts from her shin – 'And quite a *pin*cushion,' she told him smartly."

The children and girls laughed, and Andrew himself had to stifle a chuckle, lest he be discovered. Quickly, though, he sobered as Caeleigh laughed with them. He slipped out of the barn as soundlessly as he'd entered, turned the corner around the door, and pressed his fists to the wall, head dropped in frustrated prayer. The altered behavior he'd observed in Caeleigh of late correlated directly with his presence – or her awareness of it, at the least. He did not think her to be intentionally rude; he would, nonetheless, need to address the matter.

He re-entered the doorway and cleared his throat loudly. "Caeleigh." He spoke her name as an isolated statement, a summons. "I would have a word with you."

Displeased to begin with at having to speak so sternly to her, Andrew cringed inwardly at the dread in Caeleigh's eyes as she approached, drying her hands on the apron tied about her waist. Stoic and firm, he led her outside and away from the hearing of those around them.

No sooner had he turned to face her than Caeleigh spoke: "Have I done anything to give offense?" she asked timidly without meeting his eyes.

"I would ask you that same question," Andrew replied. "You've been aloof and evasive toward me for weeks."

"I haven't meant to be." Caeleigh's eyes darted repeatedly between her apron-wrapped hands and the lower portion of Andrew's face. "I've... been afraid. I'm sorry for causing you to think otherwise."

The tremor in her voice as she fought not to stammer undid Andrew's resolve to maintain a stern comportment. "Afraid? What of?"

"Of myself, I suppose. I am lost for how to relate to you or interact with you, anymore. Ever since..." Caeleigh trailed off, gesturing aimlessly with her hands as the apron fell free of them, then began to speak again. "Whenever I look at you, now, I begin to have thoughts I never *had* before. Nothing *sinful,* but still worrisome. My heart is unsustainably romantic, and I dare not trust myself not to get carried away with my emotions."

Through all of this, the most she had spoken directly to him since Bonding, Caeleigh never looked into Andrew's face. She stared at the ground between their feet, or her hands – again wound up in the apron, or once – briefly – over his shoulder. "I have built up *so* many hopes, *so* many dreams, that my expectations are *bound* to be unreasonable."

"Caeleigh."

She continued as though she hadn't heard him. "To demand *any* of it from you is certain to be unfair at the least, and more than likely unrealistic."

"Caeleigh." Andrew spoke louder the second time. Part of him wanted to laugh with relief that there was no dire problem. But seeing how genuinely beset she was, he suppressed all but a smile. "Caeleigh, look at me," he said more softly. "Before this happened, how did you view me?"

"You were among the dearest of my friends, and I loved you as a brother." Near tears, Caeleigh had scarcely managed to whisper the words.

This was the answer Andrew had anticipated she would give. "Then *that's* how you relate to me now," He replied gently. "That's how you interact with me."

"But everything has *changed*," she demurred piteously.

"And *nothing* has changed," Andrew insisted firmly.

"But now you're *stuck* with me." The moment the words were out, Caeleigh slapped both hands over her mouth, wishing they could be unsaid.

"*I* Bonded with *you*, first, Caeleigh," he reminded her in low tones, "during which time you weren't afraid to be yourself around me. Besides, even if all other factors did not exist, I would choose you for the friend and sister you have been. I regret again my assumption that I would have more time before your Bonding with me, after watching you interact with those children more warmly than you have regarded me in weeks."

Chastised and truly sorry, Caeleigh willed herself to look Andrew in the eye. "I will try to do better," she promised. "I never wanted to lose your friendship, either."

"You haven't yet and never will." he placed a hand on her shoulder. "But I would be grateful if you wouldn't withhold *your* friendship from me. I am still the same man that I was before you Bonded with me. I haven't changed – only your perception of me has."

They stood in that moment only a bit longer, then Andrew took Caeleigh by the elbow and turned her back toward the barn. "Your charges have been unmonitored quite long enough, and I'm certain they are just as eager as I am to find out what happens next to the prince and the pincushion."

"*You–?*" Caeleigh looked up in time to see Andrew's teasing grin, one that had been directed at her many times before.

"I must repair a table and some of the chairs that were brought to you this morning. There's little else I can do at this stage until it is time for work related to the structure of the meetinghouse itself." Andrew inhaled deeply and exhaled slowly, seeking for Caeleigh to meet his eyes. When at last she did, he instructed gently with the offer of the only compromise he could design, "Continue as you were before. Forget that I am in the room at all. Do this, and you can tell yourself that you're avoiding me, and I can tell myself that you aren't, but rather are only doing as I have asked."

Chapter 19

Late September 2148

Late the following morning, Sarah looked up from the simple mending in her hands. "I'm grateful to you for these lessons, Miss Caeleigh," she said with a smile. "My mother meant to teach me, but then she became so busy with preparations for the new baby and with sending my father and me here ahead to help with the Planting of the Settlement, that there simply wasn't time."

"You needn't make excuses, Sarah," Caeleigh smiled from where she was seated at Philip's dining room table. "I enjoy teaching you. You're a bright and thoughtful girl, and you apply yourself diligently to the lessons. Besides, it gives me a means to do what I most enjoy, until I'm able to resume working in my trade full-time."

"And I'm sure that my mother will be greatly pleased when she arrives and sees those lovely new drapes you're making for the dining room windows. The ones that were damaged in the storm were pretty enough, but these are much nicer."

"Mind you watch your stitch sizes. Try to keep them even and uniform," Caeleigh reprimanded gently. Carinne had made the original drapes herself, and Sarah did not need to walk so close to the line of criticizing her own mother, a woman whom Caeleigh considered a dear friend.

Perceptive for a girl of twelve, Sarah understood the unspoken correction as well as the spoken. "Would you please tell me more of the story of the maiden? *With* the parts you left out yesterday because of the younger children? You are one of the best storytellers I've heard, and I'm glad we'll have you here in the new Settlement."

"Nothing of worth can be purchased with flattery, Sarah." Caeleigh wished it were as appropriate to reprehend and deflect the adulations of adults, and of a certain carpenter in particular, as it was with children.

"I'm sorry." Sarah kept her eyes on her work as instructed. "But would you *please* tell the story, anyway?"

Caeleigh had to laugh at the girl who was caught in-between the responsible young woman she was growing into and the child who had been without her mother for the past two months and would likely be without her for another two or more yet. It was precisely because of that awkward position that Caeleigh had taken care to invest time and interest in Carinne's daughter. "Very well, then, where did we last leave off with *your* version of the story?"

Sarah was quick to reply. "The maiden had run away from the prince because of something he said to her."

"Oh, yes. Something I know a thing or two about. Misunderstandings can be very frightful." Caeleigh inserted a metal disc inside the pocket she had stitched in the hem of the drape before stitching closed that portion of the hem. The drapery hem weights had been another 'invention' of her devising that Adeline had praised. Carinne had not requested the addition, but Caeleigh had chosen to provide them for her friend, anyway – she herself preferred the resulting straighter-hanging lines of drapes with weighted hems, and knew that Carinne's tastes tended to be similar to her own.

"You ran away from someone who said something that you misunderstood?"

"In a manner of speaking." Caeleigh had a great deal of affection for the girl, but no inclination to discuss the details of her personal life with her. "I thought you wanted to hear the story?"

"Did the person forgive you?" Sarah pressed curiously to know.

Again Caeleigh redirected Sarah's attention from herself to the story. "Indeed, just as the prince forgave the maiden, although, having run away, she didn't know it yet. All she knew is that she wanted to hide, and needed to be clever about it in order to hide from the prince in his own castle, a place he knew well and she did not.

"Having found a side entry to the castle that led into a stairwell, she descended several levels, below the kitchen cellars. There she found a room full of wardrobes, all of them spilling over with fine clothes that had been set aside for the wedding guests who had no fine clothes of their own. In a drawer, she found a gown of midnight blue velvet, thick as wool and supple as satin. She changed into it, and tied the belt of matching silk cord about her waist. From a box on the table in the center of the room, she selected some plain silver hairpins, with which she dressed up her hair in imitation of the styles she'd seen some of the courtiers wear."

"No one saw her do this or accused her of theft?"

"The maiden was alone in the room, and she was one of the people for whom the clothes were intended, those who arrived at the castle wearing the only clothes they had, who owned no fine things." Caeleigh laid aside her own project temporarily. "Bring me your work so I may check your progress."

Sarah did as she was told.

From the corner of her eye, Caeleigh saw Sarah smile as if at someone in the doorway behind her, but presumed it to be Philip returning from checking his young vineyard for storm damage. When no one entered the room, the moment was forgotten as she approved the neatness of Sarah's work and resumed both the slow but easy task of hemming the drapery panel by hand and the story. "In the corner of the room stood a tall mirror and, upon examination of her disguise, the maiden didn't recognize her own reflection. Thinking it to be sufficient to hide her from the prince, she left the lower levels to explore the castle and hide in plain sight.

"Eventually she found herself in the royal library, a vast room filled floor to ceiling with bookcases, all of them full of more books than she had ever seen in one place before. Having not seen anyone else for the several past minutes and having definitely not seen anyone else in the library, the maiden decided it was a fine place to hide. She perused the nearest shelf and found there a copy of one of her most favorite novels. Slipping the leather-bound volume from the shelf, she carried it across the room to a cushioned window seat, where she sat and read for several chapters before sensing that someone else was present in the room."

"Speaking of someone else being present in the room ..." Sarah interrupted.

"Hm?" Caeleigh, who had been thoroughly engrossed in both her stitching and her storytelling, looked up to see Sarah indicating that she look to the door ... where stood Andrew, leaning against the jamb with his arms crossed, as if he had been there for quite some time.

Caeleigh felt her face grow hot then immediately cold, as she flushed and paled in quick succession at the sight of him. In her distraction, Caeleigh pricked her finger with the thick upholstery sewing needle; though she gasped at the pain, she welcomed it, as it quickly refocused her befuddled mind. Dropping the needle, she pinched the injured fingertip lest she bleed on the pristine fabric.

In a few strides Andrew was across the room and at her side. "Are you alright?" He hovered over Caeleigh, attempting to examine her hand.

Meanwhile, Sarah cast aside her own sewing and hurried into the kitchen in search of first aid supplies.

Caeleigh restricted her answer to the most concise possible without being overtly impolite. She had taken Andrew's correction the day before to heart, but felt no less uncomfortable in his company. "I'll survive. What are you doing here?"

"Replacing the windows." Andrew indicated the two front windows through which the storm's high winds had sent branches from a nearby tree.

Caeleigh quirked an eyebrow at him. "The same way you mended chairs yesterday?"

"I'm glad to see you're speaking to me again," Andrew murmured softly, taking advantage of Sarah's absence as the girl could be heard searching through a kitchen drawer.

The comment, offered innocently, hit its mark more deeply than he intended; he saw in Caeleigh's eyes how severely he had grieved her.

They both spoke at once:

"I'm sorry, Andrew."

"Forgive me."

This whispered conversation ended abruptly with Sarah's re-entry into the room, carrying a small adhesive bandage, which she delivered to Caeleigh. "In case it's still bleeding," she offered.

"Thank you, Sarah." Caeleigh opened the bandage and applied it to the wounded fingertip, which did persist to slightly bleed.

Andrew, who had stepped back at Sarah's approach, repeated his apology. "Forgive me, Caeleigh, for startling you and causing this."

Caeleigh caught his meaning, but for Sarah's sake treated the apology as though he were referring only to the pricking of her finger. With a nod of acceptance, she replied in a warm tone, "It will heal, and it's nothing uncommon to the work I do. What I would like is to know exactly how long you were standing there."

"Not *that* long."

Caeleigh turned to Sarah, knowing the girl would answer honestly.

Sarah hesitated, torn by what felt to be a need to choose between two of her favorite people. They seemed to have grown upset with one another; choosing one of them over the other might increase that tension and earn her disapprobation from whomever she chose against. After as brisk an assessment as the girl could make, her need for the conclusion of the story won Caeleigh her favor. "He was there when you last checked my work," she confessed.

Caeleigh looked at Andrew, truly looked into his face for the first time since his appearance in the room, and found herself annoyingly incapable of staying angry with him. The impish grin he wore told Caeleigh that Andrew could read in her eyes the exact nature of her irritation.

"Don't be angry," the carpenter sought to appease. "I was waiting for a pause in your conversation so that I wouldn't frighten you with the disruption when I brought in the new windows. They need to be installed from the inside." With that, he returned to the doorway and picked up the large box awaiting him there. He crossed the room and set it down gingerly between the two broken windows.

Caeleigh bit her tongue to keep from responding with a disrespectful remark.

"I swept up the broken glass as best I could," Sarah told Andrew, eager to please, and perhaps delay, him, as he slid the new windows out of the box and set them against the wall. He had given no indication to Sarah whether tattling on him had cost her his good humor. She was desperate to reingratiate herself to the man whose attentions made her feel special.

Instead, Andrew urged Sarah back to her seat and her project. "Neither one of us will find out what happens next in the tale if you don't sit down to listen to it," he told her with a conspiratorial wink, "and if I know Caeleigh and her stories, something significant is about to happen." After bending back the flaps of the cardboard box, he pulled on a pair of thick leather work gloves and gently eased the first windowpane out of the frame.

"Exactly *how many* of my stories have you listened to, that you would think so?" Caeleigh asked suspiciously while she followed the length of thread in search of her needle.

Bent over as he was to lower the damaged pane into the box without rattling loose any shards, Andrew's expression was obscured by the hair hanging in his face as he answered innocently, "Enough."

"Is he right?" Sarah nearly bounced in her chair. "Is something about to happen? Who was in the room?"

The storyteller countered with a wide-eyed question of her own. "Whom do *you* think it was?" Caeleigh suspected that Andrew knew that she sought yet again to use the tale to distract Sarah from the tension in the room, thankful that the girl was in some regards yet young enough for it to be possible to do so.

"It was the prince, wasn't it?!"

"It *was*. 'You look truly lovely,' he told the maiden, and as he came closer she saw that he held in his hands a small cherrywood box. Holding it out to her, he said, 'This is for you.' But the maiden didn't take the box or even reach for it." Though she had paused for dramatic emphasis, Caeleigh took the opportunity to peek surreptitiously over her shoulder to be sure that Andrew continued to work, and hopefully also to ignore her.

Satisfied that his attention was on the safe removal of the broken windows and not on her, Caeleigh continued. "She looked at the box in the prince's hand, uncomprehending. He laid it beside her on the cushion and turned to walk away, clearly disappointed, when the maiden remembered herself and the respect she had neglected to show. Quickly she put aside the book from her lap and stood. 'I must beg your forgiveness, your Highness,' she called after him. 'I regret my ungracious behavior; I have never received kindness from a man before.' The prince had already turned back, but now he quickly returned to the window where she stood. 'Never?' he asked.

"Shyly the maiden nodded her head. Before her stood the person she had *so* wanted to avoid, and she had invited a conversation with him!" At this point Caeleigh stopped for a moment while she tied off and snipped the thread, having completed the panel's hem.

By the time Caeleigh had begun hemming the next panel, Sarah was beside herself with the suspense. "What did the prince say next?" she begged to know.

"He indicated that the maiden should sit once more, and he also sat, at the far other end of the window seat, with the cherrywood box between them. 'Have you, then, been treated *un*kindly?' He asked the question gently so that he wouldn't frighten her and cause her to run away again.

"She nodded a second time. She knew that to not answer a direct question from the prince was *great* disrespect, but the maiden could not speak the words. So she nodded, daring only once to look his way. When she did, it was as though he could read the whole of her broken heart and all its shame, simply by looking into her eyes... and he looked as though it wounded *him*, too."

Andrew worked as quietly as possible, though whether to not disrupt or to better hear, Caeleigh could not determine. Unfortunately, she was too far into the story to change its course now. She would have to hope that Andrew would presume the story to be completely fiction.

"Just as the maiden was hoping that the prince would pose no further questions, he did. 'What was done to you?' the prince asked, almost as if he were afraid he would not like the maiden's answer. So much did the maiden regret having to give an answer that she gave the shortest one possible. 'I have been abused,' she whispered."

"Someone had *struck* her?!" was Sarah's distraught cry.

"Worse than that, and as the maiden saw the compassion in the prince's eyes, the whole story spilled out of her against her wishes. She told him of a man who had insincerely professed love, who had manipulated her emotions with a long string of untruths, who had spoken harshly and critically to her countless times, who had slandered her good reputation, who had through all these things and more brought her to a point of sincerely believing that she was of no value at all. As tears streamed down the prince's face, the maiden told him of how this man had, on the single occasion she dared stand up to the man and speak truth to contradict him, placed his hands about her throat, then told her that he did not hate her enough to kill her because hatred would require him to care more about her than he ever had.

"After she had finally finished speaking, the prince picked up the small box and offered it to the maiden again. 'Now more than ever I want you to have this,' he stated. This time the maiden accepted the gift and opened the lid of the box. Inside, on a bed of creamy satin, lay a large white oval pendant on a thin silver chain. 'What is it?' she asked in wonder. Never had she seen anything so beautiful, and she said as much.

"The prince lifted the necklace out of the box and turned it this way and that, so that the stone would catch the sunlight and reflect all the colors of the rainbow in cold fire. 'The stone is an opal,' he told her. 'The reason I want you to have it is because you are very much like it. What makes an opal beautiful is the fact that it is broken on the inside. The more fractures are inside the heart of the stone, the more radiant the opal is. Its *brokenheartedness* is the source of its beauty. So, too, with you. *Your* heart has been bruised and broken, and yet it is all the more beautiful than the hearts of the courtiers who have looked disfavorably upon you since your arrival here. For despite their treatment of you, you have not spoken against them.' The prince smiled at the maiden and opened the clasp of the chain, then waited for her to turn so that he could fasten it around her neck.

"The stone settled perfectly over the hollow of her throat, the maiden saw, as she viewed her reflection in the window. When she met the prince's eyes in the glass, she realized that she still had her back turned to him – a sign of *great* discourtesy! Quickly she turned around once more to face him, fearful of his anger. She found only a smile. 'I thank you for this precious gift,' she murmured as she curtsied.

"The prince lifted her chin with a finger so that she would look into his face as he told her, 'I want you to understand that you are of *great* value to me. I will do whatever you ask, to prove my affection for you and earn your love in return.' 'You deserve better love than I can give,' protested the maiden, 'for my heart is one that has loved not too *wisely*, only too well.' The prince, however, disagreed. He insisted that hers was exactly the kind of love he desired, and pledged to marry the maiden to prove it."

The interruption of Sarah's sniffling brought Caeleigh out of the story and into the room. At some point, she remembered not when, she had finished the last of the drapery panels.

Andrew cleared his throat behind her, and Caeleigh feared that he would reprimand her for including such unspeakable and visceral trauma in the story for yet so innocent an audience. Then she saw him pass a hand over his face and realized he had been as affected by the story as Sarah, who sat with cheeks shining with tears of her own.

Andrew spoke with his hand still to his face, his voice slightly raw. "*That* is why I listen to your stories. That was a beautiful allegory of the Christ's redemptive love for His bride."

"What's allegory?" inquired Sarah.

"An allegory is a symbolic representation." Andrew surprised Caeleigh when he spoke before she did in answer to the question. "In this story, the prince is the Christ and his father the king is Kadosh. Their kingdom is the kingdom of heaven."

Caeleigh turned to face Andrew and wondered how much else she hadn't known about him. In the few years their friendship had grown, she'd become well acquainted with Andrew's patient nature, but had always thought him to be more of an outdoorsman than a scholar or an aesthete.

Chapter 20

Early October 2148

After the rebuilding of the meetinghouse, construction elsewhere throughout the Willow Springs Settlement resumed as had been planned. The main thoroughfare took shape as buildings began to flank either side of it, in varying stages toward completion.

Caeleigh approached Andrew as he was beginning work on the porch of her new millinery. She waited quietly, watching the intensely focused care he took at each step of the process, until he became aware of her presence and set down his tools.

"Have you come to check on my progress?" Andrew enquired with a grin as he came nearer to where Caeleigh stood.

"I came to ask a favor – a rather embarrassing one. But I thought you would be the best person to ask, since we – I mean, you – I – " Caeleigh stared at the ground, her hands flexing and curling at her sides, fingertips teasing the texture of the fabric of her skirt.

Andrew extended his work-worn hands and grasped her shoulders. "*Relax,*" he told her. "It still is only me. You can ask of me whatever you need to ask." Sensing her discomfort with such closeness, he dropped his hands and stepped backward half a pace.

"I've never learned to ride a horse ... Would you teach me?" Caeleigh cringed, twisting the fourth finger of one hand in the pinch grip of the other.

Andrew responded with a brief nod that betrayed nothing of what he might think regarding Caeleigh's request. "Of course – I'd be glad to. It's a bit too late in the day to head out this afternoon, but how about tomorrow? We'll leave from the stables about midmorning."

The following morning, Caeleigh arrived at the stables, wearing a split riding skirt Elizabeth had lent her. Confessing her ignorance of horses to Elizabeth had been easier than the first such confession, and Caeleigh's once-and-again roommate had in fact recommended that she ask Andrew to instruct her, without knowing that she had already done so.

"You look nearly ready," Andrew smiled in greeting as he approached. "Come join me." He extended a hand in invitation.

Caeleigh followed him to a small table near the tack room, surprised when rather than beginning any instruction, Andrew offered her a seat and served them each a mug of tea. "I know that you don't care much for coffee," he offered in explanation as a response to her questioning glance.

"I don't understand," Caeleigh shook her head between sips of the hot liquid, "how this has relevance to horseback riding."

Andrew smiled patiently. "It's to calm your nerves," he explained. "Horses are emotionally intuitive creatures. They tend to perceive and mirror with fair accuracy the mood of their riders. As I rightly guessed, you were trembling worse than an oak leaf in a windstorm when you arrived. You'd've prompted an uncooperative response from them, in so anxious a state."

"They would have been as frightened of me as I am of *them?*" Caeleigh questioned based upon the logic that had been presented, humiliated after she spoke at her boldness in confessing her fear.

Still, Andrew remained patient and continued to smile. "They're a good deal larger than you are – what have they to fear? Besides which," his grin became mildly more audacious, "they've spent months listening to me extol your virtues and what a wonderful, caring woman you are. They suppose you worth fearing no more than I do."

"I'm going to need more tea if you continue to speak thus," Caeleigh stammered into the nearly-empty mug ensconced in her quivering hands.

"You never minded my candor in the past," Andrew intoned with the forbearance of Job. He rose to retrieve the kettle from where it warmed in the sunlight beneath a window nearby.

"You were never quite *this* forward in the past, Andrew. I'll admit, part of me enjoys the attention... but part of me is a bit frightened by it, to be truthful. I'm sorry to say such things, but I have no desire for my fear to escalate because of your being unaware. It would be unfair to us both."

Andrew set down his own mug to refill Caeleigh's as had been requested. "I appreciate your honesty. What might I do to set your mind at ease?"

Caeleigh flushed in guilt at the generosity of spirit being shown her. "I feel terrible for asking."

"Don't." Having restrained himself against physical contact up to this point, Andrew now placed a hand over hers, resting on the tabletop. "Caeleigh, it's selfish of me not to consider how my behavior might make you feel. I may have waited a long time to show you these attentions, but that does nothing to excuse me for overwhelming you now. I apologize if that's what I've done." He allowed Caeleigh to slip her hand from beneath his, without complaint.

"If it isn't too selfish of me to ask... may we keep the pace slow at first? It has been an exceptionally long time since I last received advances, however mild, that were entirely honorable." Caeleigh rushed through her latter words as tears stung her eyes. "To be transparent with you, Andrew, I need the time to alter my frame of mind and train my instinctive reactions *not* to believe that I'm being mocked or ridiculed."

Andrew's hand still flattened on the tabletop slowly curled into a fist. "I would have strong words with whoever has taught you that reflex." He forced himself not to growl the threat, adding, "I say that as a brother to my sister, understand. What is between us now only increases my anger in your defense."

"Don't contemplate it now," Caeleigh implored the carpenter, wishing she had never opened the subject. "For today, I ask you one thing only."

Andrew closed his eyes momentarily, dismissing his ire. "Name your wish," offered in a much softer tone.

"Will you help me not to make an absolute *fool* of myself as we leave here?" Caeleigh requested. "By now, Elizabeth has spoken with her husband, which means half the Settlement is aware I've asked for riding lessons. I know you love Peter as a brother, but the man seems to care little for my dignity or shame."

At last Andrew's features drained of their tension, returning him to a smile. "I shall do my best to serve you, dear student," he promised. "Finish your tea while I finish preparing our mounts. Take your time, calm your nerves. There's nothing to fear."

Ten minutes later, Caeleigh found Andrew cinching the saddle on the second of the horses.

"Come and meet them," he called with a smile as she approached. Andrew eased a bridle over the horse's head, tightening and buckling its strap beneath the animal's jaw.

"This is Elam. I've had him for a number of years. He's gentle, I promise."

Elam, a sorrel paint stallion whose nonwhite patches were bright as new copper, bowed his large head as Caeleigh reached tremulously to stroke his forelock.

Andrew grinned. "You've now made a friend for life. He loves to be petted exactly as you've done. Don't you, boy?" The steed bobbed his head as if nodding in the affirmative, causing Caeleigh to laugh.

Andrew took her by the hand and led her around to the second horse, which seemed a bit smaller in stature than Elam. "You've already met Noya previously," the carpenter introduced.

Gone was the gangly awkwardness of the yearling in front of which Andrew had struggled not to confess that he was to be sent in the Planting of a new Settlement. In its place were the proportioned lines and stately grace of a comely young chestnut mare. "She's *grown,*" Caeleigh murmured.

"In wisdom as well as stature," Andrew boasted as he applied Noya's bridle. "Normally it would be better that your first lessons be on an older horse, but I've been training her particularly for you, for the past year. She'll also respond to my verbal commands if necessary, though I truly doubt she'll get out of hand. I've given Ezra's children rides on her, and she's handled that well."

Caeleigh found the reassurance Andrew had intended, in this knowledge. Any horse mild enough in temperament for children wouldn't be too wild for her.

Andrew draped the reins over Noya's neck, just above the saddle horn, as he had done with Elam before. "Do me a favor," he directed, "and hold Elam's reins, both of them together, several inches beneath his chin, and stand aside with him. I'll show you a few of the basic things you'll need to know."

Caeleigh did as she was instructed, as Andrew swung up onto Noya's back. "The first thing, always, is if and when you need to stop, you pull back gently on the reins and say 'Whoa.' Don't pull too hard, or the bit between her teeth will begin to cut at the corners of her mouth. You don't want to hurt her, only to get her attention," He instructed. "To get her to move, you keep your feet in the stirrups and nudge her sides with your heels. It'll only take a small nudge. The more pressure you apply or the harder you kick, the faster she'll want to run – so keep that in mind." Andrew demonstrated the barest of nudges, which prompted Noya to take several steps forward, before he gently tugged the reins, calling her to stop.

Elam nudged Caeleigh's shoulder as she stood rooted.

"He means to reassure you," Andrew translated for the steed as he dismounted the mare. "He can tell you've grown nervous again."

Caeleigh touched Elam's muzzle with her free hand and murmured a brief 'Thank you' to the creature.

"You can let him go, now," Andrew summoned Caeleigh, as he reached for a mid-height stool beside the wall. "It's time for you to try." The carpenter set the stool beside Noya and patted its surface with his fingertips. "Step up onto this." He rounded the mare and held Noya's bridle with one hand, and the stirrup with the other to keep the saddle balanced against Caeleigh's pull, as Caeleigh held onto the saddle for balance. "Now, put your left foot into the stirrup. Good. Now you'll need to kick up and over while balancing your weight on your left foot, to give yourself a push."

Caeleigh followed Andrew's instructions, feeling as though she looked far from dignified while doing so, but managing to successfully seat herself in the saddle.

"Good!" Andrew praised her. He handed Caeleigh Noya's reins, instructed her on how to position them in her hands, and moved the stepstool aside. "We're ready to go." With a click of his tongue Andrew summoned Elam to himself and mounted with an agility and grace that Caeleigh determined she would never be able to master.

The carpenter sat comfortably astride Elam's back, as at ease in the saddle as Caeleigh had ever seen him. He held the reins in one hand, the other braced against his thigh. With an imperceptible nudge, Andrew urged Elam into forward motion, and out into the sunshine. Obediently, Noya followed her master.

As Caeleigh's eyes adjusted to the brighter light, she soon began to wish that they hadn't. A group of young women, whom Caeleigh had noticed watching Andrew on a number of occasions, giggled amongst themselves as they watched her, spine rigid, jostle awkwardly on Noya's back.

With a brief whistle and a small hand gesture, Andrew called Noya to walk abreast with Elam. "Pay them no mind," he murmured to Caeleigh. "You're doing fine. Relax and try to move *with* Noya, rather than attempting to remain so still on her back."

Tears of shame stung Caeleigh's eyes; she refused them and kept her gaze forward. "I want to go *far* away," she whispered, the plea inaudible over the creaking of leather and the snorting breath of the horses.

"I shall speak with those girls, *and* with Peter, after we've returned this afternoon," Andrew promised, glancing over his shoulder in an attempt to hear the words of one of the women who believed them out of earshot and spoke mockingly of his pupil. He might have reprimanded her in Caeleigh's defense immediately, but that to do so would have embarrassed his companion further than had already been done. "For now, focus on your lesson, Caeleigh. Noya will be good with you, but you'll both feel more at ease with one another once you learn how to communicate and cooperate with her."

Chapter 21

Early October 2148

They had traveled slightly over an hour beyond the outer boundary of the Settlement when Andrew commented, "Are you *certain* you've never ridden before? You're doing quite well."

"I'm absolutely certain I never have. Any success on my part is solely coincidental beginner's luck."

Andrew chuckled. "Well, then, if beginner's luck it is, you seem to have gotten quite a measure of it."

"A measure which is soon to expire. Could we stop for a while?" Caeleigh asked as they neared a large pond, with a grove of trees just beyond.

In response, Andrew reined in his horse to a halt and dismounted. Caeleigh waited, after he had helped her down from Noya's back, while Andrew loosened the girths of both horses' saddles for the animals' comfort and explained that he had trained Elam and Noya both to something he called 'ground tying' so that they could move freely to graze near the water's edge.

"They'll be fine where they are," he informed Caeleigh when she looked back over her shoulder as he led her into the shade. "We've kept a leisurely pace, so they won't mind the heat of the day as much. *You*, however, look as though you need to get out of the sun for a while."

"Yes, that would help. Thank you." Caeleigh's voice carried a fragility that confirmed Andrew's judgment.

The pair arrived at a mossy clearing, and there they stopped. From the saddlebag he had slung over his shoulder, Andrew offered Caeleigh a bottle of water, and withdrew a second for himself. "Tell me truthfully," he said after he'd half-finished his water, "did you ask for a riding lesson because you wanted to delay completion of the millinery, or did you simply want to have my attention all to yourself?"

Caeleigh flushed at his teasing. "Neither," she answered between sips of water. "I've been thinking about it, and the truth is that while I know you as a friend, I don't know much *of* you. And if we're to be ..." She trailed off, unable to finish the statement in her lingering disquiet with the thought.

Andrew finished it for her, patiently: "Bonded."

"Yes. Well, I feel I should know more *of* you than what I know by acquaintance." As she spoke, Caeleigh fidgeted with the bottle cap, twisting and untwisting it.

Andrew offered a genial shrug. "That's fair enough. What would you like to know?"

Caeleigh pondered what to ask. "Did you grow up in the Blue Creek Settlement? I've never heard you mention any family."

"I grew up in the Saint Joseph Settlement, in Missouri." Andrew returned both empty bottles to the saddlebag where he had slung it over a low branch. "My mother passed into eternal reward when I was a young boy, and my father several years later. After he was gone, I had no other family in the Settlements in that area, so I came out here. Let's sit and rest while we talk," he offered as he watched Caeleigh lean against a low-hanging tree branch, only to lose her balance when it proved weak and sagged under her weight.

Andrew sat on the ground, his legs stretched straight out in front of him, leaning back against the stump of a fallen tree. Caeleigh knelt and then settled by his feet, facing him.

"What is this?" she asked, trailing a fingertip along the edge of an empty leather sheath strapped to his boot.

"A mark of my great shame. I wear it to remind myself not to follow my own ways."

"What do you mean?" Caeleigh had never heard anyone speak in judgment against Andrew.

"I have never told anyone about it, but if you are to be my wife, perhaps you ought to know."

Caeleigh understood the implicit request that she closely guard as secret what she was about to hear.

"Twenty years ago, when I was just barely a man, I nearly Pledged myself to a girl... Margaret. She was coy, and attractive ... and she enticed me. One particular afternoon, she told me that she wanted to speak with me privately. She took me by the hand and pulled me a few yards away from the friends around us. She let go of my hand briefly, to see if I would take hold of hers again – which I did. When we were far enough away to be considered alone, she asked me if I considered her lovely. I stumbled over my answer, until she kissed me. It was forward of her, and I ought to have known better than to allow it, but I was young and stupid. So I kissed her in return. Then I told her that yes, for as long as we had been friends I had always thought her to be lovely, and that once I was a man, I wanted to Pledge with her – and she agreed to it. A few months later, when I reached the age of sixteen, I began to court her according to the traditions for a Pledged marriage."

Andrew's story astounded Caeleigh – not for the confession, but rather for the reason that never had she witnessed him speak to such great length at a single stretch. She was not unfamiliar with the tendencies of young women to toy insincerely with the affections of men; in truth she likely understood more than he the thoughts apt to have been behind Margaret's behavior. What Caeleigh struggled to comprehend was the great ease with which Andrew behaved uncharacteristically in speaking so extensively to her.

"A short time later, something happened in our Settlement. A woman had decided that she wanted to be a storyteller. She stood up at communal gatherings and told stories and jokes, but they were laced with crude allusions and inappropriate suggestions. The Elders asked her to either stop or leave the Settlement, but she refused, claiming she had the right to do according to her talent. And she *did* have funny things to say, observations of what truly *was fact*, but from a perspective that most never considered. The problem was that she often took it too far. The Governor and the Elders of the Settlement were unanimous in their call for her to leave, lest she create a foothold for corruption among the people. Again she refused, and so the Elders sent for help from the city of Atlanta, to escort her away." Andrew, who had primarily to this point been speaking to the ground between them, raised his eyes to attempt to read Caeleigh's. Thomas had been present for her discussions with Abram regarding the Border Settlements and the outside world, and cautioned Andrew that the subject might be a point of discomfort for Caeleigh. She, however, gave no indication of alarm. Andrew proceeded with his story.

"The police officers that arrived, like all people from the outside world, were vehemently bigoted against followers of Kadosh, and they antagonized the people of the Settlement. One of them had a gun and was about to fire it into a crowd for no reason at all beyond his own hatred. I rushed toward him and pushed his arm upward so that the shot fired straight up into the air – he struck me in the face with the butt of the pistol and the gun discharged again. I was deaf for weeks as a result. Eventually, though, they did leave, and took that crude woman with them." Again, Andrew paused. He had revealed himself to have knowledge of things that had no place in their society, and *had not* had any place there for nearly a century. Having grown up in one, he knew that the Border Settlements, of course, were something of an exception by virtue of, or perhaps more accurately by demerit of, their proximity to the outside world. Caeleigh continued to listen intently, unflinchingly.

Andrew redirected his gaze to the empty sheath affixed to his boot. He found himself growing increasingly uncomfortable speaking of Margaret with Caeleigh, the woman with whom he had Bonded. She did, however, deserve to know the truth of the man Kadosh had given her, his transgressions included. To ease his mind as much as could be done given what he had to say, Andrew approached from the perspective of his regret, giving concerted effort to the task of keeping his voice even and his emotions detached. "Margaret was ... kind to me as I recovered. She asked my father to teach her some Native American signing, which she knew I had learned from my grandfather when I was a boy, so that we could continue to communicate until my hearing started to return.

"Unfortunately, it took a long time for my hearing to *fully* return, and before it did, there was an ... incident. I was working for my father, clearing brush, and Margaret approached from behind me – she afterward insisted that she called my name several times, but I never heard anything. I didn't know anyone was there until she grabbed my arm. Thinking I was being attacked, perhaps by that police officer from Atlanta whom I had confronted in the crowd, I took hold of the hand on my arm and spun around, twisting her arm behind her back. I also drew the knife I carried in that sheath, and held it to her throat – until I realized who she was. I hadn't hurt her, and I threw away the knife for good, but the damage was done. No matter how much I apologized to Margaret, she never would trust me again. She thought me a violent man. From the things she said to me – and the fact that she found it no trouble to her conscience to entice a new suitor exactly as she had done to me, within a week – it became clear that she had not loved my heart; she had only chosen me to make herself the envy of her friends."

The unexpected quiet empathy he sensed from Caeleigh strengthened Andrew to continue. "After that, I knew that living in one of the Border Settlements, where the codes of personal conduct are more lax, and the influence of the outside world has a tendency to infiltrate unbidden, wasn't enough for me. I needed to go deeper. Margaret promised never to speak of what happened and we agreed that we would both say that the reason we ended our courtship was because I wanted to move further west and she did not. Such disagreement was – *is* – permissible grounds for dissolution of a Pledged courtship in the Border Settlements. The only other person who could have known what happened that afternoon was my father – and if he knew anything, he took the knowledge with him that winter when he followed my mother into eternal reward."

Andrew's speech had begun to rush, until he reached the subject of his father. The unexpected passing still gave him pause, two decades later. He hesitated in brief memory of both of his parents, sorry for the opportunity he had lost to share his present joys with them. "Soon after we buried my father, I saddled my horse and started west. With no family to leave behind, I couldn't get far enough away. I ended up in the Blue Creek Settlement because that's all the farther my horse could carry me. I declared myself an orphan and became apprenticed to a carpenter. I sought out one of the leaders to disciple me and teach me to seek deeper knowledge of Kadosh. I was determined that I would conduct my life *only* according to *His* ways in all things, so that such an incident could *never* happen again."

Caeleigh had listened in respectful silence while Andrew spoke, never looking away from his eyes. Now, she chose her words carefully. "Andrew, that was *nineteen years* ago. If you're seeking my forgiveness, which I suspect you are, you have it. But you don't need *my* forgiveness – you need to forgive yourself." She leaned over his ankle and untied the thin leather straps of the sheath and gently but firmly stated, "You are not that boy anymore, Andrew. You must stop living as if you are in danger of becoming him once again. It won't happen. You are *nearer* to the heart of Kadosh than most men I have known, and guided by His hand upon your life." She handed him the sheath. "The old man is dead, Andrew. Stop chaining his corpse to the man you are now."

Moved by her rebuke, Andrew accepted the object, staring at it through her perspective. "You are a remarkable woman," was all he could say.

Caeleigh stood and pulled him to his feet, then led him to the edge of the pond, several yards away from their horses. "Cast off the old man," she insisted. She bent to pick up a large stone, and indicated to Andrew that he should bind the sheath to it. "Bury him for good. Forgive yourself."

"I'm not certain that I can," he avowed. "I nearly harmed a woman."

"You *must*." Caeleigh grasped Andrew's wrist. "Otherwise you have stood before Kadosh and told Him that His forgiveness of you is insufficient. Do you *dare* such arrogant blasphemy?" She spoke softly but decisively.

"Caeleigh," he murmured. Dropping the rock, with the sheath now tied to it, at his feet, Andrew pulled her into his arms and held tight. Startled at first, Caeleigh soon returned the embrace. With tears in his eyes and in his voice, Andrew sought for words. "You speak the truth to cut me, marrow from bone. I thank you for your correction." Releasing her, Andrew retrieved the sheath and stone, ensured that they were lashed tightly enough not to separate, and hurled them as far across the pond as he could.

In silence Andrew watched the resultant ripples make their way across from the center of the pond to the shore where he stood. He reached for Caeleigh's hand, which she gave willingly.

"You are forgiven, and you are that man no more, Andrew," she reiterated.

Chapter 22

Early October 2148

Andrew's original intention had been to wait a week until he allowed himself to spend another day with Caeleigh. But by the time they had returned to the Settlement that afternoon, he knew he would have difficulty waiting so much as a day. For fear of overwhelming her or causing her any anxiety, he forced himself to wait a full twenty-four hours before approaching her to ask, "Would you like to go for another ride, to show me how much you remember of what you learned yesterday?" Caeleigh had agreed, and when she quickly proved to be doing well, Andrew took them in a different direction toward more various terrain.

Still saddle-sore from the prior day, Caeleigh had not lasted long before asking that they walk for a while, rather than ride, so that she might stretch her aching muscles. Given that, after the encounter at the pond, they had returned to the horses and ridden for several hours more, Andrew readily agreed, not wanting to push too hard. Since she was yet needed to participate in the labor of the construction of the Settlement, he knew he needed to be mindful of Caeleigh's physical discomfort, lest she become unable to work. That very thought, however, caused Andrew frustration – he wanted to provide *all* for her, so that she would never be required to so labor again, and he wanted to begin that provision immediately.

Some of the impatience must have shown in his eyes, for after he had helped Caeleigh to dismount, she apologized for needing the respite. "No, it's alright," he assured her as he gathered both horses' reins in one hand and began to lead them up the incline. "You're doing quite well. I have too many things on my mind, is all."

"Would it help you to talk about any of it?" Caeleigh offered.

"No, but I thank you for the thought." Andrew returned his mind to safer subjects: "You've learned very quickly. I must say that I was impressed by your determination yesterday."

Caeleigh smiled shyly. "I wanted to improve enough that I wouldn't embarrass myself when we returned, since we were so watched when we left." After a brief pause, during which she retrieved from a saddlebag the wrap she had brought in anticipation of cooling temperatures toward the end of the afternoon, Caeleigh fell into step with Andrew. "What, then, *would* you like to talk about?" she asked as she unfolded the shawl and allowed him to take it and drape it around her.

"Yesterday we spoke of how *I* came to be here; what about *you?* Tell me about your people, where you come from."

The one question Caeleigh had hoped to have never been asked was the first. She pulled her shawl tighter over her arms. "That's a rather vague question."

"Fair point," Andrew conceded. "I know you haven't lived the entirety of your life in the Blue Creek Settlement. How long have you lived here, and where before then?"

"I came to the Blue Creek Settlement not quite five years ago." Caeleigh prayed this answer would satisfy him.

"And before that?" Simply curious and believing himself to be making benign conversation, Andrew knew nothing of the turmoil his questions had begun to cause.

Rather than reply, Caeleigh hesitated, twisting and wringing the hem of her wrap.

Signaling Elam and Noya to stop, Andrew stepped around into Caeleigh's path, and placed his hands gently on her shoulders. "What is it? Are you afraid I might disapprove of you? How *could* I," he insisted when she nodded, "after you rendered no judgment against me yesterday for what I told you of *my* past?" He took hold of her hand to reinforce the sincerity of his words.

Caeleigh took a deep breath. "I haven't lived my entire life in the Settlements, as you have – not even one of the more liberal Border Settlements. I came to the Blue Creek Settlement from the outside world." At Andrew's stunned silence, she attempted to pull her hand from his and back away, intending to flee. His declaration that all natives of the outside world detested the followers of Kadosh, returning to her mind from the prior afternoon, elevated her fear.

"No," Andrew spoke quickly, tightening his grip. "Caeleigh, it *isn't* what you think. I'm startled because you walk in a faith so deep and so assured, that I presumed you must have been brought up in it, in the environment of a Settlement that would have fostered it from a young age. The fact that you came to the Settlements of your own volition, that you *chose* this life over another, speaks *more* of you, not less."

"Truly?" Caeleigh veritably begged for reassurance.

"Truly," Andrew asserted. "It causes me to want to know more of your history and how you came to such great faith." Tucking her hand in the crook of his elbow, he held it there with his other hand and resumed their ascension of the hill. Obediently the horses followed, despite absent tension in their reins.

"The increase of faith is achieved in trials, and of *those* I have known no shortage... until I came here, that is." Caeleigh trained her eyes upon the ground ahead of her feet, thankful for the terrain's demand of her attention.

Having known nothing other than life in the Settlements, and stories of the outside world tendered third-hand through as many generations, Andrew could not reconcile the idea that Kadosh had been known outside his homeland in less than one hundred years. "But faith first comes from hearing the Word regarding the Christ. How could you have heard it in a world that has rejected Him?"

"Not everyone has." The guileless tone of her companion's inquisition reminded Caeleigh of her young storytelling audiences. From the security she found therein, she chose to utilize her gifts as a storyteller to relate the less comfortable chapters of her history. "There are some followers of Kadosh who are yet 'underground,' so to say. I came to know Him through some such people when I went away to university. By the time I came of age, I still didn't know what I wanted for my life. Society – *that* society – dictates that everyone must go to university if they want to have any worthwhile place in the world. So I went, and I studied literature because nothing else appealed to me. I was thrilled at the opportunity to read all the classics from the nineteenth, twentieth and twenty-first centuries... What I read of C.S. Lewis filled me with questions. Questions to which He is the answer. Kadosh used my love of reading and of stories to show me Himself and lure me to Himself. A classmate of mine was a follower, and she introduced me to the answer to all of my questions."

"That would explain why you're such a wonderful storyteller." Andrew's simple compliment brought a rosy flush to Caeleigh's cheeks.

"After I completed university, I knew I didn't want to stay in the outside world," Caeleigh continued. "I took whatever respectable jobs I could find and worked until I paid most of my debt, then sold off nearly everything I owned to pay the remainder. As soon as I was able, I came to the Settlements."

"What of your family?" Andrew wished to know. Caeleigh had made no mention of family, and it had been presumed in the Blue Creek Settlement that she was an orphan, as he was.

Caeleigh bent down and plucked a strand of grass from the earth, permitted herself a fleeting moment of grief, then cast both aside. "I left them behind. I haven't heard from them in years. Kadosh is my Father, my family, now."

"So will I be, too," Andrew corrected gently, "when the season is right."

"Forgive me, Andrew, but I cannot fathom... I – I'm *overwhelmed* by the idea that I could experience the Bonding at all. I was well past coming of age, according to the customs of the Settlements, by the time I came here. I was not born, nor raised, among these people – *How* can I lay claim to their inheritance under the First Elders' covenant with Kadosh?"

Andrew smiled at the woman by his side. "Because, He has told me, you are so dear to His heart. This 'inheritance,' as you aptly called it, belongs to you the same way the inheritance Kadosh covenanted to Abraham's descendants belongs to *all* who call on His name – by faith. And *that*, you have in no small measure."

Caeleigh stopped abruptly and laid her free hand over her eyes and forehead.

"Are you feeling ill?" Andrew worried.

"I'm feeling reprimanded." Caeleigh gathered her hand to pinch the bridge of her nose, much of her face yet shadowed by her hand. "I ought to have known that – I *do* know it, in my heart; but I haven't lived as though I truly believed it."

"Are you certain that's all?" Caeleigh's lingering silence as they continued prompted Andrew to press. "Or has something else set you at dis-ease?"

Caeleigh stumbled as the stones beneath her feet tumbled downhill, bouncing and clattering much like her thoughts had begun to do. "Could we sit down somewhere?"

"Of course." Andrew led Caeleigh to the crest of the hilltop and ground tied the horses beneath a tree; not far from there they sat, looking down on the valley below. "What's on your mind?"

Caeleigh feared how Andrew might respond, but chose to risk his anger in favor of honesty. "I'm thinking about what you told me yesterday of that girl from the Saint Joseph Settlement."

"Margaret? What about her?" Absently Andrew reached for the sheath no longer strapped to his boot.

Caeleigh's eyes were drawn to the motion of his hand, compassion welling as she spoke softly both in tone and volume. "She deceived you about her intentions. What was that like for you?"

Andrew dusted away the nothing along the side of his boot. He answered frankly, attempting to be reserved but not too much so. "It was painful, to be honest. The discovery that she had been using me, that she'd never genuinely *cared* for me, pained me more deeply than her accusations of violence. Considerably quickly I came to deeply regret choosing to Pledge rather than wait for the Bonding."

Caeleigh picked at the hem of her wrap, again. "So you would not charge it against me if I were to carry a similar regret?"

Never had her voice sounded more fearful or forlorn to Andrew's ear. He turned toward her and struggled with an overwhelming desire to shelter her from all the world's ills and evils. Instead, he simply offered her his hand, if she might be willing to take it. "Who wronged you so severely?"

With her other hand Caeleigh toyed with the oblong pendant hanging from the chain around her neck, as Andrew waited patiently for her to speak. When she finally did, the strength in her own voice surprised her. "In the outside world, there is neither Bonding nor Pledging. There is no courtship and no declaration of intent. No code of decorum that is followed. I don't know how to explain what it *is*, except to say what it *isn't*. Women *aren't* regarded as lovely or precious or something to be valued and treasured. There's little trust and less honesty in the way relationships are conducted. Instead, there's selfishness, domination, suppression, manipulation, oppression, infidelity, objectification..."

Andrew stopped her, appalled. "You endured this?"

"I didn't know any different."

This time Andrew didn't resist the impulse – he took Caeleigh into his arms and held her so tightly that even he could scarcely breathe. *"Oh, Kadosh..."* he groaned the prayer more than spoke it.

"Kadosh *sustained* me, Andrew. It's thanks to Him that I was not completely broken by it all." Slowly she coaxed him to release her.

"... *'Completely'?"* Andrew repeated.

Caeleigh replied haltingly, far from eager to confess. "I ... have my own version of Margaret. It was during my time at university. I'm so ashamed of what happened – because of it, I'm not *worthy* of the Bonding, or of a man like you. I don't deserve such a future, because of the past."

"What happened, that could make you feel this undeserving?" Fear began to rise like bile in Andrew's throat, that Caeleigh might attempt to refuse him and their Bonding.

"Do you remember the story I was telling young Sarah the other week? About the maiden at the wedding feast in the kingdom?"

He nodded. "It's a beautiful story."

Caeleigh kept her words few to answer the man before her, exactly as her character had done in the tale. "The maiden was me."

Andrew understood, and responded as calmly as he could manage. "You mean to say you were abused the way she was, in the story?"

"Mind, soul, heart, and ... worse." Caeleigh could not bring herself to speak the words she might have said. "By the time it was truly over, I believed myself *worth* so little and *deserving* so little, because of all I had been through. What's worse is that it happened *after* I became a follower of the Christ. The man with whom I was in relationship told me that *he* likewise was, and I allowed myself to be deceived and maltreated. Andrew, I am *truly sorry* for what I became long before I ever knew you. Might you forgive me for being so ... less than right?"

"Of course you're forgiven, Caeleigh." Andrew dared to reach out and touch the side of her face. "And you are no longer what you may have been at that time. Kadosh has purified and restored you."

"But I am un– " Caeleigh began to protest with vehemence.

He cut her off: "*No,* you're not. What Kadosh has made clean, do not consider unclean."

To his great surprise, Caeleigh dove, face-first, against Andrew's shoulder and wept silently. Uncertain of what was needed of him, Andrew put his arms around her, tugging her shawl up over her shoulders where it had slipped. He considered Caeleigh and all the things he'd learned of her, and marveled at the woman Kadosh had chosen for him.

*I chose **you** for **her** equally as much, My son.* The word entered quietly into Andrew's heart.

Wanting to live up to the trust Kadosh had placed in him, he began to murmur until Caeleigh's tears subsided. "This is what it is to have the Christ as your *go'el*, Caeleigh. He purchased you out of the slaver's stockade that bound you to sin and death of the soul, not to make you His own slave, but to grant your freedom. He's paid in full all debts claimed against your life at the price of His own, and now you bear *none* of those marks upon you any longer."

As she pushed away from Andrew's shoulder, Caeleigh chuckled with embarrassment. "Now it is *you* who cuts *me* to the heart with truth." She swiped at her eyes with both hands, then scrambled to collect her wrap as it fell from her shoulders. Self-conscious, she apologized, "I'm sorry for reacting the way I did; I didn't intend to fall apart on you like that."

"It's alright." Andrew smiled reassuringly. Extracting the handkerchief from his pocket, he offered it to Caeleigh to dry her eyes. She doubted he had been able to fully comprehend what she'd confessed to him. Yet something prompted her not to question that he continued to accept her despite it. Belatedly she realized that, in her emotional decline and outburst, she had allowed less-carefully-articulated expressions to slip into her speech; she attempted to recount everything she'd said, fearful that she may have said something that might have caused Andrew to misunderstand what she'd intended to convey.

As she did so, Andrew continued, "What you did for me yesterday showed me the importance of two people speaking truth over one another. Not only in correction, which we have now both done, but in affirmation as well." Dearly he wished to touch her in some small way, at her elbow or shoulder perhaps, but restrained himself out of a greater desire not to overwhelm her. "Caeleigh, when I look at you, I don't see the summation of your mistakes and regrets. I see the strength, faith, and wisdom you have gleaned *from* those experiences, however ill-begotten you may feel those benefits to be. You have sought after Kadosh, and continue to seek Him, with your whole heart. You have pursued Him to the length of traveling halfway across a continent, and He is honored and enthralled by your pursuit."

"You always lead and instruct by example," Caeleigh returned, bolstered by his words. "It's clear to see why Kadosh has ordained that you should be Governor of a Settlement. You have the gifting of leadership, wisdom and integrity. When the Planting of the Willow Springs Settlement was announced, I knew rather immediately that you were a candidate for Governor, and because of that, it was not a difficult decision to volunteer. Not for *that* reason," she disclaimed at Andrew's teasing grin as he reached out and gave her hand a meaningful squeeze. "What I meant to say is that I knew a Settlement under your leadership would be a safe place for a woman alone. I had no idea *this* would happen. My thoughts were of the other Settlements I passed through on my way here; some of them were less ... hospitable toward a solitary woman. The Blue Creek Settlement was reputed not to be that way, which is why I chose it."

Andrew shifted onto his knees, saying, "I appreciate your words and your insight, Caeleigh. Every time you speak, it becomes more apparent what a gift you are and shall be to my life and my duty. Will you stand in agreement with me in prayer for our new Settlement?"

"Gladly." Caeleigh moved to stand until Andrew motioned for her to stay where she was. She waited while he rose and extended his hand to her, to help her up. Once on her feet, Caeleigh added her other hand to theirs still clasped, as Andrew did likewise.

Standing thus, Caeleigh pondered the significance of the arrangement of their joined hands: at the center, right hand to right hand in an unbreakable grip of strength, a blending of his authority and hers, surrounded and covered by their left hands, symbolic of intimacy. She voiced this observation to Andrew, prompting him to smile appreciatively and to say, "If you are agreeable to it, I would like always to greet you in this way."

Caeleigh nodded her assent, warming ever more to the man.

Andrew neither bowed his head nor closed his eyes, but rather looked out over the valley that would soon hold the fullness of the Willow Springs Settlement as he spoke: "Blessed be the Lord God of Israel, for he has visited and redeemed his people. To You, Kadosh, O Holy One, we commit this valley and the Settlement we are building here in obedience, according to Your command. We ask that of this place and this people it may be that You can say, 'I will set my eyes on them for good, and I will bring them back to this land. I will build them up, and not tear them down; I will plant them, and not pluck them up. I will give them a heart to know that I am the LORD, and they shall be my people and I will be their God, for they shall return to me with their whole heart.' Blessed be the Lord God of Israel, for he … has raised up a horn of salvation for us ... that we should be saved from our enemies and from the hand of all who hate us; to show the mercy promised to our fathers and to remember his holy covenant, the oath that he swore to our father Abraham, to grant us that we, being delivered from the hand of our enemies, might serve him without fear, in holiness and righteousness before him all our days."

"May it be so," Caeleigh intoned after he had concluded. Looking from the valley back to Andrew, she followed his gaze to their still-entwined hands. "What are you thinking?" she enquired of him.

"I'm thinking on what you said a short while ago, and about what we have prophesied in the joining of our hands in this manner. What I see is unified authority within the environs of intimacy – I see the shared headship of a Governor and his wife." Andrew spoke as confidently in this as he had in his prayer.

Caeleigh tilted her head to one side as she studied the image in light of what Andrew had described. "Don't you feel it might be presumptuous to call out such a thing at this juncture? You have not been selected by the people."

"*Yet*. You yourself have already guessed that I'm a candidate and presupposed that I will be the candidate chosen. You said as much in your reasoning for volunteering to join the Planting of the Willow Springs Settlement." Andrew released Caeleigh's hands at last, as she gently tugged them away from his.

She turned toward the vista before them, aglow with the beginning of the sunset. "You aren't even technically *eligible* to *be* a candidate, as far as anyone else is concerned. You haven't announced yet that you have Bonded. A candidate for Governor must be not only Bonded, but married as well."

Andrew stepped in close behind her, his hands upon her elbows, his head leaned over her shoulder as he spoke softly into her ear. "I told you before what my reasons were, and since then my silence has been in deference to the comfort of your soul. Your heart must have seemed as though it rebelled against you when you Bonded with me entirely unaware, and I have not wanted to do anything that would cause you to feel rushed. Kadosh has cautioned me that I must be patient, and so patient I shall be." Andrew paused to inhale deeply, slowing his heartbeat. "There *is* still time."

"The construction of the millinery is nearly complete." Caeleigh cited Andrew's spoken intention from the month prior, regarding commencement of open courtship. The number of weeks it had been since that conversation were still too few for her comfort; she had not yet made sense of the idea that she could possibly have Bonded with any man, let alone a man such as Andrew.

"I didn't say there was *much* time," Andrew grinned.

Chapter 23

Mid November 2148

"I suspect we may soon be found out," Andrew whispered to Caeleigh as they worked side by side in the mercantile. Several weeks had passed since they had shared their histories with one another, and they had taken great care not to be alone together since.

With October's passage into November, a deeper cold was beginning to settle in the valley, turning all work of the Planting of the Settlement indoors.

"How is that possible?" Caeleigh fretted in reply. "I – "

"*Relax,*" he urged her. "You'll spill the paint if you don't." Andrew took the paint can from her hands and set it on the floor. "Many of the unmarried young women are frequently watching me," he continued softly as they both resumed painting around the frame of the same window. "Most of them stayed behind in the Blue Creek Settlement, but a few are here now. From what I have heard of their whispers, they're beginning to believe that I'm infatuated with you."

"Even I can see that you are *exactly* that." Caeleigh smiled wryly at the wall as she spoke under her breath. "What do you plan to do about it?" she asked more seriously.

"Disappear into my workshop. My remaining tools have been transported here from my former workshop back in the

Blue Creek Settlement, and my first full shipment of materials and supplies arrived yesterday."

"I look forward to resuming *my* trade, as well," Caeleigh confessed. They had both by now recommenced speaking in normal conversational tones, as they finished the area around the window and were progressing in opposite directions. "My tools and supplies have also been delivered here, and Elizabeth and Peter have been generous to store it all in their home, but now that the millinery is done, I'm eager to begin to set everything in place."

Andrew could not stop himself from smiling at her openly, no matter who else might see. "Be truthful – you're thrilled about it, aren't you?"

"Do I hide the fact so poorly?" Beyond being in no mood to be teased, Caeleigh immediately began to fear what other emotions she might have inadequately concealed in the past few months.

"Very much so, but your excitement is understandable, and richly deserved. You made a strong case in your proposal at the planning meeting when you spoke."

Caeleigh eyed him warily. "Is *that* why you supported it?"

Upon catching her meaning, Andrew set down his paintbrush and stepped toward her. Placing his hands on her shoulders, he told her firmly, "Caeleigh, I tell you truthfully: your proposal stood and was approved *wholly* on the basis of its merits. I supported it because I, like everyone else in that meeting, saw the wisdom of the plan." He released her, though not without reluctance.

"I have heard other motives suggested," she whispered timidly while he was yet near enough to hear. "In keeping with what you mentioned before."

"Well, those suggestions were wrong." Andrew playfully tapped the tip of Caeleigh's nose with a fingertip before retrieving his paintbrush. "Though if you will force me to confess it, I *did* have reason to be rather inclined to listen to what you had to say that day. Don't worry about what is being said," he instructed her gently. "After all, infatuation frequently precedes a man's Bonding. This will only make what will play out in the near future seem all the more natural." Looking around to be assured they were unobserved, Andrew leaned closer and murmured, "It does also, however, cause me to regret that I won't see as much of you over the next few weeks as I would prefer."

Quickly he turned away to resume painting, leaving her to speak to his back. "What about the tables and shelves you promised to build for the millinery?"

"They are among the work orders I've accumulated. Have you determined the dimensions of everything you want?"

"For the tables, I think so, but I'll need help about the shelves." She, too, resumed painting as she spoke.

"I have had some ideas for the shelves, actually," the carpenter replied. "But I'll start with the tables. Bring your specifications for them to my workshop, and we'll schedule a time to see about the shelves."

Shortly before the evening meal, Caeleigh took the time to measure out the space in her new millinery and make note of the width and depth of the two tables she would need for her machines in the sewing room. The primary worktable, she decided, would be in the front area of the shop. It would mean a great deal of walking back and forth to and from the sewing room, but she had plans for this table. Adeline would tell her she was being innovative again if she knew; Caeleigh could hear the dear woman's voice in her mind, speaking the words.

Before nostalgia for her friend and mentor could paralyze her, Caeleigh decided on the dimensions and specifications for the worktable and wrote them down along with the others. Done for the time being, she closed the vacant millinery and headed up the street toward the carpenter's shop.

She arrived there to find the only man present was Ezra.

"He isn't here?" she questioned, somewhat surprised. When Andrew had ceased painting at the mercantile earlier than she had, Caeleigh supposed it had been to begin working on what had sounded like an extensive list of work orders.

Ezra shook his head. "He left some time ago, said something about having remembered a responsibility that he needed to see to over in the Cypress Ridge Settlement."

"Oh." Caeleigh frowned briefly before devising a justification for her potentially suspect emotional response. "I was under the impression he would be here to receive work requests. I finally figured out the tables I'll need for the millinery, though I'm not certain *how* I'll be able to compensate him for *all three* of them, not to mention everyone else who has done so much."

The orchard-keeper smiled. "I wouldn't worry about that. We're all aware of how hard you have worked toward the Planting of the Settlement. You've cleaned, weeded, dug, painted, and volunteered for every assignment of which you're capable. Besides which, I know Philip is grateful for the time you've spent with Sarah in her mother's absence. Our Settlement will be the first of many to have a millinery, I suspect, and we'll want to set the precedent properly. You'll have whatever you need."

When Caeleigh entered the meetinghouse an hour later, it was with the full expectation that she would find Andrew already there, waiting for her. This expectation was disappointed, however – he was nowhere to be found. Fearing that to enquire would draw unwanted attention to any attachment she might be perceived to have toward Andrew, Caeleigh said nothing regarding his absence to anyone. The most she dared was to choose a place at the table surrounded by empty chairs so that, should he arrive after the evening meal had begun, there would be an available seat near her for him.

But Andrew never appeared. The meal was finished and cleared away, and still he had not arrived. Left in silence and isolation throughout the evening, Caeleigh examined her heart and was stunned to realize how deep her despondency ran – how lonely she was for him in his absence. Despite Elizabeth's announcement that she had baked a special dessert in honor of Caeleigh's birthday, Caeleigh excused herself, claiming that she needed to retreat and spend time in prayer for someone, without mentioning that the party in question was herself. Making sincere apologies to her friend and promising to eat whatever of the treat Elizabeth would save for her, Caeleigh took her leave.

She returned to the women's lodginghouse and the room that was now hers alone, knelt by her bed and pleaded with Kadosh to forgive her for using Him as an excuse to hide, before pouring out her anguish and confusion. She continued to pray and weep until she had drained herself to the point of exhaustion and crawled into bed for a fitful night's sleep.

"Rough night?"

Hearing any voice when she thought she was completely alone in the mercantile the following morning was enough to startle Caeleigh; hearing *his* voice filled her with a conflict of emotions, soothing and agitating at once.

Unconsciously she smoothed the apron covering her skirts with her free hand. "What would cause you to think so?" Caeleigh forced herself to concentrate on the job she was doing, dipping her brush into the paint cup she'd set on a nearby windowsill and applying the paint carefully around the fixtures that had been installed. As long as she kept her hands full, Andrew wouldn't be able to greet her.

"You missed breakfast and the morning teaching, then insisted on working alone."

Caeleigh continued to paint, leaning close to the wall and keeping a focused eye on the neatness of her work. "The mercantile is nearly finished, and there are too many other things that need to be painted before it gets too cold to leave windows open for ventilation. The work to be done here yet is little enough that one person can accomplish it in a day."

"I spoke with Ezra. He's … concerned about you." Andrew lingered at the mercantile door, rolling his shirtsleeves back from his wrists for something to do with himself until he felt he had been granted entry.

Caeleigh saw the remark for the passed-blame that it was. "Why would *Ezra* have reason to worry?"

"He told me of your conversation yesterday." Finally Andrew stepped in from the doorway and crossed the room. "He told me you expressed that you feel you will be required to repay everyone for the millinery. He asked me, as your friend, to make certain you understand that you don't need to overexpend yourself out of a sense of obligation."

Andrew's tone belied him.

"Is that all? You're here only because Ezra is worried about my having a fit of conscience?" Still Caeleigh kept her back turned to him, her attention on her task.

"*I'm* concerned about you," Andrew conceded. "Elizabeth told me that last night you were antisocial throughout the evening meal then retired early, and now this morning you're avoiding as many people as possible."

Caeleigh closed her eyes. "I can't bear the way I feel *watched* lately. I never wanted such attention – I only wish to go about my life quietly and with very little notice."

"There's more to it than that. Answer me truthfully." Andrew spoke gently but firmly.

With a defeated sigh, Caeleigh set down her paintbrush, slid to the floor and buried her face in her hands.

Andrew sat beside her, wrapped an arm around her, and pulled her toward himself to rest her head against his shoulder. "I wish I knew how to help you," he murmured regretfully. "I never wanted to see you suffer hardship such as this on my account."

"I'm simply *weary*, is all, Andrew." Caeleigh rubbed her eyes with paint-speckled fingertips. "You were right in how you directed that all the buildings should be constructed while the weather was warmer, and the indoor work left until now. But I have done *nothing* but paint walls for *five straight days*. I know I oughtn't complain – "

"But you're not doing what you're best suited to do. I understand." Standing, Andrew turned and offered Caeleigh his hands to help her up. "I have an idea. I'll help you finish painting here, and after the midday meal, we'll the take the horses out for the remainder of the day."

"How can you justifiably do that two days in a row?" Caeleigh worried. "Won't you be accused of neglecting responsibilities?"

"Yesterday I was conducting business on behalf of the Settlement. We're in need of a farrier, and Thomas, as the blacksmith who has volunteered to join us from the Blue Creek Settlement, cannot fill that role. I went to the Cypress Ridge Settlement yesterday because we received word that there was someone there who was willing."

Chapter 24

Mid November 2148

Once Elam and Noya were saddled that afternoon, Caeleigh was impatient to put as much distance between herself and the Settlement as possible. Turning north, she urged her mare to a gallop. Only after she slowed, fearful of riding at such speed for too long, did Andrew catch up, having chosen, it seemed, *not* to overrule and command Noya with a whistle that would've superseded any order given by her rider.

"What was that about?" Though his voice was even, Caeleigh could tell that he was less than pleased.

She permitted Noya to amble at a significantly more relaxed pace. "Are you angry with me? I thought you would be eager for us to be able to speak freely again."

"No, I'm not angry. I simply didn't expect you to take off with such haste, else I would have told you that I wanted to keep to a slower pace. Elam and I returned from the Cypress Ridge Settlement early this morning, and I didn't want to push him very hard after insufficient rest." Andrew leaned forward and patted the paint stallion's neck affectionately as he added with a smile, "Especially given what a hurry we were in to return home."

"I honestly didn't think Noya would run so readily with me," Caeleigh apologized. "You told me last time that she was sensitive to my apprehension and wouldn't do anything to frighten me."

"She's also usually eager to run when she knows she's given the opportunity." Andrew's tone was forgiving in its correction.

"I'm sorry." Caeleigh bowed her head in contrition, Noya mimicking the gesture.

Andrew smiled affectionately at the runaway pair. "Now that we're over a mile away from any other soul, are you willing to tell me what's been bothering you since last night?"

"How did you know I had a difficult night? What I mean to say is, *how could* you know?" Caeleigh immediately knew she'd caught her slip of the tongue too late.

"I have travailed for you in prayer more than a few times. Whatever kept you from sleep had *me* awake in the middle of the night, as well."

When Andrew stopped them – for Elam's benefit, he said – Caeleigh waited until Andrew was dismounting to confess, so that he would have his back to her as she spoke. "I missed you last evening… I was unprepared for how lonely I felt without you."

By this time, he had come around and offered to help her down; he was becoming bolder with her, Caeleigh noted, when he did not immediately release his hold on her waist once her feet were on the ground.

"I missed you, as well," Andrew replied. "I had intended to be back in time for the evening meal, but business took longer than I had planned, and I ended up spending the night in the Cypress Ridge Settlement." At last he released her.

"I thought you said the farrier was willing to volunteer?"

"The farrier wasn't the only reason I was there."

At her inquisitive tilt of the head, Andrew took Caeleigh by the hands and led her to sit on a boulder not far away. "When we met, you told me that you avoided thinking about your birthday at all costs because you hated marking the passage of another year of your life spent alone. Yesterday evening you had your first birthday *not* alone, and I wasn't present for it. I'm sorry I failed you in that. I know your forgiveness can't be bought, and it shouldn't. ...All the same, I hope that this helps to make up for its own lateness and my absence." With that, he withdrew from his coat pocket a small box and offered it to her.

Mistaking its purpose, Caeleigh pushed Andrew's hand away with both of her own. "Please, Andrew, don't – " she began.

"No. It's only a birthday gift. I know you aren't ready yet for more than that. But I wasn't willing to allow the milestone pass without being celebrated somehow." Again Andrew offered the box, this time almost apologetically. "I know it isn't cherrywood. I was hoping cedar would be ruddy enough that you would catch the inference."

Her curiosity piqued, Caeleigh opened the box and gasped at what she found. Lined with midnight-blue satin, it held a pear-cut opal pendant on a delicate chain of white gold so pale it closely resembled silver.

"Your stories are always so vivid and rich with symbolism," Andrew spoke tenderly as he lifted the necklace from its nest. "Always some significance to take to heart. When you told me that the maiden in this story was modeled after yourself, I knew you deserved such a gift as she received, though I *did* deliberately modify the design from your description in one way." Draping it across his palm, he held the pendant forth for her inspection.

That's when she saw it. At the top of the pendant, the narrowed end of the teardrop was crowned by a small diamond.

Caeleigh picked up the pendant with trembling fingers as he told her, "I wanted to remind you that your heart will not always be broken."

Andrew waited while Caeleigh strove to find her voice. "*This* is why you went to the Cypress Ridge Settlement?"

Andrew grinned. "You and I both know that my purchasing something of this nature in the Blue Creek Settlement would have started too many speculations and rumors. Besides, I honestly *did* go to recruit a farrier. The volunteer simply happened, conveniently, to live in a place where I could enjoy a bit more anonymity."

Caeleigh opened the clasp of the necklace and held it out toward Andrew. "Would you – ?"

"Of course."

She shifted to turn away from him while he fastened the clasp. The pendant settled just below her collarbone; she ran her fingertips across the smooth, domed surface of the opal. Behind Caeleigh, Andrew reached into the inside pocket of his coat once more, and handed her a small mirror. She raised the mirror to examine her reflection.

"Do you like it?" he asked, meeting her eyes by way of the mirror.

"Very *much* so. It's beautiful, Andrew, thank you." Turning to face him, Caeleigh wrapped her arms around his neck in an impulsive hug.

"You're welcome. Happy birthday." He held her only for a moment longer before removing her from his embrace and gently distancing himself for the sake of propriety and self-restraint.

Caeleigh, still holding the mirror, returned to studying the pendant, tracing around its edge with her fingertips. Several minutes passed before she became aware of Andrew's bemused chuckling as he watched her. "What?"

"You." Andrew silenced his laughter. "You're utterly entranced by such a simple gift."

"Andrew, you had this necklace custom designed and crafted, derived from a description in one of my stories. I would hardly call that *simple*... it's nothing short of extraordinary, truly."

Taking Caeleigh's hands in their way as she had not permitted him to do in the mercantile, he responded, "It is your *stories* that are extraordinary. Your characters are genuine people with relatable adversities. To follow one of your characters through the course of their tale to its conclusion brings *edification* and *hope* to the hearer – " Andrew cut himself off as his speech began to sound increasingly impassioned the more his emotions engaged. He cleared his throat and began anew: "*Please* tell me you comprehend the value of what you offer a soul through your parables – for truly, it is *exceedingly* great."

Caeleigh lowered her eyes to the ground with an unreadable expression which Andrew feared meant she had interpreted his words as a rebuke.

Aware that a response was needed of her, she spoke the first thing that came to mind: "The Proverbs of Solomon caution that one is a fool who loves to receive such high praise."

"Is *that* what worried you in what I said?" Andrew's anxiety fled in the form of outright laughter. In her remark he'd seen, for the first time since her Bonding, a glimpse of the woman Caeleigh had been before that night. Though Andrew adored the woman before him presently, it would be a falsehood to deny that he missed his friend, who had a unique ability to surprise him as she had just now.

While he considered these ruminations, Caeleigh secured the jewelry box in Noya's saddlebag. Tugging at the neckline of her blouse until it covered the pendant as she returned, she apologized timorously as she disclaimed, "I am grateful for your gift and desire to honor it. However, allowing it to raise questions may not be wise – most likely, the first question would be from whom did I receive it, and there would be no stopping the firestorm of speculation after that."

"Indeed." Andrew gave in a single nod his wholehearted agreement.

Caeleigh's voice and hands trembled as she misread his diminutive reply. "Truly, I assure you I am *not* ashamed – "

Andrew stood and placed his hands on her shoulders to silence her unnecessary protest. "I never supposed you were."

"You are far too good to me, beyond my deserving." Caeleigh bowed her head, her own life continuing to play out as prescribed in the tale it had begun to imitate.

Andrew hooked his fingers beneath Caeleigh's chin, raising it until she looked into his eyes. He spoke gently, precisely as she had imagined the prince in her story would have spoken to the maiden. "Then perhaps I ought to advertise my faults, to caution you against setting me upon a pedestal, for I am as flawed and mortal a man as any. I do and shall struggle and fail, at times."

Chapter 25

Late November 2148

The copper bell over the door to Caeleigh's shop jangled, heralding a visitor. Looking up, she smiled at the sight of what she presumed to be Andrew, bearing an armload of shelves so high that she was unable to see him over them. He set his burden on the large, high worktable and clasped Caeleigh's hands in the manner that had become their customary greeting for one another. "I'm glad now that you asked for a table so tall," Andrew grinned. "It helps reassure me that I don't drop anything!"

"*I'm* glad that your new building technique proposal was passed – it's been comfortably warm in here all day, despite the bitter cold outside."

"I can tell," Andrew teased, lifting her hand and pressing the backs of her fingers against his cheek.

Blushing furiously and slipping her hands from his grasp, Caeleigh turned her attention to the shelves. "These look wonderful, Andrew, thank you." She lifted one and ran her fingertips along the wood grain. Its finish was satin-smooth, perfect for its purpose.

"You're welcome," he smiled. "I'm glad they turned out to your liking."

The tailor carried one of the shelves to the frame Andrew had constructed against the nearest wall, in essence creating built-in cases. "Will you show me how to install them, myself?"

Caeleigh's request intrigued him. "Certainly, but why? You know I don't mind to do the work. It provides me a chance to enjoy your company."

"Well…" Caeleigh turned shy, smoothing her skirts. "My inventory will begin arriving soon, and there is something else I thought it would be useful to have. I'm afraid it may be too much trouble, though."

"For you, it's *never* trouble. Name your wish."

"I would like an apothecary's chest. But not a very tall one – I don't care to be too high off the ground."

"Would you prefer it to be made with all same-sized small drawers? Or a variety of sizes?"

"A variety, but about half of them small." Caeleigh began miming approximated dimensions with her hands. "There are quite a few small notions that won't take up much space, and also some larger. But *please,* Andrew, if it's too much to ask, *don't* be afraid to say so." With this last remark, she once more turned shy.

"Caeleigh, I *want* to do this for you. Shelves and tables are such plain, utilitarian things. I will be glad to build a beautiful cabinet for you, though since it will be a significant undertaking, I will do it on one condition."

"What's that?"

"That you allow me to give it to you as a courtship gift."

Caeleigh abruptly busied herself stacking papers and clearing miscellaneous items from the tabletop. "Oh… Andrew, are you certain that's wise?" she questioned with worried sincerity. "You *do* wish to be named Governor, don't you?"

Andrew's brow furrowed in perplexity. "I don't see what relevance that has, but yes. And for a man to be appointed Governor, he must be Bonded and married."

"But he must *also* be approved by a majority vote..." Caeleigh turned her back to Andrew as she continued, afraid that she would be unable to maintain a straight face as she added, "...and this could cost you the unmarried women's votes."

Andrew laughed heartily as he wrapped his arms around her from behind. "Caeleigh, while it may have been only a few months that you have known, I have been in love with you for years. I am ready for the world to know it."

He released her as she turned around to face him and replied, "Very well, then. I accept your condition and I will accept your gift."

Later that evening at the communal meal, Caeleigh arrived clearly in pain. She cradled one of her forearms in the other, in an attempt to be as still as possible.

"Are you alright?" Andrew asked as he pulled out a chair for her.

Caeleigh eased into the seat as motionlessly as she could manage. "I'm not injured, only sore. Putting up those shelves was more strenuous than I thought it would be."

"Wait here." Andrew disappeared into the kitchen and returned with a small towel soaking in a bowl of hot water. Depositing the bowl beside her place setting, he wrung out the steaming towel. "Where is the pain located?"

"My shoulder and the side of my neck." Caeleigh winced as she attempted to raise her arm to pull her hair out of the way. "I can't lift my arm at all."

Andrew chuckled compassionately. "You ought to have allowed me to install those shelves rather than taking on so much yourself," he told Caeleigh as he moved her plaited hair aside and applied the towel.

"I *wanted* to do it. And I challenge you to find any fault with the job I did."

"I'm certain you did fine," Andrew grinned, "but you're not accustomed to that manner of work." He took his now-regular seat beside her and pressed the towel gently against the side of her neck.

In this manner they sat, silent, Caeleigh with her eyes closed, Andrew sideways in his chair, each peacefully aware of the comfort of sharing such plain company between them, for several minutes.

"Caeleigh! What happened?" Elizabeth fretted as she hurried to her friend's side.

"Caeleigh has decided to learn a new trade and had a difficult first day," Andrew teased.

Between them, Caeleigh grimaced. "Can we please speak of something else?" she asked. "The more we discuss the pain I'm in, the worse it feels."

Andrew chuckled again, earning himself a feeble swat on the arm and a reprimand: "You are entirely too amused at my expense for someone who did not do the work I did this afternoon – wholly by myself, I might add."

Andrew did his best to calm himself to seriousness as he pulled several folded sheets of paper from his pocket. "You're right, and I'm sorry. Here are the sketches I promised you; choose the one you like best." He handed them to Caeleigh as with his other hand he removed the now-cooling compress from her shoulder and returned it to the bowl. "Let that warm again before reapplying it," he instructed.

"What are they?" Elizabeth enquired, dropping into the chair at Caeleigh's left and peering over her shoulder as she unfolded the pages.

"You'll see ... Where is your husband? I must speak with him." Before he'd finished speaking, Andrew had risen from the table and started toward the door, upon sighting Peter's entry.

The women, meanwhile, opened the sketches. They were of the apothecary's chest Caeleigh had requested that morning, wider than it was tall, with a number of possible options for the arrangement of the different-sized drawers. Notations, carefully block-lettered, indicated the dimensions of all features and included some questions regarding details that the carpenter wanted to be to her preference.

Before Elizabeth could question her friend further, Governor Caleb's booming voice filled the room. "Friends! Once again I have the joyous privilege of announcing that a Bonding has taken place. Our brother Andrew has informed me that he has Bonded and that just this day the young lady has accepted his declared intention of courtship!"

The reactions throughout the room varied. Unlike most men who could not keep their gazes from the women with whom they'd Bonded, Andrew had and yet looked only to Caleb during the announcement. Older women sighed and *aww*ed; many younger women and teenage girls whimpered and swooned.

Elizabeth nudged Caeleigh's hand. "You?" she whispered.

"These sketches are for a courtship gift," Caeleigh whispered back. "It was the only provision under which he would agree to build it."

Moments later Peter arrived to sit beside his wife, with Andrew immediately behind him coming to resume his earlier seat with hands extended. Knowing that every eye in the room was on him and thus by his proximity also on her, Caeleigh hesitantly reached out her hands to be taken in their greeting. She found fortification in the warmth and strength of his grip.

"Forgive me if this has embarrassed you," Andrew apologized softly. "It was a bit awkward to explain that I had already Bonded ... some time ago, and only ... more recently ... made my declaration of intent." Andrew chose his words carefully, mindful of the fact that everyone within earshot was listening.

"I understand. Thank you for your consideration. I'm aware of what you did to spare me from scrutiny as much as possible – I appreciate that."

Andrew smiled warmly as he seated himself at her side, and Caeleigh was grateful for the giving of thanks diverting the room's attention from her.

As soon as Caleb had finished, though, Peter leaned forward to see around the women between them and all but pounced upon Andrew. "Would you care to tell me what '*some time ago*' means? You only confided in me five minutes ago that you had Bonded."

"Give me a moment," Andrew intoned calmly. "There's something else to see to before I begin explaining everything." Reaching for the soaking towel, he again withdrew it from the bowl, wrung it thoroughly, and gently placed it once more on Caeleigh's shoulder in the spot where she had earlier indicated the pain to be located. "There?" he asked her.

Understanding that the care he was taking – emphatically slowly – was partially a diversion, Caeleigh looked into Andrew's eyes, panicked at the prospect of what he might explain. "Please!" was all she could breathe out without moving her lips, fearful that the slightest word could bring suspicion. With her eyes she begged him to perceive the rest of her plea.

"Don't worry," he whispered in reply, his head tipped toward Caeleigh's so that his face was hidden by his loose-hanging hair, and could be seen by no one other than her. "I understand; it will be alright, I promise you." Andrew repositioned the towel further toward the back of her neck and enquired, in a more natural conversational tone, "Is that better?"

"Yes, thank you." Caeleigh turned, self-consciously, toward the table in time to see Caleb himself take the seat opposite Andrew.

The Governor of the Blue Creek Settlement grinned. "I love hearing a good uncommon love story."

Andrew tucked his hair behind his ears, took a deep breath, and gave Caeleigh's hand a gentle squeeze. "Peter, I was not dishonest with you, my Brother. What I said to you was 'I have Bonded' – I didn't say it was today. I Bonded with Caeleigh more than three and a half years ago."

"What?!" Elizabeth and Peter cried out in unison. Both of them had assumed, not altogether incorrectly, that Andrew and Caeleigh had only first met shortly before the stonemason had Bonded with Caeleigh's best friend, no longer ago than two years.

"Truly," Andrew confirmed. "Shortly after I Bonded with Caeleigh, Kadosh spoke to me, instructing me not to approach her yet and saying that I would be required to wait. When our two paths crossed when you announced that *you* had Bonded, Peter, I made an overture of friendship but continued to keep anything more than that in reserve. A few months ago I received a sign that the time had come."

Andrew watched Elizabeth as she calculated backward, attempting to pinpoint the occasion.

"Yes," he answered the unvoiced conjecture, "it was the evening when she and I had our misunderstanding – the occurrence that at the time I had called a 'misunderstanding' was my receiving the sign that my season of waiting was over; I'm sorry to say that Caeleigh was caught entirely unaware and the incident justifiably frightened her. Thus I have taken my time since then, before declaring my intent of courtship."

At this account of the events of that night, Caeleigh gripped Andrew's fingertips, still wrapped around her hand, with profound gratitude.

Caleb nodded and grinned approvingly. "You've done well, to honor Kadosh in such a difficult request. And for such a long time! Nearly four years!"

"His timing is perfect," Andrew replied. "For the first two years, it was easy, because we were not in the least acquainted. After I came to know her better, then it became more of a challenge. But," he glanced toward Caeleigh with an affectionate look in his eye, "this woman is *more* than worth the waiting. I could say a great deal more in that theme, but I fear it would distress her." Andrew grinned as Caeleigh flushed crimson, proving his point.

"And what is this situation here?" Caleb asked, well aware of Caeleigh's discomfort with so much attention to the subject of her relationship with Andrew. "Please don't tell me that you swept the young lady off her feet so vigorously that you've injured her!"

Finally Caeleigh relaxed enough to laugh. "No! No," she replied, as the servingwomen set bowls and platters of food before them.

"Earlier today I delivered the shelves for the millinery and she insisted on installing them herself to free my time for another project. The hot compress is to relax her sore muscles." Andrew removed the towel to the bowl once again as Caeleigh massaged her slightly heat-reddened shoulder. He handed the bowl to one of the servingwomen with thanks before she returned to the kitchen. "How is the pain now?" he enquired; after having kept his attentions from her earlier, Andrew seemed eager to make up for the lost time.

"A great deal better." Caeleigh picked up the sketches from the tabletop and handed them back to him as she continued, "And these were well worth it – this is a beautiful piece you've designed."

"I'm glad you're pleased," Andrew returned, noting that Caeleigh was less withdrawn when the attention of everyone around them was focused on him rather than on herself. "Though I do feel somewhat guilty for my comparatively lesser amount of exertion." He winked. "I could have done both the shelf installations *and* the sketches, but you were determined that I should give these my full attention." Andrew refolded the pages and slipped them back into his pocket.

"You're unusually quiet tonight," Andrew commented as he escorted Caeleigh back to the women's lodginghouse. "Is something on your mind? I know you don't care to be at the center of attention, but I did everything I could to minimize it."

"I know – and again, I thank you for that. But..."

"Yes?" He placed his free hand over hers, slipped into the crook of his elbow. "I enjoy it when you take my arm in this manner, by the way," he added when she remained silent.

Caeleigh stopped in the middle of the street. "May I be entirely candid?"

Andrew stopped beside her and stepped closer so that they might keep their voices low. "Please do."

"I feel set at a disadvantage, Andrew." Caeleigh's eyes darted furtively in all directions as she spoke, as though she feared their conversation might be eavesdropped upon. "It turns out that you have misled even *me* about when it was that you Bonded with me. I thought it was – "

"The night that Peter announced he had Bonded with Elizabeth? When we spoke at the meetinghouse after the evening meal?" Andrew supplied as his intended fell near to tears.

She nodded without speaking.

Andrew took Caeleigh by the elbow and guided her away from the center of the street, into the lamplit figurative shadow of the chapel, which stood primly nearby. "I intended to tell you, Caeleigh. I'm sorry to say that I simply haven't known how to broach the subject."

"Consider the subject officially broached," she bit off, refusing to make eye contact.

"There isn't much to tell, really," Andrew apologized. "I saw you, but you didn't see me – you never knew I was there. The moment I laid eyes upon your face, my heart was stirred, then Kadosh forbade me to approach you. He instructed me that I would have to wait, though without specifying how long the wait would be. There's not much of a story to be told in that."

Caeleigh's anger subsided; she sighed, frustration giving way to resignation. "I suppose it would have been an awkward moment if you had come to me and said, 'I have nothing much to tell you' – forgive me my temper?"

"Of course." Andrew took one of her hands in both of his own. "I understand that so much attention is never comfortable for you, as is being caught unaware publicly. I apologize for my part in creating your discomfort. I ask that you would understand that I have been waiting an exceptionally long time to make it known that I have Bonded with you and how deeply in love with you I am." With those words, he drew her close and held her, still standing in front of the chapel. "How long I have waited to be able to hold you thus," he murmured.

Chapter 26

Late November 2148

When the front door opened to reveal Peter, Caeleigh was immediately worried. "Where is Elizabeth? Is she alright?" She took a step into their home, searching for her friend.

"Elizabeth is well. She's at Ezra's home, assisting Sophia with the children."

"Then why – ?"

"She didn't call you here – *I* did." Peter spoke more gently than Caeleigh was accustomed to hearing from him. "Please, come in," he urged, closing the door and ushering her into the front parlor. There, he sat in the chair opposite the one Caeleigh had chosen.

With a heavy sigh, the stonemason leaned forward and rested his elbows on his knees, his hands dangling listlessly between them. "My brother has been suffering."

Caeleigh said nothing, to allow Peter to speak what was on his heart, uninterrupted. "After Kadosh and my wife, Andrew is the one person I love most. I spent half of last night reviewing what I have observed in him the past few years, and I am going to attempt to speak solely from those observations, so as not to betray the things he's confided in me. Though, as I'm certain you observed yourself last evening, there are things he *hadn't* confided, even to me."

She nodded.

"I understand that the circumstances for him and you are not … usual. I trust that Kadosh has had a plan and a reason for orchestrating it so, and I know that if any man living has the fortitude of heart to stand up under such difficulty, Andrew would be that man."

"But you said that he's suffering," Caeleigh half-stated, half-asked.

"Indeed. Knowing Andrew, he hasn't spoken a word of it to you. He *scarcely* has hinted at it to me. I suppose that, having known life only this way for several generations, we've come to take the Bonding for granted. This has been a considerably unique exception to the proverbial rule, and *entirely* without precedent… I consulted with Caleb and David last night, and neither of them could recall having ever heard of such a thing happening in the history of the Settlements. I fear that in his fathomless nobility, Andrew has neglected, to his own detriment, to explain to you the experience and perspective of a man who has Bonded." Peter shifted in his chair, meaning to sit back, but shortly thereafter leaning forward once more.

"To be fair, it hasn't been necessary, until now, for any man to make such an explanation," the stonemason continued. "Once a man has Bonded, he's free to make his declaration of intent and proceed with courtship. Andrew hasn't had that luxury, but I don't doubt that the emotions he has had have been no different. I know that he has been travailing for you, often with deep agony, since before my marriage to Elizabeth."

At the mention of travail, and the memory of another conversation on the subject that it had resurrected, Caeleigh subconsciously raised a hand to touch the opal pendant she was wearing without purposeful concealment for the first time since Andrew had given it to her a few weeks before. Whether Peter had noticed it or fully knew its significance, she had no way of determining. She remained silent.

"Caeleigh… his heart has been breaking, continuously and ongoing, quite likely for *every one* of the days that have passed since the moment he Bonded with you. It wounds me to watch him *will himself* to withhold the affection he wishes to lavish upon you. The thing you need to understand of a Bonded man's love for his Beloved is that it is a deep and urgent passion very much like the heart of Kadosh for His people. Every day that Andrew cannot fully express that love is *forcing* him to live contrary to the truest part of his nature – and it is *absolutely wrecking* him." By this point, Peter's hands were shaking. He raked them through his hair in an attempt to mask the tremor.

"I don't know what to say … I had no idea," Caeleigh stammered. "He has never so much as *hinted* at distress." She began to wring her hands in her lap.

"He wouldn't. Not because he is a private man or closed to emotion, but because he loves you *so deeply* that he thinks nothing of putting your every wish above any of his needs. Part of that is Andrew himself, and part of it is the Bonding. It is a reflection of the depth of sacrificial love Kadosh has for each of us – extending so far as to be willing to sacrifice the life of His only son, the Christ, in order to redeem us to Himself. *Our* love is a living representation of *His* love."

Again Peter dragged his fingers through the curls atop his head to camouflage the quaking of his hands. Though achieving his intended purpose, the action also drew Caeleigh's attention to another fact, one of which she'd not previously taken notice: in the months that he'd been laboring in the initial stages of Planting the Willow Springs Settlement, Peter had allowed his hair to grow long, seemingly in imitation of Andrew. It wasn't as long as Andrew wore his, but longer than the more conservative men kept theirs. Caeleigh recalled the several times Andrew had mentioned that Peter was a number of years younger than he and that they'd known each other since not long after Andrew had moved to the Blue Creek Settlement... which meant their friendship dated back into Peter's youth and late childhood. For Peter to so emulate the man he'd loved as an elder brother for most of his life, the adoration must run deep – He genuinely did internalize Andrew's pain, and, assuming the experience of Bonded men to be fairly universal, he was distraught at the mere imaginings of what that pain might entail.

Caeleigh replied to the last thing Peter had spoken. "I'd been aware of the comparison, but always thought it to be more of a metaphor, to explain Kadosh, whose ways are beyond our comprehension, in terms that *are* within our comprehension."

"Oh, no ... It's *much* more than that – much deeper and *infinitely* more tangible." Peter could not have been more emphatic without raising his voice.

Caeleigh pressed her fingertips into her eyelids, willing the tears to stay confined behind them. "I appreciate you telling me this, Peter."

"What will you do with this knowledge?" Peter's relative youth shone through in the question. For all the ways he had surpassed her in life milestones despite being younger, in this moment he was the one looking to her to set things right. How quickly their places had reversed since the conversation had begun.

"I'm not yet certain. I need to pray."

Thanking Peter for bringing the matter to her attention, Caeleigh left her friends' home and went in search of a quiet place.

Agitated, Andrew wiped his hands on a shop rag and tossed it against the wall of his workshop, where it slid to slump on the counter. "Rabbi," he employed Caeleigh's favorite endearment for David, "with all due respect, I soundly disagree. I can't explain to you why without betraying her confidences, but believe me when I say that such a course of action would only heap undue pressure upon her."

David sat calmly on a stool, hands folded in his lap. "You need to consider the well-being of your own heart, as well, though. I know you consider such a thought selfishness, but you've fled too far in the opposite direction. If you've so wounded yourself, what good can you be for Caeleigh then?"

Leaning back against his workbench, Andrew passed his hands up over his face and then through his hair, pushing back what had fallen loose to hang in his eyes. "I don't see that I have any other choice, David. Kadosh has set before me a path that no other man has walked. *He* must be the one to guide my steps. *He* must make a way."

From where she hid just beyond the side door of Andrew's workshop, Caeleigh perceived these words to be a timely cue. She had not been there long, only these past few minutes as she waited for their conversation to conclude and attempted to muster her courage. This side of the workshop conveniently happened to face the grove of willows where she'd slipped away to seek answers and understanding from Kadosh Himself, and the state in which she'd been left by the encounter was not one in which she wanted to meet any more people than necessary, so she'd come straight across the meadow rather than through the Settlement proper.

Exhausted by the weight of grief, Caeleigh stumbled while trying to slip in through the partially open door, thus drawing attention to herself before she meant to do so.

The way Andrew cried out her name told her that she must appear worse than she had feared she did.

"I – " Her voice cracked so terribly that she could speak no further.

While the two of them were distracted by one another, David saw himself out, closing the front door of the shop behind him.

Trepidation and worry overriding every concern he had voiced to David in the previous hour, Andrew went to Caeleigh and lifted her out of her crouched position against the door-frame. He settled her on a nearby bench along the wall, took both of her hands in his own, and lowered himself to be at eye level with her. "What's wrong? You look as though you've stared into the eyes of Death itself."

"In a manner, that's precisely what I've done." Caeleigh studied the lines of Andrew's features, the illustrations of so many emotions she now saw which where warring violently with one another. It quite nearly broke her resolve to have him be the first to speak on the matter at issue.

"What happened?"

Let go of your pride and ask him, Daughter.

The softspoken behest of Kadosh Himself was the pebble that initiated a landslide.

"*Why?!*" Caeleigh's voice came out in so fierce a whisper that Andrew nearly thought her angry. "*Why,* Andrew, did you not *once* tell me what you have been enduring, how you have been *suffering?*"

He dropped to his knees before her. "How did you learn this?"

"I've beheld it within my own spirit, Andrew. You've told me yourself that you've travailed on my behalf – I went before Kadosh and requested of Him the same for you… I asked for a firsthand knowledge of what you've had to forebear, particularly the past few months since my Bonding." Had she not already wept herself dry crying out in the throes of the experience, Caeleigh's eyes would have flooded anew. "I was all but certain that the desolation would rend my soul in two."

If Andrew had been stricken by her account to this point, now he had no words for the horror of seeing his personal tribulation in the eyes of one who was never meant to know it. He raised a trembling hand to her tear-stained cheek. "Why would you ever take such a burden upon yourself?" He spoke in the hushed tones of the bereaved.

"I needed to understand." With both of her own hands, Caeleigh removed Andrew's from her face. When he reached for her again, she firmly held to his fingers with her left hand, watching her own movements to draw his eye to the significance of her choices. Right-handed, she grasped his shoulder and probed his face with pleading eyes. "Do you not know, Andrew, how *deeply* you have aggrieved those who love you – Kadosh, Himself, among them – by continuing on in this way now that you *no longer* have no choice?" She prayed that her voice carried half as much authority as she'd implied with her body language.

When next Andrew spoke, it was in equal parts admiration and compassion. "I may be innocent of the manner of cruelties your heart had befallen before Kadosh entrusted it to me, but I am not naïve to assume it hasn't any wounds as a result. I have been loath to act in any way that would cause you to fear, or to feel coerced."

"It is my own responsibility to face my fears," Caeleigh reminded Andrew with more staid courage than she felt.

Yet loath to relinquish *all* fault, Andrew began to protest: "My duty as a man constrains me to – "

She cut him off. "To explain, perhaps, why you delayed so many years before confessing your Bonding to me."

Less than half a moment's hesitation passed before the carpenter relented with a nod. "I owe you that much and more, I agree. But you truly ought to get some rest, now – what you have been through will prove more draining than I'm certain you could have anticipated." He stood and retrieved a clean shop rag, dampening it with some of his drinking water before returning to wipe away the evidence of her tears.

"I have travailed before, Andrew."

"Not for something such as *this*, you haven't. Heed my advice and rest, please. You have my assurance that we will continue this conversation later. Come, now." He offered his hand and helped Caeleigh to her feet. "I'll escort you to the lodginghouse."

Chapter 27

Late November 2148

An hour before the evening meal, Andrew closed his workshop for the day and headed toward the women's lodginghouse, praying that he might meet someone to assist him there along the way.

He exhaled a prayer of gratitude when Beth called his name from the porch of the mercantile. Briefly Andrew thanked her for her congratulations on the news of his Bonding after she'd approached, then wasted no time in making his request. "Beth, I am in need of your assistance. Earlier today, Caeleigh came to me having undergone a more arduous travailing than she had previously experienced. I admonished her, from my own experience, that she would be wise to rest after such an ordeal. It appears she has slept through the noon meal and much of the day. My ability to look after her is confined by the restriction against men entering the women's lodginghouse; would you wake her, lest she miss the evening meal, as well? She's been strained already by her experience, and further weakening by malnourishment would cause her to fall ill."

Beth gladly obliged his request, leaving him to thank Kadosh that she was the woman whose aid he'd enlisted. If there was anyone to whom he could have explained the situation with confidence of freedom from judgment, aware of how he must have sounded, Simeon's wife was without question the one. A short time later Beth returned to where Andrew waited outside the women's lodginghouse to inform him that Caeleigh would meet him momentarily, then took her leave to return to her own home.

When Caeleigh emerged from the lodginghouse, she appeared to have benefited from the prescribed rest. Despite proving yet to be unsteady as she faltered on the porch steps, she was undeterrable.

Andrew stepped forth, grasping Caeleigh's elbow to steady her. "Did you rest well?"

"I slept deeply, but my sleep was filled with disturbing and confusing dreams."

"An effect, no doubt, of what you witnessed whilst you travailed for me." Andrew cradled Caeleigh's face between his hands, smoothing the furrows from her brow with his fingertips. "You oughtn't have done that."

Though Andrew's reprimand was given gently, Caeleigh's reply was obstinate. "I've already given you the reasons why I did so."

Andrew offered his elbow. "Take my arm as we walk. I am at fault for your condition; thus I have a responsibility to look after you and aid your continued recovery."

Little was said by either as they made their way to the meetinghouse.

They entered the dining room well in advance of the evening meal and sat across from one another at the end of an empty table. The servingwoman who'd been setting the other tables asked if she could offer them anything.

"Don't allow us to inconvenience you while you're busy, Theresa," Andrew replied with an apologetic smile. "I can see to our needs."

Theresa set out the last of the plates she'd brought from the kitchen. "It's no trouble, truly. What may I provide you both?"

"A glass of water for us each, please," he requested, relieved that Theresa had spared him the need to abandon Caeleigh for any length of time, however brief.

"You've kept busy these past weeks," Caeleigh commented regarding the table between them and its many chairs, recent additions to the room, as the servingwoman set a glass of water before each of them before disappearing into the kitchen.

"We're preparing in anticipation of more arrivals after the first homes are completed. Most of the families who have been separated for four months already don't intend to be separated through Thanksgiving and the winter, yet, as well." Andrew slid his glass across the table to stand beside Caeleigh's. "Drink slowly, but drink it all. Quite likely you're more dehydrated than you realize."

"Will you answer me now what you would not explain this morning?" Caeleigh traced her fingertips through the accumulating perspiration on the outside of the nearer glass.

Andrew reclined slightly in his chair. "I will. Though I fear the explanation I have to offer may prove unsatisfactory to you, as it has become unsatisfactory to me, the more I've reflected on the matter to choose my words for you."

He waited until she'd raised the first glass to her lips before proceeding. "Before I commence with making apologies, I'd like to thank you. Your aversion to being at the center of public attention has been more of a help to me than I have the words to say. You've lived in the Settlements enough years to know well the tradition of Bonding announcements – the attention they draw to the Bonded is meant to be in celebration of their happiness, but it isn't always universally so. After the Planting of this Settlement was announced and I was sent, I'd hoped to wait until the work of the Planting was complete before announcing anything to you or to the community at large. Being one of the sent ones, I'm" – Andrew dropped his voice to a whisper, despite the otherwise vacancy of the room and the sounds of laughter and conversation ringing from the kitchen – "at the least *suspected* to be a candidate for Governor, the requirements for which are well known. I've been loath to subject myself to the speculation, or the attentions of women wrongly assuming – or willfully attempting to assert – themselves to have won the place in my heart that has firmly been yours for years already."

That he paused at this juncture implied to Caeleigh that Andrew was providing her an opportunity to speak. "Could you not have spoken only to me of it, and kept the matter between us as we have these past few months?"

"Recall from the account I related last night at Caleb's request, that when I first Bonded with you, Kadosh forbade me to speak or act upon it. I was instructed that I must wait – though I knew not what for, nor for how long." With a nod Andrew approved Caeleigh's progress as she was soon to finish the first glass of water, before he continued.

"There was a single instance, years ago, when I gave rein to my impatience. Confident of the outcome heedless of the timing, I presumed to cause things to happen ahead of what Kadosh had apparently intended – and the consequences were wholly brought to bear upon you. Do you recall the occasion of which I speak?" He watched Caeleigh attempt to reexamine two years' worth of memories in the light of this revelation, and quickly determined from her expression that she was working backward from recent days. "It was when we danced the night of Elizabeth and Peter's marriage celebration."

Andrew closed his eyes against the guilt that lingered in his memory. "Everything I said that evening in vague and anonymous terms – I was speaking of *you*, Caeleigh. I had already

Bonded with you long prior to that day. Some selfish part of me hoped that if I spoke in such a way, you might Bond in return. I'm deeply sorry for having attempted to manipulate you so, and for how I wounded you in the process."

"What do you mean when you say 'long prior'? A few months?"

Andrew nearly laughed outright. Of all the things he'd confessed, many of them severe, *this* was the one she'd chosen to question. It was the second reappearance – the first having occurred the day he'd given Caeleigh the opal pendant she now wore proudly, he noted – of the woman he had fallen in love with; he welcomed her return. The tone of her query, moreover, implied summary forgiveness.

Andrew reached for Caeleigh's free hand and pressed his palm to hers. "More than a year, by that point." He smiled warmly but honestly, knowing that she'd become able to read the pain and grief in his countenance, where once he'd easily concealed them from her. "As I said last evening, it's been more than three and a half years; though I'm little surprised if the strain of what you've been through today pushed that out of your memory. Peter ought never have set you on that path."

"How do you know it was Peter who spoke with me?" Caeleigh had held confidential their conversation and felt relatively certain that Peter had done likewise, particularly considering that he had waited until Elizabeth had been absent to address the matter.

Andrew gentled his tone after his last words had appeared to have caused a measure of apprehension. "Only two men know me well enough to have been able to begin to guess what I told no one, and Thomas would have approached *me* about it, not you – as he has done on past occasions."

"Thomas has known? I thought you'd told no one?" Caeleigh put aside the empty first glass and reached for the second. Andrew had been correct in his anticipation of her thirst.

"Thomas has mistakenly believed that I have loved you without having Bonded with you; I've merely never corrected the misperception. I've deeply regretted having to deceive him, and I would that he had been present last evening when I was free to reveal the truth at last."

"Perhaps it is best as it is, then. Not his father's prolonged illness and passing into eternal reward, of course," Caeleigh quickly appended, self-conscious of what she may have implied. "It sounds to me, though, that you owe it to Thomas to give him the news, and explain the circumstances, more directly than simply to have had him another person at the table, if he has stood by you so steadfastly, especially unaware of what your true situation has been."

"Agreed. In that same spirit of honesty and disclosure, there are some things I need to tell you, Caeleigh." Andrew cleared his throat, rose, and moved his chair around to the end of the table to sit nearer beside her. "I have been travailing in prayer for you since not long after I Bonded with you. In the first year I was able to tell others truthfully, whenever I needed to isolate myself, that it was anonymous intercession, as I hadn't yet learned your name. Early in the second year, when I discovered that you and I were indirectly connected through Elizabeth and Peter's acquaintance, I learned a bit about you by way of that connection, but not much, and few details. I was restricted yet only to pray from a distance. I prayed for you always with ardor, having no other means to touch your heart; in return, my soul began to seem to hear more of yours whenever you were distressed. In one aspect, it enabled me to know better when and how to pray for you. In the other, it became unendurably painful and I could no longer forbear it." As Andrew had detailed the timeline of these events, he'd drawn an invisible line along the tabletop with his fingertip, tapping at randomly selected points upon it.

He and Caeleigh both had watched his hand's movements; as it came to rest, Andrew raised his eyes to meet hers. "The last time I travailed for you in that manner, the heartache I sensed from you was so intense that I experienced it as physical affliction. I couldn't simply pray for you and return to my life as it was – I had to ask Kadosh for help for myself. I begged Him to grant me some other way to aid and support you. Shortly thereafter, Peter Bonded with Elizabeth."

"That's when we met," Caeleigh replied, comprehending the fullness of what he was telling her.

Andrew nodded. "The reason I watched you so closely that evening, aside from concern for your emotional state, was that I was attempting to discern whether I truly ought to approach you, or whether I simply wanted it so keenly that I was mistaking my own desire for a spoken word from Kadosh.

"Which brings us to the final, and most important, thing I have been waiting years to be able to tell you: By the time you and I met" – Andrew slipped his hand beneath Caeleigh's and held it loosely – "I already long since loved you. I loved you with compassion as a result of a year and a half of intercession and travailing prayer. I loved you with *Phileo,* brotherly love, as a kindred child of Kadosh as Divine Father. As we became acquainted, I realized that I had entered your life already loving you more deeply than I had been aware. My infatuation with you began fairly immediately; I'm certain I concealed it so poorly any of a number of occasions over the past two years that to this day I cannot fathom how you never noticed."

His mirth quickly faded as he considered his next words. Hoping to soften their blow for himself as much as for her, Andrew brushed the hair back from Caeleigh's face with his free hand and let his fingertips linger against her cheek. "Love so deeply felt is meant to be expressed. Suppressing it is as unnatural and aberrant as consuming poison and expecting to live. Yet that's what was required of me. For two years daily I died to myself, and told myself that the sacrifice was in its own way a means of demonstrating my love for you. That is the pain you witnessed this morning. I won't lie to you – there have been days that it was a torment exceeding death. That's why telling you I had Bonded and then behaving as if I had not wasn't an option I had considered. No man in the history of the Settlements has done such a thing; I had no desire to be the first. I had already waited more than a year between Bonding and making your acquaintance – which is also why, when I returned to the Blue Creek Settlement last winter, I found it nigh impossible to continue in mere friendship with you and avoided you completely. My desire had been that once I received a sign that my time of waiting was concluded, I would announce my Bonding and proceed with courtship as is customary. Only your fear when the sign occurred in the form of *your* Bonding has deterred me from that course these past months."

"I would that I had known all of this sooner," Caeleigh replied. "I fear I've caused you more pain than you needed to endure."

Andrew offered his Beloved a bittersweet smile. "Wishing away the past is naught but a chasing after the wind, my dear one. I chose to withhold from you the pain I've endured because I did not desire to cause you any guilt or regret. My sole aim in disclosing much of what I've told you is to make amends for the deceit I have had to carry out all these years in order not to reveal until the proper time that I had Bonded with you. I have many such apologies to make in the coming days – you, for obvious reason, had a right to be the first."

Caeleigh took Andrew's hands in their manner of greeting, grasping firmly; it was the first time *she* had been the one to initiate the gesture, and the significance thereof did not escape his notice. "All is forgiven. Let us move forward from this point on a pledge to always be forthright with one another. Truth withheld, albeit with the best intentions, tends to bear undesirable consequences."

"Indeed." As the room had begun to fill before the meal, Andrew found himself reverting to his habit of sparse words.

"Not wishing to overstep my bounds, but if I may advise you?" Caeleigh asked delicately.

Andrew welcomed her suggestion with a squeeze of her fingers. "Please do."

"Speak with whomever here you urgently must, this evening, to set matters aright. Peter and Ezra in particular seem to be watching for an opportunity to speak with you at the moment. Then return to the Blue Creek Settlement – tonight. The news has already had a day's head start, and it would be best that Thomas hear it from you directly rather than via idle gossip."

Chapter 28

Mid December 2148

That Caeleigh had volunteered to aid in the preparation of an evening meal would have raised Andrew's suspicion, if not for the fact that so many of the fledgling Willow Springs Settlement's residents had returned to the Blue Creek Settlement to spend Christmastide with extended family and to forbear the worst of the winter cold there. Her failure to emerge from the kitchen with the other women after the meal was laid on the tables, however, prompted him to pursuit without first pausing to ask after her.

He found Caeleigh at one of the large kitchen sinks, washing pots still hot from use. Stepping closer, he spoke her name, calling her away from the chore.

"I wanted to get a head start, so that we won't be here so late afterward – it gets so dark so early this time of year."

"Caeleigh, stop. You needn't do this right now. Come, eat and fellowship with everyone."

She continued scrubbing, a thin attempt at concealing the heaving of her shoulders as she sobbed.

"Stop." Reaching around her from behind, Andrew took hold of her hands and pulled them out of the sink; he inhaled sharply at the sight of her wrists. Keeping her firmly encircled

in his arms, he turned hers outward to examine the jagged lines tracking down nearly half the length of the insides of her forearms. The angry red cuts and scratches stood out in stark relief against her hot-water-pinkened skin. "What is this?"

"I slipped and fell."

"This looks to be the result of more than a simple fall." Though offered mildly, Andrew's words fell upon Caeleigh's hearing as an accusation.

"Please don't interrogate me." Caeleigh quickly unrolled her rolled-back sleeves, to cover her injuries.

With an apology, Andrew released her and stepped back. When Caeleigh stood silent before him, he ventured one further question: "Why are you doing this?"

"I received a letter from Adeline's nephew. She ... has gone to join her husband in eternal reward." Fresh tears filled her eyes and promptly spilled over.

Andrew opened his arms to Caeleigh and drew her close when she fell into them. "I'm so sorry," he murmured into her hair. "I know how much she meant to you... But you have no reason to hide. Passing is a part of life."

"My grief is my own."

"It needn't be that way, Caeleigh. There are others here in our Settlement who knew and loved her – perhaps not as well as you have, but yet they did. You will not be alone in your grief."

With that, Andrew shepherded her toward the door to the dining room. He kept his hand placed gently behind Caeleigh's shoulder as they emerged and he called for the attention of all seated at the tables. "I regret to announce that we have lost a dear sister in the Blue Creek Settlement. Some of you knew the widow Adeline; she's the tailor under whom Caeleigh apprenticed and with whom she worked there. Adeline's nephew has sent word that his aunt has passed into eternal reward."

Ezra and Sophia, Simeon and Beth, Philip, Elizabeth, and several others responded as Andrew had predicted. Sarah, Philip's daughter, flew from her seat at the table and wrapped her arms around Caeleigh's waist to comfort her.

Peter spoke from where he sat beside his wife, "Let us come together to seek the comfort and peace that can only come from Kadosh for those of us she has left behind."

After the meal had been concluded and cleared away, Andrew permitted Caeleigh to return to the kitchen, but discreetly asked Sophia to join her.

Sophia took a dry dish towel from the shelf in the kitchen and took her place beside Caeleigh, who was once again washing dishes.

"Andrew is worried about you, you know," she offered gently, as Caeleigh handed her a large bowl.

"He does that rather often – it must be all those years' worth of pent-up affection," Caeleigh huffed in frustration. Ezra and Sophia had been sitting near enough, the evening when Andrew's Bonding had been announced, to hear him tell Caleb the story.

Sophia had known Caeleigh long enough to be confident in her suppositions of the tailor's mood. "Do you resent him for it?" she asked gently.

Caeleigh washed and handed over several more bowls while she contemplated her answer before giving it. Irritated as Caeleigh was, Sophia had done nothing to deserve her ire. "When I view the situation from his perspective, and knowing now what I do, I understand why he behaves toward me the way he does. From *my* perspective, though, this has been sudden and unexpected, and I'm not yet accustomed to it. I suppose I feel somewhat … smothered, at times."

"Unexpected how?" Sophia ached to help her friend in what ought to have been happy circumstances, so long-awaited.

"I learned the truth of the details of his Bonding at the same time as everyone else." Caeleigh realized, at Sophia's expression, that this information was news greatly unforeseen.

Sophia, however, responded graciously. "So you wish he might have told you privately, ahead of time?"

Though desirous not to direct her frustration with Andrew toward Sophia, Caeleigh failed to suppress all bitterness from her tone. "I would have appreciated it, yes."

"If you don't mind my making the recommendation, I would advise you to tell him that. What's done cannot be undone, but it would help him to understand."

After that, Caeleigh and Sophia shared some of their memories of Adeline as they finished the last of the dishes. The tailor admitted that the late elder woman had provided much more than a vocational training and relationship, becoming as a second mother to the young woman who had come into the Blue Creek Settlement with no family to accompany her.

Within a half-hour the chore was done, and Caeleigh urged Sophia to go without her. "I want to wipe down the countertops and rinse the soap out of the sink, and then I'll be ready to leave. You can tell Andrew I won't be long," she remarked with a teasing grin when Sophia looked from her to the dining room and back, from where she stood in the doorway between them.

Andrew waited as five minutes had passed, then ten. Sophia had advised him that Caeleigh was feeling overwhelmed by his recent attentions and needed some time to herself. As the ten minutes after Sophia's departure stretched into fifteen, he could wait no longer.

The carpenter entered the kitchen and found it vacant and dark. Through the window above the sinks, he saw the full moon's light reflected on the newly-fallen snow… and in that snow, the set of footprints crossing the meadow. Footprints that led from the kitchen's back door.

Quickly Andrew doubled back to the dining room, collected his coat from the hook beside the front door and turned off the lights there, then returned to the kitchen to exit by the same door through which Caeleigh had escaped.

Grateful that the snow wasn't deep enough to hinder him, he ran toward the grove of weeping willows. By the time he'd reached the first trees, he'd nearly caught up to Caeleigh.

"What are you doing?" he called after her.

"Grieving," came the reply; short though it was, it was enough to tell him that she was shivering.

Andrew approached cautiously at first, then more assertively when he saw how insufficiently dressed Caeleigh was for the falling temperatures. "It's too cold for you to be out here like this." Removing his coat, he wrapped it around her, pulled her close and began rubbing her back to warm her.

"I'm only c-cold b-because my s-sleeves are wet from the d-dishwashing," Caeleigh stammered through chattering teeth. "I didn't w-want to roll them up again b-because I didn't want Sophia to see m-my arms."

"Why are you out here?" Andrew's heart broke as she began to cry.

Caeleigh hesitated before leaning away slightly within his embrace to look into his face and whisper, "She knew, Andrew.

Enclosed with her nephew's letter was one he'd found among her things, addressed to me. She *knew*."

"About us?"

Caeleigh nodded regretfully, confirming Andrew's belief that she hadn't confided in the woman who had been as a mother to her. "She said in her letter that she had known for years … she knew as long ago as the day of Peter and Elizabeth's marriage."

"I recall the day," Andrew replied slowly, contemplating his memory of the event. "I had been more conspicuous about caring for you than I had before, because it was a difficult day for you. She must have been watching."

Caeleigh nodded. Adeline had known, more than Andrew had, how Caeleigh had struggled, as the two women had worked together to construct Elizabeth's bridal gown. Many tears had been shed during that time.

"She must have heard of the announcement of my Bonding," he mused.

"I suppose so. She also said that she didn't understand why you remained silent for the past two years, but trusted that you had a good reason."

Beginning to grow chilled himself, Andrew repeated his earlier question as he released her and rubbed his own arms. "What are you doing out here, Caeleigh?"

She looked over her shoulder. "Trying to figure out what to do with that."

Andrew followed her gaze to a wild rosebush, its roots wrapped in burlap, tucked beneath a shrub.

"I brought it here earlier this afternoon. It's a betrothal gift, from Adeline – she wrote that she wanted to send it earlier rather than later, since they're best transplanted over the winter and she expected that I would Bond with you before next winter." Caeleigh hugged herself as her grief washed anew over her countenance.

"At least I know now what happened to your arms." Andrew grinned, hoping that the levity would draw Caeleigh out of the sorrow of her loss.

Caeleigh chuckled in spite of her tears. "I was carrying it when I slipped," she confirmed.

"I'll assist you with it in the morning," he promised. "For now, let's get you indoors as quickly as possible, because I'm too much of a gentleman to take back my coat when you yet have need of it."

Chapter 29

Late January 2149

On a sunny, unseasonably warm Tuesday afternoon, Caeleigh took a break from her work. Andrew had agreed to help break some newly acquired horses for the message runners – this would be her best opportunity to observe him inconspicuously, to measure the man without being seen by him. Plus, the training of horses was something of an event to watch; it was not uncommon for a small crowd to turn out.

A few exuberant shouts from the men working with the animals echoed off the barn as she approached – everyone else watched with quiet excitement, mindful not to startle the already-distressed beasts. Caeleigh found herself a place along the southern fence, far enough away from the action that she thought fair her chances of not being seen by Andrew.

A youth by the name of Joseph had minutes prior dismounted and was leading a young palomino back to the barn. Moments later frenzied whinnies erupted from the paddock beside the corral where the men were working. Peter and two others – one of them Thomas, recently returned from the Blue Creek Settlement after having been recalled there by his ailing father – ran to assist Andrew as he led forth a greenbroke Percheron. Caeleigh held her breath; the sheer panic in the animal's eyes frightened her. Even normally jovial Peter remained serious. It took all four men to restrain and attempt, without success, to saddle the stallion. Before undertaking another attempt to place the saddle, Andrew retrieved an additional long-sleeved shirt one of the men had hung over a fencepost and tied it by the sleeves in such a fashion that the body of the shirt covered the horse's eyes. The Percheron resisted this blindfolding, tossing his head, but Andrew prevailed. Though still intermittently kicking skittishly, the animal was now more approachable. Andrew saddled the horse with relative ease, took the reins and stepped into the stirrup. After hoisting himself over, Andrew lowered himself into the saddle and nodded to Peter, who let go of the bridle and stepped quickly away before dashing back to the fence.

As Peter perched himself on the top rail, the stallion exploded in fury. Andrew held fast, moving with the Percheron as it bucked and leapt, desperate to throw him off its back. Man and beast wrestled in a contest of will as much as strength, the horse lathering from the exertion, perspiration dampening the horseman's brow, as well. Eventually, and after longer a time than most required, the stallion began to exhaust itself. Caeleigh grinned, feeling proud of the man who would be hers. She began to relax as the horse grew more submissive to Andrew's commands.

Moments later, a dog barked, bolted into the corral and veered toward them. Spooked, the Percheron reared. Andrew lost his grip and was thrown, landing hard on his shoulder on the hard-packed earth. Caeleigh clutched the fence in terror. Immediately half a dozen men launched into the corral – four toward the panicked horse and two to pull Andrew to safety out of the way, lest he be trampled. Among the latter Caeleigh recognized Stephen, newly returned from medical school and ready to become the physician for the Willow Springs Settlement. Andrew shouted in pain as the man on his left gripped his bicep and attempted to haul him to his feet.

As soon as he was satisfied that Andrew could walk, Stephen hurried the injured man to his offices.

Caeleigh followed, quaking with trepidation. Nicholas, the little boy whose dog had ignited the incident, ran beside her, his short legs working double-time to keep up with her brisk strides, hauling the guilty hound behind him.

"I'm so sorry!" Nicholas repeatedly exclaimed. As they reached their destination, she looked the boy full in the face and saw his wide eyes were full of apprehension.

Caeleigh knelt beside the lad and put her hands on his shoulders. "It's alright," she soothed him. "Doctor Stephen will take good care of Andrew. That horse is wilder than most, and Andrew knew the risk he was taking. He will be fine, I'm certain. But I hope you see now why dogs don't belong among untrained horses," she could not stop herself from adding.

"I do, and I'm sorry. I won't bring him along ever again," Nicholas promised as he gave the dog a reprimanding look. "I will say a prayer that he heals quickly."

Caeleigh smiled. "Run home, and do that."

As the boy darted down the street, pup in tow, and she turned to open the door to Stephen's offices, Caeleigh fought to remain brave. Showing courage in the face of reality was a tremendously different proposition from showing courage in front of a little boy. The unknowns of the reality that waited behind that portal shook Caeleigh to her core with a fear deeper than she had expected to encounter.

Closing the door softly behind her, Caeleigh searched for Andrew and Stephen. Following the sound of their voices, she found the men returning from a back room to the front of the building. Outside the open door of Stephen's examination office she hesitated, anxious.

"Caeleigh?" Andrew's voice carried a note of hope amidst his obvious pain.

She stepped into the doorway. "Forgive me if I have been overbold in coming here." After the fleeting glance she had taken at the sight of Andrew, shirtless, cradling his left arm in his right, the shoulder improperly askew, Caeleigh kept her eyes cast to the floor. Courage had fled her.

A soft knock at the rear door of the room preceded the entry of Stephen's assistant, his wife Martha, with a handful of x-ray films. Martha tucked the films onto the light board for her husband, providing Caeleigh with a focal point upon which to turn her gaze. After examining the images, Stephen turned to his patient, saying, "You're fortunate. Obviously your shoulder is dislocated, but you have no broken bones. There is nothing for me to do but reset the joint."

The physician gave Caeleigh a sparing look, indicating that she may wish to leave rather than witness the act.

Andrew, however, said to her, "Please, stay. It would help me greatly to have you here to distract me ... if you can endure it." He sat on the forward edge of the chair Stephen placed in the center of the floor. Resting his left arm across his lap, he reached his right hand toward Caeleigh. She knelt beside him, holding his hand in both of hers and focusing exclusively on his face.

When Stephen took hold of his arm and shoulder, Andrew's breaths came shallow and rapid as he braced himself for the pain. His expression begged Caeleigh to hold his attention. Then came the snap of the shoulder resetting and Andrew's agonized cry, brought more by the sound of it than the sensation. He sagged forward, panting, then dropped his face heavily against her shoulder.

Caeleigh barely caught him as Stephen lifted Andrew's unconscious form before he fell. With Martha's assistance, Stephen carried Andrew to the next room and laid him on the waiting bed.

"He passed out from the trauma, is all," the physician informed the anxious Caeleigh. "I'll bind up his shoulder so that it will be immobilized until it heals, and he will be fine."

An hour later, Andrew woke to find his shoulder wrapped in bandages and his arm bound in a sling. He had been dressed in a clean homespun shirt, though it was merely draped over his left side and left unbuttoned. In the chair beside the foot of the bed, Caeleigh was bent over something, sewing.

"Caeleigh?" he murmured hoarsely, "What are you doing?"

"I'm mending your shirt." She held it up for his inspection. "You tore it when – " Tears threatened to overcome her with the memory.

Andrew reached out his right hand toward her, beckoning. "Come here." When she obeyed and came within his reach, he pulled her closer until she sat beside him on the edge of the bed. "I'm sorry you had to see what you saw."

"Beloved, I was so terrified! I thought for certain that you would be trampled and I would lose you!" The words rushed forth as Caeleigh clutched the fabric with both hands, tears streaming down her face.

Andrew smiled, attempting to calm her. "I was referring to the fact that I fainted veritably on top of you. I hate the idea of you seeing me in such a state of weakness." He paused, thoughtful for a moment. "Did you call me 'Beloved'?"

Caeleigh gasped and covered her mouth with a trembling hand. "I didn't mean to; it just slipped out. And you haven't said it first, yet – I'm sorry!"

"Don't be." Now Andrew was genuinely grinning. He pulled her hand away from her flushed face, and caressed her cheek. "It doesn't matter who says it first. Caeleigh, Beloved, it blesses me to hear you address me thus."

Still embarrassed, Caeleigh resumed stitching. "It looks like Stephen cut whatever didn't rip, to get this off of you…"

"He had to – my arm was useless. Let me see what you've done."

Caeleigh held up the shirt, its sleeve nearly completely reattached with miniscule stitches. "It won't last for long; but hopefully long enough until I can make a new one, after I've finished making the shirt to replace the one you're wearing and the bandages I promised Stephen in compensation for your treatment. He says it will be weeks before you can resume working at the level of vigor to which you're accustomed."

"It looks perfect, to my eye. Help me sit up."

She set the shirt aside and obliged, supporting his back while taking great care not to touch Andrew's injured shoulder as he pushed himself up with his strong arm. "You should rest. Why do you wish to sit up so soon?"

"So that I may hold you properly – as best as I am able, anyway." Andrew wrapped his arm around Caeleigh and pulled her close, until she rested her head on his good shoulder. "It's alright to cry, Beloved," he whispered, keeping his hand pressed to the middle of her back. "I will be fine, but it's acceptable to cry if you need to."

"I was so afraid," Caeleigh wept, her face pressed into the side of his neck, rapidly dampening the collar of his borrowed shirt

"I know," Andrew murmured. "I don't recall the last time I prayed so hard, myself."

After a few minutes, when her tears had subsided, Andrew lifted Caeleigh's face. "I would like to ask something of you that I have never asked of you before, but I feel the situation calls for it. ...Will you allow me to kiss you?" he made his request almost shyly.

"If you wish," she whispered, equally nervous as she sat back a ways from him.

Her expression caused Andrew to smile all the brighter. "Don't fear me so," he nearly chuckled, as he kissed her forehead. "I only wished to convey my thanks."

"For what?" Caeleigh began trembling vigorously enough to mildly shake the bed upon which he reclined and she sat.

"For being here when I needed you most, in spite of your fear. For staying faithfully by me, for mending my shirt, for compensating Stephen on my behalf, and for finally addressing me as 'Beloved.' For your strength" – Andrew told her as he kissed Caeleigh on one cheek – "and for your courage" – and on the other. "You have a greater measure of each than you believe."

Chapter 30

Late January 2149

A short time later, Andrew was released from the physician's care. He escorted Caeleigh back to her shop, clutching the front of his shirt closed from the inside with his left hand and from the outside with his right.

"You can't go about like that," she chided him as they entered the millinery. "For one thing, it isn't proper, and for another, you look ridiculous. Have a seat and give me a few minutes."

He stationed himself in one of the more comfortable chairs to the side of the room and watched his Beloved as she perched on a stool and settled in at the table to work. When Caeleigh began deftly ripping out the stitches attaching the left sleeve to the body of the shirt, he spoke up.

"What are you doing? You spent more than an hour reattaching that!"

"I'm fixing it."

"Isn't that what you already did?" Andrew decided that the medication he'd been given for pain was confusing his mind.

"No," Caeleigh smiled at him briefly, patient. Returning her attention to the work in her hands and not diverting it again, she explained, "That was mending. Repairing. This is fixing. Making it workable for your need, at least for as long as you're going to be bound in those bandages." She continued ripping down the side-seam of the body of the shirt a short distance.

"Now what are you doing?"

"Wait until I'm through, and it'll make sense." Caeleigh left the sleeve lonely on the table and seated herself at one of the sewing machines in the adjoining room. When she returned, the armhole on the left side of the shirt was neatly finished and slightly larger. "If you can remove the sling long enough to put this on, you ought to be able to work it over and around the bandages without too much trouble."

Andrew rose from the chair and turned his back to her, in an attempt to maintain some measure of modesty.

"I'll do my utmost not to look," she promised as she lifted the shirt from his left side and held it so that he could easily withdraw his right arm from the sleeve.

When the sling was removed, Andrew fumbled with the modified shirt, unsure of how to attempt the feat. "I'm sorry; I'm going to need your assistance." He cringed as he turned toward her.

"I'm going to be your wife, soon, anyway," she teased with a wink, though she kept her eyes on his face. "Besides, you certainly can't attend the evening meal barely half-dressed as you were."

"I suppose you're right about that." He handed over the shirt, to which Caeleigh kept her gaze turned.

Starting with the left side, she gently eased the shirt over and along the length of his forearm and adjusted it around his elbow. Pulling the shirt up as she circled behind him, she extended the right side so that Andrew could slip his arm into the sleeve. She then continued around until she was in front of him once more, and began to close the shirt. She spoke more to the buttons between her fingers than to him: "You'll have to wear it untucked, though. I won't..."

"I was never going to ask." As she finished with the last of the top buttons, leaving the collar of the shirt open, Andrew caught both of her hands in his right one, and held them to his collarbone. "Caeleigh, look at me." He waited until her eyes met his before continuing. "Thank you, Beloved. Thank you for taking care of my needs and for safeguarding propriety. You have no reason to feel shame."

She turned to the chair and picked up the sling, saying nothing. As she assisted him in resecuring his injured shoulder, Andrew spoke again.

"We *will* need to announce a betrothal, soon, you know."

"But ... not ... You – you haven't ..." Caeleigh stammered, her voice quaking as much as the rest of her. She began to wring her hands.

Again Andrew grasped her two hands with his one, stilling her anxious habit. "No, not tonight. I know I haven't proposed marriage to you yet, and I want to. I'm waiting for a particular day for that. I have been praying that we – both of us – would Bond with one another a second time, to let us know when it is the right time. I feel that time is soon to come."

His Beloved said nothing in reply. Eyes bright with tears conveyed more messages than words could shape.

"Come here to me," Andrew murmured as he raised his right arm.

Caeleigh tucked herself against his ribcage and wrapped her arms around his waist, careful not to jostle his left side. "Thank you," she whispered against his chest as he kissed the top of her head.

Pulling back from the embrace, Caeleigh lightly brushed some of the dust from Andrew's shirt. "I'll modify the other shirt the same way so that you'll have a clean one to wear, but this will suffice for this evening. People will be wondering what's become of you, by now." Collecting the white shirt from the chair, she carried it across to her work table and pulled a pincushion from a shallow drawer beneath the tabletop.

"Sometime soon you will need to stop evading the discussion we seem to never completely have."

"I'm not evading anything," the tailor defended, running pins through several points surrounding the shirt's left sleeve. "I'm marking this for later so that I will remember exactly what I did the first time, so that this one will turn out correctly." She completed the task and put away the pincushion.

"We *will* continue this conversation soon," Andrew warned.

"But not now. Please, it's been a difficult enough afternoon already," Caeleigh pleaded. Retrieving a shawl she had left near the door, she glanced through the front window. "And Peter is anxious over you – he's waiting outside."

They both reached for the door handle at the same time. After a moment's hesitation, Caeleigh acquiesced and turned off the lights while Andrew waited for her. As she passed him out onto the porch, he smiled. "You've done enough for me today; the least you can allow me to do for you is hold a door."

"It is not in my nature to expect others to do for me," was her reply as she locked the door after he had closed it behind himself.

Any response Andrew had been about to make was cut off by Peter's call from across the street. "Glad to see you about! I told that Powderkeg you would never be bested by the likes of him."

"Powderkeg?" Andrew inquired as he and Caeleigh joined Peter in the street.

"It's what we named him. Too much volatility in his nature for any other name to fit half as well. It took four men to get him unsaddled. Not a one of us dared try again after the way he tossed you. Miss," he tipped his head toward Caeleigh in greeting; she nodded in reply. She feared Peter yet counted her singularly responsible for his beloved brother's continual suffering, unaware they'd resolved the matter privately; his cool if unforgiving civility, she posited, was to appease his wife.

"Which means it will fall to me to tame him, yet," Andrew concluded.

Beside and behind him, Caeleigh wilted. He turned to her.

"We are not given a spirit of fear, Beloved," he simply reminded her, a hand raised to silence Peter against commenting on the endearment. "What happened today was an accident, and need not happen again. I shall heal in due time, and then Powderkeg will be dealt with."

Andrew took the shawl from Caeleigh's hands and held it toward Peter. "My friend, would you do me the favor of compensating for my infirmity?"

"Of course." Peter held open the shawl and draped it around Caeleigh's shoulders. "Joseph has volunteered to assist, as well," he offered to Andrew. "After seeing how well he did today, I would trust him. The lad has an innate gift with animals."

"Have you decided whether you will take him on as your apprentice, Peter?" Caeleigh asked as they, along with the rest of the community, proceeded toward the meetinghouse for the evening meal. With the Willow Springs Settlement yet in its early stages, the stonemason had more work than one man could handle alone.

"I have. He's a capable young man with a good eye and a steady hand. I plan to approach his father as soon as he is of age." Though a young man who wished to become an apprentice sought out the tradesman himself, the tradesman sought the blessing of the young man's father, in deference to the latter's paternal authority over the son, before anything would be made official. Joseph was a few weeks away from his sixteenth birthday; once his father's blessing was obtained, he would become Peter's apprentice the very day he became a man. "Have you approached Alexander's father yet, since the young man has already made known his intention to you?" Peter asked Andrew.

"I have, but I'll be speaking to him again. Alexander is not yet sixteen, but these are somewhat exceptional circumstances – I can no more wait for him to come of age than I can wait for my shoulder to heal. There is more work to be done than I can allow to back up for a month. I need another pair of hands."

As they stepped onto the porch of the meetinghouse, Peter opened the door; pausing, he turned and said, "You'd best let me go in first, or they'll crush you. Everyone, from the young girls to the widows, has been fretting about you since the accident."

In reply, Caeleigh took hold of the door and held it open so that Peter could enter. Following directly behind him, Andrew reached back for her hand and, when she gave it to him, pulled her close. "Be my left arm," he whisperedly entreated. "They'll want to lay hands upon me to pray for healing, but I'm in too much pain to bear the pressure of a dozen hands."

Caeleigh squeezed his hand in response as a wave of overlapping cries and questions crashed upon them. Contrary to Peter's exaggeration, there were as many men as women wanting a report. Dozens upon dozens from the Willow Springs Settlement and nearly as many from the Blue Creek Settlement were present, though the evening meal was yet an hour away. Caeleigh understood now why Elizabeth had been needed to help in the kitchen, along with all the women who usually were responsible for preparing the communal meals.

Andrew released his hold on Caeleigh and raised his right hand to quiet the crowd. "I thank you all for your concern," he spoke loudly enough to be heard in the back of the room. "It is with gratitude that I boast to you all of how Kadosh sheltered me in the moment of what I'm certain you all have either witnessed or heard about. My shoulder was dislocated when I fell, but I suffered no broken bones, nor other trauma." He reached again for Caeleigh and pulled her close to his side. "Caeleigh, here, would have it that the worst I suffered was the damage I did in tearing my shirt, and even that she has already repaired." He grinned at her as many near them chuckled.

Caeleigh blushed more than she smiled. It wasn't uncommon for courted women to share in the attentions given to their men, so she did her best to hide her uneasiness and accept it graciously. She knew that Andrew was less teasing her than attempting to downplay the severity of his injury.

"Then we shall pray in thanks for your safety as well as for your healing," Governor Caleb announced from behind, having made his way around the perimeter of the crowd. Andrew and Caeleigh both turned at the sound of his voice.

Now on Andrew's left, Caeleigh edged closer to him as everyone pressed in around them. Her left arm she placed under his to support it somewhat, and her right hand she placed, gently, high on his shoulder, just beside the curve of his neck, careful to keep her touch featherlight so as not to hurt him further. In this posture she blocked his arm and shoulder with her body. She turned her left palm face-up as his left hand, peeking out of the sling, grasped her fingers.

"And the woman was made from the rib of the man, so as to be fitted at his side, to guard his heart and to protect him from harm," Caleb murmured in blessing and approval, for their hearing only. Placing his hand upon Andrew's bowed head, he raised his voice and began to pray.

Chapter 31

Mid February 2149

"Andrew, *you* recruited her here; *you* must convince her to see reason!" Thomas nearly exploded into the millinery, disrupting Andrew's efforts to convalesce.

"What are you talking about?" Andrew had never seen the smith so agitated.

"Abigail. She's decided that *she* is the one who's fit to tame Powderkeg." Thomas stammered frustratedly, searching for words. "The woman is mad – if she dares the attempt, she'll get herself killed! You're one of our best horsemen, and look what happened to you!" He paced immediately within the doorway, incapable of containing his distressed energy.

Andrew grimaced as he pushed himself out of his chair. "My thanks for the less-than-gentle reminder, my friend." He called to Caeleigh, who had not heard them from her workroom over the running of her sewing machine. "Beloved, there is a matter to which I must attend."

The glance she gave him when she entered the main room of the shop carried clear directives to mind the physician's orders.

This Andrew acknowledged by adjusting the sling as it rested against the back of his neck. "You needn't fret," he added when she did not soon break off her stare. "Thomas will see to it that no harm befalls me."

"Indeed I will," the latter added, relying on his own friendship with her to submit his appeal to the tailor.

The two hurried to the stable at the quickest pace Andrew could manage without disrupting his shoulder.

Upon their arrival, Andrew stopped Thomas for a word of caution before they proceeded. "Listen carefully, Brother. Under *no* circumstances can you rush in, raise your voice, or speak in sharp tones – not even toward Abigail. This horse is a volatile creature and will respond with violent panic to anything he perceives as hostility."

There was more Andrew would have said, but Thomas' impatience denied him the opportunity. They followed the all-too-familiar sound of Powderkeg's anxious vocalizations around to the corral, in time to see Abigail leading the Percheron by a mere halter from there to the paddock.

Thomas was a heartbeat away from vaulting over the corral fence in pursuit of them until Andrew grabbed the smith's arm. "Thomas!" he hissed in forceful reminder of the warning he'd only moments before issued. "I don't yet see evidence that Abigail is in any danger," he continued in a low voice. "Let's give her a chance."

With obvious effort Thomas restrained himself and followed Andrew across the corral at a less urgent speed. What they found in the paddock was the last thing either could have expected: Powderkeg, though fighting Abigail's command of him, was decidedly *under her command*. Thomas grunted in dumbfounded shock and, Andrew suspected, a bit of admiration.

The carpenter grinned. "Had you exercised a bit more patience earlier, I'd have had the chance to assure you of the likelihood of this. You see, beyond her skill as a farrier, Abigail is also a veterinarian." He fought to contain his laughter.

"Exactly how long did you intend to withhold that information from me?" Thomas blustered.

"Withhold? How long and how often were you denying me the opportunity to speak?"

Thomas had no choice but to accede Andrew's point, and managed as well to join in his laughter.

Their levity dissipated rapidly, however, as Abigail bent to examine Powderkeg's foreleg, probing with one hand while attempting to hold the halter with the other, her upstretched arm half-twisted behind her. The position was awkward enough to render her grip on the strap insufficiently secure, and the animal seized upon his opportunity, tossing his head and knocking the woman beside him off-balance. Andrew's blood ran cold as he stood helpless while the stallion reared over the woman, knocking her to the ground.

Thomas wasted no time before reacting, though it was difficult to tell whether the greater portion of his outrage was directed toward the Percheron or toward Abigail. He charged toward them both, screaming in fury.

Powderkeg's flight to the opposite side of the paddock did little to quell Thomas' rage. Instead he turned on Abigail, who was picking herself up, as he grasped her arm and attempted to haul her toward the fence. "Have you no sense?!" he shouted. "This beast is too dangerous! It took no fewer than four men to subdue him – what made you think you could handle him on your own?!"

To her credit, Abigail tore her arm from his grip and stood her ground. "*You're* the one who's behaving as if he's lost his senses, Thomas," she returned angrily. "I had the situation well in hand, and accounted for the risks." She gestured toward Joseph, who had come from inside the barn at the first indication of trouble and followed the ill-tempered horse where it had fled to a corner.

"He nearly *killed* a man three weeks ago" – Thomas stabbed his finger in Andrew's direction – "and easily could have killed *you* a moment ago! He should be put down!"

"I will permit no such thing! Now get out of the way and I'll thank you to stop antagonizing the poor creature." With that, Abigail spun and left him standing in a figurative cloud of dust as she joined the young lad who had been struggling to calm the animal while they'd been shouting at one another. She took hold of the halter once more and led Powderkeg away from the fence a short distance, speaking in low, soothing tones.

Once they were positioned safely away from the fence, Joseph took over control of the halter, holding firmly with both hands. Meanwhile, Abigail petted and massaged the stallion's powerful withers, continually speaking to the creature as though he could be reasoned with: "Relax now, my friend. No one means to harm you. I've put that vicious beast in his proper place; you needn't worry about him anymore."

Andrew, who'd dared venture closer in case Thomas might require further restraint, chuckled despite his best efforts at self-control.

"*That* is the 'vicious beast' – and there she stands *pandering* to it as if it were a child!" Thomas seethed through clenched teeth.

"Peace, Thomas." Andrew spoke without removing his eyes from the woman who once again was working her way along to the horse's pastern, this time with both hands. As he had before, Powderkeg kicked and screamed, dancing away and pulling Joseph with him.

"Easy now, easy!" the youth cried, struggling to hold onto the halter.

Abigail stood, dejection in her bearing. "I've seen enough, Joseph. Take him back to his stall." With a sigh she approached

Andrew and reported, "This horse is unfit for message running. He's had a prior fracture of the canon bone that was improperly set – possibly not set at all – and the bone re-fused incorrectly aligned."

Andrew took in the news staidly. "You're certain of this?"

"It's minimal enough to miss on visual inspection, but I think it's obvious that he's in pain when pressure is applied to the site of the break. And *you* know better than anyone," Abigail added, her eyes on Andrew's bound shoulder and arm, "he's unable to bear the weight of a rider. He communicated that to you the only way he could, three weeks ago."

The carpenter nodded, massaging his shoulder. "What, then, is your recommendation?"

Abigail shook her head, prohibiting Thomas' suggestion before he could repeat it. "I don't want to see him put down," she insisted. "It's an extreme and inhumane punishment upon him for the poor treatment he received at the hands of a negligent human being. I'll take him on as my own, and bear responsibility for his care."

"You're certain you won't be extended beyond your means by the undertaking?" Andrew felt it his duty to ensure that Abigail was pursuing a viable option, as opposed to merely acting to spite the man fuming silently beside them.

"Indeed." The farrier remained adamant, though she calmed her tone when speaking with the man who not only had recruited her to join the Willow Springs Settlement, but had expressed belief in her capabilities in the work of her trades. "From what Ezra has told me of the families planning to move here from the Blue Creek Settlement to establish farms, I should have enough work to provide amply to cover all of his needs and rehabilitation."

"Rehabilitation?" Thomas sputtered.

"Yes, rehabilitation," Abigail veritably spat toward the agitant blacksmith before once more addressing her intentions to Andrew. "Once I've worked through his psychological traumas" – she availed herself of the opportunity to cast a disparaging side-eye in Thomas' direction – "not the *least* of which have occurred here, I believe it may be possible to surgically correct the physical trauma, as well. Despite whatever fears and foul memories he suffers, he's a fine animal, and worth the effort." With this, her final pronouncement on the matter, Abigail exited into the barn.

"That woman is impossible," Thomas seethed.

Andrew stifled a bemused grin. "Tread carefully, my friend. Your anger stands very near to the line of infatuation."

Chapter 32

Late March 2149

"What troubles you, Brother?" Andrew strode unceremoniously into the blacksmith's workshop and posed his inquiry without the courtesy of prefacing it with a greeting.

Thomas deflected the question by offering his friend a cup of coffee.

"You *know* I know you better than to allow you to get away without answering," the carpenter warned, testing the strength of his left arm to hold the mug steady, before supporting it with his right hand.

"What troubles *you*, Andrew? You're the one who's come to *my* workshop at mid-afternoon, seemingly with no cause to be here."

Andrew stood squared with his friend and drove straight to the heart of the matter. "What troubles me is *you*, Thomas. For a month you've shown Abigail civility, respect, and on occasion kindness. For weeks, the two of you have seemed to work harmoniously where your vocations coincide. Yet in the past number of days, you have not been yourself." With his stronger right arm, he picked up an axe that stood nearby, knowing Thomas alone would comprehend the inference behind the gesture. "What troubles you?"

As anticipated, the smith indeed grasped the unspoken invitation. Smiling in spite of himself, he took the axe from

Andrew's hand. "Whatever else the circumstances may be, I am far from willing to incur the wrath of your Beloved for allowing you to reinjure your shoulder before it's fully healed."

"In that, we are agreed," Andrew laughed. Quickly, though, he sobered when Thomas' mood returned to melancholy. "Without the felling of trees, then, allow me yet to return the favor you once extended to me when I walked in darker days."

Thomas conceded with a nod. "Judah," he called to his blacksmithing apprentice. "We're closing early today. Put out the fire and you may go home."

The youth did as instructed and, before taking his leave, paused to say, "I, too, have noticed your spirits growing lower of late. I didn't consider it my right place to enquire when you didn't seem to want to discuss it, but I wanted to let you know, sir, that I've been praying for you and shall continue to do so." Though yet in the early season of his apprenticeship, Judah had come to regard Thomas as a second father. Given that his own father was a somewhat emotionally distant man, Judah had taken to seeking Thomas' counsel on matters he felt less than confident addressing at home.

The young man's concern further exhorted the smith on the state of his heart. "Thank you, Judah. I appreciate your concern. Mind you tell your father you have my permission to take the remainder of the day off. I don't want him thinking you've disobeyed me or shirked your duties."

"Yessir." Judah departed with great reluctance.

An hour later, the two men had ridden north of the Settlement, through the foothills, and entered the canyon that opened into their valley.

Andrew deeply exhaled with contentment. "I don't mean to belittle whatever is weighing on you, but I feel … refreshed … to reclaim a part of myself."

"You've been housebound too long."

"We're not out here for *my* sake, Thomas," Andrew reminded him.

More than a quarter hour longer they continued without a word spoken between them. The trail ended at a small lake, fed by a waterfall that Andrew estimated to be between eighty and ninety feet high. Thomas continued to say nothing.

Choosing to take ease in the saddle rather than attempt to dismount, Andrew broke the persistent silence. "This place reminds me of a story I heard as a child from my grandfather – one of the ancestral legends he heard as a boy from *his* grandfather, of a tribal princess who cast herself over such a waterfall as this. Her father the chief of their tribe deemed the man she loved unsuitable and prevented their marriage by having him executed. After her beloved was cast over the falls to his death, the princess followed him rather than be separated and constrained to live without him. To this day, those falls bear her name, to honor what she did in the name of love."

Thomas' sigh fell heavy with the weight of dejection. "I truly hope it was not your intention to cheer me with so grim a tale."

"It fell to me to speak, since you refused." With his inflection and a look, Andrew both gently chastised and urged Thomas to confess. "It's unlike you not to be forthright with me, Brother."

The smith massaged his forehead and pushed the hair out of his eyes. "I understand that a great deal of the administration of the Settlement has been given to you to spare you from idleness while you've been unable to perform the work of your trade, and I admit you have the gifts and abilities to carry out those duties well. Yet there are times I wish you were not so skilled at exercising the authority of a Governor."

Andrew chuckled, knowing full well that the praise was genuine and the complaint good-natured and affectionate. "What if that should be the role Kadosh intends for me to fill? Would you submit to my authority if I were to become your Governor?"

"You know I would honor whomever Kadosh places in that office – even *you*." Thomas grinned, beginning slowly to feel more himself. He swung out of the saddle and to the ground. Andrew followed suit in order to remain on equal footing, lest his friend find any cause for reluctance to speak.

"The great irony of your childhood tale is its theme of love lost to death," Thomas mused as he approached the lake and crouched beside the water's edge.

The revelation caught Andrew unprepared. "I wasn't aware your thoughts yet turned to her often after so many years."

"It isn't so much a deliberate contemplation of memories as it is … I feel as though I have betrayed her as the one I've held beloved for nearly twenty years."

"In what way?" Though Thomas had spoken of his affection for Benia only once, it had been with such firm certainty that Andrew would never have questioned its steadfastness.

Idly the smith picked up a small stone from beside the toe of his boot and tepidly flung it into the water. "In the weeks since Abigail and I have been seeking to regard one another amenably rather than adversarially, I have grown a strong affection for her. That woman can be quite endearing when she isn't infuriating."

"I'd venture that at those times she was endeared to you despite your anger." Andrew stepped nearer as Thomas rose to his feet.

Though offered harmlessly, Andrew's words bit deeply. "I beg you, do not jest with me on this."

"Truly, I would never disrespect *you,* with whom I've entrusted so much of my own struggle. What I am saying is that I believe this affection for Abigail began well before you were aware of it – and that your anger toward her served to mask your fear of those rising emotions. I have been watching you closely since the incident over the stallion, Thomas. Something has been altered in your demeanor with Abigail since the moment she refused to be intimidated by you."

Thomas stared at the falls, as if transfixed by their relentless pounding against the rocks. "I fear that I am very near to Bonding with her, Andrew."

"What is it that brings you fear of a match instituted by Kadosh Himself?" Andrew was aware he must tread carefully with his words, but the need to pose the question was no less great.

Thomas glanced momentarily at his brother before once more studying the landscape. "I made a promise to remain faithful in my love for Benia. How can I honor that promise if I love another? Nor would a divided loyalty be honoring to Abigail." He spoke with equal parts regret and frustration.

Andrew placed a firm hand on Thomas' shoulder. "The fact that you have asked these questions at all should assure you that you are a man of honor. As for the promise you made, was it spoken before Benia's passing, or after?"

"Sometime in the year that followed the news of her passing."

The carpenter gentled; the matter had become plain to him as one of self-castigation for events not anticipated. "Then be lenient with yourself, Thomas. You made the agreement with yourself, rather than with her. Truly, would Benia desire to see you set in such a condition as this, obligating your fidelity to someone with whom you cannot share this life?"

"Are you suggesting I didn't love her?" Though Thomas' anger had not fully sparked, he found himself adopting a defensive stance.

"I'm suggesting you lay that affection to rest – *with* her. If you yet desire to honor her for the place she once held in your heart, find another means to do so. Brother, if you are as near to Bonding with Abigail as you say, don't resist what Kadosh has for you. In the past four generations of the history of the Settlements, I don't know that there has ever been an incident of a man refusing the Bonding – don't be the first. I have no desire for yours to be the life in which we discover the consequences of that ungrateful rebellion."

Thomas refused to smile in the least. So much as a wry smirk would be to concede victory to an idea with which he found little comfort. "For a man of spare words such as yourself to have so much to say all at once on the matter, you must consider it vital that I allow myself to love the woman I have scarcely been able to tolerate from the day I first encountered her."

At this Andrew broke into an easy grin. "I can think of no one better suited for you. For all your bluster, she stands her ground and matches you wit for wit. Abigail is a woman who both complements your strengths and counters your flaws."

Some time later as the two men rode back toward the Settlement, Thomas reined in his horse and reached for the bridle of the other, stopping him as well. He spoke before his actions could be questioned: "Brother, if I am to follow this path, I would seek your counsel. Should I tell Abigail everything of my history?"

The earnest seeking was borne so transparently in Thomas' countenance that as he met his eyes, Andrew understood what was meant by the expression in the scriptures that said that the Christ, upon 'looking at him, loved him,' which he'd read many times, but never grasped as deeply as he did now.

"I cannot make that decision for you, my friend. I will, however, share this with you – I chose once to withhold a small measure of the truth from Caeleigh, believing it to be for her protection. As it were, she learned what I had kept from her by some other means, and came to more harm than had I simply been forthright with her." Andrew concealed from his brother none of the pain and regret that had come of the event to which he referred. Thomas had already endured enough of both and needed no more of either.

Chapter 33

April 2149

The moon hung lonely in the cold sky, giving light to the world below in a manner that reminded Thomas of the emptiness that had long occupied his heart. Andrew would have some ancestral Indian legend passed down from his grandfather's grandfather, no doubt, to share about the moon. Likely some nonsense about how the moon had come to be in the sky, and in the company of the stars – whatever the tale, it would have no relevance to the guilt and pain Thomas suffered.

He understood well that his friend's intentions were all for his best, but Andrew had never been able to fathom the full depth of his loss. Speaking of the matter improved nothing, and silence explained less. Benia's passing into eternal reward had left a void that would not be filled.

Yet, there was Abigail. Though the chill of love lost in Thomas' heart lingered like the winter reticent to loose its grip on their Settlement's valley, Abigail stood as the sunshine that gently, tacitly warmed his days. Life without her had become as unwelcome a prospect as the task of releasing Benia into the presence of Kadosh.

A soft knock on the open door of the smithy interrupted his thoughts.

"Thomas?"

"Abigail. What brings you to my door?" Thomas might have commented on her going about unescorted at so late an hour of the evening, but that he was in no mood for the recurring argument it would have raised.

The neglect to foment the ongoing debate over the propriety of her choice to eschew male escort after dark did not pass unnoticed by Abigail. She chose, however, to offer only the benign explanation she'd chosen on her short walk from the stables to the smithy. "The new shoes you promised me for Simeon's horse."

Thomas looked to his worktable and found it vacant. "I must apologize, Abigail. I've been distracted of late and haven't finished them."

Reining in her impatience, the farrier stepped further into his shop. "I've noted you have been lost in thought quite often the past few days. What troubles you?"

"You do." Thomas attempted to both make light of his mood and deter further inquiry.

He failed at both pursuits. Abigail collected a stool from the other side of the worktable, set it before him, and sat knee-to-knee with the slouched man folded in upon himself before her. She pertly crossed her arms and delivered a stare that informed the smith she was prepared to wait all night for him to speak.

Long minutes passed until with a sigh Thomas ended yet another stalemate with his concession of defeat.

"You spoke the truth just then," Abigail coaxed the man to open up. "Is there any offense I have given for which I owe apology?"

"No. Of course not. Absolutely never," Thomas replied in haste.

To this, Abigail was equally quick to respond with a jest. "I wouldn't be so quick to say '*Absolutely never*' – there was that initial matter over Barnabas..." she alluded to the Percheron she had rescued from Thomas' ire, to rehabilitate and rename against his strongly – and repeatedly – expressed will.

Thomas shook his head, chuckling despite himself. "Powderkeg," he spoke the animal's former name. "I maintain that you have succeeded with that beast only by being more stubborn than he."

"I prefer to be considered resilient," she countered, her satisfaction at his change in countenance evident. "There, now – Are you willing to share your burden?"

"To be fully truthful with you, I am not yet certain." Thomas stared into the smoldering coals of his hearth. "I have spoken on the matter with Andrew, and he insists that I ought to confess all to you, for your own good. I fail to see how his reasoning extends as far as he believes it to do."

Abigail reached out and covered the smith's strong hand with one of her own. "Then I would have you not speak until you are ready to do so. Commit the matter to prayer tonight, and I will return after the morning meal tomorrow for the horseshoes you owe me. If you haven't completed them by the time I arrive, we will talk while you work."

"This place is magnificent." Abigail stood in awe of the waterfall towering over them.

Thomas grinned at her pleasure, feeling ever the fool. Never before had he heard her speak in this manner... Or perhaps merely he had never before noticed.

He turned to the falls himself, recalling his last visit to the place. It was the same place – the same cut into the mountain. But, as his companion would be quick to point out were they to engage in another of their robust debates, the falls were not technically the same. The water presently pouring over the cliff, tumbling over the rocks and into the lake below, was not the same water that had been so doing weeks past. That water was already well beneath, churning the lake-bottom into a cloud through which he could not see.

Though the time that had passed was insufficient for any change to be marked enough for the eye to note, he knew that the rocks as well had been – and were continuing to be – changed. Continually pounded as they were, their surfaces were being altered, hard edges rounded and softened over time.

Much like his heart.

"The atmosphere is so fresh," Abigail broke into his thoughts, pulling his gaze back toward herself, haloed in the mist.

"It is," Thomas agreed, inferring more than the external environment.

The smith afforded himself several moments to collect his thoughts while Abigail dismounted the horse she'd ridden and checked on the other who had been trailing on a lead tied to the horn of her saddle.

"How have you fared, my dear Barnabas? Have you enjoyed your exercise this morning?" She kept one cautious eye on Thomas as she knelt to examine the bandaging she'd wrapped around the stallion's previously-fractured foreleg. "This has held up well," she continued to speak to the Percheron. "I don't want you becoming dependent upon it, but the support was better than having you become too fatigued so far from home." She beamed as he nuzzled her shoulder, nickering softly.

Thomas watched in awe. The woman before him was capable of the impossible. If she could tame the beast that two months prior had thrown and nearly trampled the best horseman in their fledgling Settlement, then he could certainly swallow his pride and speak his heart. He cleared his throat and mustered his courage. "Abigail."

Abigail blushed as she granted the human her attention. "I was doing it again, wasn't I?"

"You were only beginning to." Thomas chuckled. "I brought you out here so there would be *fewer* distractions, you do realize...?"

Chagrined, Abigail tethered Barnabas a cautious distance from the other horses while Thomas tethered them and loosened their cinches, having taken them while she was preoccupied. She lingered with Barnabas, seeing to it that he was settled and calm before turning away from the animal. Returning to where Thomas waited on the lake shore, Abigail seated herself on a large rock and waited for him to speak.

"I..." Thomas got no further before stopping to clear his throat. He began again. "I'm reminded, by these falls, of an ancient ancestral legend that Andrew shared with me. I'm not by any means a storyteller, so I'm certain I won't do the tale justice, despite my effort."

Abigail bid him to continue.

The words issued forth in a torrent, proving the smith's dearth of both narrative finesse and mental imperturbation. "As the legend goes, the daughter of a native tribal chief was in love with a man of whom her father did not approve. The chief prevented the marriage by having the young man flung over such a waterfall to his death, and the princess chose to send herself likewise rather than live without her beloved. The falls were named for her after that act." With mild surprise he noted the fluctuated movements of his hands mimicking his narration, a behavior that was in turns both a deliberate activity and a nervous proclivity in his friend Caeleigh.

Thomas forced himself to slow his words and quit pacing as he had been, and stand before the woman who waited for the explanation he'd promised to give. "There have been days in my life – in my history – when I have longed for a waterfall to fling myself over, in the grief I have known. Abigail, despite your protests, I know there stands a record of apologies I owe you. I have been a cold, bitter, and angry man... I have been living out of a deadness in my heart that has ruled me for nearly twenty years." With this final pronouncement, Thomas' shoulders involuntarily sagged, broken at last by the weight of their decades-long burden come to bear upon the innocent woman before him.

He raised his hand as Abigail stood, silencing her before she could begin to speak. "Do not forgive so quickly – I am not so deserving."

"Not one of us deserves the forgiveness Kadosh has extended to us, Thomas," Abigail contended. She wrapped both of her hands around his as it was still raised, the boldest she'd dared to be with him in the full length of their acquaintance. "That's the very definition of His grace. As freely as I have received both forgiveness and grace, freely I extend them both to you – regardless of what you may say of your deserving or undeserving."

Thomas observed the woman before him, seeing her as though for the first time, through new eyes. After a moment's silence, he spoke the first words he could assemble. "It's when you say such things that I find myself wishing to excise the sorrow that has too long been my companion and leave the past behind. Abigail, despite my original dislike of you, you have been good for me – a valuable friend and truly an instrument in the healing process I hadn't realized was occurring." He wrapped his free hand around both of hers, his grip tight with disquietude. "More than that, I recognize you as the one my soul was created to love. Forgive me if I seem somewhat surprised at that; to be utterly forthright, I'd grown certain I would never speak those words to any woman. I thought it a privilege long lost to me. But now that it is not, I mean to court you until our hearts are in one accord. ...Perhaps along the way we may become more of like mind, as well." He winked.

Chapter 34

Early May 2149

"It's a lovely day, Caeleigh. How can you be content to stay indoors?" Andrew called in greeting as he crossed the millinery threshold.

Across the room, Caeleigh kept her head bowed and turned away. "I propped the door open. I have work to do."

He stepped closer, persisting, "It's midday. You need to eat something. I thought you might enjoy a picnic."

Caeleigh shied away from him, almost fearful as she insisted, "I can't." She stepped backward, stumbling slightly.

Andrew caught her elbow. "What is it?"

Slowly Caeleigh raised her head and turned to face him directly, revealing the curvature of a swollen bruise on the right side of her face, around her eye.

At the sight of it, Andrew assumed the worst, recalling the similar injury he had received as a youth in the Saint Joseph Settlement. "Who struck you?" he demanded. "Who would *dare* strike a woman?!" he roared with murderous anger as he headed for the door.

"No, Andrew, please!" Caeleigh stopped him. "No one struck me. I fell."

"You fell?" he repeated, his rage beginning to dissolve. "Truly?"

"No one has been here all day. I have been alone, until you arrived. Will you please close the door before you draw attention?"

Andrew did as she requested and returned promptly to her side. Guiding her to the nearest chair, he urged Caeleigh to sit. "Allow me to see to that."

"I was about to take care of it myself," Caeleigh indicated the cotton gauze and bottle of antiseptic on a nearby counter.

"And now I'm here to do it for you. Sooner or later you *will* need to become accustomed to the idea of having someone to take care of you," Andrew smiled gently. "Are you in any pain?"

"My head aches," Caeleigh reported.

"I shouldn't wonder," Andrew murmured, as he gently cleaned the narrow cut that slashed across Caeleigh's brow and angled toward her temple. "What happened?"

"I was standing on a stool" – Caeleigh gestured toward a tipped-over four-legged stool a few feet away – "putting bolts of fabric on the high shelf. When I turned to get another from the table, I lost my equilibrium and fell."

"And struck your head on the edge of the table," Andrew concluded. Leaning back to examine the injury, he declared it not as severe as it had initially seemed. "No permanent damage. I presume that part of the problem was that you're lightheaded from hunger. Where would you like to take our picnic?"

When it became clear that he refused to take 'no' for an answer, Caeleigh chose to go to the place to which she'd fled from him on more than one occasion. Andrew did not miss the significance of the choice.

As they reached the grove of willows, Caeleigh allowed her tears to fall unabated. "I'm sorry, Andrew. I can't do it. I can't marry you. Not if you're appointed Governor."

"Why not?" Setting the basket down, he took from Caeleigh the blanket she had carried and shook out its folds.

"Because I fell today. The wife of a Governor is constantly under scrutiny. If people were to see me falling all over the place they would assume that I was drunk, and say that I'm addicted to wine." In the shelter of what had become 'their' spot, she stood wringing her hands. "It would disqualify me from leadership, and, by extension if I were your wife, disqualify you as well."

He paused. "Beloved, you fell once. What are you talking about?"

"I'm not well, Andrew. I don't know what's wrong, but I am so dizzy all the time that if I so much as turn my head too quickly it overwhelms me. I can barely cross a room without trouble, anymore."

He put down the blanket and offered her the handkerchief from his pocket. "We'll take you to a doctor in another Settlement if you're embarrassed to be seen here."

"I've been to doctors in *five* other Settlements, Andrew. None of them know what's wrong or what's causing it. And there's no cure for what cannot be named." Caeleigh paced, twisting the handkerchief already soaked with her tears.

Andrew remained where he was, watching her. "And so you expect me to turn my back on you? Caeleigh, we're Bonded. Do you think that was a mistake?" In need of a task to occupy his hands, Andrew retrieved the blanket and spread it over the grass. "Kadosh doesn't make mistakes, and He ordained it that you and I should be Bonded and that I should be Governor of the Willow Springs Settlement, with you as my wife. Do you dare call Him short-sighted that He would allow this to break apart what He has brought together?"

"Andrew – "

Caeleigh's soft cry for help turned him quickly to her side. "What can I do?" he asked, reaching for her.

"Hold me tight and stay *absolutely* still," she whispered.

Andrew did as she asked, and breathed a desperate prayer: "Give me the strength to be strong for her as You have set my purpose to be."

Several minutes later, she relaxed. "It's passed now. It always gets worse when I'm upset. I'm sorry."

"Have you prayed asking for healing?" Leading her to the blanket, he lowered her slowly to sit upon it before seating himself opposite her.

"Many times." Caeleigh accepted the bottle of water he offered, reminding herself to take small, slow sips while she continued to feel off-balance.

"And have you believed for it?" Andrew pressed the point gently, undesirous to convey condemnation, but wanting to understand as fully as he was able.

She struggled with the question. "I... I don't know. What do you mean?"

He searched for the words to explain. "When you ask, what are you believing? Do you believe it could happen?"

This she was able to answer easily and quickly. "Of course. Kadosh is the Creator of all good things – He can do whatever He wishes."

Andrew was equally quick to append further inquiry. "Do you believe He wishes to see you well?"

"I suppose so. If He loves me, and I believe He does, it follows that He wouldn't want to see one He loves suffer. In fact, He promised me years ago that He intended to heal me. It used to be worse, and has gotten somewhat better; He promised me that He would complete the good work of healing He had begun in me. I believe that promise is coming – I simply don't know *when*, is all."

"Caeleigh, that isn't enough." Leaning forward, Andrew knelt before her and spoke with soft, pleading urgency. "I accepted your correction when it was offered; please accept mine now. You are so unabashed for the sake of others – Why not for yourself? You *must* believe for your own healing as readily and as deeply as you believed for my forgiveness regarding the incident with Margaret. You believe that Kadosh wills it; you believe that it's possible. But only believing that it '*may* occur someday' deters it. To receive it now, you must believe it now. Otherwise, you're not truly requesting it when you ask."

"But I *do* believe," she protested. "I simply also accept the fact that it may not come immediately and I must be patient as I wait."

"No," he replied firmly. "That's false piety the Liar has spun to keep you too desolate to truly seek. Kadosh is the Holy One, yes, but He is yet also a loving Father, Who wants you to ask for that which He wants to give you. In the asking is your pursuit of Him."

By now her tears had resumed, yet he pressed on. "You believe that He *wants* to heal your illness, and you believe that He *is able* to do so. Do you believe that He *will* do so? Do you see the difference?"

Caeleigh fell on her face before Heaven, weeping violently. Andrew physically ached with the yearning to take her in his arms and comfort her, but he held himself back. This moment was between her and Kadosh. The carpenter did the only thing he could: bowing so low that his forehead rested on clenched folded hands, he prayed, silent tears streaming down his face.

As she pushed herself up into a kneeling position, he felt released to reach for her. Not a moment too soon, for he caught her in the moment that her arms buckled before she was upright. Holding her steady, he adjusted his posture so that she could lean against his shoulder for as long as needed. A few minutes later, Caeleigh sat back, working to compose her emotions, a feat made more difficult when she saw the evidence of Andrew's profuse grief on her behalf.

He cleared his throat and yet choked on his words as he cupped her damp cheek with his hand and instructed her, "It is as He said: All things are possible for one who believes."

"Even this, for me..." she spoke slowly as he withdrew his hand.

"Yes, even this." Andrew assured, repeating her expression, which to him felt awkward.

"Will you join with me in agreement as I ask?" she pleaded.

"Always." He clasped her hands in his own, in their way.

"Kadosh, I *do* believe – help me to overcome my unbelief!" Caeleigh began, her face lifted to the sky. "You have promised that when two or more agree, in Your name, that You will hear and honor what is asked according to Your will. We are two, together according to Your purpose, in agreement seeking You with this request: I ask You to make me whole in health. I believe You for Your promise to me, and ask You to make this the day that you fulfill that promise. Complete that work which You began in me."

For the week that followed, Andrew strove not to worry over Caeleigh. Yet every time she paused, or closed her eyes for a moment longer than he deemed reasonable, he found himself holding his breath and praying furtively.

"Not all healing is instantaneous," she repeatedly reminded him. "A gradual healing is every bit as much a healing and equally full when it's complete."

Frustrated in his powerlessness, Andrew pulled her close to his side and kissed the bruise that had begun to discolor as it healed. Though it had been concealed with translucent mineral powder, he had become incapable of not seeing its garish glare.

That evening as they took seats at a table for the evening meal, they were joined by Stephen and Martha. The physician enquired after the recovery of Andrew's shoulder and thanked Caeleigh for the shirt she'd made in replacement of the one he'd given Andrew the day of the accident. Andrew found himself fighting not to seek Stephen's professional advice concerning Caeleigh's illness.

Martha delivered the carpenter from overstepping the promise he'd made: "Is that all you intend to eat?" she asked Caeleigh, indicating the salad, albeit substantial, the tailor portioned for herself.

"I've missed fresh vegetables all winter. Now that they've begun to become part of meals again, they're my preference." Caeleigh could not conceive that a meal comprised of vegetables could win disapproval.

"You need more than that, though, dear," the soft-spoken nurse replied. "Healthy though they are, they don't provide everything you need. A diet off-balance could cause seeming ailments."

"How do you mean?" Caeleigh was altogether bewildered by the suggestion.

"You cannot neglect to regularly include red meat in your diet," Stephen joined the conversation. "Iron deficiency anemia, over a prolonged period, results in such symptoms as fatigue, dizziness, weakness, cold extremities, or rapid heartbeat."

Andrew took hold of Caeleigh's fingers and canted his head toward her meaningfully, staring her directly in the eye. Stephen and Martha watched as the pair fell into one another, laughing.

Chapter 35

Mid May 2149

Caeleigh knocked on the door to Andrew's workshop before entering, more from habit and courtesy than expectation of a response. She was aware that he had begun construction of Elizabeth's new bakery and would be at that worksite most of his days until it was complete. As a result, she was entirely unprepared to hear Alexander call, "Good morning!" upon her arrival.

"Alexander," she greeted the apprentice with consternation. "Are you not assisting Andrew with the construction?"

"He sent me to retrieve a few things we couldn't carry between us earlier this morning. May I assist you while I'm here?"

She handed him a metal ring two inches in diameter. "I need to borrow a mallet large enough to pound in grommets of this size."

Alexander scanned the pegboard wall and found the required item. Retrieving it for her, he asked, "Will you need anything for beneath the grommet?" At her raised brow, he flushed and added, "Andrew has explained the process to me, so that I'd know how and why you use his tools from time to time."

Caeleigh smiled at the youth. "I see he has imparted to you already his diligence for safeguarding his tools. You're right, though – I will need something, lest I damage my worktable."

"I don't mean to be contradictory, but it's your worktable he means to preserve. He's as proud of your design as his own craftsmanship in that." Alexander stood from the bin of scraps and returned with a small piece of pine, the end of a plank. "If I sand down the rough ends of this for you, will that work?"

She accepted it from him and studied it. "Perfectly. Thank you." She returned the block to Alexander, to be sanded as he had offered.

The young man made quick work of the task, swept up the dust it had created, and handed both the block and the mallet to Caeleigh. She asked if she might compensate for the delay she'd caused him by assisting him with the tools he needed to carry to the worksite.

"I thank you for the offer, but I had best decline," Alexander replied. "Andrew wouldn't hear of it, subjecting you to such labor. He insists you've already contributed more labor to the Planting than should be asked of a woman."

"Then I shall accompany you to apologize and take responsibility for your tardiness. He cannot refuse me that."

At the site of the bakery, she found what was becoming a familiar tell at play. Andrew stood with his left foot braced on a pile of materials, his forearm resting against his thigh.

"Alexander," she spoke quietly to the carpenter's apprentice, "has he complained of pain this morning?"

He followed her glance and understood the inference of the question. He'd been permitted to begin his apprenticeship a month before coming of age due to Andrew's need of him. "No, ma'am, but it's possible he and Peter have been moving heavy items in my absence."

"You're quite strong, aren't you?"

The young man nodded. "I am, and Joseph, as well. I'll be certain that we take on more of the heavy lifting today, to spare his shoulder."

"Thank you, Alexander." She turned and raised her voice to interrupt the men's conversation. "I apologize for having waylaid your apprentice," she called to Andrew as she approached.

He stepped away from the future building's foundation to greet his Beloved, his left hand drooping notably lower than his right as he extended them to her. "Don't fret; Stephen said it would take time," he replied to the worried expression she made no effort to conceal. "Working is therapeutic. It allows me to stretch the muscles that have gone four months without proper use. Did you find what you needed to borrow?"

Caeleigh nodded. "Alexander is much like you in finding innovative solutions for my needs." She showed him the pine block to be placed beneath the grommet. "You made an excellent choice in apprenticing him."

"He chose me. I merely agreed to his request to take him as my apprentice."

Beth intercepted Caeleigh upon her arrival in the meetinghouse for the evening meal that evening, asking, "Have you been unwell?"

"No. In fact, I've felt better the past few weeks than I have in quite some time. Why?" The question confused Caeleigh.

Beth leaned toward her friend with a confidential whisper, her brow creased with worry at the now-conflicting accounts. "You were seen leaving Stephen's offices this afternoon. The report has found its way to Andrew, by the vehicle of genuine concern for your welfare, I'm certain – nonetheless he's been beset with worry since then, Simeon says. My husband sent me to warn you, in fact."

Caeleigh shook her head in contradiction, eyes closed. "I must see to something in the kitchen. Will you give Andrew my firm assurances that the situation is not as he fears? Tell him there has been a misunderstanding that will shortly be resolved."

During the giving of thanks for the meal, Caeleigh stood with the servingwomen at the kitchen door. She'd had to wait longer than she had estimated, and though she'd stitched as quickly as she could, she hadn't been able to finish before Ezra had called the room to attention. Having held the object by its newly-closed seam, now she juggled it from one hand to the other, distributing its contents evenly, while also attempting not to burn her hands.

Andrew nearly erupted from his chair at the sight of her. She noted immediately that his left arm hugged his waist, his fist clutching the hem of his shirt. Caeleigh quickened her pace, lest he shout and draw the attention of those around him to the conversation.

"Where have you been? What's wrong?" The carpenter's anxiety was beyond containment.

Caeleigh closed her eyes and reminded herself that his words were not intended to accuse, no matter how they sounded.

"Sit down; you're causing an unnecessary scene," she replied. Andrew obliged, initially subdued by the effect his tone had borne, then deflating with the abatement of his adrenaline. "Yes, I went to Stephen's office today – to consult with him about how best to care for you." Caeleigh draped the object she'd made over Andrew's left shoulder, tugging it up against the side of his neck and adjusting it to hang evenly in front and back. "He instructed me that heat would be the best course of treatment after a hard day's exertion."

Andrew turned his head to study the heavy muslin bag that lay hot against his aching muscles, touched it with his free hand. Whether out of shock, shame, or a combination of the two, he remained silent.

"It's filled with dried beans," Caeleigh continued. "I heated them in the oven before filling the bag. They'll need to be removed to be reheated, but the stitching is simple enough to be quick." She took the seat to his right.

Andrew bowed his head in disconcertion. "Forgive me. I apologize for my harsh words and tone a moment ago."

"You must learn that my desire to care for you is as great as your desire to care for me. There is no weakness in allowing yourself to be cared for." Caeleigh spoke without turning toward him.

"Look at me, Beloved." Andrew extended his hand in reconciliation.

Caeleigh not only turned, but leaned close toward him. "Marriage is a *partnership,* Andrew. I understand what your intentions are, and perhaps what and where I've come from has caused me to be more independent than what you're accustomed to a woman being," she whispered fiercely. "But I don't want you for my valet. If I had wanted to be coddled and waited-upon by servants, I would have stayed... where I *was,* accumulated wealth, and hired them."

She said no more, realizing that her pique of temper had led her to the brink of publicly betraying her own secrets. To still the trembling in her hands, with which she'd been gesturing animatedly while speaking, she picked up the cotton napkin from her lap and began wringing it nearly to the point of straining the fibers.

"It has not been my intention to imply that you're incapable of doing anything for yourself." The pitch and timbre of Andrew's voice fell with the weight of failed intentions and the graveled texture of one wounded. "Yet I see that I've done so. My heart is grieved that I have injured you in this way." Wrapping his arm around her shoulders, he pulled her closer, kissing her forehead. "You are an extraordinary woman, and I would not have you be anything other than what you are. I need everything Kadosh has made you to be."

Across from them, Thomas dared speak up, though he'd given their conversation as much privacy as possible in such proximity. "The two of you don't communicate love the same way."

His comment roused their curiosity. Caeleigh asked him to explain, as she straightened once more in her seat.

"Serving as a demonstration of affection communicates clearly to you." Thomas nodded to Andrew. "The conversations we've had confirm it, as well as your reaction when Caeleigh brought you this new hot compress. That simple, small act spoke to you, and you heard her love calling in it. You," he turned to Caeleigh, "don't have that same response to receiving acts of service. You aren't ungrateful, but you don't hear more than simple kindness being spoken. It's akin to hearing a language you speak conversantly but not fluently: you receive the words, but not their full meaning."

"What must I do?" Caeleigh asked.

"Nothing at the moment," Andrew insisted. "I must discover the language that will speak to your heart clearly. You must tell me when I've found it."

Chapter 36

Mid May 2149

"I wish to speak with you, unless a pressing matter requires your immediate attention." Andrew briefly took hold of Caeleigh's hand as she rose from the table at the conclusion of the evening meal a week later. "However, I am required to speak first with Simeon on a few matters. Are you able to wait here?"

"I'll help the women serving in the kitchen with clearing the tables," Caeleigh offered.

Andrew smiled his thanks. "I won't be detained for long."

For the following quarter hour that she spent removing tableware and serveware to the kitchen, the tailor fretted over what it could be that Andrew might wish to say to her. His eyes and tone had given her no indication of whether the conversation would be congenial, or less favorable. Her hands shook in rising trepidation, rattling the plates she'd collected to carry to the kitchen.

Caeleigh had been diligent, she believed, in better managing her diet according to Stephen and Martha's instruction. It had taken no more than a few days for her to begin feeling noticeably less feeble or unbalanced, as Caeleigh disciplined herself to ensure inclusion of more iron-providing foods at most meals.

Upon emerging from the kitchen empty-handed after delivering the last of the soiled dishes there, Caeleigh found Andrew standing in patient wait. The dining room now vacant, Caeleigh started toward an empty chair away from the kitchen, lest the reprimand she feared was soon to come might be overheard by the women washing dishes.

"No," Andrew corrected ambiguously. "Come with me." He led her down the hall to the series of smaller rooms, in which – in the former meetinghouse, before it had been destroyed and replaced by the present one – the few women who'd come for the Planting of the Willow Springs Settlement had resided until their homes and the women's lodginghouse had been built. The last of these doors Andrew opened, indicating that Caeleigh was to follow him into what was now a music room, containing a baby grand piano. Caeleigh had been greatly pleased, after her initial arrival in the Settlements, that music was highly valued and allowances made for the purchase of such instruments. The availability of music had softened the blow of having made the irrevocable decision to submit to this society.

"Close the door behind you," Andrew instructed, continuing to speak in indiscernible tones. He had already crossed the room.

"What are we doing here?" Caeleigh asked as he seated himself at the piano.

"Showing you another facet of myself," was the reply he offered without turning to face her.

With that, Andrew had begun to play an old ballad, a bittersweet tune full of yearning. He had been prepared to shock Caeleigh with his largely unknown talent. He had not been prepared, however, to find that she knew the song.

Caeleigh began to sing as she crossed the room to slide onto the bench beside Andrew. It became all he could manage to remember the proper chords to play. He'd searched a significant amount of time to find a song that communicated things he'd wanted to say, then rehearsed it so that he might not undignify the gesture with poor performance. To hear those very words lilting back to him on the voice of his Beloved had not been an eventuality Andrew had anticipated.

Caeleigh stared, nearly mesmerized, at his work-roughened hands moving over the keys. She hadn't noticed him watching her face more fixedly than she ordinarily would have found comfortable.

Truthfully, Caeleigh was cringing inwardly at what she considered the insufficiency of her own performance. For much of her life she had wished for a better singing voice than the one she possessed. To camouflage the lack of polish in her voice was easily done while harmonizing with others, but a solo performance left all flaws to stand bare with no hope for concealment.

Silence thundered in the small room at the song's conclusion, inciting Caeleigh to pinch the tip of her thumb, turning the bed of the nail white. Apprehension of Andrew's disappointment grew, roaring in her ears, until at long last he spoke.

"It would seem that surprising you is the thirteenth of Hercules' labors," the carpenter intoned with a wry smile, his hands yet resting upon the piano keys.

"You are acquainted with ancient mythology," Caeleigh smiled in return. "And music I would not have expected you to know, having lived here the whole of your life. I *do* concede to being amply surprised."

"I sought to find a song that expressed capably what I wished to say," was Andrew's reply. "Music is a language that speaks to your heart."

"And yours as well, I would venture," Caeleigh returned.

He turned to face her. "I've done some study, since Thomas said what he did, last week. There's an old school of thought saying that there are essentially five different means of communicating love to someone. The proponent of the theory asserts that each is as disparate from the next as speaking two different languages, exactly as Thomas described it."

"Does Thomas agree with this theory?"

Andrew nodded. "He's quite familiar with it – his parents believed deeply in it, and put it into practice in their family throughout his childhood and youth. He has seen firsthand its fruit proven."

"I trust Thomas' endorsement. I'm quite aware of the close relationship he had with his father, and how well all of his family care for one another," Caeleigh spoke reverently of their friend, remembering how deeply the man had been affected by his father's passing into eternal reward the year prior. "If he believes in the merit of this, then I shall take him at his word."

"I agree," Andrew smiled. "Now all that remains is to discover which of these veritable languages you and I each speak. Thomas is firm in his assertion that they are not the same."

"Is music one of them?"

"Not directly." Andrew rose from the piano bench. "We ought to leave. They'll want to close the meetinghouse for the evening soon, if not already."

"Nor should we be alone together for too long," Caeleigh added, as she followed him to the door.

Her words perplexed Andrew. "I don't understand your inference," he told her, seeking that she might explain.

"Not here, where we might be heard – please," Caeleigh whispered, sighting the women from the kitchen exiting at the opposite end of the hall toward which she and Andrew were headed.

"Very well," the carpenter acceded patiently. "Will you join me for a stroll among the willows?"

"Yes. Thank you."

The pair departed the meetinghouse and crossed the meadow behind it, Andrew recalling yet again the first time they had done so – Caeleigh fleeing and he in pursuit – the evening she had Bonded with him, neither of them having been prepared for the event to occur at that time. He smiled at the curious pattern that had begun to develop, of, as Caeleigh expressed it, 'coming full circle' in certain matters.

The moment they reached the first of the trees' shadows cast, Andrew took her hands and turned her to face him. "Will you tell me now what you meant by your words?" he queried. "Correct me if I misheard, but you sounded nearly frightened by them."

Caeleigh drew and released a deep breath, her eyes closed.

"Is this a matter from life in the outside world?" Andrew inquired delicately. Such issues had begun to rise from time to time, as his open courtship of Caeleigh had advanced. He'd interpreted it as a matter of fear on her part, and dealt gently with each occurrence. "Tell me," he requested in reply to her timid nod of confirmation.

"In the outside world, when an unwed couple is alone for a ... long enough ... period of time, especially behind a closed door, it is generally presumed that they are engaged in ... *untoward* behavior." The words embarrassed and horrified Caeleigh to speak aloud.

Andrew lifted her chin so that she would meet his eyes. "Such is not the way of life in our world, Beloved. It would occur to no one to level that manner of accusation against us. We are people of honor. Depravity has no place among us. Nor could I presume you capable of such in the days when you *did* live in that culture. I see only the godly woman before me, who valued and chose this life over that other." With his thumb he brushed away the tears that had sprung to her eyes.

"You always know the words that chase away my fears," she thanked him.

Andrew smiled. "Kadosh gives me the words, Caeleigh. Just as He has given me you."

"If music is not one of those heart-languages," Caeleigh abruptly redirected the conversation, "then what are they?"

"Kind words is one of them," Andrew accepted the indirect request. "I spoke as I did, then, to obtain a sense for how you would respond to the words. At times you receive them well, but at others you shy from them."

The tailor watched her fingers as they laced and unlaced repeatedly. "Forgive me," she murmured in contrition.

"You needn't worry, Beloved," Andrew soothed, placing his hand on her shoulder. "There are yet four others that might speak more to your heart. There are time well-spent together, physical gestures of affection, the giving and receiving of gifts, and committing acts of service toward another."

Caeleigh mused the list. "Do you know which of those might be the one that most speaks to *your* heart?" she asked, hoping Andrew's reply might assist in guiding her own discovery.

"I've reduced the list to two possibilities. Perhaps you might make observations to direct me further in choosing between them."

Chapter 37

Late May 2149

"Elizabeth, what fortunate timing – Would you hold the door open for us before you go?"

The sound of Andrew's voice in the middle of the afternoon surprised Caeleigh. Even moreso did the sight of him staggering into the millinery bear-hugging a narrow chest of some kind in order to lift it over the threshold.

Caeleigh stepped forward from her back workroom as Andrew set down his burden. "What is this?"

The carpenter turned to Alexander, who had come in behind him carrying a number of boxes, which the youth handed over. Andrew thanked and dismissed his apprentice before replying, "I've brought you a gift."

She flushed, flustered by the material attention. "You spoil me." She shaded a deeper crimson as she grew aware of the giddy grin betraying how greatly she enjoyed it.

Andrew grinned as he clasped her hands according to their customary greeting. "No, Beloved, I *know* you. I know how your heart responds to me whenever I give you something. Gifts make you feel loved. No, it's nothing to be embarrassed by," he told her gently as she blushed. "As Thomas had said the other week, every one of us has things that speak love to our individual hearts. I've concluded that I feel most loved when you do things to serve me – the way you compensated Stephen for my medical treatment when I injured my shoulder, for example; that act on your part communicated to me that you wanted to meet my needs, out of love. I've realized that your heart responds similarly to the giving of gifts."

"What is this?" Caeleigh could no longer contain her curiosity.

Andrew knelt beside the object, inserting the boxes he had placed on the floor after receiving them from Alexander. They were drawers. "It's something I thought you might be able to use, something to help you in your work." He rose and stood back, inviting Caeleigh to see for herself.

She gasped, raising a hand to cover her mouth. Before her stood a miniature variation of the apothecary's chest he had built for her a few months before. She looked to the larger chest now. "You've already given me one of these ..."

"No, this one is different. This isn't for your wares; it's for your tools." Andrew hefted the new gift and carried it into the back room. "Help me set it in place – here," he instructed, indicating that the cabinet was to stand between the two large tables upon each of which were set the sewing machines. "Now bring over a chair," he told her once the new furnishing was situated.

Once she had seated herself before the cabinet, Andrew pulled out one of the tiny drawers and handed it to her. Long and narrow, it was subdivided into square compartments. "I've seen how you try to organize your things, the spools of thread and those little..."

"Bobbins," Caeleigh supplied. "They're for the first machine."

"Yes. You have them stacked in pairs on the ledges, which can't be ideal. In here, each pair can be kept together and they won't become lost or mixed-up." Andrew took the nearest spool-and-bobbin pairs and set them in the first few segments of the drawer. "This one," he continued, pulling open the single shallow drawer the full width of the chest above the rows of tiny square drawers, "is for your scissors and other tools, and the larger ones on the bottom are for the thread for the other machine." Andrew gestured toward a basket full of cone-shaped spindles of thread much larger than the spools.

Cradling the drawer Andrew had handed to her, Caeleigh fought tears. "It's beautiful. It's perfect. Thank you."

"You're welcome. I'm glad you like it." Andrew took the drawer from Caeleigh's lap and reinserted it in the cabinet, then pulled her to her feet.

"You're missing a button," she informed him, plucking closed the gap in his shirt over the middle of his chest.

"I know. That's why I had to have Alexander carry the bottom drawers separately – the hardware got caught." Andrew extracted the wayward button from his pocket with a smile. "I knew you would want to repair it immediately, so I made certain to save it."

He stepped behind the privacy screen standing in the corner and held out the shirt once he'd removed it. Caeleigh took the damaged garment from him and made quick work of reattaching the button. She returned the shirt to Andrew where he waited, and stepped back as he dressed. A few moments later he emerged to find her already busy putting away her spools and bobbins of thread in their new home.

"It's perfect," she repeated.

"You're beautiful." Andrew had scarcely breathed the words, overcome by awe, as though he feared the sight before him had been woven of finest gossamer, at risk of dissolution by the least misstep or movement.

"What?" The unexpected compliment stopped Caeleigh where she stood.

"You're absolutely radiant right now, Beloved. You feel my love for you and it shows in your countenance." Andrew crossed the room, rather than raise his voice. Arriving before Caeleigh, he slid his hands down her arms to take hold of her hands as he knelt before her.

She remained fixed on the spot, waiting for him to explain the uncharacteristic extreme of his behavior.

Softly, his voice lanced with the grit of emotion, he did so. "Caeleigh, I have received as I have asked. I have Bonded with you a second time. I am overwhelmed by the affection in my heart for you, my Beloved. Like the first, this chest also is a Bonding and courtship gift."

This time Caeleigh surrendered to the tears that burned her eyes. "When did it happen?"

"Last Sabbath. When you sat with me at the piano."

She recalled the evening. After the evening meal had been finished and cleared, and nearly everyone had left the meetinghouse, Andrew had taken her to the music room with the intention of surprising her, only to have the situation turned upon his plans when Caeleigh sang with his accompaniment.

"You were so lost in the song," Andrew stood as he broke into her reverie, still holding both of her hands. "It was beautiful to behold, watching you sing for the joy of music, and hearing your voice alone. I've heard you sing in worship, and you harmonize wonderfully. But this was a wholly other experience." As Caeleigh dipped her head, blushing profusely, he gently took hold of her chin, lifting her face toward his and caressing her lips with his thumb. "I had set out to shock you, and instead you shocked me... not terribly unlike how you did the night you first Bonded with me."

"So you *did* react in repulsion when I touched your arm!" she exclaimed, striving unsuccessfully to feel indignant. "I *knew* something had to be remiss when you hesitated before telling that tale about my fingers being cold and giving you a chill."

Andrew laughed as she pulled her hand from his grasp and swatted at his arm. "Calm yourself, Beloved. Yes, I did feel a shock then, too, but I wasn't certain at first how well you would take to the accusation of having Bonded with a man you were convinced hadn't Bonded with you. And your fingers *were* cold and *did* give me a chill. Now," he changed the subject, "are you ready yet to tell me why you were so fascinated with my hands?" Though he had asked her that night, she hadn't had an answer for him.

Caeleigh lifted his left hand in both of her own as she mulled over her reply. She trailed her fingertips down the back of his hand and along the length of his fingers as she spoke: "These hands are used for hard labor – breaking horses, laying floors, building things..." Turning over his hand, she studied its many callouses as she continued. "In some ways, they are the hands of an artist: the gifts you've crafted for me are truly lovely. But I never imagined that these hands could or would ever bring forth such beautiful music." Finally she looked up from his hand and into his eyes. "It was so unexpected – I was entirely captivated."

"As am I, with you," Andrew murmured.

"Is that why you didn't sing?" Caeleigh asked as she released her Beloved's hand and reached for the basket of thread spindles.

Andrew seated himself in the chair set before the sewing machine and watched her kneel to transfer the contents of the basket into the lower drawers of the cabinet. "No. I'm a terrible singer."

"You can't be that bad."

The carpenter smiled indulgently at his Beloved as he permitted himself a brief self-derisive chuckle. "I can follow along well enough when others are singing, but I don't sound that wonderful by myself. That's why no one would ever believe that I could have any talent as a musician."

"You mean no one knows? You've told no one that you're gifted with an art beyond your trade?" Caeleigh finished her task and slid the drawer closed.

Andrew shook his head in reply. "You're the first. Once I Bonded with you – the first time – I reserved it as something special to share with you, to surprise you. Actually, I meant to do it sooner, but then the incident with Powderkeg incapacitated my arm for more than a month."

The mention of Andrew's injury reminded Caeleigh of an observation she had been intending to make. "You're still in pain, aren't you? Answer truthfully."

"Some, yes. I try to ignore it. I didn't realize I was giving any indication."

"You've massaged your shoulder no fewer than three times since you arrived, and even now you're favoring that arm again," Caeleigh pointed to the way Andrew held his left arm across his lap. "Have you seen Stephen about it?"

Andrew rolled his shoulder stiffly, unwilling to reach for it after having had attention drawn to the number of times he had unconsciously done so. "I have. He says the pain will subside once I've reconditioned the muscles more; they're still rather tight from weeks of stillness and limited use."

Chapter 38

June 2149

"It's *my* turn, now, to tell *you* a story." Andrew grinned in that cheshire manner that Caeleigh had come to associate with his teasing of her efforts to demonstrate her own capability in an area in which her Beloved was skilled.

"Is that why you've brought me out here?" Caeleigh enquired in reply, taking in the wilderness of the seldom-if-ever-traveled trail that led away from the Willow Springs Settlement in a southwesterly direction. The trail had been so long neglected that it could scarcely be found, for the severity of overgrowth it suffered. Had Andrew not been leading, Caeleigh had little doubt she'd have been lost within minutes.

"Partly so," Andrew admitted, as their horses ambled on at a leisurely pace. "I admit that I don't have your gift for creating vivid scenes with words – so I wanted to show you what I would have done a poor job attempting to describe."

Caeleigh smiled at the ironically eloquent apology for lack of eloquence. "Fair enough, though I hope you'll not altogether abandon the endeavor."

Drawing in a deep breath and adjusting his grip on Elam's reins, Andrew began his tale. "Some years ago, on a day much like today, a young man was riding, alone, on a trail much like this. It wasn't in fact a trail, yet, that day, but would become one in the weeks and months to follow. That day, it was only the path laid before him by Kadosh – and as he prayed regarding his future, Kadosh was setting, at different points along that path, many of the pieces of his future for which the young man was praying, though he knew it not in the moment."

"You've rehearsed this, haven't you?" The effort required to filter her bemusement into a tone nearer to admiration surprised Caeleigh with its diminutiveness. Having been the discomfited object of Peter's jesting on a number of occasions, she daren't extend the same treatment she had no care to receive. "While storytelling may not be your first gift, you're better at it than you suppose of yourself," she offered in heartfelt probity. "I could easily see small boys and youths gathered in your workshop listening to you tell stories as you work."

Andrew acknowledged her praise but deflected, "That might be, some day, but *this* would not be the story I would tell. This tale can only be for you."

"Why is that?" Caeleigh was bewildered at the suggestion of a tale for an audience of one.

"The reason the young man was out in such a wilderness is not something that would be explained, in any degree of detail, to anyone," Andrew shook his head as he clarified. "Given what our future holds, however, it is something that you and I may see someday in the role that will be mine to fill – and yours at my side – so I don't see much harm in explaining it to you. When the time comes to begin preparing to Plant a new Settlement, the Governor of the Settlement sending out the Planting assembles the three men whom he has chosen as candidates to be Governor of the new Settlement, and sends them out in three different directions to scout for a place for that Settlement to be located. The principal instruction given is to be at least an hour's hard ride or two hours' easy ride away. The second is that the location be isolated enough to have ample space for expansion as the Settlement grows over the years."

"I never knew that."

"No one does, outside the men involved. I only know because I was sent, myself, once. I am only able to tell you because someday, I trust, the Willow Springs Settlement will have grown and prospered enough to send out a Planting of a new Settlement, and you'll be at my side when the three candidates are chosen and sent, so you will have knowledge of it at that time. Call it marital privilege, if you like," Andrew offered with a playful wink. "Now if you'll allow me to return to my story…"

Caeleigh noted the accumulating sum of presumptions Andrew had made, until reminding herself that she no longer resided in the outside world. "Please do."

"The young man had been out on a scouting ride of the type I described a moment ago. He had ridden out until the plain ended in a cliff that overlooked a beautiful valley, embraced by the surrounding hills. The moment he looked upon that valley, he felt assured that he had found the place Kadosh was promising to him. He had arrived at it by a more northern route, quite direct, and decided that he desired to explore the surrounding country on his return trip, so he turned his horse to the south. Despite not having entered the valley, the young man had felt a confirmation in his spirit that Kadosh would have the Governor who had sent him choose the land he had found as the location for the new Settlement, and that he would be the one chosen as its Governor. His certainty on both of these points was unshakable. He had but one hindrance between himself and his future – he was unmarried, and neither had he Bonded.

"This was his other reason for the detoured return path. It afforded him time to pray about this newfound predicament. 'Kadosh,' he spoke into the surrounding silence, 'You know I have no ambitions to seek out a position of leadership for my own gain, but if it is what You will for me, then I am honored by it and will seek to pursue Your will. If it is Your will for me to become Governor of this new Settlement, I need for You to make me eligible according to the rules of the Settlements.' No sooner had he uttered the words and the stillness of the late morning was shattered by a cry of distress. He turned his horse toward the direction from which it had come and raced as fast as he dared for what felt like much longer a passage of time than it truly was."

Andrew paused and dared a surreptitious glance at Caeleigh. He knew that he was reaching a point where the details would become unmistakably personal, and he might slip. Promising himself that if that happened, he would simply massage into the story whatever comment he accidentally made, Andrew halted Elam and dismounted. Walking around to hold Noya's bridle while Caeleigh slid to the ground, he took the long moment to gather his thoughts while he loosened the cinches of both animals.

Upon completing this task, Andrew continued his tale. "When the young man reached a grove much like this one, he dismounted, knowing that it would injure his horse to charge through the growth, as well as make such a noise as would alert whatever or whomever might be the source of danger for the person who had screamed. Though he scarcely spent more than the space of a heartbeat taking in his surroundings, that grove was forever burned into the young man's memory by the events that followed. He would be able to find it unmistakably no matter from which point of the compass he approached it, for years to come. Cautiously he crept through the brush as quietly as possible, following the voice he had heard."

Taking Caeleigh by the hand, slowly he led her in retracing the steps he had taken the day that had changed his life. Through all of his tale she had remained silent, for which he was both grateful and uncertain. She gave no indication of suspecting whose story he was actually telling her.

"Just before the trees broke, Kadosh stopped him from progressing further." Likewise Andrew stopped their progress, but shorter of the mark so that she would not be able to see past the tree line.

"Crouching beneath the cover of the foliage, the young man watched a young woman in the clearing beyond pacing and gesturing with her arms, crying out to Kadosh. Some of the words she spoke sounded like the Psalms of David son of Jesse, but they weren't any of the Psalms that the young man had ever read – not exactly. She spoke of unmet heart's longings and deep despair. When she flung her hands out at her sides and turned her face to the heavens and shouted, 'This is not the life I desire!' it broke his heart such that he had to remove a glove from one of his hands and bite down upon the leather to keep from crying out."

Trembling, with her arms wrapped across her midsection, Caeleigh stepped around Andrew and beyond the tree line into the clearing without a word. He followed her as she found a rough-stacked stone bench upon which to sit. He sat beside her and searched her eyes for some indication of how she had accepted the revelation. Stolid serenity, for Caeleigh, was often a mask for anxiety, Andrew knew.

He reached for her hands, deceptively folded in her lap. Her fingers trembled within his light grip as he spoke his tender confession. "Yes, Beloved – I haven't told you *a* story, I've told you *my* story. I was that young man. The valley 'he' found is the one where the Willow Springs Settlement, our home, now stands… And this is the place where I first Bonded with you, four years ago today."

"This place," Caeleigh finally spoke, "was my secret. No one knew of it. I called it my vesper grove. It's nearly an hour's walk from the Blue Creek Settlement, and from anyone or anything else, far enough away that I could pray and offer up laments without fear of being witnessed. You're telling me that you did witness me… ?"

"Your privacy that day was and still is intact," Andrew assured, quelling her fear before it had opportunity to rise further. "I didn't know you and had never seen you before that day – recall that the population of the Blue Creek Settlement was already more than substantial by then. It wasn't possible to know everyone. I was out riding … I had been assigned by Governor Caleb to ride out scouting for a location for a new Settlement Planting, as I explained before. I'd ridden out early in the morning, and was on my way back when I heard a terrible scream – I thought someone was in trouble. I turned aside from the trail and raced to where the sound seemed to have come from."

"I never knew anyone else was there." Caeleigh spoke with the numb detachment of one struggling to process unanticipated news.

"Kadosh stopped me before I was near enough to be seen, and commanded me not to interfere with your …"

"Lament," she supplied. "I had gone out to the vesper grove to offer a lament."

"I see." Andrew sat in recollection for several moments. "So much of what I heard you say that day makes more sense, now."

"You heard me?" Caeleigh's eyes widened in distress.

"Your voice rather carries out in the wilderness when you're wailing as you were that day." Gently he pulled her hands away from her face as she hid. "Don't hide from me, Caeleigh. You have no reason to feel shame."

"You witnessed me at my most vulnerable and my worst, and you tell me I have no reason to feel shame?" No longer in torment but in desperation for reassurance, Caeleigh's expression remained wide-eyed as she questioned him.

"If you look at it from a certain perspective, my being present was a fairly immediate answer to your prayer that day," he replied gingerly. "No sooner had you asked Kadosh if there was a man who would love you than I had crept near enough to catch sight of you in the clearing. The moment I saw your face, my heart was stirred in Bonding. In the next moment, Kadosh instructed me not to go near you, that I must wait… Although I must confess to you that you were as much an answer to *my* prayer as I was to yours. As I told you earlier as part of the story, the scouting ride I'd been sent on is only assigned to those who are chosen as candidates for Governor. I knew I was chosen for something I could never become unless I were to have Bonded and married, and I had yet to Bond. Shortly before I heard your scream, I had prayed that if Kadosh willed for me to be appointed Governor, He was going to have to rectify the fact that I was entirely ineligible for it."

Feeling a subtle nudge of courage, Andrew rose to his feet, taking Caeleigh by the hands and pulling her to stand with him. "Caeleigh, it was four years ago today in this place as I watched you offer your heart in excruciating honesty to Kadosh that my life was changed forever, when I Bonded with you. Kadosh has entrusted to me the greatest honor and privilege that could ever be bestowed upon a man, in the charge of loving you. Will you change my life again in this place today? Will you bring me even greater honor and joy by consenting to become my wife?"

Andrew hadn't meant to propose quite so quickly, but now that the words were spoken they could not be recalled. Truthfully, neither did he desire to retract them. Instead, he reached into the pocket of his coat and produced the box

Thomas had gone and retrieved from the Cypress Ridge Settlement for him, so that Andrew could avoid having a conspicuous absence that might have betrayed his plans.

Before he could open the box, Caeleigh's response was arriving through their connected hands, just as it had the first time. Her second Bonding had occurred as Kadosh had promised.

She shivered, chuckling as she withdrew her fingers from his grasp. "Does that happen with *everyone's* Bonding, or is it unique to us?" she asked.

"I honestly don't know," Andrew laughed with her, pulling her tight in a brief embrace. He then released her and stepped back to open the jewelry box. "However, I would like you to answer me before I give you this." He held out toward her the betrothal ring he had spent hours designing and selecting stones for with the jeweler of the Cypress Ridge Settlement, the last time he had been there. It had been the real reason he'd missed Caeleigh's birthday, and now that lost time was counted more than worth it, as he watched delight brighten her features at this significant gift.

Caeleigh blinked away joyous tears. "Of course I will. Whom else could I find who would treasure my heart the way you do?"

"No other man on earth, since I am the one Kadosh created specifically to fill that role," Andrew replied as he slipped the ring on Caeleigh's finger, attempting to quote as accurately as he could recall the words she had used in her lament that day four years before.

Chapter 39

June 2149

The following day, Governor Caleb stood before the gathered assembly. Now that the lingering winter had fully ended and the thaw of spring had given way to the bloom and warmth that heralded summer, the Willow Springs Settlement was truly beginning to *become*. The families who had waited behind in the Blue Creek Settlement while the hardier initial work was done over the previous seasons had now joined those who had preceded them to complete that work.

Paternal pride was evident in Caleb's eyes as he stepped forward to speak. "Friends!" he called out for all to hear, "Your awaited day has come. A year and a half ago, when I announced that I would be sending out a Planting for a new Settlement, *this* Settlement, I named more than the customary three men to be sent. I did so for a number of reasons, one of which is that all of their gifts and skills were needed to prepare this piece of land and establish the Settlement for you. However, I have not broken with the rules of the Settlements concerning the appointed candidates for your Governor. At this time I will present to you those men, so that you may make your choice. Despite my express directive that their shared leadership until this point be completely anonymous, all of them have led commendably and with great integrity through the challenges your young Settlement has faced. They are Simeon, Andrew, and Ezra."

As their names were called, each man rose to stand behind Caleb, each with his wife – and in Andrew's case, Caeleigh, though she was not yet his wife – at his right hand. Their smiles reflected the solemn weight of the moment; the responsibility, which they had heretofore shared, was about to be placed solely upon the shoulders of one of them. Already they had met privately and agreed that whomever was chosen, the other two would willingly serve as Elders, as would those other men who had been sent in the Planting but not appointed.

The stillness was broken by a low-uttered protest from the back of the room: "Andrew cannot be eligible to be Governor. He is not married." There wasn't a soul present who hadn't heard the damning proclamation.

Andrew clenched his hands, clasped behind his back, and kept his facial expression dignified and neutral. Reaction to the baiting would not serve him well. Surveying the crowd, recognition served to eliminate surprise when he saw who had spoken; it was Michelle, the woman he'd chastised in Caeleigh's defense after the fire that had claimed their first meetinghouse. He exchanged a glance with Simeon, who had also spoken in correction to her that day. Without a word, Simeon cautioned Andrew to hold his peace – neither of them, nor Ezra, were in competition for the position for which they had been potentially named. They had been working together for more than a year and would sooner protect one another than allow trouble to befall any one of them.

Caleb looked over his shoulder at Andrew. "I'll bear the fault for that," he apologized to the younger man. Caleb turned back to the room and raised his voice once more. "It was my intention to make the announcement, as I traditionally do, at this evening's meal. It is my great joy to inform you all that Andrew's Beloved has Bonded with him and they were betrothed yesterday afternoon. The fulfillment of their marriage is forthcoming in due time."

He didn't know how it caught his eye, but Andrew noted the flexing tremor of Caeleigh's fingers seeking something to hold onto; she was having another episode of dizziness, likely brought on by anxiety caused by the dissenting remarks that could be heard spreading amidst the crowd. Wrapping his arm about her, Andrew tucked Caeleigh close to his side and kissed the top of her head. "Lean into me – I'll hold you steady," he whispered, his face yet close enough that her hair concealed the movement of his lips.

Caeleigh hummed a single note of assent and thanks, grateful for the reputation Andrew had developed, in recent months, of being overtly affectionate with her.

The hushed slander campaign persisted, Andrew sensed. Immediately he prayed against the anger that welled up in his heart. Surely the people knew him well enough to know that he would not use a woman to falsely legitimize his eligibility for the Governorship of the Settlement, especially not such a woman as Caeleigh. Barring that, surely they would never believe that a woman – especially such a one as she – would *volunteer* to be so dishonestly used. Reaching across himself with his left hand he took hold of hers and lifted it high enough to show off the betrothal ring he had so recently placed there. He tilted it back and forth with his thumb to catch the sunlight, as if sending coded light-signals with a mirror. Andrew wanted it assuredly known that in terms of commitment he truly was as good as married. He had waited too many years not to be.

Am I travailing for my Beloved again, Kadosh? he asked as he took into consideration his highly unexpected last thought.

She hears the words as well as you do, My son, but that does not mean that what she hears being said matches what you hear being said. It simply was a gentle reminder of that fact.

Andrew raised Caeleigh's hand to his lips and kissed it. It wouldn't be appropriate for him to speak to her at the present moment, and might in fact exacerbate their slanderous accusers. He could, however, exploit himself as a man newly betrothed and hope that Caeleigh received his unspoken affections as clearly as he intended them. Her tightened grip encouraged Andrew that she understood.

Andrew watched as Philip approached the antagonist and attempted gently to quiet her. At the same time Andrew and Simeon had been having their wordless communication, Ezra had in the same manner dispatched Philip to prevent further damage.

"Kadosh is the one who instructs me whom to name," Caleb reminded those who seemed to have begun to be influenced by Michelle's outburst and continued mutterings. If anyone had already intended to choose Ezra or Simeon, that would be acceptable; turning those who would have chosen Andrew against him out of one's personal resentment, however, was not. "It is my place to obey Him, not to question Him. He would not call a man to a duty that He did not mean to qualify him for. I ask you all to consider each of these men not in terms of their circumstances, but in terms of their character. Of greater importance than that, I ask you to seek the will of Kadosh – ask Him whom He desires to set as your Governor."

Ezra, Simeon, and Andrew exchanged glances, confirming their agreement, after which Ezra stepped forward and placed a hand on Caleb's shoulder. "We will leave the room until the matter is concluded," he offered.

Caleb agreed. He was as aware of the history of the situation as they, having received a report shortly after the fire. It was, in fact, one of the reasons he had visited the Willow Springs Settlement two months thereafter; the three had requested his guidance and counsel on their handling of the matter.

The three couples retreated to the music room, simply because it was the one of the smaller rooms in the meetinghouse. The moment the door closed behind them, a collectively held breath was released in sighs of frustration.

"How could anyone dare speak so disrespectfully of Andrew?" Sophia demanded.

Ezra put an arm around his wife's shoulders. "Peace, Beloved," he soothed.

"Michelle bears a bitterness against him for having given her a public chastisement," Beth replied.

"And against me, as well," Caeleigh added, still leaning against Andrew for support, "for the same reason."

After ushering his Beloved to a chair, Andrew finally spoke for the first time since the altercation had begun. "We must pray for her ... for all of them." Despite his best efforts, he was unable to prevent a tone of defeat from edging his voice.

Simeon took note of it and stopped him from continuing such a stream of thought, placing a hand on the carpenter's shoulder. "Your actions that day were not in the wrong, Andrew. I supported you then and I support you now. Do not allow someone else's foothold to take root in your soul. However, you are right that we should pray. One person's bias should not sway an entire community. That's why there are three of us here, to begin with."

They remained in sequestration until the evening meal, praying for each member of the Settlement by name to be filled with peace, breaking the influence of divisive spirits, and asking Kadosh to guide their hearts to His choice for their Governor.

"Above all things, we seek that Your will be done," Andrew concluded his turn of petitioning. His heart had found comfort with the passage of the time they had spent before the throne of heaven; he had little doubt that his companions beside him had been silently interceding for him as he interceded for their people.

The atmosphere in the dining room was positive. Whomever had been chosen, it appeared nearly everyone was pleased, or at least satisfied, with the choice. Neither Andrew, nor Ezra, nor Simeon was eager to receive the news immediately; rather they kept to the company of one another and their women. Continuing to behave in concert as had become their habit, they sought a report from Philip on the situation in which he'd engaged.

Other than Philip, whose presence they had requested, the only person to approach them was Thomas, whose sole purpose in so doing was to congratulate Andrew and Caeleigh on their betrothal. They had already shared the news with those closest to them the prior evening, privately; Thomas would have been one of those to be informed, but for his absence to visit his family in the Blue Creek Settlement for the day.

After every other stage of their relationship had been so contrary to convention, albeit not deliberately, they had decided to continue it so, and not make the public announcement immediately. Caeleigh had questioned that the timing would have appeared suspect, announcing their betrothal less than a day before Andrew was disclosed to have been one of the men named as a candidate for Governor. He had agreed, not wanting any suspicions cast to detract from their joy. Now, Andrew sensed, Caeleigh was doubting, if not altogether regretting, the decision.

Leaning in closer, he told her gently, "Do not fear that you worsened my circumstances today by the choice we made – *together* – not to speak last evening." Taking her left hand, Andrew raised it to bring the betrothal ring into Caeleigh's line of sight, kissing her fingers as he continued, "If you have done anything for my circumstances, it was to improve them by enabling me to not have to stand alone before the people today." At last he was able to coax a smile to her lips.

Caleb, after observing this exchange, made the determination he had been delaying for the young couple's sake. All three elect-candidates, as well as Philip and Thomas, stood out of respect for his authority as he approached, until he waved them to be seated once more and joined them.

Until the authority of the Governorship of the Willow Springs Settlement was bestowed upon one of them, they all would defer to his, he knew. Such were all three of these men; at moments Caleb wished he had been instructed to Plant three Settlements, to give one to each of them. Their people would be well-served by any one of the three as a leader.

"Have you come to hear the uncommon story?" Andrew asked, glancing briefly to his newly betrothed for her consent, reminding Caleb of his fondness for the ways Kadosh had worked in the young man's life.

"I would greatly enjoy it, yes, but I have something to ask of you that you may find personally difficult." Caleb paused a moment to look from Andrew to Caeleigh and back. "In light of today's events, and perhaps future challenges that may present themselves, I believe it would be best for you to tell not only me, but everyone here gathered."

Caleb watched Andrew close his eyes in prayer and clasp hands with Caeleigh in a characteristic manner exclusively theirs, as with very few words – and none of them direct – they consulted on what was to be said. Having decided, Andrew stood, caressed her cheek affectionately, and went to the head of the room.

"My friends," Andrew called out, in a voice stronger than he felt as he prayed for the proper words. "It has been placed upon my heart to share with you the story of how I have come not to meet many of your expectations – as well as my own, if I am to be entirely truthful. A few of you already know this" – he locked eyes momentarily with Peter – "but my

Bonding was not as recent as it was announced. I chose to make my proposal of marriage yesterday, specifically, because it was four years to the day from the morning I had Bonded with Caeleigh." He allowed a moment for that news to be received.

"For those of you who have known one or both of us that long," the carpenter grinned, "yes, that outspans our acquaintance." A few chuckles rose throughout the room, bolstering Andrew's courage. "I had taken my horse out for a ride and to spend time in prayer for my future, when I happened upon a young woman pouring out her heart before Kadosh with a level of honesty that humbles me to this day. She never was aware of my presence; Kadosh forbade me to move or speak toward her, and instructed me that I was to wait. In obedience, I waited, I prayed, and on occasion I travailed for the stranger for whom love had been planted in my heart, until Kadosh brought our paths together two years later."Andrew looked to Peter and Elizabeth; the latter smiled, while her husband remained begrudging to forgive. "Even then it was not yet time; I was permitted to be no more than a friend and brother to the one I loved more dearly than my own life. Only in the past half-year out of four have I been *permitted* to make my affections known." Andrew felt a need to emphasize the word in demonstration of a reporting of events beyond his command, rather than a mere telling of a sentimental tale. Thus far, Andrew feared, he had won favor only with a number of women. It was a nod from Thomas that encouraged him to press on.

"Just as our Father Abraham of old was asked to sacrifice his only and late-begotten son Isaac, daily have I had to lay my most deeply longed-for promise upon the altar of obedience."At last, Peter's attention had been won. "My obedience has not been blind; my eyes have been wide open and my choices very much an act of will. The wait was long and at times much more than difficult, but were Kadosh to ask it of me again, I would willingly agree without a moment's hesitation – for His purposes, no matter how little we may comprehend them, are perfect. As I speak these words, I see that it is right that I am telling you these things now, after you have made your choice. You have needed to hear me tell you this, not to plead my case before you as a candidate for the Governor of your Settlement, but to plead *your* case in matters of obedience."

Again Andrew paused, allowing his words their time to resonate. Peter, upon concluding not long after the announcement of Andrew's Bonding that Andrew had confided more in another than himself, had maintained a subtle derision at having been spurned. The stonemason had been the last to award Andrew his heedfulness. The carpenter felt now that his brother had forgiven whatever perceived slight had exchanged between them.

"We are about to step into new days and a new beginning. While it is much like what we have left behind in the Blue Creek Settlement, it is still new, and somewhat different, and separate. There will be challenges. This *is*, after all, already our second meetinghouse. But Kadosh is faithful and will watch over and provide for us. We must heed the things He asks of us and obey, no matter how difficult, contrary, or painful they may be. Believe me when I say: it *can* be done, and great is the reward."

The applause that followed Andrew back to the side of the room stunned him. Though he'd been granted the calm and confidence for which he'd prayed while speaking, now that he was returning to his seat, a slight tremor began to settle in throughout his frame, whether from adrenaline or nervous energy, he could not determine. The nodding smiles received from Ezra and Simeon eased some of the tension in his shoulders. Caleb met him a few paces ahead of the table and shook his hand firmly, congratulating him with words that shocked him further.

"Well said, Governor. Well said."

Chapter 40

June 2149

David found Andrew prostrate in the chapel the following morning. "Have you been here all night?"

"I've had many things to pray over. It's taken that long, I suppose." Slowly Andrew uprighted himself. The Governor-elect stretched as though he hadn't moved in countless hours, passing his hands over his face and through his hair, which had been let loose from confinement during the course of the night.

David recalled long sessions of prayer he'd spent in a similar posture, though usually for circumstances of a more dire nature. "You didn't believe you'd be the man chosen?" Though inflected as a question, it was clearly intended as a statement.

Andrew rubbed the long night's vigil from his eyes and joined David on the pew. "Only in the last hours," he admitted. "This valley is the one that *I* found. I've known for four years a sound confidence that Kadosh has meant for me to be the Governor of this Settlement. I scouted the land, helped to dig the wells and set the streets, laid the foundations and raised the buildings. I've covered every corner of this place in prayer and covenanted with Kadosh for our faithfulness to Him. Through all of that I have continually felt assured of the role He intended for me. Until..."

"Until there was a dispute of your fitness for it," David supplied when Andrew showed himself reluctant to complete the thought. "Are the plans Kadosh has made so fragile that they may be uprooted by the will of one mortal rebellion?" He stood, indicating that Andrew ought to follow suit, and the two men began slow progress along the chapel's center aisle.

Andrew's response was a fatigued and chastened, yet genuinely appreciative, smile. "I oughtn't have doubted for a moment that which I have known for years to be truth. I repent of my unbelief, and I am beginning to truly understand why Caeleigh prefers to call you 'Rabbi.' While I am reminded and we have the moment to discuss it," he added as the two men exited the chapel, "I would like you to serve as the primary teacher for the Settlement. I am not officially installed as Governor until after I am married, so I can't ask you officially until then. But will you agree to serve?"

David bowed his head in affirmation with a grateful smile. "I would be honored."

Beth and Simeon met them in the street.

"Are you ready to do what must be done?" Simeon enquired of Andrew.

"My heart is at peace. I am prepared." The ease in Andrew's countenance was genuine. "And Caeleigh?"

"Worried to the end of her wits by your disappearance," Beth chided him, "but also prepared. Sophia and I kept watch in prayer with her late into the night, as well. They both await us at the meetinghouse."

For this, Andrew thanked her earnestly. That Simeon and Ezra's wives were becoming for Caeleigh what the men themselves were for him was invaluable. Andrew had long worried for Caeleigh, and how she would inexorably be affected by the consequences of her association with him.

Caeleigh's hands were extended to him, to be taken in their greeting, by the time he reached her in front of the meetinghouse.

"Forgive me, Beloved, for causing you distress," he apologized, as he removed his left hand from their joined hands and raised it to brush her hair back from her face. "I had need to slip away and ensure that my heart was set aright on more than a few matters."

Caeleigh responded to Andrew's use of her own words from years and situations past with a knowing smile. "I understand. All is now well?"

"Indeed. Your heart is likewise prepared?" Andrew took in the exhaustion that creased his Beloved's features and underlined her eyes, worried that their cause might derive from her fear of confrontation.

Caeleigh nodded resolutely.

"Then let us conclude the matter. I will not abide any festering malevolence to take root in our Settlement." Andrew found a patriarchal spirit of territorial possession rising, as it had begun to do over the course of the night's prayers.

Sophia, who'd stood quietly beside Caeleigh, spoke then. "Ezra has already gone to prepare the meeting. He's waiting at Philip's home and we are to meet him there."

Parting ways with David, the remainder of the company turned toward the vintner's home.

Philip and Ezra greeted them warmly upon their arrival. Seated in self-imposed isolation on a bench not far from the house, Michelle regarded them all with stony silence. Sophia joined Philip and her husband on the porch, while the others approached the one they had summoned there.

Beth sat beside her on the bench, positioned as advocate. Caeleigh took care to seat herself in a chair situated to Michelle's side rather than directly opposite. Andrew positioned another chair to sit beside Caeleigh, while Simeon stood to the side, slightly removed, yet present.

"I want to begin by saying that I forgive you for what you did yesterday." Andrew spoke directly but gently, looking Michelle in the eye as much as she would meet his. "I understand that you were displeased when I contradicted your self-defense and stood in Caeleigh's defense against your accusations, after the fire that destroyed the first meetinghouse. Trust me when I say my reproof of your words against Caeleigh was not personal. It was based upon the testimony of witnesses, including my own; I saw that you were safely out of the meetinghouse before the fire spread to that part of the building."

Caeleigh reached for Andrew's hand, grasping it tightly as she picked up where he had left off. "And *I* forgive you for the accusations and the words you spoke against me. I won't ask for, or expect, an apology. I simply choose to forgive. I'm sorry that you did not receive correction well."

Michelle's dyspathy toward them had not lessened in the least. Beth looked to her husband to intervene. Simeon, however, wanted to give Andrew another chance before stepping in.

"Michelle, the scriptures instruct us to respect and obey those whom Kadosh places in earthly authority over us." Andrew released Caeleigh's hand and leaned forward, resting his elbows on his knees. "I am not officially in the position of authority here yet, but I will be as soon as Caeleigh and I are married. I want your assurance that you will respect and obey me as the Governor selected by majority vote according to the rules of the Settlements. I am not instituting disciplinary action against you, but I wish to make myself plainly understood: I will not allow the Willow Springs Settlement to develop from its first days a legacy of impudence and rebellion, not from any one of its members." He laced his fingers to still his hands while waiting for a response.

When none came, Simeon stepped into the figurative circle and lowered to one knee so that he would not be standing over everyone else. "If you are not prepared to give an answer immediately, Michelle, take a day or two to consider whether you can agree to what has been asked of you. All we ask is that this matter be resolved within a reasonable amount of time, and not drawn out indefinitely."

A short time later, Andrew, Caeleigh, and Simeon retired to the porch, leaving Michelle in Beth's care.

Upon reaching that safe distance, Andrew deflated in the aftermath of the confrontation. "Not a word spoken. She was absolutely unresponsive," he reported to Ezra and Philip, whose wife emerged from the house at that moment to serve the men coffee.

"Do not despair, Governor." Simeon smiled as he employed the title. "If anyone can open a closed heart, it's my Beth. Her gentleness can reach the most obdurate wounded soul."

As the day progressed, Andrew grew increasingly withdrawn. At last Caeleigh could bear it no longer and took him aside. "You are not yourself."

"I feel as though my heart is being rent in two, split between that to which I have been called, and that which is dearest to me. Kadosh never told me I would have to choose between the two; yet now I am being made to feel as though I must, because the timing of it all has been so misaligned." Andrew's despondency was palpable as he verbalized his frustration.

"Do you truly believe none of this would have happened, were we to have already been married?" With a pointed look Caeleigh forced the carpenter to closely consider the question.

Andrew strove to soften his tone toward her. "I am uncertain what to believe, at this point."

"Then do not for one moment believe that the events of your life have happened in any sequence or timing other than that which Kadosh has purposed for you." She spoke firmly yet gently, reminding him of the countless times he'd spoken thus to her. "Who are we, that He should be made to answer to *us* for how He has ordered our days?"

"You've done it again." Andrew stretched out to caress her cheek. "This is why I need you by my side."

"To remind you of the truths you already know?" Caeleigh winked as she teased him, eliciting a brief laugh.

"I've refrained from speaking of this to anyone for fear of seeming to stand in judgment," she continued, subdued. "I speak to you now as who you are to me, not as the Governor-elect, in order to find the courage to speak at all. The night of the fire, Michelle *chose* her fear, as though she preferred it. I observed her closely and watched her make the decision. She considered fear an acceptable and desirable response to the circumstances we were facing that night – when she deemed to incite that response among others, I felt it my responsibility to stop her before she incited a panic. Perhaps the way I went about it may not have been the best approach – "

"Peace now," Andrew stopped Caeleigh, placing a hand over both of hers, between which she'd by this time begun twisting a minute object. "What is this?" he asked, turning one of her hands palm-upward to reveal the item.

"It's for you. I'd intended it to be your birthday gift, but in light of the struggles you've confessed, I would rather give it to you early." She handed over the data drive.

Andrew received it and turned it over, studying it, then looking back to her with a raised eyebrow. The markings on the data drive's case implied that it contained a textile manufacturer's catalog.

"This was the only dispensable data drive I could find. I'd be embarrassed for anyone else to see what this contains, but if you're reading it on your tablet, people may think you're working, reviewing designs for a project, or a work order; I have seen other tradesmen carry their tablets with them outside their workshops. I know that is generally not *your* practice, but perhaps, I thought, you might be willing to make an exception ..." she trailed off, more self-conscious than she'd felt in his presence in longer a time than she could recount.

He smiled, seeming to recall the same past day she had in mind as she stood fidgeting before him. "I am still the man you've always known."

As it had done before, the reminder calmed Caeleigh. "I've written a story for you. This one is more than a mere children's tale; I purposed it solely for you – you gave me the idea with the things you said the day you presented me with the opal necklace you devised from one that had been described in a story you'd heard me tell. I believe Kadosh has set within it a theme that will speak to you against these questions that have raised themselves."

Andrew stared, agape. "Do you *know* how you bless me?"

Chapter 41

Late June 2149

"This is remarkable." Andrew gestured toward the screen of his tablet, upon which was displayed the story Caeleigh had written for him. "You truly are gifted, Beloved. I consider it a mark of your talent that I found the characters' manner of speech unfamiliar."

Caeleigh blushed under his affectionate praise. "That is how they speak in some parts of the outside world," she murmured in timid explanation.

"It differs from the few experiences I recall from my childhood and youth in the Saint Joseph Settlement," he replied, knowing she would remember the story he'd told her of why he'd left there.

"Different peoples in different parts of the world speak differently. In Japan, not only speech, but *everything*, is significantly more formal than on this continent, but not in the same way that it is here in the Settlements. It's part of what differentiates one culture from another."

"I see. Yet there's a casuality in some of their expressions, as well; when ...one of them... says..." Andrew pointed at a passage of text, reticent to attempt to pronounce the character's name.

Caeleigh smiled as she peered over his arm to read the passage he'd indicated. "Yes, *'fess up* is meant as something of an abbreviated manner of expressing 'to confess,' but I presume you could glean that from context."

"I did. Though it's still an odd way to speak. I can't imagine you ever spoke in such a peculiar manner, articulate and well-spoken as you are." The carpenter grinned in bemusement.

The storyteller merely smiled, giving her Beloved pause, before she changed the subject. "Will you tell me which parts of the story you most enjoyed, what resonated most deeply with you?"

"Gladly. Let's wait until after the midday meal, so that we're more apt to have uninterrupted time." With a few taps to the screen, Andrew had hidden the story and replaced it with a list of names. "Look this over and let me know if there's anyone else from the Blue Creek Settlement you wish to invite to our marriage ceremony."

She accepted the tablet from him and perused the list as they walked to the meetinghouse. "Do you ever feel as though we're conducting subterfuge?" she whispered, tilting the tablet screen toward him for emphasis. "First there was the matter of our …first… Bondings; now this…"

"Some things are meant to be held close rather than disclosed widely," he returned.

Caeleigh gathered a handful of her skirts to avoid tripping on the steps of the meetinghouse porch. Upon looking up from watching her feet, she caught Andrew staring at her from the door, where he stood waiting. "What?" she questioned the inscrutable expression that had come over him as she passed through the door he held open.

"There are moments yet when I must consciously remind myself that the long – *very* long – season of waiting for my bride is nearly over."

Caeleigh glanced at her betrothal ring, uncomprehending. "It's scarcely been a y– "

"Four years, Beloved," Andrew interrupted. *"More than,* in fact."

She dipped her head with an apologetic smile. "Forgive me. I was counting the time from my own Bonding, not yours."

Despite their habit of arriving early to meals, they found Simeon and Philip already waiting in the dining room. "A decision has at long last been made, I presume," Andrew greeted them by saying. Both men knew how heavily the conflict with Michelle's rejection of Andrew's authority had weighed upon his mind, and had promised to report the moment there was resolution.

Simeon rose from his seat as the Governor-elect approached. "Michelle returns permanently to the Blue Creek Settlement this afternoon. Beth learned little in the way of detail, but suspects that the root of the matter may have lain in Michelle's motive for joining the Planting."

"This matter will have no bearing on your authority as Governor," Philip was quick to assert. "We've sent our account to Governor Caleb, ahead of any complaint of expellment she may attempt to raise. Ezra is expected to return this evening with his reply."

Tension he hadn't known himself to be holding eased from Andrew's shoulders. "I thank you both, gentlemen. You've proven yourselves wise and adept, and make me grateful that I will have you both at my side as Elders of this Settlement."

Thomas entered a short time later, Abigail on his arm. Once the farrier had stepped aside to greet a friend, Andrew approached the smith with a gleam in his eye. "Have I any announcements to make today?"

"Not yet, Brother," Thomas returned with a grin. "Apparently I am not charming enough to woo so quickly."

Andrew laughed. "Either that, or you've a longer record of apologies to make than I thought."

"That's where you're wrong." Thomas watched his Beloved across the room as he spoke, all jesting now gone from his voice. "*She* is the one who insists I need to forgive myself. That's the only argument we have, anymore."

"And I'd wager it's as rigorous as any of the others you've had." Andrew clapped a hand on Thomas' back. "She's good for you, my friend. I have had few greater joys than the day I was privileged to announce your Bonding." Until the events of his marriage and installation as Governor of the Willow Springs Settlement transpired, Andrew continued to share the responsibility of such announcements with Simeon and Ezra. When Thomas had confided his Bonding with Abigail to him, he had consulted with the other two, who had readily given the now-Governor-elect leave to announce and bless his friend's courtship.

Involuntarily both men looked to Andrew's betrothed where she sat, not far away, adding to the list she'd been asked to review. Andrew stepped closer and attempted to read over Caeleigh's shoulder. "Whom did I neglect to include?"

"Abram the coppersmith. He is – was – a dear friend of Adeline's, and also is a friend of mine – she sent me to him to be taught the art of storytelling."

Andrew turned briefly once again to Thomas, still standing nearby. "Isn't he the one under whom you had your first apprenticeship?"

The smith managed to suppress most of a chuckle. "It would seem I've been acquainted with your Beloved longer than you have."

"Exactly how long had you been planning that surprise?" Andrew clasped Caeleigh's hand against his forearm as she slipped it into the crook of his elbow after they departed the meetinghouse. Though the midday meal generally did not include a dessert course on working days, an extraordinary display of berry tarts had been brought from the kitchen near the end of the meal and set before Andrew, in celebration of his birthday.

Caeleigh, walking beside him, insisted upon her innocence. "Why do you assume the idea principally was mine?"

"Whose, then, if not yours?"

"Peter wanted to do something to raise your spirits," she confessed in a demure murmur, reticent to betray the stonemason's confidence, had she been expected to keep it. "This matter with Michelle's challenge of your stature has borne increasingly heavily upon you as the weeks have gone by, and it has become plain in your countenance."

Andrew spoke no more as the pair entered the copse of weeping willows. This time *he* had been the one to choose it as their destination, citing the privacy it afforded them. Several yards further in, and Caeleigh would discover his ulterior motive for the choice.

"What is this?" she cried, looking to him, then back to the ornately carved park bench that stood with its back toward the largest of the tree trunks, tucked within the languorous branches.

"It's ours," he informed her. "Yours and mine. This place was our beginning, and we've both returned to it over and again since that evening, in good times as well as difficulties. I decided that if we continue to do so, we ought to have somewhere comfortable to sit."

Caeleigh had been running her hands along the back and arms of the bench as Andrew spoke; the finish of the wood was as satin-smooth as the shelves he'd made for the millinery. "How do you achieve such a soft finish? It genuinely feels more like fabric than wood."

He stepped in close behind, wrapping his arms around her. "If I told you, not only would I be divulging the secrets of my trade, but we'd certainly become lost in a lengthy discussion of a topic other than what we're here to discuss."

They seated themselves, Andrew retrieving Caeleigh's story on the tablet once more. "The first thing I appreciated was your forenote – certain individual character summaries provided enough of each character's personality that I felt I could easily anticipate their responses to events, while others were appropriately vague enough to provoke intrigue. Your explanations and descriptions of things and places with which I have no acquaintance were sufficient to aid my understanding without spoiling the discovery while reading. The fact that you wrote all of it in a similar voice to that which the narrative and the characters speak helped me acclimate to…" he searched for the words to express what he meant to say.

"What essentially feels akin to a foreign language?" she suggested.

"Exactly. I appreciated that you translated the customs of their culture into terms somewhat synonymous with ours. While their way of conducting courtship, for example, is unfamiliar, you presented it in a manner that it didn't seem unnatural or abnormal."

"That *is* what is considered normal courtship in the outside world," she reminded him. "It's merely the misfortune of many that there is little honor left in humanity to go about it properly."

"You sound like your samurai, speaking of honor," he teased.

Caeleigh accepted the compliment in his jesting remark. "What of the story itself?"

"I don't believe I could select a single favorite moment," Andrew replied, paging slowly through the digital text. "There is a considerable number of beautiful images, moments, and expressions throughout. Here" – he pointed at an early passage – "the words are simple but the emotion they evoke, the warrior's remorse that a peaceful life is lost to him, is powerful. The words you chose to describe his beloved gave me not only the ability to see clearly her appearance, but also the equally clear understanding that I was seeing her *through his eyes*. It is my deep hope that you understand that I see you the way he saw her."

"I am not her," Caeleigh protested. "I wrote the character to be everything I *wish* myself to be: courageous, honorable, strong, and beautiful."

"I defy you to read your own words and tell me there is neither courage, nor strength, nor honor, nor beauty in you," he insisted. He searched forward through the story for a later chapter he had marked.

Caeleigh looked at the passage he had highlighted:

> *That you still love me and whether I am welcome in your heart are two separate questions.*

Andrew pressed his point further, gently insistent. "The line is beautifully written. It is artfully phrased, nearly musical. The woman who spoke those words is a pillar of courage, strength, honor, and grace – and she, along with the whole of this story, is a product of your heart, Beloved… which means all of those qualities originate in you. I see you in that character quite clearly.

"While I am on the subject, I saw a great deal of myself in the protagonist, in his thoughts and struggles" – once more Andrew pointed to the name on the screen, loath to attempt to pronounce the patently Japanese name that in print looked unlike any name he'd heard in his life; Caeleigh pronounced it for him – "...yes, him. And this other" – again he pointed and she pronounced the name – "strongly resembles Peter in personality. Did you base those men or their friendship on us?"

"Not deliberately, no," Caeleigh replied. "I had already established the characters in my mind altogether outside of anyone I know – Peter, you, and myself included. Any resemblances you recognized, *you* brought to the reading. If an element herein resonated with your soul, it was the work of the Spirit of Truth, Who guided me as I wrote; I did not plan every element of the story through to its completed state."

Andrew searched through the text for the line that had lingered with him through the watches of a sleepless night. "You're telling me that this primary theme – a man's torment over feeling that he must choose between duty and love because one life conflicts with and complicates the other – *that,* so resemblant to my own current struggle, was *not* your deliberate design?" He read out the line, the assemblage of words tasting as odd as they sounded to him, yet otherwise they perfectly summarized his heart: *"I just don't know how to reconcile the life I want to lead with the life I am called to lead, especially when one precludes the other."*

"Truly. Recall, Andrew, that I began writing this months ago, during a season when your heart was at peace. I will accede that it was my prayer and the desire of my heart that this torment you're presently experiencing would be spoken to – but I assure you that this vein of the tale was established independent of true events. It was inspired by the Spirit of Truth, working in, with, and through me as I composed it."

Caeleigh leaned over his arm and paged a bit further through. "What did you think of this scene?"

Andrew reviewed it briefly and grinned. "I enjoyed it thoroughly. This character – truly? That's how it's said?" He shook his head as she repeated the pronunciation of the name. "Poor man, I have greater sympathy for him now than I did upon the first reading. You've archetyped him as a Shakespearean buffoon, with such a name. Nonetheless, while I did find several of his expressions both here and in the finale confounding, they easily conveyed the essence of his disposition.

"This," he turned to the final two chapters, "was an apt crescendo. Each word and phrase of the dialogue placed so articulately as to impart not only the characters' intentions but also each respective frame of mind. This – '*the most precious gift I could never have dreamt to seek*' – that is an exquisite means of depicting precisely what you are to me. You've shown me that *I*, like the samurai, must and can choose *both* of the things I feared I might be required to choose between. Like him, in choosing the one, I will be more greatly empowered for the other for which I am called."

Andrew placed his hand on Caeleigh's shoulder, high against the side of her neck, according to the custom of the First Followers of the Christ, which David had described in a recent teaching. "You, *my* dear one," – he employed the endearment that the samurai had used for *his* beloved in the story – "are the most precious gift in my life. Not merely with the encouragement, humor, and suspense you've woven into this tale you crafted for me, but by your heart: the strength, courage, wisdom, and love you offer me every day. I bless Kadosh for Bonding my soul with yours."

Chapter 42

Mid July 2149

While scrolling through the fabric catalog on her digital tablet, Caeleigh found herself aching for her mentor in the elder woman's absence. Adeline's wild rosebush bloomed vigorously where Andrew had planted it the winter prior in front of the millinery, filling the front room of the shop daily with its wistful fragrance. Carinne had marked its prolific growth after her arrival to the Willow Springs Settlement in the spring months and promised Philip's assistance in taking a cutting to cultivate and plant beneath the workroom window later in the year.

The cheery jangle of the millinery's copper bell brought Caeleigh's misted eyes to the door.

"Good afternoon," spoke the vintner's eldest daughter.

"Welcome, Sarah." Caeleigh greeted her future apprentice. "I had forgotten we scheduled a lesson for this afternoon. It is, however, favorable timing. We can discuss more formal fabric types today. I'm attempting to make a selection for my gown."

Sarah seated herself on a stool around the corner of the table from the tailor, after setting a small flat-bottomed basket on the sideboard. In a short half-year, the girl had become a young woman, trained and tempered by her mother's resumed presence and the birth of her younger sister. Yet two years away from coming of age, Sarah had decided and expressed her desire to become apprenticed under Caeleigh. Philip and Carinne had given their blessing to the pursuit, and the Settlement's unofficial council of leadership, at Philip's request, had approved that in the interim time, Sarah might receive general lessons and assist in the millinery, until reaching the appointed age to begin her official apprenticeship. "You're missing Adeline," she submitted, after assessing the tailor's demeanor and posture.

Caeleigh nodded. "I had hoped she would be available to guide me in training my first apprentice," she admitted. "It may be poor form to confess this to you, but it is at these times when I miss her most. I wish to train you in the skills of the trade as thoroughly well as she instructed me."

The young woman smiled. "Miss Adeline always spoke well of your abilities. I heard her boast once that you had surpassed her own skills, in fact. I have no fear of being insufficiently prepared for the trade." Sliding from the stool, she retrieved the basket, as well as two of the teacups she knew Caeleigh stored in the sideboard drawer. "Perhaps this will help. I've been experimenting."

The small announcement unsettled Caeleigh more than it soothed. "Do I dare inquire regarding the nature of your experiment?"

Unruffled, Sarah poured two servings from the towel-wrapped two-quart jar she'd lifted from her basket. "At the worst, I've accomplished nothing and this will be plain chilled tea. I'm confident, though, that I will've succeeded." She offered a cup of the beverage to Caeleigh and quickly afterward raised her own to her lips, lest the elder woman fear giving offense by not wishing to drink first.

Sarah's triumphant grin prompted Caeleigh to take an inquisitive sip. The sweet flavor that greeted her proved rewarding of the risk. "Well, young lady," Caeleigh smiled, "please tell me how you achieved this."

"You were telling me of cheese cloth last week, and some of the ways it had formerly been used. It prompted me to think. Fresh raspberries are sweeter than dried ones, and while I know the tea maker has ground dried raspberries and mixed them in with tea leaves to create a raspberry tea to be brewed hot, the berry flavor thins and becomes bitter as the tea chills." Sarah untied the strips binding the towel to the jar and unwrapped it. Within the vessel semifloated a bloated-looking object. "I brewed the plain tea last night and picked fresh raspberries while it cooled. I had already made the pocket of cheesecloth and only needed to fill it and sew it closed, then add it to the tea to steep. The weave is close enough to keep the seeds out of the tea, but the fabric is thin enough to allow the flavors through."

Caeleigh smiled approvingly. "That's quite a well thought-out plan."

"I intend to attempt it with peaches, next. Though I fear the flesh of cut peaches will not resist well to being pressed into the pocket." Sarah refilled each of their teacups.

"What about blackberries?"

The suggestion so animated Sarah that Caeleigh momentarily saw in her eyes the light of the girl who had requested story after story whenever she was near. The thought resurfaced a memory, at which Caeleigh removed the pendant she wore around her neck and laid it on the tabletop between herself and her student. "Do you recognize this?"

Sarah stared thoughtfully at the necklace for a few moments, until realization dawned. "It's the pendant the prince gifted to the maiden at the wedding feast in the kingdom from your story! I didn't know it was real!"

Caeleigh nodded her permission for Sarah to pick up the necklace for closer inspection. "It wasn't, until Andrew had one made for me, based upon the description in the tale. What do you think?" she asked her young friend. "Shall I wear that on the day of my marriage, or allow him to gift me another between now and then?"

"I'll gift you another, whether you permit me to do so, or not." The carpenter grinned as he intruded upon the women's moment.

"Oh!" Sarah exclaimed, shocked by the unexpected entry through the door to which her back had been turned. The pendant clattered upon the tabletop.

"You must sample this flavored tea that Sarah has devised, Beloved," Caeleigh invited him further into her millinery.

"Indeed I shall," Andrew returned, crossing the room to greet his betrothed with their clasping of the hands and a kiss upon her forehead. "Allow me first to install your screen door. The days grow warmer, and you'll be in want of the cross-breeze. I know how you detest allowing the ingress of insects."

Caeleigh thanked him, adding afterward, "When begin ...other projects?"

The carpenter smiled over his shoulder as he crouched in the doorway to retrieve his tools, the inference of the question well-caught. "Construction of the Governor's Home – of *our* home – " he corrected, "begins later this week. Your requests have all been incorporated into the design, Beloved. You have quite an eye for aesthetics. Simeon was as impressed as I had been."

"It was necessary to wait construction of your home on the selection of a Governor, wasn't it?" Sarah interjected into the conversation as innocently as she could think to manage.

"I'd have been building at least one structure either way," Andrew replied to the young woman through the open doorway as he set the screen door in place and marked the placement of its hinge plates while his apprentice, unseen from within, held the door steady. "Only one, however, would be designed to my bride's preference, and it needed to be the correct one. I waited, lest another man be chosen, and I be required to build the Governor's Home to the preference of that man's wife. Little would have changed in the layout, but there are details that make the difference between a house and a home – these are what a woman brings to the architect's table. The uniquely feminine gift of creating a haven within the walls of what otherwise is merely shelter from the elements."

Sarah looked at Caeleigh over the rim of the teacup the younger woman held between her hands. "You've made a poet of him. Andrew has been friends with my father more than all of my life, and I have never heard him speak in this manner until he met you."

The tailor demurred the compliment.

"What are your thoughts of the necklace, Sarah?" Andrew rescued himself as much as Caeleigh with the redirection of conversation. "Is it sufficiently radiant for my bride, or must I find something that more greatly accentuates her beauty?"

Sarah contemplated the pendant before her. "It is genuinely amazing," she replied. "But brides already wear white. I believe a colored stone would stand out more in its contrast."

"For my utter lack of knowledge on the subject, I am inclined to agree, sir," Alexander contributed, further flustering Sarah with *his* undisclosed presence.

"The majority rules in favor of your receiving a new jewel, Beloved." Andrew grinned, in part over his victory in the debate, and in part over the flush that had risen in Sarah's cheeks as the younger man followed him into the millinery.

Caeleigh retrieved two additional teacups from the sideboard and served both men Sarah's raspberry tea. Alexander was generous in his praise of its sweetness and depth of flavor, causing the young woman to turn crimson.

Wordlessly, Caeleigh beseeched Andrew to spare the girl. He heeded the request, reminding his apprentice that they had additional work yet to be done before the noon meal. After the men's departure, Caeleigh noted the additional color draining from Sarah's face.

"The young man flusters you," the tailor opened the topic delicately.

"We've known one another all our lives," Sarah explained, "but since he's come of age, Alexander seems to have begun to look at me differently."

"You're nearer to coming of age, yourself," Caeleigh reminded the girl. "Neither of you are children anymore. He's become aware of the fact. It is becoming time to cease behaving with one another as though you yet were."

As Caeleigh arrived at the meetinghouse for the midday meal, Thomas approached the table where she'd chosen to sit with an urgency that would not be stilled. The smith shifted from one foot to the other with an effervescence bespeaking either unspeakable tragedy or unrestrainable joy.

"Dearest Sister," Thomas implored in a low and harried voice, "I require your assistance with a matter of urgency. Are you available to accompany me on an errand immediately following the conclusion of today's noon meal?"

Caeleigh was taken aback by the request. "Wouldn't you rather Abigail's company?"

"No," Thomas replied quickly, his eyes darting to where his Beloved stood in conversation with Andrew and Ezra near the entry to the meetinghouse dining room. "She must not, or the surprise will be ruined." Thomas bowed his head, leaning closer to the shorter tailor. "Andrew has told me that many of the jewels he has gifted you have been designed based upon descriptions from your stories. I wish for you to assist me in selecting a betrothal ring for Abigail."

The unmade announcement contained within Thomas' request caused Caeleigh to smile for her friend. "I will be glad to help you," she promised, rising to embrace him tightly. Quickly the two separated, lest they cause suspicion of Thomas' news.

Andrew approached momentarily, with a cryptic smile. "Do you congratulate my betrothed, Thomas," he winked, "or she, you?"

"Caeleigh has consented to aid me in the selection of a betrothal ring," Thomas confided. "I believe Abigail may soon become amenable to accepting my entreaties of marriage."

"My dear friends!" Ezra's raised voice interrupted the trio's conversation. "Upon receiving news of great joy this afternoon, I am unable to wait until our evening meal to announce that our sister Abigail has recently Bonded with her Beloved Thomas! Blessings and felicitations to you both, as you prepare to take the next steps in the journey of life together."

"It seems that day has come," Andrew murmured betwixt chuckles.

Thomas was less amused. "She seeks to confound at every found opportunity, as if it delights her," he grumbled. His disposition lightened, however, when Abigail sidled up to him and wrapped her arms about his waist.

"You're displeased," the farrier observed with mild chagrin.

Thomas, who had settled his arm about Abigail's shoulders the moment she'd tucked into his side, shook his head. "No, Beloved. Not terribly so, anyway. I only wish you hadn't chosen to make the announcement without consulting – or *informing* – me."

"I apologize," Abigail offered sincerely. "It's what I was accustomed to from the traditions of the Cypress Ridge

Settlement. I hadn't realized it wouldn't be the same here. Forgive me, Thomas." She bowed her head, clearly disappointed in her error and the disharmony it had caused.

The smith hooked his finger beneath her chin and raised it until her eyes met his. "Already done, Abigail," he told her affectionately before gifting her a gentle kiss to further reinforce his pardon.

Chapter 43

Late August 2149

Beneath the cover of the wild roses she held, cut from Adeline's rosebush planted in front of the millinery, Caeleigh pinched the tender skin between her thumb and forefinger with her fingernails. This was real. Implausible, inconceivable, unimaginable – yet truly happening.

She had arrived at the entrance of the Willow Springs Settlement's crowded chapel, attired in a gown of a design she'd unexpectedly come to love more than the one she had gifted to Elizabeth two years prior. The lines were simpler, straighter, cleaner. The style had required fewer modifications to meet Caeleigh's ideal, and the work of its construction had been assisted by Carinne and Sarah both.

Upon looking downward, as she'd climbed the few steps outside the chapel with Peter's assistance, Caeleigh had smiled at the flash of cornflower blue in the front of her hem. She'd murmured the ancient rhyme *Something old, something new, something borrowed, and something blue* one afternoon during the last of the workdays on the gown when Carinne had jestingly quipped that the tailor was borrowing her daughter, yet too young to be an apprentice. Sarah had immediately leapt on the balance of the list, calling the gown's fabric new, and Adeline's roses, which Caeleigh intended to carry, old. The young girl had then retrieved the blue thread from the thread-and-bobbin chest in the sewing room of the millinery and run a quick, neat topstitch over a handswidth of the center front of the skirt hem of the otherwise-nearly-completed gown.

Clearing his throat, Peter called the bride out of her reverie. "Are you ready?" he asked, his tone carrying the paternal gentleness of the father-to-be he'd recently become, but his eyes twinkling with the mischievous jesting that had ever been Peter.

"You *are* welcome to escort me," Caeleigh repeated the invitation. Upon learning that Andrew intended to ask Thomas to stand as his man of honor during their planning of this day, she had feared that Peter would feel slighted, and asked Peter to stand in the place of her absent family, since his wife was standing as her woman of honor.

Peter shook his head with a smile. "No, dear Sister. You've walked on your own with none but Kadosh beside you for many years. This is the one final walk you ought to have Him alone escort you on. I shall join Abigail. I mind it no more than she. We've already agreed to keep company today while our Beloveds are engaged in honoring you." With these, his parting words, Peter stepped around the closed door through the one propped open, leaving Caeleigh to draw and release a number of deep breaths in a final attempt to slow the staccato drumming of her heart.

Alexander stood in the doorway with an eager grin to offer his hand to her as she stepped across the threshold. He released her fingers and stepped back to the wall, pleased he'd been offered a role of direct service to the ceremony, however small, as the bride entered the aisle and the congregation stood with the rise of the processional music.

Caeleigh, however, progressed no further than the midpoint of the chapel's length before Andrew arrived at her side and offered her his arm to escort his bride the remainder of the distance to the altar. There, they stood before David, adjoined by Elizabeth and Thomas.

"On behalf of those who stand before us all," David beamed, "I welcome you all to this long-awaited day. Today – and all the days that have led to it – are a testament to the faithfulness of Kadosh to stand watch over His promises, to see them to completion, for those who trust and abide in Him."

At David's nodded invitation, Caleb, Governor of the Blue Creek Settlement, rose from his seat in the front pew and moved as though to step between the bridegroom and his bride. Andrew tightened his grasp on Caeleigh's hand and warned the elder man aside with a grinning glare. Laughing, Caleb stepped around the couple to join David behind them.

"Dear friends," the visiting Governor's voice filled the room. "I add my welcome, and bring greetings from your family and friends in the Blue Creek Settlement." The younger-than-his-years man clapped a hand on Andrew's shoulder, addressing the groom directly. "I am blessed to be present for this day, and gratified to speak. You honor me by having asked."

Andrew nodded, smiling in solemnity.

Caleb removed his hand from Andrew's shoulder and stepped back, raising his voice for the room at large. "My affinity for love stories is no secret," he began with a wink, prompting a ripple of laughter that began as near to him as the bride and groom themselves. "Those whose love we celebrate today have asked that I tell you *why*. The reason is that all love stories carry within them the echo of *the* Love Story, the first of all time – that which is recorded in the account of the Genesis of Creation. We all know that story, of beauty and perfection, of flawless oneness and relationship with Kadosh, where man and woman were created expressly to know the communion of love with Him and with one another. All was well in Eden's Paradise until the Rebellion created an insuperable division where once stood love. Thus began the indomitable pursuit, the inexhaustible passion, of Kadosh for the hearts of His Beloved, to restore us to perfect love within our now-imperfect world. Every love since then, every courtship, every pursuit of a man seeking to win the heart of the woman whom Kadosh has written into his soul, reflects as in a shaded glass that Divine passion."

Caleb smiled upon the couple standing before him, paternal affection and pride for both earthly-fatherless parties raising a swell of emotion. "*These* two people's love story, I must tell you," he pointed to the bride and groom, shaking his hands thrice for emphasis. "In all of my lifetime, I have *seen* no greater such reflection. Caeleigh, to have heard it told that your prayers asking to be granted the partnership of marriage subverted piety in favor of honesty reminds me of the Christ Himself, as does your choosing to obey and submit to the will of Kadosh *over* your desires. Andrew, *your* story, son, is a testimony to the resilience of the soul of Man and the faithfulness of Kadosh to stand watch over His promises and see them through to fulfillment, no matter how long the journey or how little events unfold as preferred. You have shown us all the diligence, the patience, the persistence, gentleness, and longsuffering devotion, the *ardence* that is in the heart of Kadosh toward each and every one of His chosen Beloved with whom He has entered into covenant. I rejoice over you both as we celebrate with you today."

Andrew embraced the man who had selected and sent him, before Caleb ceded to David and resumed his seat.

"The groom and his bride have elected to compose their own covenant vows," David announced. He nodded to Andrew to begin. Caeleigh laid her roses on the altar beside the round textured-glass charger upon which their covenant rings were displayed, then offered her hands to her bridegroom.

Andrew gave Caeleigh's trembling hands a light squeeze before lifting his left hand to slide it high on her shoulder, against the side of her neck. Not until he held fast to her did he begin to speak, directly and solely to her. "My Beloved Caeleigh... I am compelled to begin with a confession: It had been my long-held opinion that I should appropriately have been married ten years ago – if not longer. Yet I am now converted, for had I married then, it would not have been to you and I would have missed out on the greatest of treasures. I regret that I am not as gifted with words as you, to say this more artfully: You are worth all of the waiting that has been asked of me."

Feeble was Caeleigh's effort to pull her hands from her Beloved's unsurrendering grasp, for want to brush away the tears he'd prompted to her eyes.

Andrew smiled at his silently weeping bride as he continued, "Your talent with words, and the care you take to express exactly what you mean, blesses everyone within hearing. With your voice as well as your hands you put forth exquisite beauty that bespeaks of the artistic nature of our Creator Father, Kadosh. Of your servant's heart and charitable spirit I have been but one of a multitude of beneficiaries."

Without pausing, Andrew slipped his right hand from Caeleigh's grasp and reached into the inside pocket of his suit coat for a handkerchief, which he pressed into one of her hands for her to dry her tears and reclaimed the other as he continued with a broadening smile. "Your love is a vast ocean, the depths of which no fathoming line can reach. I am blessed beyond imagination to be the man to receive such affection.

"I promise here before Kadosh and all these witnesses that I will do my utmost always to cherish you, to love you, to honor you, to lead you rightly by example, to seek and consider your wisdom when making decisions that will affect us both, and to be faithful to no woman but you every day of our lives. I am my Beloved's and my Beloved is mine." The bridegroom drew his hand upward from Caeleigh's shoulder to her cheek, stopping an errant tear with his thumb, before lowering it to resume hold of her right hand, still clutching the handkerchief.

Caeleigh's left hand trembled as she set her fingertips to the curvature of Andrew's neck, her palm hovering above his shoulder. She hesitated, throat dry at the prospect of speaking before the gathered assembly. Andrew nodded slightly, encouraging her to proceed. At his direction Caeleigh flattened her hand and properly held fast, her eyes never once breaking from his. "Andrew, my Beloved, I must confess that when I learned that Kadosh willed for me to be your wife, as I embraced that truth into my heart, I laughed – I laughed as Sarah laughed when she overheard Kadosh informing her husband Abraham that she would bear him a son at 99, and he at 100, years of age... for truly I felt that her chances of that were greater than my chances of this."

Recounting her laughter, Caeleigh found herself unable to suppress the chuckle that rose up within her. "Yet as it was, Sarah did bear not only a son, but the forebear to the one who was called and became the father of the nation of Israel – and so likewise here I stand today." She smiled more soberly, thankful that the implausibility had not been firmly rendered an impossibility. "You are a greater gift to my heart than I could ever have dared to *conceive* to wish or ask or imagine. You stand as a constant reminder that I am dearly beloved of Kadosh, and that His desires for my life are greater than my own, for He has chosen to give you to me as friend, lover, and husband in the covenant of marriage. A year from the day I learned this to be true, I continue to stand in awe that both He and you consider me so deserving."

Caeleigh found herself in need to clear her throat of the tears that had welled there before proceeding to conclude her marital vows. Andrew grinned, and winked nearly imperceptibly, as her fingers trembled against the firm musculature of his neck and shoulder. "I – " the bride began, succeeding no further before her voice faltered and failed entirely.

She inhaled deeply and found success on her second attempt. "I promise before Him always to love and respect you, to honor you, to obey your headship in kind as the Christ is head of the Church, to stand by your side and share in whatever labor to which you are called, and to be faithful to no man but you for every day of our lives. I am my Beloved's and my Beloved is mine."

After she finished speaking, Caeleigh waited for David to retrieve their rings from the altar behind him. Instead, Andrew surprised her by reaching up and removing her hand from the back of his neck. To her questioning expression he replied quietly, "I have a gift for you first."

He led his bride by the hands to the chapel's piano and seated her in a chair positioned beside it such that they could see one another once he took his place on the bench. Tentatively he placed his hands over the keys, issuing forth a single note, joined by a second, a third ... a simple melody emerged, then grew into whole chords.

The tune was delicate both in its higher notes and its lower tones; sweet, inquisitive, promising. Caeleigh sat entranced, and equally astonished – not only was Andrew playing publicly, but the piece was a technically complex composition.

As quickly has it had broadened, the song thinned once more, until he was playing no more than one or two notes at a time, then the final triad. Bride and groom sat unmoving, eyes only for one another. The last sounds from the piano dissipated in the stillness of the chapel.

Caeleigh held her breath and waited, apprehensive for the reception Andrew's surprise performance would receive. Her thumb worried the hem of the handkerchief she yet held in her lap from when he'd given it to her as he'd spoken his thanks and his vows.

At the right-hand side of the altar, Thomas broke the silence, slowly beginning to applaud. Opposite him, Elizabeth set down the flowers she held and followed suit. Peter and Abigail, as well as Caleb, David, Philip, Ezra, Simeon and their families joined moments thereafter; soon the entire population of the room had risen in ovation.

Andrew stood, flustered by the attention. Caeleigh extended her hands to him. He helped her to her feet, pulling her close to speak so that she might hear him: "Did my surprise please you? You smiled, but uneasily so."

"I was afraid for you," she replied in his ear, "for what response your revelation might be given."

"My sole concern is to know my bride's response."

As the applause subsided and those not standing for the ceremony regained their seats, Caeleigh stepped backward out of her bridegroom's embrace and smiled. "My response is this: Please tell me there is a piano in our home."

Andrew grinned and leaned toward his bride as though he meant to kiss her.

"Not yet!" David called to them, index finger extended. "We have a few matters to address before it's time for that."

Andrew pressed his forehead to Caeleigh's as laughter cascaded through the chapel. "There isn't at the moment, but I will see to it that the oversight is corrected," he promised.

Bride and groom returned to their former places at the center front of the chapel. The covenant bands were exchanged. Elizabeth, Carinne, Peter, and Thomas each in turn spoke blessings over the couple, having been asked to do so, as the closest of their friends. Matthias, the carpenter under whom Andrew had trained in their trade, also rose and blessed his former apprentice. Andrew drew Caeleigh closer to his side, knowing she wished Adeline could be present to do the same for her. He looked up when Thomas nudged his elbow, drawing the bridegroom's attention to the fact that Abram had stood and come forth.

"Storytelling may not be a trade for commerce, or in which one takes an apprentice, Caeleigh," the coppersmith addressed the bride with damp eyes, "but you set yourself as my student in that art, so I hope that excuses my desire to speak in Adeline's place. You know she wanted to see this day for herself, and in the last days of her illness, she told me that this was what she was sorriest to miss. Adeline and I were good friends for many years, during her marriage to my best friend, and after his passing into eternal reward – I knew well her mind and her heart, and I can say with assurance that she loved you as a daughter. I see that you carry a piece of the gift she sent you." Abram nodded to Caeleigh's roses, once more held in hand. "She would be honored that you've chosen to include a remembrance of her in your celebration today. Before she" – he cleared his throat of building emotion – "joined her own Beloved, Adeline and I spoke of what she might have said to you today, had she been here." He withdrew a worn half-sheet of paper from the inner pocket of his suit coat.

Abram blushed as he took Caeleigh's hand after Elizabeth relieved her of the roses. "Forgive these words coming from an old man. Adeline asked that I speak them as though they were coming directly from her. 'I bless you, dear girl, with the happiness I have known in my own life and marriage, and with the love you have showered upon me and all others in your life, for which I have watched you yearn and submit obediently to Kadosh in waiting upon the promise that has stood long unanswered, but not unforgotten. I have trusted alongside you that the time it has taken for this promise to be fulfilled was spent setting every piece of it to perfection, and that it will prove to have been well worth the wait. I am deeply sorry not to be present on this most significant of days. But *know* that long ago, before the day was set and before I knew I would be absent, that in my heart, I had already given you and Andrew my blessing. Yes, dear girl, I've known – only a man in love is as gentle with the heart of a woman as he has ever been with yours. Treasure one another, both of you, always grateful for that which you have long awaited.' "

Caeleigh nodded tearfully as Andrew exchanged his handkerchief in her hand with the dry one offered from Thomas' pocket. No further blessing necessary, David moved to conclude the ceremony as Abram returned to his seat.

At long last, David turned to Andrew, saying, "Andrew, it pleases me to say this woman is your wife. Caeleigh"– he turned to her – "this man is your husband. Andrew, you may now claim your bride."

"I've certainly waited long enough to do so," Andrew murmured, smiling capaciously as he pulled his wife to himself to kiss her.

Chapter 44

Late August 2149

When Caeleigh woke the following morning, she needed a moment to remember why she was in a different bed, in a strange house. She turned over from her right side to her left and found Andrew beside her, watching her.

"Good morning, wife." He grinned.

"Good morning, husband." A thought occurred which caused her to immediately begin smoothing and fussing with her hair.

Andrew took hold of her wrist. "You're beautiful. Stop worrying and simply enjoy the peace of the morning." He stretched out his right arm, inviting her to cuddle against his chest, and kissed her forehead as she rested her head on his shoulder.

"So yesterday truly happened, then?" Caeleigh asked in wonder, staring at the covenant band he now wore on his left fourth finger.

Her husband's laughter shook them both. "Yes, Beloved. I can pinch you if you believe you're dreaming yet," he volunteered.

"Don't you dare!" She laughed before falling silent, her fingertips studying the overnight growth of stubble along his jaw.

They remained in that tableau for several minutes until Andrew broke the silence, asking gently, "Tell me what you're thinking?"

"I don't really have the words to articulate what's been rolling around in my mind," Caeleigh began, then cringed in the manner that he had come to recognize as her reaction whenever she caught herself reverting to words and expressions from life before the Settlements.

"Don't worry." He winked. "No one heard you but me – and I won't repeat it; I wouldn't know how to properly apply the expression."

"You're mocking me."

"I adore you," he quickly retorted, punctuating the statement with a kiss on her forehead.

"Were we in outside world, I would say you need to consult a therapist."

"My shoulder has healed perfectly well, thank you."

She surrendered, descending into laughter. Whether Andrew had misunderstood or ignored what she had said was irrelevant. What mattered was that they couldn't lounge about all day in newlywedded bliss. "We oughtn't be late this morning," she insisted, as they both sat upright. "A Governor mustn't behave like a slacker on his first official day in the position." This time, her application of foreign vernacular was playfully deliberate.

"A what?" he was baffled at the employment of so abstruse a term.

His wife laughed and expelled him from the bed with a light shove. "I'll explain later. Promise me that you won't repeat the word."

Though compliant, he turned back toward her with a grin. "Kiss me."

"Shave that scruff off your face first." Caeleigh rebuffed the advance with a turn of her head.

Andrew laughed and crossed the room to carry out the directive. "Spoken like a true wife."

"Simply trying to do my best on my first day on the job," she called as the door to the master bath closed behind him. His laughter echoed over the running water in the sink.

Caeleigh quickly changed out of her nightdress, then sat down at the vanity to brush and pull back her hair when Andrew emerged. "How's this?" he asked, nuzzling his cheek against hers.

"Much better." She allowed him a single quick kiss before slipping from his grasp. "I've laid out a new shirt for you," she called through the closed door before she began to brush her teeth. As she was finishing, he knocked on the door and opened it a crack.

"This was laid out on the vanity. Do you wish to wear it?" Her husband held up the necklace he'd gifted her the previous Christmastide, its circular pendant a luminous, champagne-colored diamond that, now, matched the accent stones in her betrothal ring.

"Yes. Will you fasten the clasp for me?" Caeleigh allowed him entry, smiling. "Finally I'm able to wear it openly and tell people who gave me such a marvelous gift."

"*You* are the marvelous gift that Kadosh has given to *me*."

With a well-humored roll of her eyes, Caeleigh called for the cessation of their repartee. "Enough flattery. Breakfast," she demanded tartly.

Andrew grinned and took his wife by the hand. "As you wish, Beloved."

They arrived at the meetinghouse to find that the celebration of their marriage seemed to be intended to continue in the morning meal, absent the wine that had been served the evening prior.

When Andrew questioned Peter and Thomas on the matter, their reply was that a marriage so long awaited deserved greater celebration. Elizabeth had stored all of the flowers in the bakery's refrigerators overnight to keep them fresh another day, and risen early to decorate the dining room with assistance from Carinne, Sarah, Lydia, Beth, and Sophia.

The meal was a festive time, filled with laughter. A significant amount of discussion centered on Andrew's previously unknown talent as a musician, which he declined to explain.

After the tables had been cleared, David deferred the morning teaching. Caleb rose from his seat beside Andrew and stood at the head of the room. "My dear friends of the Willow Springs Settlement!" he called in his joyous booming voice. "You have Planted and labored to establish this new Settlement without the headship of a Governor. This is the first time in the history of the Settlements that such has occurred.

"Nearly five years ago, when Kadosh guided me in selecting the three men who were to be the candidates for Governor of this Settlement, I worried only briefly when He instructed me to name an unwed man in contradiction to the rules of the Settlements set forth by the First Elders. I took this young man aside and spoke with him, telling him of what Kadosh had told me of His intentions for his life that stood in contravention to the apparent circumstances of his life. Andrew responded with utmost confidence in the faithfulness of

Kadosh. Things haven't gone exactly as he expected at the time that they would, since then" – Caleb made eye contact with the young man, who shook his head and laughed before kissing his new bride – "yet he has remained unwavering in his faith and his faithfulness both to Kadosh and to this community. It brings me great joy and greater pride to install and commission Andrew as your Governor today."

Andrew stood with Caeleigh beside him before Caleb, surrounded by the Elders and their families, as the Governor who had sent Andrew instructed him of the responsibilities of his position, then wrapped his right hand around the back of the younger man's neck and blessed him. "My son, my son, my son," Caleb began, if at all possible with a paternal delight brighter than that which had lit his countenance the previous day. "Twenty years ago, you arrived in the Blue Creek Settlement an orphan, with no more direction to your life than a ship cast about upon stormy seas. It has been my great joy and privilege to disciple you and watch as Kadosh has formed you into the manner of man I count it an honor to know. His hand has surely been upon you for all of your life, and decidedly so in these past few years. Now these people have chosen you to shepherd them as a father. This is the wisest counsel I am able to offer you: Regard yourself as father to this community, and your leadership shall always be directed by proper motives. Stay near to the Father-heart of Kadosh. And submit to this beautiful wife of yours – she will keep you humble." This final admonition raised well-natured chuckles from the men surrounding as Caeleigh gave her husband a cautioning glance and a prod in the ribs with her elbow.

"Truly, Andrew," Caleb resumed as the laughter dissipated, "to bless you seems unnecessary, for already you are truly blessed with all good things that you will need – a steadfast heart, a steady mind, and an excellent woman at your side. Therefore, the only words I feel it necessary to leave you with are those with which Kadosh instructed Moses to speak over his brother Aaron and his sons, instructing them to bless their people Israel: 'The LORD bless you and keep you; the LORD make his face to shine upon you and be gracious to you; the LORD lift up his countenance upon you and give you peace.' Govern well, my dear son." He pulled the new Governor into an embrace, to the congratulatory applause of the Elders.

Caleb stepped back as the Elders – Ezra, Simeon, Philip, David, Thomas, and Zachary, the gristmiller, who had been selected by popular vote and approved by the others whose places had been assured by Caleb's selection – each in turn prayed for their new Governor and blessed him. Then it was Andrew's turn to speak.

Andrew cleared his throat as he stepped forth from those surrounding him. "I'm not the one who's gifted with words – that would be my wife's blessing." He turned and looked at Caeleigh momentarily while several individuals chuckled at his self-deprecation.

"For the past two years I have covered every corner of this Settlement in prayer. From the acreage of Philip's vineyards and Nathaniel's fields, to the streets and every building we've raised. I've walked all of the land here and carried the blessing of Kadosh everywhere my foot has trod. I've prayed for each of you by name. I've ridden up to the cliff that overlooks our valley and covenanted with Kadosh for our home and our people. Now let us join together and covenant with Him for our future.

"...'Lord, you have been our dwelling place in all generations. Before the mountains were brought forth, or ever you had formed the earth and the world, even from everlasting to everlasting you are God. Blessed be the Lord God of Israel, for he has visited and redeemed his people ... to show the mercy promised to our fathers and to remember his holy covenant, the oath that he swore to our father Abraham, to grant us that we, being delivered from the hand of our enemies, might serve him without fear, in holiness and righteousness before him all our days.' "

About the Author

J. Anne Lezsley has been a voracious reader and avid valuer of the written word since childhood. She has been composing stories, poems and sonnets of varying forms and themes since the age of eight, occasionally daring to set them to the page. *The Unforgotten Promise* is her first novel, with more to come, hopefully in the near future.

An enthusiast of many pursuits with eclectic tastes, Anne counts among her principal interests good music, sweet wine, white chocolate raspberry scones, and a well-prepared cup of tea.

She presently resides in central Pennsylvania but aspires to see more of the world.

Invitation to Contact

The three-year journey of writing this book has been and included the most significant and formational seasons of my life. I have been unalterably affected by it. If you have been impacted by this story, as well, I would love to hear your story.

Visit me on Facebook: www.facebook.com/J.AnneLezsley

Or contact me via e-mail: anne.lezsley@gmail.com

I also welcome questions. It has been the exploration resulting from readers' questions during the writing process that have led to some of the best discoveries about some of my favorite characters. So feel free to ask! You never know; the question smoldering in the back of your mind could inspire major developments for the sequel.

Significant Names, Terms and Ideas

Kadosh – This is one of God's many Hebrew names. It means "The Holy One"... in the context of this story, it is used in exclusive reference to God the Father.

The Christ – Jesus. So often Christians say "Jesus Christ" as if the latter is his surname, but really he was 'Jesus, *the* Christ.' **"Others said, 'This is the Christ'..."** – John 7:41A (ESV)

Spirit of Truth – The Holy Spirit. **"When the *Spirit of truth* comes, he will guide you into all the truth"** – John 16:13A (ESV), emphasis mine.

Go'el – This is an Ancient Hebrew concept/tradition. The Kinsman Redeemer is a male relative who served one, some, or all of four functions: delivers or rescues a person, redeems lost property, avenges wrongful death, and/or receives restitution on behalf of someone who has since died. The best example from scripture is in the book of Ruth – having been widowed left Ruth in poverty in a foreign land. Boaz (her late husband's relative) rescued her from poverty and potentially also slavery, and entitled her late husband's property (basically preserving the estate), when he married her.

Covenant – A legally-binding and soul-binding agreement and commitment. Parties who entered covenant with one another were committed upon their lives to the oath they sealed to become joined in oneness with together, for the entirety of their lives – and bound to honor it to generations beyond.

Travail – The dictionary definition of the word will provide a picture of the experience: hard or agonizing labor, as in childbirth, deep distress or anguish. The prayer definition of the word includes that intensity, and occasionally also the agony. This is prayer initiated by God for a need or person outside of oneself, bypasses the pray-er's will and conscious mind, and is marked by weeping, groans, and unintelligible speech.

Shemitah – Biblically, the seventh of every seven years (a Sabbath year, just as the seventh day of the week is the Sabbath day). The word means 'the release' or 'the letting go.' More specifically, marked on the last day of the year, the 29th day of the month of Elul on the Hebrew calendar every seven years; also connected to the Jubilee Year (see Deuteronomy 15). God had set this up for Israel to be a blessing, a rest, and a relief from debts; when neglected, it changed from a blessing (gift offered) to a judgment (it was forced upon them). In scripture, Isaiah 9:8-10:19 details how catastrophic things kept happening to the nation of Israel in those days on that date for not observing the Shemitah as they had been directed to do. Rabbi Jonathan Cahn has observed that the same has been occurring in the U.S. since 2001 due to the nation's open rebellion against the covenants the founding fathers (particularly George Washington in his 1789 inaugural address) made with God when inducting this young nation.

Holding Fast to the Head – This is a tradition from the earliest centuries A.D. When two individuals who had not seen one another for a long time met again, they would greet one another in this way. The individual doing the 'holding' would put their hand on the shoulder/back of the neck of the one they were greeting, and speak reasons for which they were thankful for that individual and bless them. The person receiving this could not speak in response, but rather had to "stand there and take it."

The significance of Right hand vs. Left hand – In ancient Hebrew and early-church tradition, many things had significance. The right hand is symbolic of authority, and the left hand is symbolic of intimacy. Which hand was used or extended, then, is indicative of the context from which one speaks or acts.

To order more copies of this book, please go to:

https://www.createspace.com/5262112

Made in the USA
Middletown, DE
19 June 2017